D1003038

THE GOLEM

by
Gustav Meyrink

Edited and with an introduction by
E. F. Bleiler

DOVER PUBLICATIONS, INC.
New York

This Dover edition, first published in 1986, is an unabridged republication of the translation by Madge Pemberton published by Houghton Mifflin Co., Boston and New York, in 1928. E. F. Bleiler wrote the introduction and emended the translation specially for the previous Dover edition, published in 1976, in which *The Golem* was accompanied by *The Man Who Was Born Again*, by Paul Busson.

Manufactured in the United States of America
Dover Publications, Inc., 31 East 2nd Street, Mineola, N.Y. 11501

Library of Congress Cataloging in Publication Data

Meyrink, Gustav, 1868-1932.
    The Golem.

    I. Bleiler, Everett Franklin, 1920-   .   II. Title.
PT2625.E95G6213   1986   833'.912   85-20527
ISBN 0-486-25025-3

GUSTAV MEYRINK

"I know a banker, a grayhaired businessman, who has the gift of writing stories. He does this in his spare time, and his work is often excellent. Despite this ability, however, he is not in very good repute, for he has served time in prison, deservedly so. Indeed, he first became aware of his gift in the prison where he was confined, and his prison experiences form a basis for all his work." From *Tonio Kröger* by Thomas Mann.

This is probably a reference to Gustav Meyrink, the Austrian-German satirist and occult novelist, at that time known as Gustav Meyer. Heinrich Mann, Thomas Mann's brother, knew Meyrink well, and it is quite possible that Thomas Mann, too, had been acquainted with Meyrink. The paragraph cited may not be correct in all details, but it offers at least a general contemporary opinion about Meyrink.

During much of his life Gustav Meyrink was a cause célèbre in the Germanic world, sometimes in small ways, sometimes in large ways. During his early life in Prague he delighted in shocking and annoying the bourgeoisie, until he was brought down by legal persecution. During World War One, as a pacifist, un-patriot and scoffer, he was considered an enemy of the Reich, and suffered for it. In 1917 his books were banned in Austria. Later, under Nazi Germany his works were among the first to be burned, probably as a result of his prolonged feud with proto-Nazi litterateurs and historians.

From a literary point of view Meyrink was one of the most talented and most annoying satirists to emerge in twentieth-century Germany, an author who had the ability to prick his victims into a frenzy that is now difficult to understand. He was also one of the earliest Expressionist writers, and certainly the foremost twentieth-century novelist of the supernatural. He is now remembered mostly for *Der Golem* (The Golem), a mystical love story of charm, tenderness and terror.

Meyrink, unfortunately, has remained a Germanic phenomenon, a mysterious figure almost unknown in the English-speaking world, surrounded by some speculation and even more misinformation.

Bankier Meyer, as Gustav Meyrink was known around the turn of the century to Mann, was born Gustav Meyer in Vienna, 1868. He

was the illegitimate son of Maria Meyer, an actress at the court thea-
ter, and an elderly nobleman, the Freiherr Varnbüler von und zu
Hemmingen, a minister of state in Württemburg. Rejection by his
father, neglect by his mother, who cared only about her career, and a
helter-skelter childhood obviously colored Meyrink's life and soured
certain areas of human experience for him. He spent much of his early
life in Munich and Hamburg, but later moved to Prague, where he
attended a commercial college.

After leaving business school Meyrink worked in the export trade
for a time, then together with a nephew of Christian Morgenstern the
poet opened a bank in Prague. This was Banker Meyer, investing and
handling securities for his clients, disposing of estates, changing cur-
rency.

But there were at least two other Meyers in habitation within his
body. There was also Gustav Meyer the aggressive playboy and bohemian, who delighted in using his sharp, sarcastic tongue to annoy the
stodgy German patricians of Prague, and wasted no chance to shock
them. He was athletic, and won many prizes as a sculler, including the
championship of the Austro-Hungarian Empire. He was a skilled
fencer, a riotous liver who rode about in balloon-decorated carriages
with troops of chorus girls, and he affronted the horses by driving the
first automobile in Prague. Like his counterparts in England he lived
in eccentric surroundings, in a tower in an older part of the city, where
his strangely decorated room contained a confessional booth, a terrar-
ium filled with exotic African mice, a large picture of Madame Blavatsky, and a sculpture of a ghost disappearing into a wall.

This strange sculpture and the portrait lead us into the third element of Meyer—Meyer the occultist, dreamer, mystic, and magician.
We do not know much about his childhood thoughts, but in his early
twenties he had decided to commit suicide and was in the act of
raising the pistol to his head when someone shoved a pamphlet under
his door, an advertisement for a series of occult books. He interpreted
this as both a warning and an invitation. This led him to consider a
way of life other than materialism, and as he states in his *An der
Grenze des Jenseits* (On the Border of the Beyond), he devoted the
remainder of his life to a spiritual quest and praxis that eventually
worked through Spiritualism, Theosophy, alchemy, Christian mysticism, Cabbalism, various yogas, Tantrism, Sufism, Far Eastern
thought and primitive religions. He joined such occult groups as were
accessible to him during his early life. At one time he was a member
of the Inner Circle of Annie Besant's Adyar Theosophical Society,

and he was well acquainted with G. R. S. Mead and Rudolf Steiner. It would be a mistake to regard him as a gull, however, for he was a difficult man either to satisfy or deceive. He attended séances together with magicians in order to catch trickery. It was Meyer who snipped off, secretly, a fragment of ectoplasm from one of Schrenck-Notzing's favorite mediums and took it to a laboratory where it was revealed to be cheesecloth and chemicals. He was usually disillusioned, as he freely admitted, and he came to regard occultism as the "religion of the stupid," but he gradually worked out an independent, eclectic position of his own that dominated his later life.

The various Meyers in Meyer continued their strange mésalliance until January 1902, at which time the primal innocence collapsed. Meyer was arrested for fraud and placed in jail for several months while being investigated.

What actually happened has never been clearly established, beyond the fact that he was charged with embezzlement and misuse of accounts. In all probability he was innocent and guilty of carelessness only, if even of that, since his remaining life displays a pattern common among artists: complete honesty coupled with a good deal of unrealism about time and money. One can only marvel that this Gauguin of the hidden worlds ever entered finance and stayed there for so many years.

According to one account Meyer was the scapegoat for the irregularities of his partner, Morgenstern; according to another theory, he was hounded because of personal grudges and official disapproval.

There may be some truth in this latter speculation about grudges, for Meyer had suddenly become a notorious figure, prominent in the newspapers, café gossip, and official documents. His first marriage had collapsed, and he had taken up with another woman, whom he later married when his first wife granted him a divorce. This second wife was slandered by an Army reserve officer, one Dr. Bauer; we can only guess what the doctor said about her. Meyer demanded an apology, which was refused, and found that under the mores of the time his recourse was to challenge the doctor to a duel. The doctor refused (although such duels were not illegal), and his refusal was backed by the military authorities, the Prague newspapers, who defended the officer corps, and the police, who took to harassing Meyer. A court of honor called by Bauer ruled that Meyer was not capable of receiving satisfaction, since he was illegitimate. Meyer fought the decision, and obtained a reversal, on the grounds of noble descent: his father was a German nobleman, and his mother came from an ancient noble fam-

ily of Styria, the Meyerincks. The doctor was saved by Meyer's oppor-
tune arrest, and it is hardly any marvel that Meyrink, as his writings
show, retained strong feelings about regimental surgeons, the officer
corps, militarism, and police commissioners.

Meyer spent almost three months in jail while his affairs were mi-
nutely scrutinized. He was completely cleared by the commission and
released in April, 1902, a ruined man. His reputation was gone; his
enemies simply winked and laughed about offenses that were just
outside the law. An illness, too, from which he had been suffering for
several months was seriously aggravated. This was a spinal affliction,
which was diagnosed as tuberculosis of the spine. As a result of this
triple crucifixion Meyer the playboy banker was dead, and in his
place stiffly stood a gaunt, tired, tortured-looking man, who eventually recovered enough to walk about carefully, but suffered periodic
relapses of his ailment until his death.

Meyer, on leaving the prison hospital, sued the newspapers which
had libeled him, but without success. He now found himself without a
livelihood and without a home, since life was impossible in Prague: he
was marked by the military and the police. His salvation came from
an unexpected source.

While in a sanatorium, not long before the Bauer affair exploded,
Meyer had made the acquaintance of the writer Oskar Schmitz, the
brother-in-law of the artist Kubin, and Schmitz, recognizing Meyer's
ferocity of wit, his bizarre and powerful imagination, and his gift with
language urged him to try writing.

Journalism was not an empty mirage for beginners in Germany and
Austria at that time, for Germanic art-nouveau culture was still bur-
geoning, and was vined with many excellent literary periodicals,
which occasionally failed for their backers, but served to keep writers
and artists in food. Following Schmitz's advice Meyer sent a satirical
story to the highest of all German magazines, the brilliant *Simplicissimus.* The story was "Der heisse Soldat" (The Hot Soldier), a sharp
fantasy set in Indo-China, ridiculing army doctors and the military.
According to a reminiscence, which is generally accepted, the subedi-
tors of *Simplicissimus* threw Meyrink's manuscript into a wastebasket.
During an editorial conference which followed, Thoma, the editor-in-
chief, being bored, began to poke around the wastebasket with his
cane. He knocked out Meyrink's manuscript, and read it with increasing excitement. "What is this?" he asked. "Something sent in by some
nut," answered Geheeb, the subeditor. "We'll publish it," replied Thoma. "The man may be stark raving mad, but he's a genius!" The

comment was not entirely untrue.

"Der heisse Soldat" was published in *Simplicissimus* in October 1901 under the name Gustav Meyrink, an adaptation of Meyerinck or Meyeringck, Meyer's ancestral name. Gustav Meyrink he now remained for all his writings; in 1917 he changed his name legally to Meyrink. This explains the confusion of library card catalogues, which variously refer to him as Meyrink, Gustav, pseud., see Meyer, Gustav; or Meyer-Meyrink, Gustav, see Meyrink, Gustav, pseud.; or Meyrink-Meyer, Gustav; or even occasionally, Meyrink, Gustav.

The debacle had taken place in 1901–02. For the next decade or so Meyrink made a scanty living from writing of various sorts. He continued to sell material to *Simplicissimus,* where he was popular with much of the readership, but was a painful experience to the balloon folk whom he pricked. Besides being an original and powerful satirist, Meyrink was also a fine hand as a parodist, as can be seen from his travesties of the regionalists. He rewrote the story of Job in Hamburg dialect, deflating Frenssen, who later became notorious as a neo-Pagan; he imitated Gerhart Hauptmann with admirable obscurity; and he played havoc with Swiss *Heimatkunst* in "Das Wildschwein Veronika," the story of a wild sow who becomes a landmark of Swiss culture and marries a music critic. In bitterness, savagery and verbal brilliance Meyrink's work is very similar to that of Ambrose Bierce. If Meyrink was not as prolific or as amusing as Bierce, he was more bizarre and more profound.

For a short time Meyrink was on salary with *Simplicissimus,* but he did not fulfill his commitments and he was dropped. He always had many more ideas than finished stories, and his correspondence was haunted with ghost projects. His books during this period, however, were largely based on contributions to *Simplicissimus* and similar magazines, such as Hermann Hesse's *März.* These books include *Der heisse Soldat und andere Geschichten* (The Hot Soldier and Other Stories) (1903); *Orchideen, sonderbare Geschichten* (Orchids, Strange Stories) (1904); *Das Wachsfigurenkabinett, sonderbare Geschichten* (The Wax Museum, Strange Stories) (1907) and a three-volume boxed set that gathered together the previous three books and a few additional stories: *Des deutschen Spiessers Wunderhorn* (The German Neanderthal's Magic Horn) (1913). This last title indicates what Meyrink was driving at in one of the strangest collections of satires, travesties, insolent essays and very odd fantasies ever published. *Spiesser* does not lend itself to a one-word English translation: it is a slang term for a person who combines smug arrogance, stupid boorishness, pettiness, philistinism and reaction. The full title, of course, is a slighting parody of Brentano's *Des Knaben Wunderhorn,* one of the sacrosanct classics of nationalism.

During this period before the publication of *Der Golem* Meyrink moved about considerably, with major shifts of residence among Prague, Vienna, Monteux, Berlin and Munich. In Vienna, 1904, he edited a periodical called *Der liebe Augustin,* a would-be competitor to *Simplicissimus.* Meyrink had a brilliant roster of contributors: Klinger, Max Brod, Paul Busson, Kubin, J. J. Vriesländer, Zille, Pascin, Kolo Moser, Stefan Zweig, Wedekind, Josef Hoffmann and many others of international stature. Unfortunately *Der liebe Augustin* did not have the financial backing it deserved, and it soon collapsed.

A good deal of routine work also busied Meyrink during this period. He undertook to translate the works of Dickens into German, and over the years 1909–14, finished the *Christmas Stories, David Copperfield, Bleak House, Pickwick, Nicholas Nickleby, Martin Chuzzlewit* and *Oliver Twist.* (In later years he translated work by Lafcadio Hearn, Ludwig Lewisohn, Sir Oliver Lodge, Kipling, and G. S. Viereck.) His English was excellent, and it is obvious in reading his later works that Dickens's concept of grotesque characters influenced Meyrink as much as had Hoffmann's.

From about 1912 to 1914 Meyrink tried his hand at the stage, and in collaboration with the Roumanian expatriate Roda Roda he wrote four plays, none of which was especially successful either artistically or financially. As a somewhat related project which had obvious linkages with his occult studies he tried to establish a puppet theatre for playing serious, symbolic works (as well as crowd-pleasers). This concept, which was never brought to actuality, finds echoes in *Der Golem.*

In Vienna and Munich Meyrink was a passionate caféteer, an important member of the various small literary and artistic coteries who met in cafés and played chess, solved the problems of the arts and the world, and also drank coffee. Meyrink was helpful to younger men, and it was in the cafés that Max Brod and Kokoschka sought him out. Meyrink sometimes joined in the discussions, sometimes played the role of the older man who bought the drinks. His coterie was avantgarde, liberal, internationally minded and very largely Jewish—a situation which Meyrink's Nazi enemies were later eager to point out.

A major change in Meyrink's life came with the publication of *Der Golem.* It appeared in periodical form in 1913 and 1914, and was issued as a book in 1915. It became an immediate best-seller. Selling over 200,000 copies, it brought Meyrink's name out of the satirical in-groups and before the general public. A good-sized part of this public did not like what it saw in Meyrink, however, and once again he became a cause célèbre.

Meyrink was strongly opposed to World War One, and as has been previously stated, he scoffed at most of the concepts that were floating high during the war years. He ridiculed the military caste and the Junkers, sneered at pan-Germanism, loathed authoritarianism in the administration, and scoffed at ideas of racial purity and the sanctity of German womanhood. As an Anglophile he even questioned the superiority of German *Kultur.*

As the war progressed through the later years and the initial feeling of exuberance disappeared in the Central Powers, Meyrink began to pay for his individualism. Both his house and his person were stoned. He was ferociously attacked in the newspapers, and suffered an onslaught of abuse from the proto-Nazis of the day. "He is one of the most dangerous opponents of German folk-thought. He will corrupt thousands and tens of thousands, just as Heine did," accused Albert Zimmermann, one of his most persistent enemies. A writer's association called him a public enemy; Hesse, Wedekind and the Manns defended him. When his friends in Munich planned to give him a gigantic 50th birthday party in 1918, it was necessary to ask for police protection against riots. In 1916 *Des deutschen Spiessers Wunderhorn* was banned in Austria.

With the money that he had received from the sale of *Der Golem* Meyrink had bought a small house on Lake Starnberg in Upper Bavaria. There, now a Bavarian citizen, he spent the years after the War as a semi-recluse. He had a small tree house built, and in it he studied and worked; or he sat by the shore of the lake practicing meditation exercises.

During this Munich–Lake Starnberg period Meyrink continued to prepare occasional journalism, did some translating and editing, and wrote a few novels. His most important work from this period includes the short story collection *Fledermäuse* (Bats) (1916) and the novels *Das grüne Gesicht* (The Green Face) (1916), *Walpurgisnacht* (Walpurgis Night) (1917), *Der weisse Dominikaner* (The White Dominican) (1921) and *Der Engel vom westlichen Fenster* (The Angel from the Western Window) (1927).

Meyrink's finances became more and more difficult as his books dropped out of fashion. Styles had changed, and his later works had become personal and obscure. Inflation cut into his royalties, and while eventually (after 19 years!) he won a lawsuit against a Nazi historian of literature, he never received a settlement. His old spinal ailment grew worse, and during 1932 it became obvious that his death was near. At that time the suicide of his son, who had become partially paralyzed in a skiing accident, destroyed his will to live. On the day that he knew would be his last he bade farewell to his wife and daughter. He refused opiates that might have clouded his mind, took a meditation posture on a chair facing the sun, and waited for death, which came to him much as it had to John Dee in *Der Engel vom westlichen Fenster.* One can only hope that he found the same illusions in passing that comforted many of his characters in similar situations.

II

Meyrink found great difficulty in writing *Der Golem.* He probably started work on it in 1906, for in January 1907 it was a topic in his correspondence with his friend Alfred Kubin. According to their first plan *Der Golem* was to have been a collaboration of a sort with Kubin: as Meyrink finished chapters of the novel he was to send them to Kubin, who would prepare an illustration for each. Meyrink sent a couple of chapters to Kubin, who made drawings for them, but then, according to Kubin's notes, Meyrink went stale and was unable to write any more. Kubin lost patience after a while and used the Golem illustrations in his own novel, *Die andere Seite* (1908).

For the next six or seven years *Der Golem* kept arising and disappearing like its supernatural prototype. Book publishers got wind of it and tried to buy rights, but for a long time Meyrink refused to sign contracts. He wanted a first publication in England, he claimed, since the Germans had no taste. Then there was the question of the manuscript itself; when asked how close it was to completion, Meyrink's reply would be, "Another week," or "In a couple of weeks." But the months continued to pass. In 1911 a fragment of the novel appeared in the periodical *Pan,* and Meyrink signed a contract with Kurt Wolff, who was to be the publisher of the book. But no manuscript was forthcoming, and the years started to pass.

The truth of the matter was that Meyrink had become lost in his own story. He had far too much material, too many ideas, too many characters, and he could not see his way clear to discarding elements and establishing a central line. Several accounts describe different ways in which Meyrink finally solved the problem, but they all bring in outside help and a geometric diagram. Meyrink and a friend (whose identity is not certain) went over the characters and plot lines, arranged them diagrammatically, probably on a chessboard, and end-

ed by discarding about half of the material. Perhaps it was this proce-
dure that gave *Der Golem* an occasional jerkiness and thinness that do
not occur in Meyrink's other novels.

While not too much is known about the earlier versions of *Der
Golem*, surviving working papers show that originally there were almost twice as many characters; that Rosina, the whore who wanders
in and out of the story peripherally, almost on a symbolic level, was to
have been the most important female character, an opposite foil to
Miriam; that Angelina was to play a larger role; that Pernath was not
so central; that Charousek (at a very early stage of the planning) was,
to disguise himself as the Golem in order to frighten Wassertrum into
suicide; and, also at this very early stage, that the Golem was to have
been simply a ghost. All these features, of course, were changed.

Der Golem as we know it today appeared serially in 1913 and 1914
in the periodical *Die weissen Blätter*, where it aroused a great deal of
attention. It appeared in book form in 1915 and almost immediately
became a best-seller. Between 200,000 and 250,000 copies were sold in
a very short time. These sales did not help Meyrink very much, however, for being in desperate need of cash, he had sold his novel out-
right to Wolff, instead of waiting for royalties. Instead of earning
perhaps $25,000 (his contemporary currency), he received only about
$2,000.

Many of the details in *The Golem* might have been recognized by
Meyrink's contemporaries in Bohemia. Vriesländer the painter, who
appears as one of the background figures, was a friend of Meyrink's,
a fellow contributor to many periodicals; Loisitschek's dive existed, as
did the blind centenarian Schaffranek and the woman who accompanied him; the student Charousek is obviously reminiscent of Charousek the chess master, while the Brigade of Thieves existed, as did the
renegade privy councillor who renounced his honors to become the
mastermind of a gang. The brutal police chief who interrogates Pernath was Meyrink's revenge on the police chief, Olič, who had hounded him, and in all probability a host of smaller details and
personalities could have been found in the Prague of Meyrink's own
life.

This Prague, however, was Romantic Prague, which Meyrink seems
to have been the first to perceive and record. It was a comfortable,
decaying city, not yet a center of Czech nationalism, a living museum
where ancient fortresses and palaces projected memories of the Bohemian kings and Holy Roman Emperors, particularly the mad Habs-
burg Rudolf II. There were the quaint, ancient architecture and

narrow twisting streets of the old quarter—the Stag's Ditch, where criminals were flung in the old days, and the Hunger Tower, where other criminals were suspended in baskets—the Street of the Alchemists, where Rudolf's assorted quacks and fanatics tried to manufacture gold—the insular, decadent German patricians and nobility, who knew no Czech and only incorrect German—the Moldau and the old statue-adorned bridge (which was partly washed away in 1890, the year that *Der Golem* takes place)—and of course the Ghetto, a strange city within a city. Surrounded by invisible psychic walls the Ghetto was still living in the experience of the great sixteenth-century cabbalist Rabbi Judah Löwe or Loew, who had created the golem of folklore. Meyrink may have hated Prague as much as he loved it, but he was obviously fascinated by it and Prague enters into his works over and over. The experiences of Pernath, just released from prison, as he wanders over the devastated Ghetto (in process of "urban renewal") looking in vain for familiar streets are obviously based on Meyrink's own experience on leaving prison.

After Prague itself, which Meyrink often considered anthropomorphically, the most striking element in *Der Golem* is the "being" that gives the novel its name. Yet the presence of the Golem is really more a matter of local color than of necessity. While Meyrink gives the "standard" version of the Golem legend in the puppeteer's narrative, he makes little use of the legend. The Golem might have been called many other things without too much loss. Indeed, Meyrink has been criticized by historians of religion like Gershon Scholem for inadequacy in both the Golem and the comments on the Cabbala. The criticism has some justification, since Meyrink in his desire to retain an element of place gave a historical name to a private symbol.

As the figure of the Golem assumed final form in 1913–14 for Meyrink, it consisted of two supernatural elements. It was the collective psyche of the Ghetto, a strange mixture of saintliness and squalid evil, first evoked by Rabbi Löwe; it was a soul that sums up the experience of the humanoid old buildings and the organic city within and below a city. On the second and more important level the Golem was the principle of individuation, the split soul within us, which could awaken and emerge under certain circumstances, and must be faced and mastered. The Golem is freedom from matter, freedom from organic limitations (and thereby all restraint), and he is the etheric body of the occultists. In this sense *Der Golem* anticipates the spiritual quests of the later novels.

In *Der Golem* the emergence of this second self may occur through various means: the nameless narrator of the frame story experiences it through a dream experience caused by indirect contact with the adept Athanasius Pernath; Pernath experiences it through mental illness and a hypnotic treatment that divided his mind into two compartments; Pernath's counterfigure Laponder the sex criminal experiences it after years of ascetic training and occult study. Pernath succeeds, while Laponder fails, or perhaps the Laponder facet of the larger personality is cast out. Above and beyond the Golem, however, stands the persistent theme of most of Meyrink's major fiction: the surmounting of death by death in life or life in death, as Pernath and the dead Miriam find one another and live in a never-ever world.

Der Golem was Meyrink's first novel, and now, 70 years after its conception, it is mostly a love story in faded old rose, with occasional flashes of fire to be seen behind the fabric. Meyrink's later novels are more individualized and more timeless. As novels of mystical exploration and occult adventure in the mind they form a unique grouping.

Das grüne Gesicht (The Green Face), which first appeared in 1916 when World War One was still in progress, in some superficial aspects embodies the frustrations and miseries of life in Austria and Germany. It is set in Amsterdam in the near future just after the World War has ended in a stalemate of exhaustion. The Netherlands are filled with refugees from Central Europe, and both social and physical dimensions are strained. The world is about to collapse; the Great War was only a symptom of this collapse; and the Kaliyug is about to end. A great spiritual revolution is about to burst upon mankind, accompanied, but not caused, by a physical catastrophe.

The plot line, following a technique that Meyrink often used, starts in a very sedate manner, with only slight hintings and murmurings of fantasy, as a German engineer, Hauberrisser by name, comes upon a magic supply shop in Amsterdam. Within a short time the engineer is whirled along at unbelievable pace through bewildering experiences: the Wandering Jew, the embodied soteric personality of the universe, supernatural judgments, the gods of ancient Egypt, reincarnation, prophecy, madness, voodoo, glamour, doppelgängers, eternal life in death, confrontation with the female principle of the universe, Cabbalism, and many other motives. This listing may sound strange and jumbled, but such is Meyrink's power of internal logic that all these strange concepts are harmonized and flow logically from the basic premises. The novel ends with the destruction of Western Europe by a tremendous wind storm paralleling the spiritual storm, and with the transcendence of life and death by Hauberrisser and his bride. It is a novel of great scope, filled with marvelous touches of style, satirical humor on occasion, and strange personalities.

In *Walpurgisnacht* (Walpurgis Night), which was first published in Leipzig in 1917, Meyrink returned to the curious lore of the strange old city on the Moldau for a wild, chiliastic fantasy. Again it is a collapsing world that he depicts. A physical and spiritual cataclysm (this time motivated from the Orient) brings an age to an end. In German Prague, set among the precious and futile older nobility, whom Meyrink satirizes with his usual savage humor, an upwelling of psychic reversion takes place. The unfulfilled personal past, the criminal, suppressed past, the ancestral past all emerge. The young noblewoman Polyxena Zahradka is possessed by a personality fragment of a wicked ancestress. By magical means she assumes control of the emergent forces of terror and raises her lover to the position of a stump king, in a situation reminiscent of Jan of Leiden. The local Czechs, roused to wild enthusiasm, revert to Ziska's medieval Taborites, and a welter of terror begins, to end horribly. Telepathy, reincarnation, psychic control (aveysha, as Meyrink calls it), prophecy all interpermeate the pathetic story of an elderly privy councillor, the Penguin, who discovers all too late that he may have been purposed for flying. He perishes in the attempt. As a strange Manchu sage reveals, just as there are yearly Walpurgis nights, there are also cosmic Walpurgis nights. All in all *Walpurgisnacht,* with its combination of local color, wild imagination and mockery is a remarkable work.

With *Der weisse Dominikaner* (The White Dominican), published in Vienna and elsewhere in 1921, Meyrink began to abandon the external story of event and action, and began to concentrate more on the inner story of mind and idea, in a combination of occult and mystical themes. A somewhat Hoffmannesque story set vaguely in a small German or Austrian town, it is heavily symbolic in detail and plot, so much so that a summary cannot represent the story fairly. It is a study of psychic evolution through the development (by mental disciplines) of an etheric body; this concept is combined with transmigratory linkages with the past. It is a story of the psychic way of life and psychic way of death; of the battle with the Medusa force of matter, illusion, constraint, and Maya that permeates the universe, and of the narrator's reception into an eternal line of adepts. It is a strangely serene story, filled with odd detail, thought-provoking for the reader who wishes to try to unravel its symbolic threads in detail, but highly personal for Meyrink, and much less accessible than the earlier novels.

Meyrink's last novel, *Der Engel vom westlichen Fenster* (The Angel from the Western Window), published in Leipzig in 1927, is a curious compound of genius and flatfooted banality. The explanation for its defects is quite simple: Meyrink was too ill to work out all his scenario, and much of the novel was written by an occultist associate and friend.

Der Engel vom westlichen Fenster is magnificent in concept, a novel of fate and reincarnation, occult perils and developments, strange linkages of past and present, occult brotherhoods with secret wisdom, black magic, alchemy, Maya, and astounding drugs. It is a double novel set in two worlds which are linked magically: sixteenth-century England and Prague, and twentieth-century Vienna and Prague. Baron Müller, the last descendant of John Dee, the English renaissance scholar and magician, receives an inheritance from his remote ancestor and discovers that he has become involved in Dee's tragedy. Dee's scrying stone, the alchemical stone, mind-expanding drugs, angelic revelations, and a supernatural weapon all play a part in the story, as the novel alternates back and forth in time, yet reveals the meaningless of time. Müller experiences episodes from the life of Dee (freely fantasized from history). He is present as Dee encounters black magic and an Isiac cult flourishing in England and he relives Dee's association with the charlatan Edward Kelly: their mystical séances, the transformation of metals, the revelations they receive from the Angel Il, and their pilgrimage to Prague. There, in Prague, they meet the Emperor Rudolf and encounter the wisdom of Rabbi Löwe. But the Dee facet of the eternal personality is defeated by the evil powers of the universe and perishes miserably. In the twentieth-century facet Müller must redeem the eternal personality by overcoming the Black Isais, the evil principle of duality that destroyed Dee. Müller emerges into a strange transcendence and interpermeation of life and death that cannot be summarized.

Those portions of *Der Engel vom westlichen Fenster* that seem obviously by Meyrink (most of the twentieth-century episodes) are remarkable, and show Meyrink at his best. If one can survive the maunderings of John Dee (which I would speculate were not written by Meyrink), one will never forget the beautiful and charmingly evil Princess Chotokalungin, certainly the most fascinating female figure in occult literature, nor the enigmatic, timeless Mascee, nor the strange wonderland when Prague and Mortlake, past and present, myth and symbol of the cosmic drama all interpermeate one another almost indistinguishably in a misty syncrasy.

In addition to the five important novels, *Der Golem, Walpurgisnacht, Der weisse Dominikaner, Das grüne Gesicht* and *Der Engel vom westlichen Fenster,* Meyrink wrote a fair amount of shorter material that can be considered fantastic in one manner or another His book *Goldmachergeschichten* (Tales of Alchemists) (1925) plays semifictionally over historical moments in eighteenth-century alchemy, including the careers of Böttger and Sendivogius. Meyrink wrote with the assumption that alchemy was valid, and cited contemporary documents in the guise of narrative, a practice for which he was criticized. It is not an important book. Meyrink also left an unfinished novel, *Das Haus des Alchimisten* (The Alchemist's House), which, to my knowledge, has not been published; I know it only from a description of the manuscript. One of its themes is the use, in a motion picture, of an emblem of Melek Taos to enslave men's minds.

Many of Meyrink's short stories use the motives of fantasy for purposes of social satire, literary parody, polemics, or as fables. These do not concern us, despite their occasional brilliance; most of them were based on issues or ideas that are now forgotten except to specialists, and much of their point is now inaccessible to a lay reader.

Certain of Meyrink's short stories, however, conform more to English-American standards of a weird tale. To mention a few: "Der Opal," a Tantric adept changes the human eye into an opal of peculiar brilliance; "Bal Macabre," visions caused by the hallucinogen *Amanita muscaria,* and vampirism; "Bologneser Träner," a witch uses Prince Rupert's drops to kill her lover; and a short series of fantastic *contes cruels* based on the remarkably wicked Dr. Mohammed Darasche-Koh, a Persian master who holds the lost wisdom of Atlantis: "Der Mann auf der Flasche," "Das Präparat," and "Das Wachsfigurenkabinett." Dr. Darasche-Koh also appears in *Das Haus des Alchimisten,* where he is revealed to be a Yezidee. Also worthy of mention are three of the stories in *Fledermäuse:* "Meister Leonhard," "Der Kardinal Napellus," and "Die vier Mondbrüder."

Meyrink's later short stories, such as those in *Fledermäuse* and the few that were written in the 1920's, tend to approach symbolism and planned allegory and bear out his statement that he wrote, as he put it, not by the rules of art, but by the rules of magic. Stories like "Der Uhrmacher" (1926) are a closed system. At times they remind one of Goethe's "Maerchen," and at other times they seem to be a Renaissance or Baroque magical diagrammatic illustration turned into prose. I know of nothing else quite like "Der Uhrmacher."

III

For some years after his death in 1932 Meyrink suffered a critical eclipse. The generation that had laughed or snorted at his jibes in *Simplicissimus* in the first decade of the century grew old, and probably forgot Meyrink for more important day-to-day things. His occult romances, so highly personal in his later years, grew less and less intelligible. And then there was the problem of finding texts. The Nazis had been rather thorough in destroying his books. Even today it is very difficult to find them. I still do not have a full set of his fiction, after some twenty years of (admittedly intermittent) search.

There was the further problem of the Golem itself. I suspect that just as *Der Golem's* partial concern with the Prague ghetto and Judaism capped Meyrink's puncturing of *Spiesser* for the Third Reich, it also served as a point of recoil in post-war years. How was Aaron Wassertrum to be taken? Or how Rosina? Are these to be read as anti-Semitism in Meyrink? Do Meyrink's comments about the horror-soul of the Ghetto indicate hatred in his mind? It is quite conceivable that these questions should be raised. Yet the answer is obvious and clear: no. Meyrink portrayed saints as well as villains, and he said no more about the Ghetto than has been said about ghettos of all sorts by generations of sociologists.

One peculiar aspect about Meyrink has, to my knowledge, never been pointed out. It is generally accepted, almost as a truism, that aspects of the German mystical and romantic traditions gave birth to Nazism, in a linkage from the early nineteenth-century storytellers, poets and philosophers through the Victorian romantics, up into the Neo-romanticism of the early twentieth century. "From Caligari to Hitler" is the phrase that sums up this interpretation of history.

An examination of the work and life of Gustav Meyrink, on the other hand, offers an opposite picture. Here we see the writer of fantasy and expressionist critic lambasting the reactionaries, the military, the totalitarians of the early twentieth century, the men who either lived to become Nazis or anticipated their counterparts who became Nazis. In Meyrink we see occultism and mysticism interpreted as the utmost in the evolution of the free spirit, the ultimate freedom of speech, action and thought. It was the uniformed *Spiesser* of the 1930's who became the final enemy of this mode of thought.

Meyrink reached his position of freedom via occultism and mysticism. Part of his system came from his personal psychic experience; part of it came from external sources. His system, unfortunately, will never be known in detail, since so much of it was lived month by month by Meyrink in his own mind, and would only occasionally be recorded. In all probability Meyrink would have followed the common practice of occultists and initiates in maintaining a level of esotericism that could not be revealed until proofs of advancement had been shown. Yet it is possible, in the most general way, to characterize his thought in historical terms: a background of neo-Paracelsian interpretation of the components of the psyche; a mixture of Renaissance alchemy and psychoanalysis for certain aspects of spiritual praxis; and an equally strong component from Indian thought, particularly the later yogic and tantric systems for physical exercises. To this would have been added interpretations from the various lodges emergent from Madame Blavatsky.

I do not know if too many people today take Meyrink's occult ideas seriously (I should add that I do not), but this does not change the fact that they offer a wonderful source of images, rich in imaginative possibilities. One can read Meyrink's novels on the thrill level, or on the level of art and ideas. As Hermann Hesse said of him, "He is a man with something to say."

E. F. BLEILER

ACKNOWLEDGMENTS

This volume is based on a previously printed English translation of *The Golem* by Ms. Madge Pemberton, who had the ability to reconstitute a translation as original English prose. Her work reads smoothly, with the independence that a good translation should have. Yet it has been necessary to make alterations in the translation. Ms. Pemberton was sometimes inaccurate on the literal level, and sometimes missed the ideas behind the story. I have made some literal corrections, have translated and inserted some passages that had been omitted, and have toned down the Cockney patois that Ms. Pemberton gave to the lower orders in Prague.

A word must be added about sources. Comments about the writings and inferred philosophies of Meyrink have been based on his original works, where described. Biographical material and some background, however, have been derived from the following invaluable studies: *The Bases of Satire in Gustav Meyrink's Work* by William R. van Buskirk. A dissertation submitted in partial fulfillment of the requirements for the degree of Doctor of Philosophy in the University of Michigan, 1957. *Gustav Meyrink, Werk und Wirkung,* by Dr. Eduard Frank, Avalun-Verlag, Büdingen-Gettenbach, 1957. *Studien zu den phantastischen Erzählungen Gustav Meyrinks* by Siegfried Schödel. Inaugural-Dissertation der Philosophischen Fakultät der Friedrich-Alexander-Universität zu Erlangen-Nürnberg, 1965. *Beiträge zur Biographie Gustav Meyrinks und Studien zu seiner Kunsttheorie* by Manfred Lube. Inaugural-Dissertation zur Erlangung der Doktorwürde der Philosophischen Fakultät der Karl-Franzens-Universität, Graz, 1970.

E.F.B.

Lithograph by Hugo Steiner-Prag from *Der Golem*, published by Kurt Wolff Verlag, Leipzig, 1915.

Lithograph by Hugo Steiner-Prag from *Der Golem*, published by Kurt Wolff Verlag, Leipzig, 1915.

Lithograph by Hugo Steiner-Prag from *Der Golem*, published by Kurt Wolff
Verlag, Leipzig, 1915.

Lithograph by Hugo Steiner-Prag from *Der Golem*, published by Kurt Wolff
Verlag, Leipzig, 1915.

Lithograph by Hugo Steiner-Prag from *Der Golem,* published by Kurt Wolff Verlag, Leipzig, 1915.

Lithograph by Hugo Steiner-Prag from *Der Golem*, published by Kurt Wolff Verlag, Leipzig, 1915.

Lithograph by Hugo Steiner-Prag from *Der Golem*, published by Kurt Wolff Verlag, Leipzig, 1915.

Lithograph by Hugo Steiner-Prag from *Der Golem*, published by Kurt Wolff
Verlag, Leipzig, 1915.

Advertising leaflet from Kurt Wolff Verlag, 1915.

Letter from Gustav Meyrink, showing his handwriting.

November 1, 1921 (?)

Dear Sir:

I would be delighted to collaborate on your periodical, *Die* [illegible], and wish you every success.

Yours very truly,
Gustav Meyrink

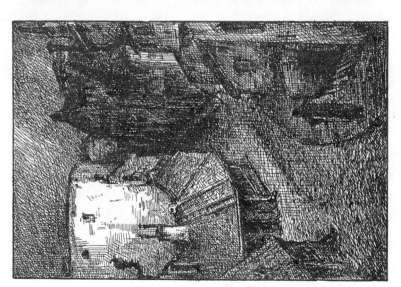

Drawings by Alfred Kubin from *Die andere Seite,* published by Georg Müller, Munich, 1923 edition; originally drawn for *Der Golem.*

The Altneu Synagogue, Prague. In left background is the Jewish Community House.

Typical alleyway in the Ghetto, Prague, 1898.

THE GOLEM

by Gustav Meyrink

Translated by Madge Pemberton

Gustav Meyrink

SLEEP

The moonlight is falling on to the foot of my bed. It lies there like a tremendous stone, flat and gleaming.

As the shape of the full moon begins to dwindle, and its right side starts to wane—as age will treat a human face, leaving his trace of wrinkles first upon one hollowing cheek—my soul becomes a prey to vague unrest. It torments me.

At such times of night I cannot sleep; I cannot wake; in its half dreaming state my mind forms a curious compound of things it has seen, things it has read, things it has heard—streams, each with its own degree of clarity and colour, that intermingle, and penetrate my thought.

Before I went to bed, I had been reading from the life of Buddha; one particular passage now seeks me out and haunts me, drumming its phrases into my ears over and over and over again from the beginning, in every possible permutation and combination:

"A crow flew down to a stone that looked, as it lay, like a lump of fat. Thought the crow, 'Here is a toothsome morsel for my dining'; but finding it to be nothing of the kind, away it flew again. So do we crows, having drawn near to the stone, even so do we, would-be seekers after truth, abandon Gautama the Ascetic so soon as in him we cease to find our pleasure."

This image of the stone that resembled a lump of fat assumes ever larger and larger proportions within my brain.

I am striding along the dried-up bed of a river, picking up weathered, worn flints.

Now they are greyish-blue, coated in a fine, sparkling dust; persistently I grub them up in handfuls, without in the least knowing what use I shall make of them; now they are black, with sulphury spots, like the petrified attempts by a child to create squat, spotty monsters.

I strive with all my might and main to throw these stone shapes far away from me, but always they drop out of my hand, and, do what I will, are there, for ever there, within my sight.

Whereupon every stone that has ever played a role in my life rises into existence and compasses me around.

Numbers of them labour painfully to raise themselves out of the sand towards the light—like monstrous, slaty-hued crayfish when the tide is at the full—as if venturing their lives to compel me to see them, so that they can give me tidings of infinite importance.

Others, exhausted, fall back spent into their holes, once for all abandoning their vain attempt to speak.

Time and again do I start up from this dim twilight of half dream, and for the space of a moment experience once more the moonlight on the end of my billowing counterpane, like a large, flat, bright stone, only to sink blindly back into the realms of semi-consciousness, there to grope and grope in my painful quest for that eternal stone that in some mysterious fashion lurks in the dim recesses of my memory and looks like a lump of fat.

At one time, as I envision it, a rain pipe must have emptied near it, but now the pipe is broken off, its edge eaten by rust; with all my might and main do I endeavour to fix this image in my thoughts, that their troublings may be conjured into rest, and sleep prevail at last.

But always it eludes me.

Again and again, with the persistence of idiocy, a voice keeps repeating in my innermost being—indefatigable as the wind-blown shutter beating at regular recurring intervals against the wall— *"That is not the way of it; that is not the stone like a lump of fat."*

Nothing can rid me of that voice.

When, for the hundredth time, I have reiterated that, anyway, all this is not of the slightest consequence, it stops for one brief moment, only to be born again, and start once more with all its old persistence: *"Very well. . .very well. . .very well. . .but that is not the stone . . . like a lump of fat. . . ."* Slowly an unbearable feeling of frustration begins to overpower me.

What happens next I cannot say.

Whether, of my own free will, I abandon all resistance; whether they overpower and stifle me, those thoughts of mine. . .

I only know that my body lies sleeping in its bed, while my mind, no longer part of it, goes forth on its wanderings.

"Who is this 'I'?" That is the question I am suddenly beset with a desire to ask; but at the same instant do I become conscious of the fact that I no longer possess any organ to whom this query might be addressed; added to which, I am in mortal terror lest that idiotic voice should re-awaken and begin all over again that never-ending business of the stone and the lump of fat.

I turn away.

DAY

All of a sudden, there I stood in a gloomy court, looking through a reddish archway on the hither side of the narrow, grubby street, at a Jewish junkdealer, leaning against the doorway of a shop, whose walls were cluttered around with old ironware, broken tools, rusty stirrups, skates, and an endless variety of derelict objects and general hamper.

And, to me, this image was steeped in that painful monotonous element, the distinguishing mark of all those impressions familiar on the threshold of our consciousness as daily visitants. It aroused within me neither curiosity nor surprise.

I knew beyond all doubt that I had been living for a long time near here.

Neither did this conviction make any deep impression on my mind, despite the startling fact of my presence there, and its utter contrast to all my previous perceptions.

"I must," the idea suddenly came into my head, as I trod the well-worn stone steps that led to my room, and received fleeting impressions of its greasy portal, "somewhere or another I must have come across some curious comparison between a stone and a lump of fat."

I now heard footsteps running down from the staircase above, and as I came to my door, saw that it was Aaron Wassertrum's fourteen-year-old Rosina of the red hair.

I was forced to squeeze past her, and she leant back alluringly against the staircase, laying her dirty hands on the iron rail and I saw the whiteness of her underarm stark against the gloom of shadow.

I did not meet her look.

I detested that insistent smile of hers and her waxy, rocking-horse face.

Her flesh must be white, surely, like that of the axolotl that I saw the other day at the birdshop in the salamander's cage.

As for the eyelashes of the red-haired, I'd as soon contemplate those of a young rabbit.

I unlocked my door and slammed it quickly behind me.

From my window I could see Aaron Wassertrum the junkdealer still standing in front of his shop.

He was leaning against the doorway of his dark shop, clipping his fingernails.

Was Rosina of the red hair his daughter or his niece? There was no shadow of resemblance betwixt them.

I find it easy to pick out the divers breeds of Jew among all those faces that crowd the Hahnpassgasse every day. But they have as little to do with near relationship as oil has to do with water; you can never say, There go a pair of brothers, or a father and son. One belongs to one tribe and one to another. That is all that their faces betray. It would prove but little if Rosina did bear a likeness to old Wassertrum.

These varied types loathe one another with an antagonism not even blood relationship can break through; but they know how to preserve this hatred from the eyes of the outer world, like the conservation of a deadly mystery. It is a secret not one human soul is allowed to penetrate; they are united in the keeping of it like a group of blind men with hatred in their hearts who cling to the same greasy rope; one holds tight with his two fists, another reluctantly with one finger only, but all are possessed with the same superstitious fear lest disaster overtake them should they relinquish their hold and go apart from one another.

Rosina belongs to the tribe of which the red-haired members are even more repulsive than the rest. The men thereof are narrow-chested, with long, bird-like necks and aggressively prominent Adam's apples. They are for the most part freckled, and suffer all their lives from the torment of suppressed passions, against which they wage a perpetual, ever-losing war, racked incessantly by apprehensions for their own bodily health.

I was incapable of resolving the problem of Rosina's blood relationship to Wassertrum the junkdealer. I had never seen her in the old fellow's company, or at any time heard them calling across to one another. Nearly always she was on this side of the courtyard, lurking around the dark corners and passages of my particular block. In any case all my neighbours took her for a close relation of Wassertrum's, or at least his ward; and yet I am sure that no one could have given a particle of proof for it.

I had had enough of thinking about Rosina, and now I looked through the open window of my room towards the Hahnpassgasse. Promptly Aaron Wassertrum glanced up, as though he had felt the force of my gaze in his direction. His same staring, greasy countenance with the goggle fish eyes and the sagging hare-lip. He looked like a human spider, registering, for all its assumed inertia, the slightest contact with its web. On what does he live? What does he think of? What possess?

That I did not know.

All round the walls of his shop are ranged, day after day, year in, year out, the same old worthless things. I could have identified them with my eyes shut: the battered metal cornet without keys, a picture of a group of soldiers, painted on a yellow paper; and, in front of the shop, blocking the entrance, a range of iron stove lids.

These things were constant, never any more of them, never any less, and should some passer-by actually stop and make an enquiry with regard to prices, the junkdealer would fall into a positive frenzy. With his hare-lip protruding at its fullest and most horrifying, he would splutter forth in his rage in a gurgling, stuttering bass something utterly incomprehensible to the intending purchaser, whose desire for information would instantaneously evaporate as he hurried away in a state of terrified dismay.

What was he looking at down there? The house stands with its back towards the Hahnpassgasse, and its windows facing the court. Only one of them looked out towards the street.

The rooms near mine on the same floor—some sort of a corner studio affair from the look of it—would appear to be occupied for the moment, for I can hear through the walls, all of a sudden, a male and a female voice in conversation.

But it's impossible that old Wassertrum, right down below there, can have noticed that!

Someone is moving, the other side of my door. I conjecture: it is Rosina, still waiting greedily in the shadows, lest I should be tempted to call her in to me. Below me, half a story again, Loisa is standing on the staircase, pock-marked and stunted, breathlessly listening to hear if I open. I can positively feel the breath of his hatred and all his frothing jealousy stealing up the steps towards me. He is afraid to come nearer and be seen by Rosina. He knows he is dependent on her as a hungry wolf upon its keeper. . .yet what would he not give to spring up there and then, giving full vent to his fury, blindly. . .madly
. . . .

I sit down to my work-table and search for my pincers and graving tools. But this was to be one of my off days. My hand was not steady enough to work on the restoring of that delicate Japanese print.

The dismal gloomy pall of life that hung over this warren of lodgings obsessed the whole soul of me. Picture after picture rose up into my mind.

Loisa and his twin brother Jaromir are hardly a year older than Rosina. Of their father, a baker of consecrated wafers for the Church, I scarcely seem to have any recollection; some old woman, I believe, now sees after the two youths. That is to say, she provides them with a roof to sleep under, for which they must pay her with whatever they can beg or steal. Does she give them their meals? I should imagine not, considering the late hour of the old crone's regular home-coming. She is a layer-out of corpses by profession, so they say.

I had often watched Loisa, Jaromir, and Rosina playing together in the courtyard as children. But that is long ago.

Day in, day out, does Loisa persist in shadowing that red-haired Jewish girl. Sometimes he will not be able to find her for hours together, and then it is he creeps in front of my door and waits for her, with wry distorted face, lest she creep by secretly. I can see him in the spirit, as I sit at my work, lurking there in the passage corner, his head, with its nervous twitch, stuck out, listening.

At times the stillness is broken by a sudden wild cry. It is Jaromir, the deaf mute, whose whole existence is bounded by a dominating lust after Rosina; he roams the building like a wild beast, half crazed with jealousy and suspicion, and his inarticulate howling cry is enough to freeze up the blood in one's veins. Always he is visualising in his mind Loisa and Rosina together, and he seeks and seeks, first in one smutty corner and then in another, in utter blind madness, impelled for ever by the one great thought—that he must perpetually be on his brother's heels, that nothing shall take place between him and Rosina without his knowledge.

And, so I surmise, it is precisely this perpetual agony on the part of the cripple that provides the incentive to Rosina's carryings-on with Loisa. The latter, should Rosina show signs of falling off ever so little, manufactures fresh atrocities to stimulate her flagging spirits. They let themselves be surprised by the deaf-mute and lure the poor mad creature treacherously into dark passage-ways, where they have erected artful contrivances of old rusty barrel hoops and iron rakes with teeth upwards into which traps the miserable man falls and emerges bleeding. Occasionally, that the pain may be provoked to the point of torment, Rosina will devise, by her own unaided genius, a plan little short of demoniac.

She will change, in a flash, her whole demeanour towards Jaromir, and pretend he has found favour in her sight. With that perpetual smile of hers, she makes the cripple a recipient of hasty confidences, which transport him to a state of wild excitement, and for this end she has evolved a mysterious language of signs, only half intelligible, that weave an inexorable web around the unfortunate deaf-mute, of babbling uncertainty and devastating hope. I saw her once, standing before him in the courtyard, and, such were her gestures and emphatic working of her lips, I thought for sheer mental torment he must needs break into little pieces. His face was sweating at every pore, in his almost superhuman efforts to understand the sense of her lightning movements, so deliberately misleading. The whole of the following day he waited, feverish with expectation, within the dirty doorway of an old derelict house a little farther down the narrow, grimy Hahnpassgasse. There did he wait and linger, wasting time enough to have begged for himself the sum of a couple of kreuzer. Late at night, when he returned, half dead with hunger and spleen, the old woman had locked him out.

The gay sound of a woman's laughter from the adjacent studio came to me through the wall.

Laughter? In a place such as this a real happy laugh? In the whole Ghetto there is no one who can laugh happily.

Then I remembered what Zwakh, the old puppeteer, had confided to me a few days ago—that a distinguished young gentleman had taken the studio over from him at a high rental, obviously for the express purpose of meetings undisturbed with the lady of his choice. Bit by bit, in the watches of the night, so as to escape the notice of the other inmates, handsome pieces of furniture had been arriving. The old boy had rubbed his hands with glee in the telling of it, childishly delighted at his own clever part in the transaction; not one of the other tenants could have the slightest suspicion of the presence of this pair of lovers in their midst.

And yet from no less than three of the houses was it possible to obtain access to this studio. There was even a trap-door that led into it! To say nothing of the fact that, if one unlatched the iron door to the basement—quite easy from above—it was possible, through my room, to reach the staircase of our house and make an exit that way.

I heard peals of laughter—and vague memories arise—a great mansion, a noble family, where I often called to make small restorations on priceless antiquities.

Suddenly from the same quarter I hear a piercing cry. I listen, appalled.

The iron door grinds open, and the next moment a woman has rushed into my room. Hair dishevelled, white as the wall, a piece of gold brocade flung over her naked shoulders: "Master Pernath, hide me—for the love of Christ! Don't ask questions; hide me—here!"

Before I could reply, my door was suddenly opened, and as quickly shut again.

For the space of a second the face of Aaron Wassertrum had grinned like an obscene mask through the aperture.

A round luminous spot swims into my vision, and by the light of the moon I become aware once more of the foot of my bed.

Sleep lies still upon me like a thick woolly mantle, and the name of Pernath is woven into my consciousness in letters of gold.

Where have I read it before, this name—Athanasius Pernath?

Once, long, long ago, it is in my mind that somehow or other I took the wrong hat by mistake; at the time I was surprised how well it fitted me, for the shape of my head I always thought peculiar to myself. I had glanced at that time, down at the lining of the hat, and there had observed, in letters of gold in the white silk:

ATHANASIUS PERNATH

And, for some reason I did not understand, the hat had filled me with fear and dislike.

All of a sudden, like an arrow from the bow, comes the sound of the voice, the voice I had forgotten, and which still persists in asking me where the stone is that looks like a lump of fat.

In a trice I conjure up in my mind the image of Rosina, with her lascivious, grinning profile. That seems to settle the voice, for the arrow is lost in the darkness.

Ah—that face of Rosina! That has ten times the strength of this babbling voice of inanity; now can I rest in peace even though I be buried again in my room in the Hahnpassgasse.

"I"

Unless my impression was wrong that someone followed me up the staircase, always the same distance behind, with the object of paying me a visit, he must have arrived at the last flight by now. He is, I surmise, making his way round the corner where Schemajah Hillel the registrar has his lodging, along the upper story passage with the red tiles. He is fumbling his way now along the wall; at the moment he must be laboriously spelling out the letters of my name in the darkness, upon my door.

There stood I in the midst of my room, gazing towards the passage.

The door opened, and he came in.

He took a few steps towards me, without removing his hat or uttering any greeting. I had the feeling that was how he behaved himself at home, and to me it seemed quite as it should be that this was the way of it.

He reached into his pocket and took out a book.

For a long time he stood there, turning over the leaves. The book was bound in metal, which was chased with rosettes and seals, in which were coloured enamels and small stones.

At last he found the place he wanted, and pointed to it. It was a chapter entitled *Ibbur, or the Fecundation of the Soul.*

Almost mechanically I noted that the initial letter, in red and gold, took up nearly half the page, and the edge of it was worn away.

It had been brought to me for restoration. The letter did not adhere to the parchment in the way I was familiar with in old books, but appeared to consist of two strips of thin gold, soldered together in the centre, and fixed to the edge of the parchment at each end.

Had it been necessary to cut a hole in the page in the place where the letter now was. . .and would the "I" show reversed on the other side? I turned over the page, and found that it was so. Involuntarily, I read the page through, together with the one that followed.

I read on and on.

The book spoke to me as had my dream, only clearer and more coherently. Like an interrogation, it pierced straight to my heart. From an invisible mouth words were streaming forth, turning into living entities, and winging straight towards me. They twirled and paraded like gaily dressed female slaves, only to sink on the floor or evaporate in iridiscent mist into the air, each giving place to the one that followed. For an instant each would pause, hoping to be the object of my choice, before making way for her successor.

More than a few of them there were that peacocked up and down in shimmering garments, with slow and measured steps; others, again, resembled aged queens, a lascivious crook to the corners of their mouths, and wrinkles foully besmirched with garish paint. They passed, and others succeeded them, a ceaseless procession of grey forms and faces, so humdrum and devoid of all expression that to memorise them seemed beyond the power of concentration.

Now they dragged in a woman, stark naked, gigantic as a feminine Colossus. For the space of a second she stood there, doing me reverence. The lashes of her eyes were the length of my whole body, and with a silent gesture she directed my gaze towards the pulse in her left wrist. It started to throb like an earthquake, and I felt within her the life of an entire world.

A throng of corybantes came rushing out of the distance.

A man and a woman were embracing. I saw them come from afar, and nearer and nearer came the throng. Now I heard the singing of the frenzied troop close to me, and my eyes sought out the embracing couple. But they had now turned into one single form, half male, half female—a hermaphrodite seated on a throne of mother-of-pearl. Its crown terminated in a piece of red wood, on which the Worm of Destruction had gnawed mysterious runic figures. Pattering blindly behind came a flock of miniature sheep, in a cloud of dust—perambulating provender that the giant hermaphrodite trailed in its wake to feed its train of dancing bacchantes.

And some of the figures that streamed forth still from this invisible mouth were risen from the dead, their features swathed in grave-clothes. Should they pause in my presence, they would let their wrappings suddenly fall, staring hungrily right into my heart with their predatory eyes that sent a stab of icy horror through my brain, and seemed to dam the swift course of my blood like a stream on which the skies have rained great chunks of stone, plumb to the very centre of its bed.

Now swept past me a woman. I could not see her face; that was turned from me; she wore a cloak made all of flowing tears.

A procession of masked forms then jigged on its way, laughing and with no thought in their heads of me. The figure of a pierrot only gazed at me, full of thought, then turned back, and stood there looking at my face as though into a mirror. The faces he pulled were so fantastic, and the motions of his arms, now slow, now quick as lightning, so bizarre, that I was seized with an irresistible impulse to wink even as he did, to shrug my shoulders and twitch the corners of my mouth. Next moment he was shouldered along by the crowd behind him, all wanting to catch a sight of me as they passed. But not one of these creatures was endowed with reason. They were so many glittering pearls strung on a silken thread, the several notes of a single melody, welling forth from the invisible mouth.

It was no longer a book that spoke to me. It was a voice. A voice that wanted something from me I could not understand, try as I would. It tormented me with its fevered, incomprehensible questionings.

But the voice that uttered these visible words was dead to all eternity, and devoid of echo.

Each noise in this our world of actuality is accompanied by its attendant echoes, just as each object casts its one big shadow together with a multitude of smaller ones. But this voice knew not its echoes any more; long ago they had faded and passed into oblivion.

I had read the book now through to its end, and still held it there in my hands, as though all this time I had been fumbling in my own brain, and not inside a book at all!

Everything the voice had uttered was there within me, had been there all my life, though smothered and forgotten, choked down beneath the weight of my own thoughts, till this, the day of delivery.

I glanced up. Where was the man who had brought the book? Had he gone? Would he fetch it when it was ready? Or ought I to take it to him? I couldn't remember that he had told me where he lived.

I tried to visualise him in my mind, but in vain.

How had he been dressed? Was he old? Was he young? What coloured hair had he? What coloured beard?

Not one single thing could I remember about him. The images I tried to conjure fled away, helter-skelter, before I could fix them in my mind.

I closed my eyes, pressing my lids down with my hand, trying to summon up a glimpse of him, be it ever so slight. Nothing. Nothing at all.

I took up a position in the middle of the room, as I had done at the moment of his arrival, and pictured the scene: thus had he groped round the corner, thus had he stolen along the tiled passage, thus had he stood outside, reading the letters on my door-plate: "*Athanasius Pernath.*" And then he had entered.

It was all in vain.

Not for an instant could I recapture the least glimmer of his presence as it had appeared to me. I saw the book lying there on the table, and conjured up in spirit the vision of that hand as it had emerged from its pocket and reached it out to me. I could not even remember if it had worn a glove or if it were bare, if it were young or old, plain or beringed.

Suddenly I was possessed with a strange idea.

It was like an irresistible inspiration.

I threw my cloak over my shoulders, put my hat on my head, and went out along the passage and down the stairs. Then, slowly, I returned towards my room. Slowly, slowly, slowly, just as he had done. As I opened the door, I noticed the shadows that already filled my room. But surely it had been full light of day when I went out?

How long had I been groping there, lost to all knowledge of time? I tried now to imitate the stranger in gait and gesture, yet still could recall nothing of him. How could I imitate him, when I had no point of contact with his personality?

Yet now it was the thing happened, quite other than the way I had imagined.

My skin, my muscles, the whole of my body, remembered suddenly, without telling my brain. They made movements I had neither willed nor desired. It was as though my limbs belonged to me no more. Without any warning my gait had become fumbling and strange to myself as I took a couple of steps within my room. It was the gait of a man for ever in fear of falling, so I said to myself.

It was *his* way of walking! Yes, it was! Yes, it was!

I knew now for certain that he was like that.

My unfamiliar face was now clean shaven, with prominent cheek-bones, my eyes were slanting.

I could feel it, even though I could not see it.

"That is not my face!" I wanted to cry out. I wanted to feel it, but my hand did not obey my will; instead, it crept into my pocket, and pulled forth a book.

Precisely as he had done a short while ago.

All of a sudden I was sitting down, without my cloak, without my hat, at my own table. I—I—Athanasius Pernath.

Terror took me by the throat; my heart beat fit to burst. Those ghostly fingers, groping in the crevices of my brain, had ceased their fumbling, yet still, deep down in my innermost mind, I could feel the cold contact of their touch.

I knew now who the stranger was, and that at any moment I could feel his personality within me at my will; yet still was I unable to conjure up his actual presence before me, face to face. I knew I never should be able to.

He was like a negative, I recognised, an unseeable hollow form whose lines I cannot comprehend, into which I must slip if I was to become conscious of its form and its impact on my Self.

In my table drawer was a little iron box; in it I decided I would place the book and let it stay there till the effects of my brain-storm had passed away; then and not till then, would I see to the restoration of that letter "I."

I picked the book up from the table. I had a curious sensation as of not touching it, and the same thing happened when I tried to raise the box. It was as though my sense of touch needs must flow through a long, dark streak of nothingness before it merged into my conscious self, as though betwixt me and inanimate objects yawned a great gulf of time; as though they belonged to an age past and gone, of which I had once been part.

The voice circling round me in the darkness, tormenting me with its queries concerning the stone and the fat, had at last passed me by! This time it missed me! I knew now that it emerged from the realm of sleep. What I had just experienced being on the plane of life, it failed to get in touch with me and track me down.

PRAGUE

Beside me was standing the student Charousek, the collar of his shabby, threadbare overcoat undone, his teeth audibly chattering from cold.

"He'll catch his death," thought I, "in this icy archway," and asked him to come up with me to my room.

But he refused. "Thank you, Master Pernath," he gasped at me, shivering, "I'm afraid I haven't time. I've got to hurry off into the town. Besides, we should get wet to our skins if we were to cross the street at this moment. One second's enough to soak you, in this!"

The rain sheeted over the roofs and trickled down the house-fronts like a storm of tears. Stooping a little, I could catch sight of my window on the fourth floor, the panes of it obscured by drops of moisture that turned it to an unhealthy blister on the wall.

A dirty drain ran the length of the street, and the archway was filled with people waiting for the downpour to end.

"There goes a bridal bouquet," said Charousek suddenly, pointing to a bunch of withered myrtle drifting along in the filthy water.

At which somebody behind us laughed out loud. Turning, I saw it to be an elderly, white-haired man, carefully dressed, with a bloated countenance, strangely reminiscent of a frog. Charousek glanced over his shoulder for a moment, then stood humming something to himself.

There was something unpleasant about that old man. I looked away from him, and gazed instead at the discoloured buildings, standing there side by side in the rain like a herd of derelict, dripping animals. How uncanny and depraved they all seemed. Erected without plan, from the look of them, as fortuitously as so many weeds rising from the ground. Two of them were huddled up together against an old yellow stone wall, the last remaining vestige of an earlier building of considerable size. There they had stood for two centuries now, or it might be three, detached from the buildings around them; one of them slanting obliquely, with a roof like a retreating forehead; the one next to it jutting out like an eye-tooth.

Beneath this dreary sky they seemed to be standing in their sleep, without a trace revealed of that something hostile, something malicious, that at times seemed to permeate the very bricks of which they were composed, when the street was filled with mists of autumn evenings that laid a veil upon their features.

In this age I now inhabit, a persistent feeling clings to me, as though at certain hours of the night and early morning grey these houses took mysterious counsel together, one with another. The walls would be subject to faint, inexplicable tremors; strange sounds would creep along the roofs and down the gutters—sounds that our human ears might register, maybe, but whose origin remained beyond our power to fathom, even had we cared to try.

Often in my dreams would I witness the ghostly communings of these old houses, and in terror realise that they in very truth were the lords of the street, of its very life and essence, of which they could divest themselves at will, lending it during the day to its inhabitants, only to reclaim it, plus exorbitant interest, when night came round again. To say nothing of the curious beings living within their walls— beings not born of flesh and blood—whose doings and strivings seem jumbled one against another, conglomerate, without a plan; as their spirits pass before me, more than ever am I convinced that such dreams as these conceal some dim truth within themselves which, in my waking hours, like the faint rainbow impress of a fairy-tale, shimmers only faintly in the depths of my soul.

Then, in mysterious fashion, comes into my mind the legend of the mysterious Golem, artificial man, whom once, long ago, here in the Ghetto, a rabbi learned in the Kabbala shaped from the elements, investing it with an unreasoning, automatic life when he placed a magical formula behind its teeth. And, as that same Golem stiffened into clay the instant that mysterious phrase was removed from its lips, so must, I thought, these humans dwindle to soulless entities so soon as was extinguished within them some slightest spark of an idea, some species of dumb striving, however irrelevant, already deteriorated with most of them, from the look of it, into a mere aimless sloth, or a dull waiting for they know not what.

Lurking and waiting . . . waiting and lurking . . . the terrible, perpetual motto of the Ghetto.

Never are its inhabitants seen in the act of work. Yet they are awake with the first dawning, and they wait, almost with stopped breath, as if for a sacrifice that is never performed.

"Toothless, degenerate beasts of prey, stripped of their strength and their weapons," said Charousek hesitatingly. And he looked at me. How could he have known what I was thinking of? "Sometimes," thought I, "so strong is the burden of a man's thoughts within him that, like spraying sparks, they leap from one's brain into that of one's next-door neighbour."

"How do they live?" I asked, after a little while.

"Live! How do they live? More than one of them's a millionaire."

I looked again at Charousek. What on earth could he mean?

But the student gazed silently up at the clouds. The murmur of voices had ceased for a moment in the archway, and the only audible sound was the hissing of the rain.

What on earth did the fellow mean, with his "More than one of them's a millionaire?" Again it was as though Charousek had been responding to my thoughts.

He pointed to Wassertrum's old shop, past which the water swirled in reddish puddles, stained with the rust of scrap iron.

"Aaron Wassertrum, for instance! He's a millionaire. Owns a third of the Ghetto. Didn't you know that, Herr Pernath?"

I gasped. "Aaron Wassertrum? That old junkdealer is a millionaire?"

"Oh, I know all about *him,*" continued Charousek venomously, as if he had only been waiting for me to ask him. "And I knew his son, Dr. Wassory. Never heard of him? Wassory the famous ophthalmologist? The whole town was mad about him a year ago. A great specialist, they used to call him. They never knew that not so long ago his name had been Wassertrum. He loved to play the part of a man of science who had renounced the world. Any awkward questions about his origin he'd turn aside with modest chat about his father in the Ghetto, his own humble beginnings, and how he had kept the lamp of learning alight despite sorrows and hardships. Sorrows and hardships! He was right there, but he never revealed whose sorrows and hardships, nor the means he had used. But I knew." Charousek seized my arm and shook it, none too gently.

"Master Pernath, I tell you I'm so poor it's almost past my own power to realise. I go about the streets half naked, like a tramp—look!—yet I'm a student of medicine, and a man of education!"

He undid his overcoat, and I saw, to my horror, that he had neither coat nor shirt beneath it; nothing, in short, but his bare skin.

"And I was every bit as poor when I dragged this dirty dog down to his ruin—this eminent God almighty Dr. Wassory—and not a soul knows to this day . . . I was the cause of it! All over the town it was believed that it was one Dr. Savioli who had exposed the rascal's methods, and driven him to take his life. But I tell you Dr. Savioli was nothing but a tool in my hand. It was I thought out the plan and collected the evidence; sapped all the foundations, bit by bit, of the house of Wassory, till the mine was laid and wanted nothing but the merest spark to fire it! Not all the money on earth or the whole accumulated cunning of the Ghetto could save him. It took only the slightest push for a collapse. The way you play chess. Exactly the way you play chess.

Nobody knows it was I! Not a mother's son of them! Though old Aaron Wassertrum, I shouldn't wonder, has some sleepless nights, with a nasty feeling somewhere in the pit of his stomach that there's somebody none too far away, for all that he can't locate him, somebody other than Dr. Savioli, who must have had a hand in the game! But Wassertrum's the sort of chap who, for all those little squinny eyes of his can see through a stone wall, never allows for the fact that there are minds who know how to use long, invisible needles with poison on the end of them, that can penetrate those same walls, beyond gold and precious stones, till they reach the vital arteries behind them."

Charousek gave a wild laugh as he slapped his hand against his forehead.

"Aaron Wassertrum will know soon enough. On that same day he thinks to have Savioli by the throat—on that identical day! I know all the moves of this game down to the last move. It's going to be a King's Knight Gambit. There will be no possible move, up to the bitter end, against which I don't have a devastating reply. Anyone pitting himself against me will find himself dangling in the air like a marionette on strings . . . and I'll have the pulling of them. Mark my words, I'll manipulate them at my own sweet will."

The student rambled on like a man in a fever, and I gazed into his face, dismayed.

"What have Wassertrum and his son done to you for you to hate them so?"

Charousek waved the question aside with a violent gesture.

"Let us forget that. Instead ask what broke Wassory's neck? Or would you rather hear about it another time? The rain's stopped. Perhaps you'd rather go home?"

He dropped his voice like someone suddenly relapsing into calm. I shook my head.

"Have you ever heard how they cure glaucoma these days? No? I'll have to tell you that, Master Pernath, so that you can get it all clear in your mind. Listen. Glaucoma is an internal disease of the eyes that ends in blindness, and there is only one way of stopping it in its course; that's by what is called iridectomy, snipping off a small section of the iris. But the operation is followed by permanent damage to the vision, though actual blindness is usually averted. Moreover, there is one extremely peculiar condition attached to this disease: there are times, especially during its inception, when the clearest symptoms seem entirely to disappear. In such cases a surgeon, though he can find for the moment no actual traces of the disease, cannot state with conviction that his predecessor has diagnosed wrongly. Once the operation has taken place—and naturally it can be performed equally well on a sound or on an unsound eye—no one can be certain whether glaucoma has, or has not, previously existed. Dr. Wassory based his plans on these facts.

"Time and again—especially with women—he would diagnose glaucoma in cases where there were only harmless visual conditions, simply and solely so that he could advise an operation which would involve him in no difficulties and bring him in lots of money. His patients were as wax in his hands; it was as easy as taking candy from a child!

"So you see, Master Pernath, there you get the degenerate beast of prey set in conditions where he needs neither strength nor weapons to shred his victims. He stakes nothing and dares less. By means of a lot of worthless articles in scientific papers, Dr. Wassory succeeded in establishing a reputation for himself as a specialist of the first water, and even in throwing sand into the eyes of his brother colleagues, all of whom were far too straightforward to see through him. A stream of patients in his consulting-room, I need hardly say, was the result. If anyone had even the slightest visual problems, Dr. Wassory would promptly set to work on the approved lines. First came the usual examination during which he would concentrate exclusively on those answers bearing upon glaucoma in order to cover himself for future contingencies. And, above all, he established the fact whether there had or had not been any previous consultation. By way of conversation, he would let drop how he had been summoned abroad in the interests of science, and was obliged to start next day. And, all the time, by means of juggling with electric light, he would deliberately cause as much pain in the patient's eyes as possible. All done, of course, with due caution. You can't be too careful!

"The examination over, followed by the usual anxious question on the patient's part whether there was real reason to fear, Wassory made his first chess move. Taking a seat opposite his victim, after a moment's impressive pause, he would deliver himself of his verdict in grave, considered tones: 'I fear that blindness in both eyes within the immediate future is all but unavoidable.'

"Naturally, the scenes that followed could hardly be called pleasant. More often than not, people would faint, or else weep and scream, and cast themselves down on the floor in utter despair.

"Once eyesight is lost, what remains? The inevitable moment arrived when the poor devil would cling round the doctor's knees imploring to know if there were not some way—any way—of saving him from his doom. On which the cur would make his second move, and convert himself thereby into God, from whom all blessings flow!

"I tell you, Master Pernath, the whole world's like nothing so much as a game of chess!

" 'An immediate operation,' he would say, *'might* be successful. . . a chance maybe. . .the faintest possible. . .' and then he would fairly let himself go, giving way to a vein of bombast in his constitution, describing this case and that, each of them strangely similar to the one in hand—how countless sufferers had owed their salvation to him and him alone, and a lot more of the same kind of bilge. He literally revelled in the idea of himself as the arch physician appointed to pronounce upon the weal or woe of his fellow-creatures.

"But the helpless victim would sit there before him, broken, sweating with agony, his mind seething with questions, but afraid to utter them from very fear to offend him—*him*—his one and only possible saviour.

"Dr. Wassory would then conclude the interview with a neatly timed expression of regret that he would be unable to operate till he returned from his journey abroad in a few months' time. 'Let us hope,' he would conclude, 'hope is a good physician—that even then it may not be too late.'

"Then, of course, the poor devil would spring up, at the end of his tether, declaring how he couldn't be expected to wait one single day, and imploring advice and counsel as to which other surgeon in the town could be recommended to undertake the operation.

"That was the culminating point towards which Dr. Wassory had been working.

"He would pace up and down, his brow furrowed with anxiety, muttering anxiously his objections to such a step: how another opinion would necessitate another examination, which—as the patient realised—was a matter of acute pain, and might end in increased complications, owing to the strong electric rays being once again applied to the patient's eyes before they had had time to recover from the severe strain to which they had been recently submitted. Another doctor might lack practice in this particular operation, and, in any case, would have to wait until the optic nerve had recovered from this examination."

Charousek clenched his fists. "That is what chessplayers call Zugzwang, my good Master Pernath! And the rest was nothing but

Zugzwang pure and simple, one forced move after another.

"The distracted patient would now conjure Dr. Wassory by all his gods to postpone his Continental trip for the space of a day, and undertake the operation himself, a case like this involving, as it did, more even than sudden death. For what greater horror could man endure than the perpetual fear of imminent blindness in both his eyes? The more the swine protested and refused, claiming that postponing his trip would cost him dear, the higher the sum that the patient would offer. Should the amount prove sufficient, Dr. Wassory would cave in ultimately, and arrange for an operation that very same day, lest chance should step in and circumvent his little scheme. His wretched victim would then be condemned for the rest of his life and Dr. Wassory would have destroyed any evidence that might have incriminated him.

"Thus did Dr. Wassory succeed in acquiring for himself a reputation as an incomparable surgeon, and satisfying at one and the same time his boundless avarice and vanity. What could be more gratifying than the thankful admiration of those he had irreparably injured both in fortune and health?

"None but a man born and brought up in the Ghetto could have gone on successfully perpetrating such atrocities for such a length of time; a man who has learnt from childhood upwards to lurk like a spider in its web, for ever on the watch, making it his business to be acquainted with the town's every inhabitant, probing into their slightest little affairs, their comings and their goings and their yearly incomes. A man with eyes in the back of his head, as the phrase goes. And, but for me, he'd have been plying his devil's trade here to-day, till he'd attained a ripe old age; sitting as an honoured patriarch in the midst of his friends and disciples, a shining example to youth, held up as an object-lesson to the rising generation, till—till at last he died— the same as anyone else.

"But I—I too was the Ghetto's own child, and my blood too is tainted with its infernal cunning, and that's how it was I was able to bring him down—struck down by the Invisible—a thunderbolt from the clear sky.

"To Dr. Savioli, a young German medical man, belongs the honour of finally unmasking him. I used Savioli for it, heaping proof upon proof, till the Public Prosecutor stepped in, and Dr. Wassory was a marked man. The dog took his own life then. Blessed be the hour!

"And, as though my shadow had been standing at his elbow, guiding his every motion, he poisoned himself with that very phial of amyl nitrite I had left on purpose in his consulting-room that day I had him examine me, egging him on deliberately to pronounce his verdict of glaucoma. I had placed it there in the burning desire he would take it, and that it might prove the last thing he *would* take! They said, in the town, it was syncope. Amyl nitrite certainly produces all the effect of syncope on the brain. But rumour let out the truth."

Absently Charousek stood staring in front of him as though immersed in some insoluble problem. Then he nodded his head towards Aaron Wassertrum's junkshop.

"He's alone in there," he murmured, "all alone with his avarice and . . . and . . . his wax doll."

My heart leapt into my mouth, and I gazed, horrified, at Charousek. Was the fellow crazy? It must be some high state of fever that wrought these images upon his mind.

Of course! Not a doubt of it! The whole thing was sheer invention—or else a dream. That hideous story about the ophthalmologist couldn't possibly be true. Charousek was consumptive and had brain fever. My impulse was to turn the current of his thoughts, with a couple of jesting words, into a more wholesome direction. But, as I sought them, there shot into my mind the picture of Wassertrum, harelip and goggle eyes, as he had peered into my room.

Dr. Savioli! Dr. Savioli! That surely was the name Zwakh, the old puppeteer, had mentioned in connection with the young gentleman who had rented his studio from him. Dr. Savioli! Almost with a cry the name surged into my conscious mind. A whole host of nebulous pictures now coursed through my brain, hard on one another's heels, chasing one another in a mad dance of conjecture.

I wanted to question Charousek, and then and there confide in him my whole uncanny story, but suddenly he was seized with a fit of coughing that racked his entire being. I was still hesitating when the poor fellow began to grope his way along the reeking archway, bestowing a fleeting nod upon me before going his way out into the rain.

No, I thought to myself. It was not the ravings of a man in fever. The fellow was right. Intangible, the spirit of crime walks through these streets day and night in its quest for a human lodgment. It floats on the air, and we see it not. Suddenly it swoops on a human soul; yet still are we impervious to its presence, and no sooner have we sensed it than it has flown away again and the moment has passed.

In a flash I had solved the riddle of all those fantastic beings in the midst of whom I dwelt. I had penetrated their secret; they were being driven, willy-nilly, through this life of theirs by some magnetic, invisible stream just as the bridal bouquet had been swept along the reeking gutter.

And now it seemed to me as if an evil, hostile spirit stared forth at me from the face of each and every house; their doors were so many black, wide open mouths with cancerous tongues . . . screaming furies, whose piercing cry rose up into the air, so full of hate that it filled the secret places of the soul with terror.

What was that last phrase the student had used about the old junk-dealer? "He is alone now with his avarice and his wax doll."

Wax doll! What, exactly, did he mean by that? Just a simile, surely—one of Charousek's sick similes—a little phrase that you don't understand at the time of hearing, while later on, in all its vividness, it gets up and hits you in the face and fills you with nameless fear, like the forms of unfamiliar things suddenly lit up by a streak of garish light.

Trying to pull myself together and shake off the disturbing impression Charousek's story had made upon me, I drew a deep breath. I looked more closely at the people gathered in the passage with me. Next to me was the fat old man, the one with the unpleasant laugh. He wore a black frock coat and shoes, and was staring fixedly, with his protruding eyes, at the house door opposite. The broad, coarse features of his clean-shaven face were twitching with excitement. Involuntarily I followed his gaze, and found it riveted upon Rosina of the red hair, who was standing on the other side of the street, her perpetual smile upon her lips.

The old boy was feverishly endeavouring to make her aware of his signs. She, of course, was fully conscious of them, but preferred to pretend otherwise. At last he could bear it no longer, and started wading through the puddles in her direction, bouncing along for all the world like a large black india-rubber ball. He seemed not to be a stranger, to judge by the comments that followed him; a tough-looking fellow behind me, with a blue peaked cap on his head, a red striped kerchief round his neck, and a cigarette stuck behind his ear, indulged in a series of grimaces I was at a loss to interpret.

All I gathered was that they dubbed him the "Freemason," which, among the initiate, meant one who had dealings with immature girls, but because of intimate connection with the police, stood in no danger of arrest.

Meanwhile, Rosina's face had vanished, together with the old man, within the darkened doorway of the house.

PUNCH

We had opened the window to try and get the smell of tobacco smoke out of my little room. The cold night wind now blew in, making the curtain that hung over the door sway to and fro.

"Prokop's worthy headgear would like to take unto itself wings and fly away," said Zwakh, and pointed to the musician's hat, which was flapping its broad brim like black wings.

Joshua Prokop's eyes twinkled.

"It wants to go . . ." he said.

"It wants to go dancing at Loisitschek's," Vrieslander finished for him.

Prokop laughed again, and started to beat time with one hand to the noises borne over the roofs on the wings of the winter breeze. Then, from the wall, he took down my old guitar, and made as though he would pluck its broken strings, while he sang in his cracky falsetto, and with fantastic phrasing a remarkable song in dialect:

> An Bein-del von Ei-sen recht alt
> An Stran-zen net gar a so kalt
> Messinung, a'Raucherl und Rohn
> Und immer nurr put-zen . . .

"He's a dab at the dialect all right, isn't he?" laughed Vrieslander, and drummed with his fingers and joined in:

> Und stok-en sich Aufzug und Pfiff
> Und schmallern an eisernes G'suff.
> Juch . . .
> Und Handschuhkren, Harom net san. . . .

"They sing that old song every evening down at Loisitschek's," Zwakh informed me. "Meshuggene old Nephtali Schaffraneck, with his green shade over his eyes, wheezes it out, accompanied on the accordion by a painted piece of female goods. Really, you know, Master Pernath, you ought to go along with us there some evening. Perhaps to-night—later—when we're through with the punch—eh? What do you say to it? Isn't it your birthday to-day, or something?"

"Yes," urged Prokop, as he closed the window once more, "You come along with us, old fellow-me-lad. It's a thing to see for yourself."

We sat around drinking hot punch, while our thoughts roamed the room.

Vrieslander was carving a puppet.

"Well, Joshua,"—Zwakh broke the silence—"you've shut us off good and proper from the outer world. Not one word has got itself spoken since you shut the window."

"I was thinking," said Prokop, rather hurriedly, as if apologising for his own silence, "while the curtain was flapping, how odd it is when the wind plays with inanimate objects. It's almost like a miracle when things that lie about without a particle of life in their bodies suddenly start to flutter. Haven't you ever felt that? Once I stood in a desolate square and watched a whole heap of scraps of paper chasing one another. I couldn't feel the wind, as I was in the shelter of a house, but there they were, all chasing each other, murder in their hearts. Next instant they appeared to have decided on an armistice, but all of a sudden some unendurable puff of bitterness seemed to blow through the lot of them, and off they went again, each hounding on his next-door neighbour till they disappeared round the corner. One solid piece of newspaper only lagged behind; it lay helplessly on the pavement, flapping venomously up and down, like a fish out of water, gasping for air. I couldn't help the thought that rose in me: if we, when all's said and done, aren't something similar to these little bits of fluttering paper. Driven hither and thither by some invisible, incomprehensible 'wind' that dictates all our actions, while we in our simplicity think we have free will. Supposing life really were nothing but that mysterious whirlwind of which the Bible states, it "bloweth where it listeth, and thou hearest the sound thereof, but canst not tell whence it cometh and whither it goeth"! Isn't there a dream in which we fumble in deep pools after silver fish, and catch them, to wake and find nothing in our hands but a cold draught of air blowing through them?"

"Prokop, you're catching that trick of speech from Pernath! What's the matter with you?" Zwakh regarded the musician suspiciously.

"It's the result of the story of the book *Ibbur* we had told to us before you came. Pity you were late and missed it . . .you can see the effect it's had on Prokop." This from Vrieslander.

"Story about a book?"

"Story of a man, rather, who brought the book, and looked very strange. Pernath doesn't know who he is, where he lives, what his name is, or what he wanted. And, for all his visitor's striking appearance, he can't for the life of him describe it."

Zwakh listened attentively.

"Strange, that," he said, after a pause. "Was the stranger clean shaven by any chance, and did his eyes slant?"

"I think so," replied I. "That is to say . . . yes . . . yes . . . I am quite sure of it. Do you know him?"

The puppeteer shook his head. "Only it reminds me of the Golem."
Vrieslander, the artist, laid down his knife.

"The Golem? I've heard of it a lot. Do you know anything about
the Golem, Zwakh?"

"Who can say he *knows* anything about the Golem?" was Zwakh's
rejoinder, as he shrugged his shoulders. "Always they treat it as a
legend, till something happens and turns it into actuality again. After
which it's talked of for many a day. The rumours wax more and more
fantastic, till the whole business gets so exaggerated and overdone
that it dies of its own absurdity.

"The original story harks back, so they say, to the sixteenth century.
Using long-lost formulas from the Kabbala, a rabbi is said to have
made an artificial man—the so-called Golem—to help ring the bells in
the Synagogue and for all kinds of other menial work.

"But he hadn't made a full man, and it was animated by a sort of
vegetable half-life. What life it had, too, so the story runs, was only
derived from a magic charm placed behind its teeth each day, that
drew down to itself what was known as the 'free sidereal strength of
the universe.'

"One evening, before evening prayers, the rabbi forgot to take the
charm out of the Golem's mouth, and it fell into a frenzy. It raged
through the dark streets, smashing everything in its path, until the
rabbi caught up with it, removed the charm, and destroyed it. Then
the Golem collapsed, lifeless. All that was left of it was a small clay
image, which you can still see in the Old Synagogue."

"The same rabbi was once summoned to the Imperial Palace by the
Emperor, where he conjured up the spirits of the dead and made them
visible," put in Prokop. "The modern theory is that he used a magic
lantern."

"Oh, yes," said Zwakh composedly. "That explanation is foolish
enough to appeal to moderns. A magic lantern! As if Kaiser Rudolf,
who spent his life chasing after such things, couldn't have spotted a
blatant fraud like that at first glance.

"I don't know how the Golem story originated, but this I know—
there is something here in this quarter of the town . . . something that
cannot die, and has its being within our midst. From generation to
generation, my ancestors have lived in this place, and no one has
heard more direct experiences and traditional stories than I have."

Zwakh suddenly ceased speaking. It was obvious his thoughts had
gone trailing off into the past.

As he sat there at the table, head on hand, his rosy, youthful-look-
ing cheeks contrasting oddly in the lamplight with his snowy hair, I

could hardly refrain from comparing his face with the little puppets he had so often shown to me. Curious how the old fellow resembled them! The same expression, and the same cast of countenance.

There are many things on earth that cannot be separated, I pondered. As Zwakh's simple life-history passed before my mind's eye, it struck me as both monstrous and weird that a man such as he, in spite of a better education than that of his forebears—he had, as a matter of fact, been destined for the stage—should suddenly insist on reverting to his dilapidated box of marionettes, trundling once more into the market-place these aged dolls that had anticked for the scanty living of his ancestors, and there making them re-enact their well-worn histories in terms of clumsy gesture.

I appreciated the reason. He could not endure to be parted from them; their lives were bound up with his, and once he was away from them they changed to thoughts within his brain, where they led him a restless existence till he returned to them. For that reason did he love them, and trick them out proudly.

"Won't you tell us some more, Zwakh?" Prokop begged the old man, with a glance at myself and Vrieslander that sought approval.

"I hardly know where to begin," the old man said hesitantly, "Golem stories are all hard telling. Pernath, here, just now was telling us he knew quite well how the stranger looked, but couldn't describe him. More or less every three and thirty years something takes place in our streets, not so out-of-the-way or startling in itself, yet the terror of it is too strong for either explanation or excuse.

"Always it happens that an apparition makes its appearance—an utterly strange man, clean shaven, of yellow complexion, Mongolian type, in antiquated clothes of a bygone day; it comes from the direction of the Altschulgasse, stalks through the Ghetto with a queer groping, stumbling kind of gait, as if afraid of falling over, and quite suddenly—is gone.

"Usually it is seen to disappear round a corner. At other times it is said to have described a circle and gone back to the point whence it started—an old house, close by the Synagogue.

"Some people will tell how they have seen it coming towards them down a street, but, as they walked boldly to meet it, it would grow smaller and smaller, like an ordinary figure will do as it moves away from you, and finally disappear completely.

"Sixty-six years ago there must have been a particularly lively scare of this sort, for I remember—I was a tiny youngster at the time—that the house in the Altschulgasse was searched from top to bottom. It is also said that there is a room there with a barred window, but no entrance. They hung washing out of every window, and the room was discovered. As the only means of reaching it, a man let himself down on a rope from the roof, to see in. But no sooner did he get near the window than the rope broke and the poor fellow fractured his skull upon the pavement. And when they wanted, later on, to try again, opinions differed so about the situation of the window that they gave it up.

"I myself encountered the Golem for the first time in my life nearly three and thirty years ago. I met it in a little alley, and we ran right into one another. I still cannot remember now very distinctly what went on in my mind at that encounter. Heaven forbid anyone should spend his life in perpetual expectation, day in, day out, of meeting the Golem. At that moment, before I had seen anything, something cried out in me, loud and shrill, 'The Golem!' At that instant someone stumbled out of a doorway and the strange figure passed me by. Next moment I was surrounded by a sea of white, frightened faces, everyone asking if I had seen it.

"As I replied, I was aware for the first time that my tongue had been released as from a clamp. I was quite surprised to find I could move my limbs, for I realised how, for the space of a heart beat, I must have endured a sort of paralytic shock from surprise.

"I have given the subject much thought, and the nearest I can get to the truth of it seems to be this: that once in every generation a spiritual disturbance zigzags, like a flash of lightning, right through the Ghetto, taking possession of the souls of the living to some end we know not of, and rising in the form of a wraith that appears to our senses in the guise of a human entity that once, centuries ago, maybe, lived here, and is craving materialisation.

"Maybe, too, it lurks within our midst, day after day, and we know it not. Neither do our ears register the sound of the tuning-fork till it is brought in contact with the wood, which it forces into sympathetic vibration.

"Think of the crystal, resolving itself, it knows not how, but in accordance with its own immutable laws, from the formless, to a definite ordered shape. May it not be even so in the world of the spirit? Who shall say? Just as, in thundery weather, the electric tension in the atmosphere will increase to a point past endurance, and eventually give birth to the lightning, may it not be that the whole mass of stagnant thought infecting the air of the Ghetto needs clearing from time to time by some kind of mysterious explosion, something potent in its workings. Something forces the dreams of the subconscious up into the light of day—like a lightning stroke—giving rise to an object that, could we but read its riddle, symbolises, both in ways and appearance, the mass-soul, could we but understand and interpret the secret language of forms?

"And, just as Nature has her own happenings that foreshadow the advent of the lightning, so do certain forbidding signs portend the arrival of this phantom within our world of fact. The plaster peeling from an old wall will adopt the shape of a running human form; and stony faces stare from the ice-flowers formed by the frost upon the window-panes. Sand from the roof-tops falls in a different way from usual, filling the apprehensive passer-by with the impression it has been thrown by some invisible spirit, trying to form, from the hiding-place wherein it lurks, all kinds of unfamiliar outlines. No matter what the object one beholds—be it wicker work, all one colour, or the uneven surface of a human skin—we are still obsessed with this disconcerting gift of finding everywhere these ominous, significant shapes, that assume in our dreams the proportions of giants. And always, through these ghostly strivings of these troops of thoughts, endeavouring to gnaw their way through the wall of actuality, runs, like a scarlet thread, a torturing certitude that our own mental consciousness, strive as we may, is being sucked dry, deliberately, that the phantom may attain to concrete form.

"Just now, when I heard Pernath tell how he had met a man clean shaven, with slanting eyes, there stood the Golem before me as I saw it previously.

"He stood there as though risen from the ground. And, for the space of a moment, I was filled with that dumb, familiar fear, the intuition of some ghostly presence near at hand, that I had felt then, in my boyhood, when the Golem had thrown its dread, ominous shadow across my path.

"Sixty-six years ago! And another memory, too, is connected with it—one evening when my sister's fiancé came to settle the marriage date with my family. We amused ourselves by casting lead. I stood by, in open-mouthed astonishment, wondering what it all might mean. The childish workings of my mind connected it somehow or other with the Golem, of whom I had often heard my grandfather talk. Every moment I expected to see the door open and the stranger walk into the room.

"My sister filled a ladle with the molten stuff, and emptied it into a bowl of water, laughing the while at my intense excitement. With his withered, trembling hands, my grandfather picked out the lump of lead and held it to the light. Immediately arose a hubbub of excitement. Everybody talked at once; I tried to wriggle through the crowd of agitated guests, but they stopped me.

"Later, when I was older, my father told me how the molten metal had shaped itself into a miniature but quite unmistakable head, smooth and round, as though cast from a mould, with features that bore such an uncanny resemblance to those of the Golem that fear possessed them all.

"Many a time have I discussed the matter with Schemajah Hillel the registrar, who has in his keeping the paraphernalia of the Old Synagogue, together with the clay figure I told you of, from Kaiser Rudolf's days. He has given much time to the Kabbala, and he held the clay image to be nothing but a presage in human form, at the time in which it was made, just as, in my case, was the lump of lead. And the stranger who haunted our precincts he held to be a projection of the thought that had sprung to life in the brain of the old rabbi before he had succeeded in giving it tangible form, and that it could only appear at stated intervals of time, under those astrological conditions in which it had been created; that then, and then only, would it come back to the earth on its agonised quest for materialisation.

"Hillel's wife, in her lifetime, had also seen the Golem face to face, and felt the same shock of paralysis that I had so long as the inexplicable presence was near. She said, too, she was quite positive that what she had seen was her own soul divested of its body; that just for a moment it had stood opposite to her, and gazed into her face with the features of a strange being. In spite of the terrible fear that had got her in its grip, the conviction had never left her that this thing confronting her was only a part of her innermost self."

"It's not credible," murmured Prokop, lost in thought.

Vrieslander, too, sat there brooding.

Then came a knock at the door, and the old dame who brings up my evening water, and anything else I happen to want, came in, placed the earthenware pitcher on the floor, and silently withdrew.

We all looked up and gazed vaguely round the room, as though awakening from sleep, though a long time elapsed before any word was spoken.

Some new influence had entered the room with the old crone, and we had first to accustom ourselves to it.

"That red-haired wench Rosina, too—she has a face that dances for ever before a man's eyes out of the nooks and the crannies." This from Zwakh, quite suddenly. "I've known that fixed, grinning smile, now, for a whole generation. First the grandmother . . . then the mother! And always the same face . . . not a feature altered! The same name, Rosina—one always the resurrection of the other!"

"Isn't Rosina Aaron Wassertrum's daughter?" I asked.

"So they say," affirmed Zwakh. "But Aaron Wassertrum has many a son and many a daughter people know nothing of. Nobody knew who was the father of Rosina's mother, nor what became of her. At the age of fifteen she brought that child into the world, and that was the last heard of her. Her disappearance had something to do with a murder, if I remember rightly, committed in this house on her account.

"Just like her daughter, she turned all the heads of the young men. One of them's alive still—I see him quite often—I can't remember his name. The others all came to a premature end—through her, probably. I only remember detached episodes, here and there, of that bygone time, that stray through my brain like a series of faded pictures. There was one half-witted fellow who used to go from café to café every evening, cutting out silhouettes in black paper for a couple of kreuzer. Once they'd got him drunk he'd sit there in the depths of melancholy sighing and crying, cutting out always the same sharp girl's profile, till his whole stock of paper was all used up. Almost as a child, so they said, he'd been caught in the toils of a certain Rosina—the grandmother, probably, of our one—and loved her so madly he'd lost his reason. When I count the years back, it can't have been anyone but the grandmother of our present Rosina."

Zwakh ceased speaking and lay back in his chair.

"Fate flits in circles," thought I, "around and around this house, returning always to its starting point." And a hideous image of something I had once seen shot simultaneously into my mind—a cat gone mad, twirling around frantically, in circle after circle.

"Now for the head"—all at once, in Vrieslander's cheery tones. And he took a small billet of wood from his pocket and started to carve.

I pushed my arm-chair into the background, out of the light. My eyes were heavy with weariness.

The hot water for the punch was sizzling in the kettle, and Joshua started to fill our glasses round again. Softly, very softly, the strains of dance-music stole through the closed window; fitfully, now coming, now going, according to the caprices of the wind.

Wouldn't I clink glasses with him?—so the musician wanted to know, after a pause.

But I made no answer. So loth was I to make any kind of movement, I would not even open my mouth. Almost I might have been asleep, such was the feeling of utter quiet that now possessed my soul. I had to glance now and again at the twinkling blade of Vrieslander's pocket-knife, as he cut small chips of the wood, to assure myself I really was awake.

From afar I heard Zwakh's rumbling voice, as he told wonderful stories about puppets, and narrated the plots of his plays.

They were talking now of Dr. Savioli, and the elegant lady—some titled man's wife—who paid her clandestine visits to him in that obscure little studio. Once again I saw floating before me the triumphant, mocking visage of Aaron Wassertrum. I wondered if I would confide that experience of mine to Zwakh, then came to the conclusion it would serve no useful purpose, to say nothing of the fact that I knew my will would be unequal to the effort of relating it.

Suddenly I saw all three of them looking at me across the table. "He is asleep," said Prokop, so loudly that it sounded almost like a question he had put to me.

Then they spoke in subdued voices, and I realised I was the subject of their conversation.

The blade of Vrieslander's knife danced here and there, catching the light from the lamp, and the glint of it burned into my eyes.

"Mental condition," were the words I caught. They talked on, and I listened.

"Subjects like the Golem shouldn't be raised in Pernath's company," said Joshua Prokop reprovingly; "just now, when he was telling us about the book *Ibbur,* we sat silent and raised no questions. I would wager that it was a dream."

"Quite right!" Zwakh nodded. "It's like walking with a lighted candle through a disused room, in which the walls and furniture are all wrapped in dust-sheets, while the dead tinder of the past smothers your footsteps ankle deep; one spark let fall, and fire'll break out of every corner."

"Was Pernath long in the asylum? Poor devil, anyway . . . can't be forty." Thus Vrieslander.

"I don't know. I haven't the faintest idea where he came from, or what his profession was before. He has all the air of an old-fashioned French aristocrat, with his slender figure and pointed beard. Years ago, an old doctor of my acquaintance asked me to do him a favour, and see if I could procure for a patient of his a lodging somewhere in this street, where no one would be likely to disturb him, or worry him with questions about the past." Zwakh waved vaguely in my direction. "Ever since then he's lived here, repairing antiques and cutting precious stones, and apparently making a modest living out of it. It's fortunate for him that he seems to have forgotten everything to do with his mental trouble. You must on no account ask him questions that might awaken his memory. That's what the old doctor used to keep impressing on me. 'Remember, Zwakh,' he used to say, 'all that's over and done with; we've evolved a system now to treat it with; we've built a wall round it, just like fencing in a place where a tragic event has taken place, because of the painful memories.' "

The puppeteer's talk struck at me like a pole-axe on a defenceless beast. Red, merciless hands were clutching at my heart. I had had this dumb kind of torment before . . . a suspicion that something had been taken away from me, and that I had spent a long time walking at the edge of an abyss, like a sleepwalker. And now the riddle was solved—and burned like an open wound.

That reluctance I had to think of the past . . . the strange recurring dream of being in a house with a series of rooms sealed off from me . . . the painful inability of my memory to function where associations of my youth were concerned . . . all these problems had suddenly achieved their terrible solution: I had been mad, and treated by *hypnosis.* They had, in short, locked up a room which communicated with certain chambers in my brain; they had made me into an exile in the midst of the life that surrounded me.

And no prospect of my ever recovering again that lost portion of my memory.

I understood now that the mainspring of all my thoughts and acts lay hidden in another world, forgotten and never to be recalled; I was like a grafted plant, a twig proceeding from an alien root. Even if I ever did succeed in forcing the door of that locked room, would I not fall immediately a prey to the spirits imprisoned therein?

The story of the Golem as related by Zwakh passed through my mind, and suddenly I recognised a connection of infinite mystery and magnitude between that legendary room without an entrance, which the unknown was supposed to inhabit, and my own significant dream.

That was it! In my case, too, the rope would break, should I but try to glance into that barred window of my inner consciousness.

This curious connection became clearer and clearer within my mind, and the clearer it grew the more terrifying did it become. There were things in the world, so it seemed to me, beyond the mind of man to grasp, riveted indissolubly together and running about distractedly, like blind horses, on a path whose direction is hidden from them.

Here, too, in the Ghetto: a room, the door of which nobody could find; a ghostly presence dwelling therein, that from time to time would walk through the streets, spreading terror and fear in the minds of men!

Vrieslander was still hacking away at his puppethead; you could hear the scraping of his knife upon the wood.

The sound of it somehow distressed me, and I looked up to see if it would not soon be finished.

The head, turning about as it did in the carver's hand, looked alive. It seemed to be peering into all the corners of the room. At last its eyes rested upon me. It appeared pleased to have found me at last.

And I, in my turn, was unable to turn my eyes away. Stonily I stared at that little wooden face.

The carver's knife seemed to hesitate a little, then suddenly made a strong, decided cut, informing the wooden head, all at once, with terrifying personality. I recognised the yellow countenance of the stranger who had brought me the book.

There my powers of discernment ended. It had lasted only one moment, but I could feel my heart cease to beat, and then bound forward agonisingly.

The face, none the less, remained in my mind. Just as it had done before.

It was I myself . . . I and none other . . . and I lay there on Vrieslander's lap, gaping.

My eyes were wandering round the room, and strange fingers laid their touch upon my head.

All of a sudden I was aware of Zwakh's face distorted with excitement. I could hear his voice: "God! It's the Golem!"

A short struggle had ensued, while they had tried to wrest Vrieslander's work from his hand. But he fended them off, and crying, with a laugh: "All right! I've made a mess of this job," had opened the window and flung the head into the street below.

Consciousness left me, and I dove into deep darkness veined with shimmering golden threads, and when I awoke again, as it seemed, after a long, long time, I heard the wooden head strike the pavement outside.

"Wake up," I could hear Joshua Prokop saying to me. "You've been so fast asleep you couldn't feel how we've been shaking you. We've finished the punch, and you've missed all the fun."

Then the sharp pain of what I had just been hearing surged over me once more, and I wanted to shriek aloud that it was not a dream that I had told them of the book *Ibbur*—that I would take it out of its box and show it to them.

But I could neither utter these thoughts nor combat the general spirit of leave-taking that had now seized my guests.

Zwakh forcefully put my cloak round my shoulders while he cried:

"Come along with us now to Loisitschek's, Master Pernath. It'll cheer you up!"

NIGHT

Without volition I had let myself be led downstairs by Zwakh. More and more could I sense the fog that was creeping into the house from the street. Joshua Prokop and Vrieslander had gone on a little ahead, and could be heard conversing before the archway that led into the street.

"It must have fallen right into the gutter. So it's on its way to Hell."

We came out into the alley, and I saw Prokop bending down, looking for the puppet's head.

"For my part I'm glad you can't find the damned thing," growled Vrieslander. He was leaning against the wall, his face sharply lit now and again by little spasms of light as he drew the flame of a match into his short pipe.

Prokop made a deprecatory gesture with his arm, and bent down once more, so low he was almost kneeling on the cobbles.

"Soh! Don't you hear anything?"

As we came up, he pointed to the gutter, and listened with his hand to his ear. For a moment we stood there without moving, listening.

Nothing happened.

"What could it have been?" whispered the old puppeteer at last. But Prokop seized him quickly by the wrist.

For the fraction of a second, hardly a heart beat, I had heard something, scarcely audible, as if a hand were knocking against a metal plate. And the sound of it revived an echo in my memory that disappeared, even as it came, to make way for a feeling of indescribable terror.

Steps coming up the street dispelled the impression.

"Come along! What are we standing about here for?" Vrieslander wanted to know.

We walked on, along the row of houses, Prokop very loth to follow.

"I'll bet the hair off my head," he murmured, "someone cried out that moment in fear of death."

No one answered him. But to me it was as though a growing feeling of apprehension had fettered all our tongues.

Soon after, we stood in front of the red-curtained windows of a tavern. On a cardboard placard ran the words:

SALON LOISITSCHEK
GRAND CONCERT TO-NIGHT

Round the placard were stuck faded photographs of women.

Before Zwakh could lay his hand on the bell, the door opened inwards, and there stood, bowing on the threshold, a thick-set fellow with black, tangled hair, no collar, a green silk kerchief knotted round his neck, and a waistcoat decorated with a cluster of boar's tusks.

"More customers . . . more customers. Quick, Panne Schaffranek, another tune," he called over his shoulder into the already overcrowded room, as he bowed his welcome to us. His dialect was heavy and coarse.

For answer came a sound as though a rat had scampered over the keys of a piano.

"Yes—yes—all the nobility of the land are at my house this evening," he replied to Vrieslander's astonished gaze, in triumph. For the latter had glimpsed a couple of elegant young men in evening dress at the back of the room, on a kind of estrade, separated from the rest of the room by a rail and a couple of steps.

Above the tables hovered a cloud of thick, pungent tobacco smoke; the long wooden settles ranged against the walls were full of folk: prostitutes, blowzy, barefooted, their ample bosoms scarcely concealed by the garish handkerchiefs fastened across them; next them their bullies, with blue peaked caps on the backs of their heads, cigarettes stuck behind their ears; hairy-handed, coarse-fingered cattle-dealers, with gestures and actions to suit; pock-marked clerks in loud check trousers; and impudent-eyed waiters prowling around.

"Here you are, gentlemen! Here's a screen for you. You'll be more to yourselves then," spoke the oily voice of mine host, and the next moment a portable screen, covered with little dancing Chinese figures, was rolled up against the corner table at which we had sat.

And now the buzz of human voices was lost in the thrumming of a harp. The whole room held its breath, and for the space of a moment there was silence.

Suddenly, with frightening clarity, the hiss of the gas fixture could be heard, as it shot its heart-shaped flames into the air—then the music swallowed its hissing.

Two curious figures seemed to rise up into my sight from nowhere, through the thick clouds of tobacco smoke. An aged man with a long, streaky white prophet's beard, and a black silk cap on his head—such as the old Jewish patriarchs often wear—with unseeing glassy eyes of a milky blue, sat soundlessly moving his lips, and plucking a harp with fingers like vulture's claws. By his side, clad in a black taffeta dress spotted with grease, jet ornaments on neck and arms—a sham epitome of bourgeois morality—sat a flabby-looking woman, with a concertina on her knee. From the instrument rose a jumble of cacophonous sounds. Then, as if tired, the melody subsided into a mere accompaniment.

The old man opened wide his mouth, as though he were biting the air, revealing the blackened stumps of his teeth in the process. Then, from the pit of his stomach, issued a sound. In a strange bass voice, with queer Hebrew intonations, he was singing:

"*Roo . . . n . . . te, blau . . . we . . . Steern . . .*"

"*Rititit,*" shrilled the woman at his side, pressing her shrewish lips tight together, as if already she had said too much.

> Roonte blaue Steern
> Hörndlach ess' i' ach geern
> Rititit . . .
>
> Rothboart, Grienboart,
> Allerlaj Stern.
>
> Rititit . . . Rititit. . . .

Now they began dancing together.

"That's the song of the 'chomezigen borchu,'" the puppeteer said with a smile, beating time with the tin spoon that, oddly enough, was fastened by a chain to the table. "More than a hundred years ago, two rascally bakers, 'Red Beard' and 'Green Beard,' on the evening of the *Shabbes Hagodel*,[1] poisoned the bread, both stars and crescent rolls, that the Jews in the Ghetto might die off like flies, but the *Meschores*—the attendant at the Synagogue—was put wise to it by divine revelation, and informed the police. And, to commemorate this miraculous deliverance from death, the *Lamdonim* and *Bocherlech*[2] of the period composed that curious song, now used to dance to in a disorderly house."

"*Rititit . . . Rititit . . .*"

"*Roote blaue Steern . . .*" the old man's quavering voice echoed down the room, ever more hollow and more fanatical.

Suddenly the melody grew more confused than ever, and by degrees slid into the rhythm of the Bohemian slapak, a kind of shepherds' dance, whereat the couple pressed their perspiring cheeks closer and closer together.

---

[1] The first Sabbath in Passover.
[2] Wise men and students.

"Bravo! Bravo! Aha! Hep—hep!" shouted from the estrade a slender young dandy in swallow-tails, monocle in eye, fumbling in his pocket and tossing a silver coin towards the harpist. It never got to him; I could see it flashing over the dancing throng; then it disappeared. An apache type—his face seemed familiar to me, and I thought it must be that same man who was standing the other day close to Charousek during the downpour—had slipped his hand out from his harlot's bosom, where up till now it had been rooted firm enough, and with one quick gesture, slick as a monkey, without breaking one single beat of the music, had snaffled the coin. Not a muscle moved in the rogue's whole face; only one or two of the couples round him grinned broadly.

"One of the famous Brigade, judging by his skill," said Zwakh, laughing.

"I don't suppose Master Pernath knows about the Brigade," Vrieslander broke in quickly, and made a surreptitious sign to the puppeteer not meant for my eyes. I understood perfectly. It was just as it had been in my room. They considered me a sick man and wanted to cheer me up. So Zwakh had to tell a tale. Anything would do.

When I saw the old man looking at me so compassionately, it was all I could do not to cry. If he only knew how his pity hurt me!

The first few phrases of his tale passed me by. I sat there feeling as though I were bleeding to death. Ever colder I felt, and more inanimate, just as when I sat on Vrieslander's knee in the guise of a wooden puppet-head. Then, suddenly, I was plunged slap in the midst of the story which seemed now to close me in. I felt like an inanimate object out of a story-book.

Zwakh began:

"The Story of the Honourable Doctor Hulbert and his Brigade.

"Well . . . how shall I start? His face was all over warts, and his legs as crooked as a dachshund's. From a lad he'd never done anything but study. The little money he was hard put to it to earn by teaching went to the support of his invalid mother. He only knew from books I fancy, the look of green fields, and hills, and coppices full of trees and flowers. As for the sun, you know how much of that gets through to Prague's dark alleys.

"He had got his doctorate all right. He would. As time went on, he became a leading jurist. So much so that judges and experienced lawyers would go to him for advice. Yet he still lived like a beggar, in his little attic room, looking out over the Teinhof.

"The years went by, and Dr. Hulbert's fame as a legal star became proverbial. That a man such as he could be subject to ordinary human emotions, or had ever been heard to talk on any subject save law, no one would have believed. Already his hair was beginning to turn white. But it's just in those hearts of reserve that desire is at its hottest.

"The very day that Dr. Hulbert attained the goal which, ever since his student days, had seemed the very highest he could strive for—the very day, that is, when the Emperor had been pleased to confer on him the title of Rector Magnificus in this our university, the rumour went round that he was betrothed to a young and beautiful lady of poor but noble birth.

"It certainly did seem as though luck had at last come Dr. Hulbert's way. Even though his marriage was childless, he adored his young wife, and was never so happy as when satisfying the slightest desire he could read in the depths of her lovely eyes.

"But he did not, in his good fortune, as do so many, forget his suffering fellow-creatures. 'God has fulfilled my desire,' he is reported once to have said, 'He has caused my fondest dreams to come true, that lighted my boyhood days; He has given me to possess for my own the dearest being the earth contains. And I would like a gleam of this, my good fortune, so far as in me lies, to fall upon others.'

"And so it came about that he took a poor student into his house and cared for him like an only son, thinking, I fancy, what it would have meant in his lean and hungry boyhood had anyone so done to him. But, as we live in a world where we seem unable to distinguish between the wholesome and the noxious grain in the deeds of our own sowing, and many an action which to us appears both noble and good bears a harvest of nothing but evil, so did it happen in this case that Dr. Hulbert's act of mercy contained the germs of his bitterest suffering.

"The young wife soon fell head over ears in love with the student, and a ruthless Fate had ordained that her husband should discover her in the arms of the very man who owed everything to him, one day when he returned home unexpectedly on his wife's birthday, to surprise her with a bouquet of roses.

"They say that the beautiful blue gentian can lose its colour for ever once it has felt the touch of the pale, sulphury lightning streak that announces the approach of a hailstorm. It is certainly a fact that the old man's soul was numbed from the day that saw the destruction of his happiness. That night he sat here in this room, fuddling himself with gin till he almost passed out, till the day dawned—he who all his life had never known the meaning of intemperance. And from that day onward he made Loisitschek's the home of his broken life. In summer-time he would sleep out somewhere or other in the shelter of some half-built house; in winter, here on a settle. He still kept the title of Professor and Doctor of the Two Laws. No one had the heart to alter that.

"Gradually there began to gather round him all the ne'er-do-wells of the Ghetto, and ultimately they formed amongst themselves that fantastic society still known to-day as the Brigade. Dr. Hulbert's inexhaustible knowledge of the law was the greatest stand-by to those members whom the police eyed askance. Should a discharged prisoner find himself faced with starvation, Dr. Hulbert would send him down to the officers of the District Council, naked as the day he was born, and they would be compelled to provide him with clothing. Should a prostitute receive orders to clear out of the town, she would marry, at Dr. Hulbert's instigation, any scoundrel appertaining to her parish, when she would immediately become eligible for permanent residence therein. He was wise to a thousand such tricks and evasions, and the police could only look on helplessly. All the 'earnings' of these outcasts of society were pooled, to the very last heller and kreuzer, for the community's general subsistence. Their conditions in that respect were drastic, and scrupulously adhered to. It was most likely this discipline that won them the title of the Brigade.

"Every year, on the 1st of December—the anniversary of the old man's tragedy—a curious nocturnal ceremony would take place at Loisitschek's. They would all assemble in this room, and stand, crowded there together shoulder to shoulder: tramps, beggars, prostitutes and their bullies, drunks, and every kind of riff-raff, while, for silence, you could hear a pin drop. And then old Hulbert would stand there, up in that corner, beneath the crowned picture of His Majesty the Emperor, and tell them his life's history—how he had fought his way up, inch by inch, to win his degree, and afterwards been made Rector Magnificus. Always, when he got to the part when he came into the room with the roses in his hand to celebrate his wife's birthday, and the anniversary of the day he had wooed and won her, his voice would fail him, and he would collapse, weeping on the table. And, as often as not, some lewd baggage of a woman would creep up, half ashamed lest the others should see it, and place a withered flower in his hand. Not one of his listeners would stir then for a bit. They're too hard a crowd to weep, but they'd look down at their feet and stand twiddling their thumbs.

"One fine morning old Hulbert was found dead, on a bench down by the Moldau. Frozen to death, from the look of him. His funeral was a thing I'll never forget. The Brigade must have simply bled themselves white, trying to have everything as impressive as they knew how.

"First of all walked the 'Beadle of the University,' in full regalia, carrying the purple cushion with the golden chain upon it. Behind the hearse, as far as you could see, walked the Brigade—dirty, bare-footed, torn, and ragged. One of them had long ago pawned everything that belonged to him; his arms and legs and the whole of his body were tied round with pieces of newspaper.

"That's the way they paid him their final homage. Upon his grave, there in the churchyard, stands a white stone with three figures carved on it—the Saviour, crucified between two thieves. No one knows who did it. It was rumoured that Hulbert's wife ordered it to be set up.

"The dead barrister had left a sum of money in his will providing for a basin of soup to be given every day at midday to each member of the Brigade. That's why these spoons are tied here to the table, and the plates sunk into those hollows. Every day at twelve the waitress comes with a huge stewpan and ladles it out. If anyone's there who can't prove himself a member of the Brigade, back the soup is ladled into the bucket.

"That table has by now got a reputation far beyond its own country, I can tell you."

I was waked out of my lethargy by the sensation of some disturbance in the café. The last phrases of Zwakh's story still simmered vaguely in my mind. I could still see the way he had moved his hands about, with a gesture of ladling soup; then images rolled by so fast before my eyes, so clearly defined, that for the time being I lost all consciousness of myself, and became just a wheel in a living clock-work.

The room seemed to be simply surging with people. Swarms of young men in evening dress upon the platform; white shirt-cuffs, shining rings. An officer dragoon's uniform, with the braid and piping of a captain; in the background a lady's hat with large, salmon-coloured ostrich feathers. Then Loisa's distorted face, staring through the railings. Obviously it was all he could do to stand on his two feet. Jaromir, too, was there, his gaze riveted high, high up, his back flat against the wall, as if pressed hard by some invisible hand.

Suddenly the dancers stopped. Mine host must have called something out to them—something alarming. The music continued to play, but very softly, as if afraid of itself. You could hear it trembling, distinctly. On the landlord's face a look of malicious, wild delight.

Suddenly, in the doorway stood a Commissioner of Police in uniform. He stretched out an arm, so that no one could pass by him. Behind him stood a policeman.

"Dancing here!? In defiance of the law? I am closing this dive. You, manager, come along with me. Everyone to the station house!"

He rapped his words out like commands.

The paunchy landlord said not a word, but still grinned his malicious grin.

The whole place is transfixed with amazement. The concertina has now resolved itself into a plaintive squeak. Even the harp has given up the ghost.

The whole crowd can now be seen in profile, gazing towards the estrade. Thence comes a well-dressed figure in black, down the steps towards the Commissioner of Police.

The eyes of the policeman are already riveted on that pair of patent-leather shoes. Their owner stands in front of the official, scanning his figure slowly from top to toe. The other young bloods on the estrade lean over the baluster, stifling their laughter in their silk handkerchiefs.

The dragoon captain screws a gold coin into his eye and spits the end of his cigarette playfully into the hair of a girl beneath him.

The Commissioner of Police has changed colour, and still stands gazing, in his embarrassment, at the pearl in the young nobleman's shirt-front. That calm, cool gaze from the immovable clean-shaven face with the hooky nose is past his powers of endurance.

It rattles him. It destroys his nerve.

The silence in the room is well-nigh unbearable.

"That," whispered Vrieslander, with a glance at the young blood, "is how the stone effigies look of the knights on tombs in Gothic churches."

The young nobleman now breaks through the silence. "Ah, hmm." He imitates the voice and dialect of the manager. "These are my guests. Look alive! Waiter!" The room resounds with a yell of laughter that makes the glasses tremble; the young men nearly split their sides with merriment. A bottle is flung against the wall, and breaks in pieces. The paunchy landlord now announces to the multitude, breathlessly, obsequiously: "His Excellency Prince Ferri Athenstädt."

The Prince has handed a visiting-card to the Police Commissioner. The poor wretch takes it, salutes repeatedly, clicking his heels together. It is quiet again. The crowd is listening, breathless in anticipation.

The young nobleman speaks again:

"The ladies and gentlemen here present are guests of mine." Then, with a languid gesture, taking in the entire assembly: "You don't desire—er—I presume—officer—to be introduced?"

With a forced smile the Commissioner declines, stutters forth confusedly something about his "painful duty," concluding with the words: "Now that I see . . . all in order. . . ."

That fairly goes to the head of the dragoon captain. He pushes his way back towards the ostrich feather hat, and the next moment, amidst the jubilations of the young sparks on the estrade, has dragged Rosina down with him on to the dancing-floor.

She sways, being drunk, and keeps her eyes closed. The huge, expensive hat perches grotesquely on her head; she has nothing else on at all but rose-coloured stockings and a man's swallow-tail coat, on her naked body.

It is a sign for the music to strike up like a mad thing. "*Rititit . . . Rititit . . .*" it goes, to the accompaniment of a gurgling howl, for Jaromir, pressed flat against the wall, has caught sight of Rosina.

We decide to go.

Zwakh calls for the waitress. But in the general hubbub he cannot be heard. The scene swims before my eyes, as fantastic as any opium dream.

The dragoon captain clasps the half-naked Rosina in his arms, and twirls her slowly round to the music.

The crowd make way for them, respectfully.

Then from the benches arises a murmur: "Loisitschek! Loisitschek's!" Necks are craned on all sides, and to the dancing couple is now added another, even more grotesque. An effeminate-looking young man in a rose-coloured "pull-over," with long, fair hair down to his shoulders, lips and cheeks made up like any harlot, and eyes cast down with an air of maiden modesty, is revolving round the room with Prince Athenstädt, his head on his partner's breast.

A honey-sweet waltz trills forth from the harp.

I feel I want to vomit. In terror I look toward the door. The Commissioner is standing there, ostentatiously half turned away, so that he will see nothing. He whispers to the policeman, who hides something. It clinks like handcuffs.

Both men gaze in the direction of the pock-marked Loisa, who tries for an instant to hide himself, and then stands there helplessly, his face stone cold, and contorted with terror.

A scene flashes into my mind, only to disappear again immediately. The picture of Prokop, listening, as I had seen him an hour before, bending over the drain, and the sound as of a soul in agony, rising from the earth.

I want to cry out. But I cannot. Cold fingers seem to seize my tongue, pressing it back from beneath my teeth, rolling it into a ball,

and filling my whole mouth with it. I cannot see those fingers; I know
them to be invisible, but none the less I can feel them—the cold
substance of them.

Suddenly it is revealed to me. They belong to that ghostly hand that
had presented me, in my room in the Hahnpassgasse, with the book
Ibbur.

"Water! Water!" Zwakh was yelling out, close to me. They are
holding my head up, and gazing into the pupils of my eyes by means
of a lighted candle.

"Take him back home . . . fetch a doctor . . . Schemajah Hillel is
skilled in these cases. . . . Take him to him. . . ." Murmurs all round
me.

Then I lie stiff and stark as a corpse on a bier, and Prokop and
Vrieslander carry me on a shutter.

AWAKE

Zwakh had hurried up the steps before us, and I could hear Miriam,
the registrar's daughter, making anxious enquiries, and he trying to
reassure her. I didn't trouble to try and hear what they were saying,
but guessed that Zwakh was telling her how I had been suddenly
taken ill, and begging her to give first aid and try to bring me round.

I could still move none of my limbs, and the invisible fingers still
clutched at my tongue. But my thoughts now were both clear and
calm, and the sensation of terror had gone. I knew exactly where I
was and what had happened to me, and didn't even find it odd that
they were carrying me up the stairs like a dead man, placing me in
Schemajah Hillel's room, laying me down, and then—leaving me
alone.

I was filled now with a feeling of peace and natural contentment,
such as a man feels on his home-coming after infinite wanderings. So
it seemed to me.

The room was dark, and the shape of the window-frame stood out,
cruciform, in the half-light that filtered in from the street.

Everything seemed to be just as it should be, and it surprised me
not at all when Hillel entered the room, carrying a large Jewish seven-
branched candlestick and bidding me "Good evening" as to someone
whose arrival he had long expected. I noticed now something that had
never struck me all this time we had been lodging under the same

roof, for all I had been by way of meeting him on the staircase three or four times a week: I realised, as he went to and fro, putting various objects straight upon his sideboard and lighting another candlestick of the same kind, the almost perfect proportions of his limbs and body, the clear cut of his features, and his noble domed forehead.

As I saw him there in the candlelight, he could surely not be older than I, forty-five years old at most.

"You arrived a little earlier than I anticipated," he observed, after a pause; "otherwise I should have had the candles ready lighted."

He pointed to the candlesticks, then came close to the shutter, fastening his dark, deep-set eyes on somebody who seemed to be standing or kneeling—for I could not see—at my head. He moved his lips, and seemed to be muttering a phrase, though no sound came.

Immediately the grip of the fingers upon my tongue was loosened, and my limbs were paralysed no more. I sat up and looked behind me. No one was in the room save Schemajah Hillel and myself.

So that friendly greeting of his, to tell me I was expected . . . that was really addressed to me.

What was stranger still, this circumstance, so strange in itself, surprised me not at all.

Hillel obviously read my thoughts, for he smiled cordially, holding out his hand to help me up from my shutter, and pointing me to a chair as he said:

"There's nothing strange about that. It's only the supernatural, the *Kischup*, that can strike terror into the soul of man. Life scratches and burns like a hair shirt, but the sunbeams of the spiritual world are sweet and full of good comfort."

I was silent, for I could think of nothing to say by way of answer. He seemed not to expect any, for he sat down opposite me, and continued calmly: "A silver mirror, if it had sensation, would experience pain only until it is burnished. Once its surface is smooth and shining, it reflects all the images that fall upon it, without pain or grief. Blessed is that man," he added softly, "who can say to his own self, 'I too have been burnished.'" And I heard him murmur a sentence in Hebrew: *"Lischuosecho Kiwise Adoschem."*[1]

Then his voice was speaking again clearly, close to me. "You have come to me in a deep sleep, and I have waked you. As David sings in his psalm: 'Then said I to myself, The Righteousness of God hath wrought this change in me!'

"When a man rises up from his bed, he believes himself to have cast

[1] "For Thy help I pray, O Lord."

off sleep like a garment; neither does he know that he has become a sacrifice to his senses, and become the victim of a deeper sleep by far than the one he has just left behind him. There is only one true state of being awake, and that is the state you are about to experience. But men will say, when you speak of it to them, that you are sick. For they cannot understand. Therefore is it pain and grief to talk to them about it.

"Thou carriest them away as with a flood; they are as a sleep; in the morning they are like grass which groweth up. In the morning it flourisheth, and groweth up; in the evening it is cut down and withereth."

"Who was that stranger who came to my room and gave me the book *Ibbur*? Was I dreaming when I saw him? Or was I awake?" Thus I wanted to question him, but, before the words had left my lips, Hillel had answered me:

"Hear and understand. The man who sought you out, and whom you call the Golem, signifies the awakening of the dead through the innermost life of the spirit. Each thing that earth contains is nothing more than an everlasting symbol clothed in dust. Learn how to think with your eyes. Think with your eyes, as you behold each and every shape. Nothing that takes shape unto itself but was once a spirit."

I felt now that concepts, which hitherto had adhered to the substance of my brain, were tearing themselves loose and floating off like rudderless ships on a shoreless sea.

Peacefully Hillel continued:

"He who is once waked can no longer die. Sleep and death are one and the same thing."

"Then . . . can I no longer die?" A dull agony took possession of me.

"Two paths there are, running parallel courses—the way of life and the way of death. You took unto yourself the book of *Ibbur* and read therein. Your soul is fecund now with the Spirit of Life." Thus I could hear him speak.

"Hillel—Hillel! Let me go the way of all flesh! The way of death!"

My whole being was centred in that one poignant cry.

The face of Schemajah Hillel was rigid in its earnestness.

"Men tread not a path at all, neither that of life nor death. They drive like chaff before the wind. In the Talmud it is written: 'Before God made the world, he held a mirror to his creatures, that in it they might behold the sufferings of the spirit and the achievement that ensue therefrom. Some of them took up the burden of suffering. But others refused, and those God struck out of the Book of Life.' But you tread a path you have chosen of your own free will, even though you know it not. You are self-elected. Do not torture yourself. As knowledge comes, so comes also recollection. *Knowledge and recollection are one and the same thing.*"

The friendly, almost affectionate, tone in which these words were uttered did much to calm me. I felt like a sick child that knows its father sits by its side.

I looked up, and suddenly became aware that the room was full of forms that stood round us in a circle. Some were in white robes like grave-clothes, as worn by rabbis of olden days; others wore three-cornered hats, and shoes with silver buckles; but Hillel made a movement with his hand across my eyes, and once again the room was empty.

He saw me out then, down the stairs, and gave me a lighted candle to light me to my room.

I went to bed, and tried hard to go to sleep. But sleep eluded me, and I fell instead into a strange state that was neither sleeping nor waking.

I had put out the light, but, none the less, everything in the room stood out so distinctly there was no shape I could not distinguish. Moreover, I felt delightfully at ease, and free from all that agonising unrest I had suffered so recently.

Never before in my life had it been given to me to think so clearly and precisely as I was doing now. The rhythm of health flowed through all my nerves, and marshalled my ideas like a regiment that waited on my commands.

I needed only to call, and forth they stepped, and fulfilled my every wish.

There was a gem which I had wished to cut for the last few weeks. But I could not do it, for the facets did not coincide with the lines I wanted to cut. This came to mind, and in an instant I had the solution—how to lead the cutter and make use of the structure of the mass.

From the slave I had been hitherto to a horde of fantastic impressions, not knowing whether they were feelings or ideas, I now felt myself transformed, suddenly, to a monarch in my own kingdom.

Calculations that formerly I had only achieved groaning, on paper, now strung themselves together in my mind, and leapt to a result. I was able, by means of this newly awakened faculty, boldly to grasp all the things which had hitherto so consistently eluded me—whether figures, shapes, objects, or colours. And when it came to abstract questions, not to be solved by means of concrete tools—philosophical

problems and so forth—my power of visualising seemed to be sup-
planted by an inward sense of hearing, whereby the voice of Schemajah Hillel played the rôle of speaker.

All kinds of curious knowledge became part and parcel of my mind.
Phrases that a thousand times had reached my ears as mere sound and
fury, signifying nothing, percolated to the innermost depths of my
mind; things I had learned parrot-wise, in a flash became *mine* in very
deed and truth. The mystery informing the creation of words, hitherto
a sealed book to my stupidity, now lay open to my probing.

The so-called "high ideals" of humanity that, like so many eminent
business magnates, flaunting their Orders of Merit on their breasts,
had deigned to exploit me from afar, with their catchwords of petty
pathos, suddenly removed the masks from their sanctimonious faces,
and excused their smug presence; they were nothing but beggars,
when all was said and done—crutches for the promotion of future
swindles!

Could it be—oh, could it be all this was nothing but a dream?

What if I had never spoken to Hillel at all?

I reached out for the chair next my bed. There stood the candle that
Schemajah had given me; and, happy as a little boy on Christmas
night, who has convinced himself that his wonderful jumping jack
really exists, and is there beside his bed, I snuggled back again into
my cushions.

Like a sleuth-hound now did I pierce into the undergrowth of mental problems which beset me.

First of all I tried to reach back to the furthest possible point in my
life where memory served me. Only from thence, I thought, would it
be possible for me to survey that part of my existence that, by some
strange stroke of Fate, lay hidden from me in darkness.

But, try as I would, I could get no further than a vision of myself
standing in the gloomy court, looking through the archway into old
Aaron Wassertrum's junkshop—as though for the course of a century
I had lived in this house as a cutter of gems, always as old as my
present age, and without ever having been a child.

I was about to abandon as useless this groping in the abyss of time,
when suddenly it was borne in on me, with lightning clarity, that,
though within my consciousness the broad path of events stopped
short always at a certain archway, yet there were a multitude of smaller lanes running alongside the principal path that I had so far continu-
ously overlooked. "Whence," almost I heard them screaming to
me, "did you receive this knowledge whereby you gain your daily
bread? Who taught you to cut stones? engraving, and all the rest of it?

And to read, and write, and speak, and eat, and walk, and breathe, and think, and feel?"

Neither did they exhort me in vain. Systematically I began to probe back into my life. I forced myself to consider, in sequence unbroken, though reversed, what it was that had recently taken place—what had led up to it, of what was this the direct consequence, and so on and so on.

Again had I arrived at that familiar archway. Now . . . now . . . now . . . one little leap into the void and the gulf that separated me from my unknown past must once for all be passed over; but then came a picture I had overlooked in the reconstruction of my thoughts: Schemajah Hillel passed his hand across my eyes, just as he had done in his own room.

On which . . . everything vanished. Even the wish to investigate further.

Only one lasting advantage had I gained: the knowledge that the succession of mere events in one's life is a cul-de-sac, however broad and accessible it may seem to be; not in the revolting and obvious scars left by the file of our outer life, but in the scarce visible lines engraved upon our being, is to be found the solution of our uttermost secret.

And, as in my childhood's days I would fumble through the alphabet backwards, in my spelling-book, to arrive at the place where they had been teaching us in school, on the same principle I saw now that I must be able to roam in that other, distant homeland, which lies beyond all thought.

The weight of a whole globe now rested on my shoulders. Hercules, I recalled, bore upon his head, for a period of time, the dome of the sky, and the legend revealed itself to me as full of hidden significance. Even as Hercules freed himself through a ruse, while begging the giant Atlas: "Let me but bind a lump of twine round my brow that my brain burst not," so perhaps, it dawned upon me now, might some small, obscure pathway exist which would lead me from the depths of the precipice.

I was seized, suddenly, with a deep distrust of the guiding powers of my thoughts. I sat up, putting my fingers into both eyes and ears, so as not to be led astray through their temptings. I would kill my thoughts.

But my will recoiled at the task: all I succeeded in doing was in driving out one thought with another, and directly one succumbed, the next would be devouring its carcase. I tried to take refuge in the pulsing of my blood—the beating of my heart. . . .

Then came Hillel's friendly voice, saying unto me: "Go on your way and fear not! The key to the art of forgetfulness belongs to our brethren, who tread the path of Death; but you are fructified with the Spirit—of Life."

The book of *Ibbur* rose before me, with two letters flaming in it: one signifying the Archetype Woman with the pulse that beat like an earthquake, the other, at an infinite distance—the hermaphrodite on the pearly throne, with the crown of red wood upon its head.

A third time then did Schemajah Hillel pass his hand before my eyes, and I slept.

SNOW

Dear and honoured Master Pernath,

I am writing you this letter in greatest haste, and distress of mind. Please destroy it, as soon as read, or, better still, bring it back to me, inside its envelope. Otherwise I shall know no rest. Don't tell a soul that I have written to you. Nor where you are going to go to-day.

"That kind, good face of yours has *recently* (I hope that word will enable you to recall an event of which you were witness, and thereby to guess the writer of this letter, for I am afraid to sign it with my name) inspired me with so much confidence . . . also the circumstance that your dear father, of blessed memory, used to teach me in my childhood . . . all this gives me courage to appeal to you as being, probably, the only man on earth who can help me.

I implore you to be, this evening, at five o'clock, in the Cathedral on the Hradschin.

A certain lady who is known to you.

I sat there for quite a quarter of an hour holding the letter in my hand. That curious religious frame of mind that had seized on me last night had vanished in a trice—blown away by the fresh, invigorating breath of a new day on this our earth.

A brand-new Fate came laughing towards me, with hands outstretched—a veritable child of Spring! A human being had turned to me for help! To me! Strange, how different my room looked, all of a sudden! That worm-eaten, carved chest of mine twinkled at me in so friendly a fashion, and the four chairs seemed like nothing so much as four old people sitting round the table, contentedly playing round games.

My empty life quite suddenly had been filled by something . . . some substance that was rich and glowing. Was the rotten old tree about to bear fruit yet?

It was as though some life-giving sap were flowing through my veins, something that hitherto had slumbered within me, deep hidden in the secret places of my soul, its egress blocked by the lumber of everyday life. It welled forth now as a spring wells through its ice when the winter breaks.

And I knew, with absolute certitude, as I held the letter in my hand, that I should be able to help, whatever it might be. My strength would be found in the joy of my heart.

Again and again I read those few lines: "your dear father, of blessed memory, used to teach me in my childhood." I caught my breath. Did it not read like the promise "To-day shalt thou be with me in Paradise"? The very hand held out to me, beseeching help, was reaching me that gift—the remembrance of my past, for which I agonised. It would disclose that secret now, and help to raise the curtain that had veiled it hitherto.

"Your dear father, of blessed memory" . . . how strangely the words sounded, as I said them over to myself. Father! For an instant I beheld the tired face of an old man with white hair, in the arm-chair next my wardrobe; it rose up, strange and alien, and yet so terribly familiar. Then my vision once again grew normal, and my heart beat, hammer-wise, its registration of the actual present.

Frightened, I pulled myself together.

Had I mistaken the time? I looked up at the clock. Thank God! Half-past four only.

I went into my bedroom, got my hat and cloak, and stole downstairs. What did I care now for the whisperings of the dark old corners, the mean, suspicious, malicious grudging that emanated from them, as I went my way: "You've not done with us yet; you belong to us; we don't desire your happiness; happiness doesn't go with this house."

That fine, poisonous dust that used to rise up and stifle me out of all the nooks and passage-ways with eager, choking fingers—before the living breath of my mouth did it now melt utterly away. Just for a moment I paused at Hillel's door.

Should I go in?

A curious shyness prevented me from knocking. My mood to-day was so completely changed, it almost seemed I had no right to enter. The hand of life was driving me along. I continued my way downstairs.

The streets were thick with snow.

Many people seemed to be greeting me as I passed along. Whether I replied to them I do not know. I kept on feeling to see if I had the letter safe in my pocket. The place where it lay felt warm.

I traipsed through streets and under archways till I reached the Altstädter Ring, and passed by the bronze fountain, the baroque bowl of which was full of ice; then over the stone bridge, with its statues of saints and monument of Johannes von Nepomuk. Down below, the river rolled on its way, lashing its embankment with the foam of its rage. Half in a dream, I saw the "Torture of the Damned" carved in the sandstone relief of St. Luitgard; the writhing, agonised figures, with the snow lying thick upon their eyelids and outstretched, manacled, beseeching hands.

I slipped through more archways still; palaces passed me slowly by, with stately portals, elaborately carved, lions' heads set in the midst of them, biting rings of bronze.

Snow everywhere—snow, snow, snow. Soft and white as the pelt of a gigantic polar bear. Proud, tall windows, their mouldings glistening and caked with ice, turned their detached gaze upwards to the clouds.

I wondered why the skies were so full of passing birds.

As at last I climbed the countless steps of granite that lead up to the Hradschin, each one of them as broad as the length of four men, the town—roofs, gables, and all that pertained to it—passed, step by step, out of my conscious mind.

The twilight was already taking possession of the rows of houses as I arrived at the deserted Square, in the midst of which the Cathedral spire towered up towards the Throne of the Angels.

Footsteps, imprinted in the snow, their edges crusted round with ice, led in a track to the side entrance door.

From what seemed very far away, came the notes of an organ, softly wailing, melting into the stillness of evening like tears of gentle melancholy.

I heard the heavy baize door slam behind me. There I stood in the darkness, the golden altar gleaming at me, like a veritable rock of peace, through the blue-green shimmer of the fading light that drifted down on to the praying-stools through the multi-coloured windows.

The enervating smell of tapers and incense.

I sit upon a seat. This kingdom of tranquillity is working its strange spell upon me.

The whole of space seems filled with a sense of mysterious, secret waiting: a life without a heart beat.

The silver shrines of the saints lie in everlasting sleep.

Hark! A long, long way away I can hear the muffled sound of horses' hooves, scarcely audible at first, but drawing nearer bit by bit—then stopping.

A dull thud as though a carriage door were shut.

The rustle of a silk dress came close up to me, and a small, soft, feminine hand touched me on the arm.

"Please, please, let us go over there to that pillar. I don't like to say what I've got to say here, by these praying-stools."

The incense-clouded images that had ringed me round came suddenly clear before my eyes. It was daylight once more.

"I don't know how to thank you, Master Pernath, for being so very kind, and coming all this long way in this dreadful weather."

I stuttered forth a couple of banal words.

. . . "But I knew of no place where I should be freer from danger and eavesdropping. They won't follow us here, surely—to the Cathedral."

I pulled out my letter and handed it to her. She was wrapped up to the eyes in costly furs, but from the tone of her voice I recognised at once the woman who had fled into my room that evening in the Hahnpassgasse, in terror of Aaron Wassertrum. It did not surprise me, for I had expected no one else.

My eyes searched her face, that, in the half-light of this niche in the wall, seemed even paler than it was. Her beauty almost took my breath away, and I stood there transfixed. It was all I could do not to fall down and kiss her little feet, thanking her for allowing me to help her, for choosing me, of all people.

"I implore you, from the bottom of my heart, to try and forget—at least for as long as we are here together—the circumstances in which you saw me last," she continued urgently. "I don't know how you feel about such things."

"I am an old man now, but never in my life have I made so bold as to set myself up as a judge over my fellow-creatures," were the only words I could find to say to her.

"Thank you, Master Pernath," she replied fervently and simply. "And now I will ask you to listen patiently, and tell me whether, in my desperation, you think you can help me, or at least give me counsel."

I could feel how possessed she was with anguish, as her voice trembled. "That time—in the studio—I had just realised the ghastly truth, that that terrible ogre was deliberately following me about. For months I had noticed that wherever I went, whether it was with my

husband or—or with Dr. Savioli—the dreadful criminal face of the
old junkdealer would appear from somewhere near by. Those squinting eyes of his would follow me, sleeping or waking. So far he had
made no sign to explain his presence, but all the more would fear
choke me in my dreams. . . . When did he mean to slip the noose
round my neck? At first Dr. Savioli would try and reassure me, saying, what, after all, was to be feared from a miserable old wretch like
that—at most only a small sum of hush money, or something of that
kind; but always his lips would go white at the mention of Wassertrum. I suspected Dr. Savioli was trying to buoy me up falsely, by
keeping something back—something dreadful, that might mean death
to himself, or me.

"Then I learned something he had done his utmost to conceal from
me: *that the junkdealer had been to see him more than once, at his house,
at night!* I knew—I could feel in every hair of my head—that something was closing around us like the coils of a snake. What did the
scoundrel come for? Why couldn't Dr. Savioli shake him off? I
couldn't bear to see it go on any longer. I must do something . . .
anything . . . before I lost my reason."

I tried to murmur a reassuring word or two, but was not allowed to
finish the sentence.

"In the last few days the nightmare that threatened to stifle me
became more and more palpable. Dr. Savioli suddenly became ill; my
connection with him was all at once cut off; I couldn't go to see him,
for fear my love for him would be discovered; he lay in delirium, and
all I could learn was that, in his ravings, he believed himself to be
persecuted by a man with a hare-lip—Aaron Wassertrum!

"I knew—none better—how brave my lover was. All the more horrible—you can imagine that, can't you?—was it to me to think of him
lying like that, helplessly at the mercy of some terrible, throttling
demon, whose hands I could feel creeping nearer and nearer in the
darkness.

"You are going to tell me, I know, that I am a coward! You are
going to ask me why, if I love Dr. Savioli like that, I could not sacrifice everything for him, and go to him . . . riches, honour, reputation,
everything belonging to me. But I cannot! I cannot! I have my child
. . . my dear, sweet little golden-haired baby girl. You don't suppose
my husband would let me keep her? See . . . Master Pernath . . . take
that!" With trembling fingers she tore open the lid of a leather box she
was carrying, and I could see it was filled full with strings of pearls
and other precious stones. "Take that, and hand it to the villain. He's
greedy . . . I know that . . . very well. He shall have everything I've

got—except my child! That will stop him, will it not? He won't tell, then? For the love of Christ, say something . . . tell me—tell me you'll help me."

It was all I could do to compose the poor creature sufficiently to allow me to lead her to a seat.

I said anything to her that came into my head at the moment. Wild, whirling words, that had no connection the one with the other. Thoughts coursed through my brain, so that I hardly knew myself what my mouth was uttering—ideas so fantastic they died of their own craziness so soon as they were born. By chance my gaze had fallen upon the painted statue of a monk in a niche of the wall. Still I talked and talked. By degrees the features of the statue became transformed; its cowl was changed into a threadbare overcoat with high, stand-up collar, from which looked forth a youthful face with wasted cheeks, hectically flushed.

Before I could get a glimmer of what the vision meant, the monk was there once more. My pulses were beating far too loud.

The unhappy woman was still stooping over my hand and weeping.

I set about transferring to her the strength that had filled me when I read her letter, and which had not left me yet. I could see it visibly helping to recover her.

"I want to tell you, Master Pernath," she continued softly, after a long silence, "exactly why I turned to you in my trouble. It was on account of something you said to me . . . something I never forgot, though it was all those years ago."

Years ago? My blood froze.

"You were saying good-bye to me . . . I can't remember now how or why it was . . . I was still a child, but you said to me, so sweetly, and so sadly: 'I don't suppose it ever will, but if the time should ever come when you need a protector, may the good God grant that I should be he.'

"I turned quickly away, and let my ball drop into the fountain, so that you should not see me crying. And then, I wanted to give you the coral heart I wore round my neck on a piece of ribbon, but I was too shy . . . it seemed so silly."

Chords of memory!

That merciless finger had got hold of my tongue again! Something flashed in front of me—a distinct glimmer, clear and terrifying, of a longed-for land, far, far away; a little girl in a white frock, in the grounds of an old castle . . . old elm-trees on every side. . . . I could see it distinctly.

I must have changed colour. I guessed it from the hurried way she went on: "I know, of course, that they were only words spoken beneath the impulse of a parting; but they have often comforted me since, and I thank you for them."

With all my might I clenched my teeth together, and pressed down that shrieking agony once more into my breast, ere it tore me to pieces.

I understood. It had been a kindly hand that had fixed the bolt upon my past. The gleam of a day that was gone had left its message written clear-cut upon my conscious mind. A love that had proved too strong for my heart, that for years had been gnawing at the root of all my thoughts, and for which no healing balsam had been found, save the merciful dark of insanity.

The perfect peace of anaesthesia stole over me, and cooled the tears behind my eyelids. The superb and solemn sound of bells echoed through the Cathedral, and I could smile now, quite happily, into the eyes of her who had come to seek my help.

Once again I heard the dull sound of a carriage door as it was slammed to, and the pad of horses' hooves.

I was on my way back through the town, amid the blue-gleaming snow in the moonlight.

The street lanterns looked down at me, twinkling, and from mountainous heaps of fir trees there were murmuring hints of tinsel and silver nuts and approaching Christmas.

Beneath the pillars of the old Rathaus aged dames, with their heads in grey kerchiefs, were murmuring prayers by candlelight to the Mother of God.

In front of the darkened gate that led into the Jewish quarter were the stalls of the Christmas market. In the midst of them, framed in bright scarlet cloth, and lit by garish, flickering torches, was the open stage of a marionette theatre. Zwakh's Punchinello, in purple and violet, rode clumping over the boards on a white wooden horse. On to the lash of the whip in his hand was fixed a human skull. The children sat in front in constricted rows, their little fur caps pulled tight down over their ears, mouths gaping wide, listening enthralled to the verses of Prague's poet, Oskar Wiener, as recited by Zwakh from his little box.

> Jumping Jack comes leaping by,
>   As scrawny as a poker.
> Ribbons and patches gaily fly
>   On the grimacing joker.

I turned into the dark corner-street that frowned forbiddingly upon the Square. Another crowd was bunched together there in the darkness, looking at a poster. A man had struck a match, and by its fitful light I read the printed lines. Dully I registered a few of the words:

MISSING
REWARD OFFERED
1,000 FLORINS
An elderly gentleman . . . dressed in black . . .
plump, clean-shaven face . . . white hair . . .
All information should be addressed to the police station.

I crept along the rows of dark houses, slowly, slowly, like a living corpse, devoid of wish, devoid of will. A handful of feeble stars twinkled in a narrow patch of sky among the gables. Full of peace, my thoughts flowed back towards the Cathedral, placid and serene.

All at once, from the market-place, clear-cut in the wintry atmosphere, came the voice of the marionette player, sharp and shrill, as though at my very ear:

"Where is the heart of stone, blood-red;
It sparkles in the sun's bright ray,
It hangs upon a silken thread."

GHOSTS

I had paced my room without ceasing, deep into the night, racking my brains how I could bring *her* the help of which she stood in need.

Often I was on the point of going down to Schemajah Hillel, to confide my secret to him and ask for his advice. But each time I rejected the idea.

He loomed so large before me in the spirit, it seemed a desecration to disturb him with things that concerned one's outer life. Added to which, there were moments when I was beset by doubts whether I had really lived through all those happenings which, recent though they were in point of time, paled so strangely into insignificance once they were confronted with the events of the last few hours.

Or was *that* my dream? Had I any right, I a man to whom the unthinkable had happened—the forgetting of his own past—ever for an instant to accept as concrete fact something with no other proof of its reality than my own memory could offer?

My glance fell upon Hillel's candle, which still stood on the chair. Thank God, at least that was still there: I had undoubtedly been in personal contact with him.

Suppose I were to hasten to him now, cling round his knees, and pour out in his sympathetic presence this inexpressible suffering that was eating up my heart?

I stood there, his bell-pull in my hand; then I let it drop again; I saw in advance what would happen: Hillel would gently pass his hand across my eyes and . . . No! No! Anything but that! I had not the right to seek out palliatives. *She* believed in me, and my help, and, even though the peril she felt threatening her seemed at moments sufficiently slender to me—to her it appeared little short of colossal.

Time enough to ask for Hillel's advice in the morning. I forced myself to be calm and collected. How could I pester him like this, in the middle of the night? It would be the act of a madman!

I wanted to light the lamp; then decided not to. The reflection of the moonlight shone into my room from the roofs opposite, and gave me more light than I could have wished. I feared to frustrate the night in its departure, once I struck a light.

To kindle a lamp and sit expectant for the day to break was a thought full of such dismal implications I shrank from the doing of it. Something whispered fearfully to me that, once I did so, the dawn would never come.

I stood at the window. Rows and rows of tortured gables, standing in the shimmering night atmosphere like some ghostly cemetery—so many headstones carved with weather-beaten dates ranged above the dark, dank graves, the "dwelling-places" hollowed beneath them by the hosts of the living.

For a long time I stood there, staring out, till slowly, very slowly, I began to wonder why I was not afraid at the noise of measured footsteps, treading, quite distinct to my ears, the other side of the wall.

I listened again. No doubt of it. Someone was there. The creaking of the boards recorded every tread.

In a trice I had pulled myself together. I literally felt myself becoming smaller, as I constricted my every nerve and fibre to my will. This was the present, and I would deal with it.

Another little rustling which broke off short, as though frightened at itself. Then, the stillness of death. That grim, alert stillness, instinct with its own betrayal, that magnifies minutes into hours.

I stood there, stock-still, my ear pressed close to the wall, a frightful premonitory fear within me that someone on the other side was doing just as I did!

I listened . . . and listened . . .

Not a sound.

The studio next door seemed utterly deserted.

Noiselessly, on tip-toe, I stole towards the chair by my bed, picked up Hillel's candle, and lighted it.

I stood, thinking. That iron door in the passage that led to Savioli's studio opened outwards.

At random I picked up a hooked-shaped piece of wire that lay beneath my graving tools on the table—the kind of thing that made short work of locks, in a skilled hand. Well . . . and what then?

It could be none other than Aaron Wassertrum who was spying next door—rummaging in boxes, probably, seeking weapons and proofs to establish his case.

Exactly how much good would my interference do?

I did not waste much time in thinking. Better to act than not to act! At least it would put an end to that terrible waiting for the dawn!

I was now standing before the iron door, pressing against it, cautiously insinuating the wire into the lock, and listening. I had guessed right. From the studio came a noise as though someone were pulling out a drawer.

Next moment the latch gave way.

I could see right into the room, although it was all but dark, and my candle dazzled my eyes. A man in a long black cloak sprang up, panic-stricken, from a table where he had been sitting. For a moment he seemed uncertain what to do, then, controlling an impulse as though to fling himself upon me, he snatched his hat from his head and quickly covered his face with it.

"What are you doing here?" I wanted to cry out. But the man was at my side.

"Pernath! You! Good God! Put that light out!"

The voice was familiar to me, but was most decidedly not that of Aaron Wassertrum.

Automatically I blew out the candle.

There lay the room in semi-darkness, obscurely lit in places only by the dim light that filtered through the window-panes—much as my own room had been—and I was forced to strain my eyes to their uttermost before I could recognise, in the emaciated, hectic countenance that emerged forth from the coat—the features of the student, Charousek!

"The monk!" The word leapt to my tongue, and instantaneously I understood the vision which I had yesterday experienced in the Cathedral.

Charousek! That was my man! Again I heard his words during the
shower beneath the archway. . . . "Aaron Wassertrum . . . will learn
. . . that invisible, poisoned needles can penetrate walls . . . on that
same day he thinks he's got Savioli by the throat . . . that identical
day."

Had I, then, got an ally in Charousek? Did he know what had been
happening? His presence here, at such a curious hour, seemed almost
proof that he did; but I was loath to question him direct.

He had hurried to the window, and was gazing from behind the
curtain down into the street.

I realised he feared lest Wassertrum should have seen the light from
my candle.

"You think, of course, that I am a thief . . . finding me as you do,
groping around here in a strange room at night-time," he began, after
a long silence, in a voice that shook a little. "But I swear to you——"

I broke in at once, to reassure him. And, in order to convince him
I had no suspicions of him, and, on the contrary, regarded him as a
confederate, I told him, with a few advisable reservations, what
brought me to the studio, and how I feared that a woman, in whom I
was greatly interested, was in some danger of being blackmailed by
the junkdealer.

I gathered, from the courteous way he heard me out, without inter-
rupting me with questions, that he knew most of it already, except,
maybe, for a few details.

"That's about the way of it," he said, brooding, as I had finished. "I
thought I could not be wrong. The rascal evidently wants to choke the
life out of Savioli, but apparently hasn't got enough evidence yet with
which to do it. What would he always want to be prowling round here
for, if he had? As I went yesterday—shall we say 'by
chance'?—through the Hahnpassgasse," he continued, in reply to my
enquiring look, "I noticed how Wassertrum had been slinking about
before the door of this house for a suspiciously long time. As soon as
he thought the coast was clear, he slipped inside. I made after him,
pretending I was on my way to see you—that's to say, I knocked at
your door, and then went on and surprised him fumbling about with
a key at that iron passageway door. Of course he gave it up directly I
appeared, and went and knocked, too, on your door, as a pretext. But
you weren't at home, presumably, for nobody opened.

By making careful enquiries around the Ghetto, I learned that
someone who, according to his description, could only be Dr. Savioli
had a secret lodging here. And as Dr. Savioli is lying critically ill at
the moment, I soon put two and two together. What's more "—and

Charousek pointed to a packet of letters lying on the writing-table—
"I've been through every drawer, and forestalled our friend once for
all. I hope that's the lot of them. That's all I've been able to find, and
I've looked pretty closely, so far as was possible in this dark."

As he talked, my eyes took stock of the room, and rested involuntarily on a trap-door in the floor. I remembered vaguely Zwakh telling
me about something of the kind, that there was some sort of secret
entrance leading up from below. It was square in shape, with a ring in
the middle to grip it by.

"Where shall we put the letters?" Charousek went on talking. "You
and I, Herr Pernath, are the only two folk hereabouts whom Aaron
Wassertrum regards as negligible quantities. Why *me*, there are special
reasons." I could see the man's face, distorted with a spasm of hate as
he spoke the last phrases—"and as for you . . . he takes you for
a——" With a hurried, and obviously affected, fit of coughing he
stifled the word "lunatic," though I knew perfectly well what he had
meant to say. I didn't care; the feeling that I was going to help *her* had
made me so extraordinarily happy, all my old sensitiveness was gone.

We finally decided to conceal the packet with me, and left the room
together.

After Charousek had gone, I couldn't bring myself to go to bed.
Apprehension niggled at my mind and prevented me. There was
something I should do, I felt quite certain of it. But what? What?

Should I sketch out a plan for the student, of the best subsequent
course to pursue?

A work of supererogation. Charousek wasn't going to allow the
junkdealer out of his sight for a moment, of that I felt quite certain. I
shuddered when I thought of the hatred implied within his words.

What on earth was it Wassertrum had done to him?

That growing feeling of unrest within me nearly drove me distracted. Something invisible was calling to me, something from the Other
Side, and I could not understand it.

I felt like a horse being broken in, that feels the tug upon its bridle,
but does not know what tricks it is supposed to perform, being unable
to grasp the meaning of its trainer's command.

Should I go down below to Schemajah Hillel? Every nerve within
me repudiated the idea.

That vision of the monk in the Cathedral, upon whose shoulders
yesterday the head of Charousek had arisen, in reply to my dumb
appeal for counsel, was sufficient indication to me not to despise
unduly those strange, inarticulate sensations. That I had possessed,

for some time now, certain hidden faculties within myself was not to be disputed. I felt the potency of them far too vividly now to attempt to ignore them.

To *sense* the meaning of letters—not only to register them in books with my eyes, but to set up within myself an interpreter who would translate to me the meaning of all those things that *instinct* whispers, without the aid of words; that, I realised now, was the one key to the understanding of my own innermost soul.

"Eyes have they, but they see not; ears have they, but they hear not" . . . the old Bible phrase leapt into my mind as a kind of illumination.

"Key . . . key . . . key." My lips kept on forming the words mechanically, while my mind played with notions, strange and—as quite suddenly I realised—not a little dangerous.

"Key . . . key." My glance fell upon the piece of bent wire in my hand, which had served me to pick the lock of the iron door, and I was obsessed suddenly with an ungovernable desire to see where the trap-door led to from the studio.

Without pausing to consider, I went back again to Savioli's studio, and tugged at the ring in the centre of the square piece of wood, till at last I succeeded in raising it.

Nothing revealed itself at first but darkness. Then I became aware of small steps leading down into nether-most gloom. I began to descend them. For some time I groped my way along with my hands, till there seemed to be no end to it: niches in the wall, full of fungus and decay; nooks, crannies, turnings, corners; straight passages—passages that wound to the right or the left; the remains of an old wooden door; alleys branching off in all directions; and steps, and steps, and steps.

Over all hung that heavy, stifling smell of earth and mould.

And still not one single ray of light. If only I had taken Hillel's candle with me! The path I trod was flat now, and seemed to go on for ever. From the crunching sound beneath my feet, I knew I was treading on gravel.

It must be one of those innumerable passages that wind beneath the Ghetto, apparently without rhyme or reason, until they reach the river. Their existence was in no way surprising. The whole town had stood, since the memory of man, upon a series of such subterranean windings, the inhabitants of Prague having had only too good reason, in olden days, to shun the light of day.

The lack of any kind of sound above my head convinced me I was still within the Jewish Quarter (that at night-time is as silent as the grave), although I seemed to have been wandering to all Eternity. Had it been otherwise, I should have heard the muffled sound of carts rolling overhead.

For an instant fear took me by the throat. What if I were going round and round in a circle? What if I fell into a hole, and broke my leg, and was unable ever to get out again?

What would happen, then, to her letters in my room? They must infallibly fall into the hands of Aaron Wassertrum.

Involuntarily I was confronted by the thought of Schemajah Hillel, with whom I vaguely associated the concepts of help and guidance.

More and more cautiously and slowly I groped my way along, holding one arm above me, so as not to crack my head against the ceiling vault, should it suddenly start to slope. By degrees it did so, and finally the ceiling was so low that I was forced to stoop as I made my way along.

Suddenly my upraised arm felt empty space. I stopped and looked up.

By degrees it seemed to me as if a faint, hardly discernible glimmer of light stole downwards from the roof.

Could this be a kind of shaft, leading down from above towards some kind of cellar?

I stood upright, and groped around with both hands over my head. The opening seemed to be rectangular and walled all round.

By degrees I was able to distinguish something that seemed to lie horizontally across the opening in the form of a cross, and at last I succeeded in gripping a portion of it, and dragging myself up and through the aperture. I stood now upon the cross and tried to take my bearings. Apparently these were the corroded remnants of a circular iron staircase, if my fingers did not deceive me. For what seemed ages I groped and groped, till at last I succeeded in finding the second step and started to climb up.

There were eight steps in all, one above another, each at the height of an average-sized man.

The odd thing was, these steps seemed to end, above, at something criss-cross, through which percolated the same regular bars of light I had noticed from below.

I stooped down as low as possible, to try and get, from a point further removed, a better grasp of the way these rays of light fell, and saw, to my amazement, that they took the form of a six-pointed star such as is to be seen inside synagogues.

What on earth could that mean?

Suddenly it was borne in upon me that this, too, was a trap-door, letting light through its edges—a trap-door cut in wood, in the shape of a star!

I heaved against it with my shoulders, opened it, and found myself, next moment, in a room filled with dazzling moonlight.

It was a smallish room, and completely empty save for a heap of rubbish in one corner; there was only one window, and that stoutly barred with iron.

I could find no door of any kind, search as I would round and round the walls.

The bars of the window were too close together for me to put my head out, but this much I was able to establish: the room was approximately three stories high, for the houses opposite rose to two stories, and were obviously built much lower down. I could distinctly make out the opposite side of the street, but the light of the moon, shining full into my face, made it impossible for me to distinguish separate details within the heavy shadow. The whole style of the buildings in the street, with masonry and lintels, made it apparent that it was part and parcel of the Jewish quarter; nowhere save in the Ghetto do houses turn their backs on one another in that crazy fashion.

In vain I cudgelled my brains to try and elucidate precisely what sort of a fantastic building this was that I now stood in.

Could it, by chance, be a kind of an annex to the Greek Church? Or did it belong in some way to the Old Synagogue? I couldn't tell from the surroundings.

I gazed round the room again. Nothing seemed there that could afford me the slightest clue. The walls were stark and bare, with the plaster and whitewash long since peeled off; no nails therein, not even the holes for them, as evidence that once human beings had lived in it.

The floor was smothered in dust, as though no human foot for decades on end had trodden it.

The thought of turning over that heap of rubbish in the corner filled me with loathing. It lay wrapped in darkness, and for the life of me I could not make out of what it consisted. It looked, at first glance, like a ball of old rags. Or was it, perhaps, a couple of old black bags?

I touched it with my foot, and succeeded in poking out a part of it into the light thrown into the room by the moon. It appeared to be some sort of a broad, dark-coloured band, that began slowly to unroll.

A glittering point like an eye! Was it a metal button?

Bit by bit I began to distinguish; a sleeve of strange and antiquated cut lay hanging out of the bundle.

Beneath it lay what seemed at first sight to be a little square white box, which disintegrated at the touch of my foot, and lay before me as a number of grubby white pieces. I gave them a gentle kick; a piece of paper or cardboard flew clear.

A picture? I stooped. A playing card? What I had taken for a white cardboard box had resolved itself into a pack of tarot cards! I picked it up.

Of all the fantastic things—to find a pack of playing-cards, here in this room full of ghosts!

Strange how I had to force myself to smile at the thought. As a matter of fact, a faint feeling of horror was beginning to creep over me.

I racked my brains for some everyday explanation of the way the cards could have got here, and began mechanically to count them. It was a complete pack all right—seventy-eight cards. But, even as I counted, I realised the startling fact that each and every one of them was ice-cold to the touch. Already my fingers were half frozen with their contact; so stiff were they, it was all I could do to drop the pack from my hand. Again I strained for a rational explanation.

It was odd, when I came to think of it, how only now I first began to realise the cold, in spite of the thin coat I had on, my long ramble in the subterranean passage without hat or cloak, the grim winter's night, the stone walls, the cruel frost; my perpetual state of excitement had, presumably, kept me unaware of the fact.

Shiver after shiver now began to course down my spine, passing, penetrating deeper and deeper within my very system. I could feel my very skeleton congeal, and every single bone in my body as so many rods of iron, round which my flesh was petrifying.

In vain I paced around the room; in vain I stamped with my feet, and beat my arms on my chest. I clenched my teeth, not to hear their chattering.

"This," said I to myself, "is death, laying his icy finger on your skull."

And I fought, like a mad thing, against the numbing sleep of frost-bite that was trying to smother me with its fleecy, stifling pall.

"Those letters in my room—her letters. If I die in this place, they will find them." The words kept dinning themselves into my ears . . . and she believed in me! I was her only hope of salvation! Help! Help!! Help!!!!

I screamed down into the street below, till it echoed again: "Help! Help!! Help!!"

I cast myself upon the floor, and sprang up again. I mustn't die—I mustn't! For her sake—only for her sake! Even if I had to smite sparks out of my bones to warm me back to life again!

Then the heap of rags in the corner caught my eye, and I rushed at them, and pulled them, with shaking hands, over my own clothes.

They stank of mould.

For a time I crouched in the opposite corner, feeling slowly, slowly, the warmth creep back into my skin. But that terrifying sensation of my own frozen skeleton still remained with me. I sat there immovable, while my eyes wandered round the room. The card I had first discovered—the *Pagad*—still lay there, in the rays of the moon, in the middle of the room.

I could not take my eyes off it.

So far as I could see from this distance, it seemed to have been clumsily painted in water-colour by the hand of a child, and represented the Hebrew letter Aleph, in the form of a man dressed old Frankish fashion, his grey peaked beard cut short, his left arm raised on high, while the other pointed downwards.

And now I began to be filled with a torturing suspicion. Did the fellow's face, or did it not, bear a strange resemblance to my own? That beard—that didn't belong on a *Pagad* from a tarot pack. I crept up to it, and threw it in the corner with the rest of the rubbish, to rid myself of the disconcerting sight.

There it lay, shining—an indistinguishable grey-white speck—out of the darkness towards me.

I forced myself to consider urgently what I had to do to get back again to my own room.

Must I wait till the morning? Call out to the passers-by through the window, so that they could use a ladder to reach me candles or a lantern? It was only too apparent to me I should never find my way back through those twisting, twirling passages without a light . . . . Or, if the window were too high up, what if someone let a rope down from the roof——

Oh, God!

In a flash I realised it all now! I knew where I was! A room with no entrance . . . only a barred window . . . the ancient house in the Altschulgasse that everyone avoided. Many years ago a man had let himself be swung down by a rope to look through the window, and the rope had given way, and . . . yes, I was in that house all right. The house into which the supernatural Golem had been known each time to vanish.

A deepset horror I was powerless to combat, even with the thought of those concealed letters, now paralysed completely all my powers of thinking. My heart began to contract convulsively.

Hastily, with frigid lips, I told myself it was nothing but the wind, sweeping with its breath round the corner, faster and faster, whistling as it went. But it was all to no purpose; that white speck over there, the *Pagad*, began to blow itself up like a balloon . . . began to edge itself over the ray of moonlight . . . began to creep back once more into the darkness! Drop . . . drop . . . drop . . . that was the noise I began now to hear—part thought, part fancied, part actually experienced—inside and out . . . deep in my own heart, and again in the very centre of the room . . . a pinging noise, as if a compass point were being darted into wood . . .

Again that white speck! That inevitable white speck!

"It's a card!"—my very soul shrieked forth the words—a foolish, pitiful, good-for-nothing little playing-card, and the *Pagad* at that! And yet—and yet—it had assumed a human form. Actually it was crouching in the corner over there—*and looking at me with my own face!*

For hours and hours I cowered there, motionless in my corner—a frost-bitten skeleton, in strange, out-moded dress. And he—he too crouched in the corner opposite. I . . . he . . . I. . . .

Not a sound. Not a movement.

We stared one another in the eyes: the hideous image one of the other.

Did he see, as I did, the moonbeams making their snail-pace track across the floor, and start crawling up the infinite wall, like the hands of an invisible clock, paler and paler.

I fixed him with my eye, and all his efforts to dissolve into the light of early morning that began to filter through the window to his aid came to nothing. I held him fast.

Step by step I wrestled with him for my life—that life which all the more was mine because it no longer belonged to me.

Smaller he grew and smaller. When day dawned, and he dwindled once more into a playing-card, I rose, and, going up to him, picked him up and put him in my pocket, the *Pagad*.

But the street beneath me was still desolate and empty of folk.

I investigated each several corner of the room in the insipid morning light: bits of broken crockery . . . a rusty pan . . . foul-smelling rags . . . the neck of a bottle; dead things, yet how strangely familiar, one and all. The very walls—how every crack and fissure seemed impressed on my mind. Where had I seen them before?

I took the pack of cards up in my hand. The idea went through my

mind, Had I not once painted them myself? As a child? Long, long
ago?

It was a very old pack, with Hebrew symbols on it. No. 12, I seemed
to remember in my mind, should be *Le Pendu*, the Hanged Man.
Head down, arms tied behind his back. I turned over. . . . There he
was.

Then again, half reality, half dream, a picture rose up before me: an
old blackened school-house, rickety and crooked; a sinister witches'
den, its left shoulder shrugged on high, its right incorporated with its
next-door neighbour. We are several half-grown youngsters . . . an
abandoned cellar somewhere . . .

I looked down again at my person, only to become more mystified
than ever. The antiquated clothes I had on conveyed absolutely nothing to me.

I started at the noise of a cart creaking over the cobbles. But when
I looked out of the window I could not see a soul. Only the butcher's
dog, standing aimlessly at the curb.

Ah! At last! Voices! Human voices!

Two old women came slowly hobbling along the street, and I half
forced my head through the grating and cried to them.

With gaping mouths they stood there, looking up. But, once they
caught sight of me, they uttered one piercing cry and fled.

I knew. They had taken me for the Golem.

I stood and waited for the crowd that I imagined would assemble
now. I could explain myself to them. But an hour passed, and only
now and again would a passer-by raise a pale face in my direction,
immediately to scurry hence in an agony of fear.

Should I have to wait now for hours on end until the police came?
No, I would try to continue farther along the underground passage,
rather than return. Perhaps now that it was day, some light might
percolate through the masonry.

I clambered down the ladder, and continued along the way, over
heaps of broken tiles, through sunken cellars—climbed a flight of
broken stairs—and found myself in the black schoolroom that I had
seen as in a dream.

A flood of recollection poured over me immediately; benches, spotted with ink from top to toe, exercise-books, the bawling of school-
songs, a boy letting a beetle loose in the midst of class, reading-prim-
ers with squashed crumbs of bread and butter between their pages,
and a pervading smell of orange-peel. I knew now with the utmost
certainty I had been here as a boy. But, without allowing myself time

to think about it, I tore myself away and hurried home.

The first to meet me in the Salnitergasse was an old Jew with white sidecurls. No sooner had he caught sight of me than he covered his face with his hands and cried aloud Hebrew prayers.

Attracted by the noise, a horde of people dashed out, and a screaming outcry arose. Turning, I saw myself surrounded by a surging sea of death-white faces, distorted by terror.

Looking down at myself in my amazement, I understood; I still was wearing the strange mediæval garments I had pulled over my outer clothes, and they were taking me for the Golem.

I dashed around the corner, slipped behind a door, and tore off the mouldering rags.

Hardly had I finished when the crowd passed me, full tilt, sticks waved in air, mouths slobbering, hard on my pursuit.

LIGHT

I had several times tapped at Hillel's door in the course of the day. I could refrain no longer. I simply had to talk to him and ask what was the significance of all these strange happenings. But each time he had been out.

His daughter said she would let me know directly he returned from the Jewish Council House. That was a strange girl—Miriam! A type I had never so far met.

She was beautiful, with a beauty so remote that one hardly seemed able, at first sight, to realise it—the kind of loveliness that leaves a man dumb, and awakens in him—Heaven knows why—a faint, inexplicable feeling of despondency. Such a face must, I thought broodingly, as I conjured her before me in the spirit, have been formed in accordance with laws of proportion lost for thousands of years.

I wondered idly how a man might congeal her beauty in a precious stone, and which would be most suited to the purpose, only to realise the hopelessness of the proposition, even where externals were concerned. Impossible to give a local habitation and a name to the blueblack of that hair and those wondrous eyes, so utterly peculiar to herself; how, then, could one hope to capture in a cameo the spiritual values of such a face, and subject them to the stupid, man-made "values" of canonical "art"? Only, I realised quite clearly, through the medium of mosaic. But, even then, what material would one choose?

Such a problem would require, surely, the natural span of a man's life for its solution.

Where on earth was Hillel all this time? I found myself longing for him as for an old and valued friend.

Strange how he had grown into my heart in the few days of our acquaintance. Strictly speaking, I had only really spoken to him that one time in my life!

To preserve my peace of mind, I must find a safer hiding-place for *her* letters, in case I should be unexpectedly absent from home for any length of time. I took them out of the drawer. They would be more secure, so I thought, in the iron box.

A photograph slipped out from between the leaves. I tried not to see it, but it was too late. Staring me in the eyes was that piece of brocaded stuff around those bare shoulders—just as I had seen "her" that first time when she had fled into my room from Savioli's studio.

A crazy pain began to bore its way through to my conscious mind. I read the inscription beneath the photograph without realising the import of the words, and then the signature: "Your Angelina."

Angelina!

As I spoke the name aloud, the curtain veiling from me the years of my youth was rent from top to bottom!

I thought the agony must kill me.

I clawed the air with my hands and moaned aloud. I sank my teeth into my hand.

God in heaven! might I but be blind once more—might I but sink again into my blessed state of living death! Thus did I pray.

Pain choked my utterance . . . anguish . . . gnawing grief. . . . Somehow it tasted strangely sweet . . . like blood!

Angelina!

The name crept into my very veins, like a sort of unbearable, ghostly caress.

With a superhuman effort I pulled myself together, and with clenched teeth forced myself to look that picture in the face till I had mastered my emotion.

Mastered it!

It was like last night over again . . . and that playing-card . . .

At last I heard steps . . . the footsteps of a man.

He was coming.

I joyfully hurried to the door and opened it.

Schemajah Hillel stood there, and behind him—I reproached myself mildly for a feeling of annoyance—old Zwakh, with his rosy cheeks and round child eyes.

"I am pleased to see that you are still up, Master Pernath," Hillel began.

His voice was cold. Decidedly. The whole room suddenly felt full of frost—biting, annihilating frost.

Dully, with only half an ear, I heard Zwakh's excited voice chattering:

"Didn't you know the Golem's in our midst again? You remember how we were just speaking of him—don't you, Pernath? The whole Ghetto's agog. Vrieslander actually saw him with his own eyes! And, as it usually does, it began with a murder!"

I listened now in amazement. *A murder!*

Zwakh was shaking me now. "Don't you know anything about it, Pernath? The police are all over the town. It's Zottmann—the Freemason, as they call him. You know Zottmann, director of the life assurance company? They say he has been murdered. Loisa, here in this house, has been arrested! And they're after Rosina, too, but she's cleared out. Not a track of her left! The Golem—ah, the Golem—it's hair-raising."

I made no answer, but looked into Hillel's eyes. Why did he keep looking at me like that?

Suddenly a guarded smile played round the corners of his mouth. I understood. I was the cause of it! For very joy I could have fallen on his neck. In my infinite relief I rushed aimlessly round the room. What was I looking for? Glasses! Where was that bottle of Burgundy? I had just one left, I knew. Cigars?

At last I found my tongue. "But—why don't you sit down?" Hastily I dragged out a couple of chairs.

Zwakh began to get annoyed. "What are you smiling like that for, Hillel? Don't you believe the Golem's abroad again? Don't you believe in the Golem at all?"

"I shouldn't, if I were to see him sitting here in front of me," Hillel answered very collectedly, with a glance at me as he spoke. I caught the double meaning that his words contained.

Zwakh stopped drinking in his amazement.

"Then you choose to ignore the witness of some hundreds of people? You mark my words, and wait! There'll be murder after murder now, committed here in the Ghetto. I know that for a fact. The Golem always introduces a weird chain of events."

"There's nothing strange in a piling up of similarities," Hillel replied, as he walked to my window and looked through the panes towards Wassertrum's shop. "When the wind of spring begins to blow, there's always stirring within the roots of things. Sweet as well as poisonous."

Zwakh winked at me as he nodded his head towards Hillel.

"If the rabbi were only in the mood, he could tell us many a tale would make our hair stand on end," he half whispered.

Schemajah turned.

"I am not a rabbi, for all I may bear the title. I am only a poor registrar, employed at the Jewish Council House. I manage the Registry of the Living and the Dead."

I could feel a certain hidden significance in his words. Even the marionette player seemed aware of it, unconsciously, for he remained quiet, and for a long time nobody spoke at all.

"I ask your pardon, rabbi—I should say, Herr Hillel," began Zwakh, after an interval, and there was a ring of earnestness in his voice. "There's something I've wanted to ask you for a long time. You needn't answer, if you are not allowed to or feel you shouldn't . . . "

Schemajah came up to the table and idly fingered a wine-glass. He didn't drink. Perhaps some Jewish custom forbade it.

"Ask, Herr Zwakh."

"Hillel . . . do you know anything about the secret teachings of Judaism, the Kabbala?"

"Only a little."

"I have heard say there's a document by which a man may learn it, called the *Zohar.*"

"The *Zohar,* yes—the *Book of Splendour.*"

"Then, if that's the case," Zwakh finally broke out, "isn't it a crying shame that such a book, which they say is the key to the understanding of the Bible and a state of blessedness——"

Hillel cut him short. "Only some of the keys."

"Very well, then, some of the keys! That this work, on account of its rarity and its great price, should be accessible only to the rich? The only copy, I've heard, is now in a London museum. To say nothing of the fact that it's all written in Chaldean . . . Aramaic . . . Hebrew. Have I ever in my life had a chance to learn them, or of going to London?"

Hillel chaffed him mildly. "Have you directed all of your wishes so eagerly towards that goal?"

"Well, I didn't mean that, exactly," replied Zwakh, rather confusedly.

"Then you've no real grievance," Hillel told him drily. "He who seeks after things of the spirit, and does not strive with every atom of his body—like a strangling man gasping for air—can never come to know the secrets of God."

"There should, still, be a book containing all the keys to the riddles of the other world, instead of just some of them." The thought shot through my mind, as my hand played automatically with the *Pagad*, still lying in my pocket; but, before I could clothe it in words, Zwakh had given it utterance.

Hillel smiled again, Sphinx fashion.

"Every question a man can find to utter is answered even in the moment of its asking if he asks it in the way of the spirit."

"Do *you* understand what he means?" Zwakh turned to me.

I made no answer, but held my breath, for I didn't want to lose one word of what Hillel was saying. He continued:

"The whole of life is *nothing* more than questions that have taken unto themselves shape, and bear within themselves the sum of their own answer: and answers that are pregnant with questions. Only fools see it otherwise."

Zwakh banged his fist upon the table. "Yes . . . questions and answers that mean different things to different people."

"But that's just my point," went on Hillel, in friendly tones. "It's solely the doctor's privilege, surely, to 'cure all men out of the same spoon'? Each questioner receives the answer fitted to his need; how, otherwise, could the longings of poor humanity ever be satisfied? Do you suppose that it is only caprice that our Jewish sacred writings are written down in consonants? Every man must find the hidden vowels which determine the meaning destined for him alone. Otherwise the living word would petrify into dogma."

The marionette player expostulated:

"Words, rabbi—nothing but words! If I could make sense of such stuff, you could call me the *Pagad ultimo* of the pack."

Pagad! The word hit me like a sledge-hammer! In my dismay, I nearly fell off my chair.

Hillel evaded my look.

"*Pagad ultimo?* And who's to say, Herr Zwakh, that's not precisely what you are?" His voice sounded in my ears as from a great distance. "We can't any of us be too sure of ourselves, you know. And, since we're on the subject of cards—do you play tarot much, Herr Zwakh?"

"Tarot? Of course. Ever since I was a boy."

"Oh, then I'm surprised to hear anyone asking for a book about the whole Kabbala who's had it in his hands at least a thousand times."

"I? Had it in my hands? I?" Zwakh beat his brow.

"Yes, you. Has it never occurred to you that the game of tarot contains two and twenty trumps—precisely the same number as the letters of the Hebrew alphabet? Don't our decks have card after card of which the painted pictures are obviously symbols—the fool, death and the Devil, the last judgment? My good friend, how loud do you want life to shout her answers in your ears? There is no need for you to know, of course, that the word 'tarot,' bears the same significance as the Jewish 'Tora,' that is to say, '*The Law,*' or the old Egyptian 'Tarut,' '*Questions asked,*' and the old Zend word 'Tarisk,' meaning, '*I require an answer.*' But learned men ought to ascertain these little facts before they give out with such certitude that tarot dates from the period of Charles the Sixth. And, just as the *Pagad* comes first in the game of cards, so is a man the first figure of all in his own picture book—his own doppelgänger, so to say. The Hebrew letter Aleph is shaped like a man, with one hand pointing to heaven, and the other downwards, meaning: 'As it is above, so it is below; as it is below, so it is above.' That's why I said to you just now, 'Who knows if your name is really Zwakh or—*Pagad?* Don't reject it!'"

Hillel turned his gaze full on me, and I realised what depths of implication now lay hidden in his speech.

"Do not cast aside the opportunity, Herr Zwakh. It is possible for a man to find himself in murky windings underground, from which he may not emerge *save by virtue of a talisman that he bears within himself.* According to tradition three men once descended into the Realm of Darkness; one went mad, the other lost his sight, and only the third, Rabbi Akiba, returned safe and sound, and related that he had met himself. Others, they will tell you, before and since, have also met themselves; Goethe, for instance, usually upon a bridge or stepping-stones that led from one river bank to another. He looked his own self in the face and kept his reason. But that was only a mirroring of his consciousness, and not his true doppelgänger; not what is called his 'breath of bones,' otherwise Habal Garmin, of whom it is said: 'As he descended into the grave, incorruptible, bone for bone, so will he arise on the day of the Last Judgment.' " Hillel's look was more and more piercingly directed upon me. "Of whom our grandmothers related: 'He dwells high above ground, in a room with no door, and one window only, through which understanding with mankind is not possible. Whosoever can both banish and *purify* him, that man will be reconciled with his own self.' As for the game of tarot, you know as well as I do how each player has his own hand to play, but he who knows how best to use his trumps wins the game! Come now, Herr Zwakh, it's time we went. Otherwise you'll be finishing off all Master Pernath's wine, without leaving him a drop for himself!"

DISTRESS

A snowstorm was raging in front of my window. The snowflakes sped like regiments—little miniature soldiers in white furry coats—past the panes of my window, on and on, one behind the other, always in the same direction, as though in universal retreat from a peculiarly formidable foe. All of a sudden they seemed to get tired of running away, and, in some mysterious manner having decided on attack, would whizz back again, till fresh hostile armies fell upon their flanks, and the whole resolved itself into a pallid hurly-burly.

Months seemed to me to have elapsed since the curious happenings in which I had been involved. Had it not been for the periodic rumours of the Golem which reached my ears from time to time, oiling the springs of my memory, I might almost, in my most doubting moments, have believed myself to have been the victim of a temporary hallucination.

The thing that detached itself most garishly from the highly coloured arabesque that events seemed to have woven around me was what Zwakh had told me concerning the still unsolved disappearance of the so-called "Freemason."

I was far from satisfied with the way they had dragged in Loisa in this connection, though I was not without my own dark suspicions. I could not help remembering how, that night when Prokop had heard a mysterious cry coming from the direction of the drain, we had seen the youth soon afterwards at Loisitschek's. But surely there was no need to connect this cry, which proceeded from the bowels of the earth, and could well have been deceptive, with a human being's appeal for help?

The whirling snow before my eyes blinded me, and I began to see everything in terms of stripes that danced. I once more turned my attention to the precious stone upon my table. The preliminary wax model I had made of Miriam's face should really look a thing of beauty when cut into that radiant moonstone, palely blue. I rejoiced thereat; it was a piece of rare good fortune, my finding something so eminently fitting amongst my stock of stones. The deep-black matrix of hornblende, in which it was imbedded, gave just the right light to the moonstone, and the lines fitted remarkably, as though nature had succeeded in perpetuating a lasting likeness of Miriam's clear-cut profile.

My intention had been at first to cut from it a cameo of the ancient

Egyptian deity, Osiris, together with the vision of the hermaphrodite
from the book *Ibbur,* still such a lasting and memorable image on my
mind. From an artistic point of view the idea appealed to me most
strongly, but, by degrees, I realised such an unmistakable likeness
between my initial cuttings and the daughter of Schemajah Hillel that
I abandoned my project.

The book *Ibbur!*

Tormentedly, I laid my graving tool down again. Incredible, the
amount of things that had trammelled me around in this short space
of time!

Like a man who finds himself transplanted to the midst of an im-
measurable sandy desert, I was aware, by a sudden self-revelation, of
the colossal and utter loneliness that severed me from other men.

Could I ever talk with a friend—Hillel excepted—of what had happened to me?

In the silence of the nights that had recently passed over me, the
recollection seemed to have returned of how, in my boyhood's days—
even from my earliest childhood—an insatiable longing had obsessed
me for the strange and wonderful, for the life other than ours on this
globe; it had tormented me almost past bearing, but the fulfilment of
my craving had come upon me now like a clap of thunder, and
crushed my soul's rejoicing with its own weight.

I trembled to think of that moment when I must wake once more
and review what had happened in the harsh, relentless light of the
actual present.

But at least that need not be yet! I could surely first taste the full
flavour of it on my lips . . . feel the utter glory of what words could
never convey!

I had it in my power! All I had to do was to go into my bedroom
and open the iron box in which lay the book *Ibbur,* that gift from the
invisible!

How long, long ago it seemed since my hand had touched it, that
day I laid Angelina's letters inside!

How quiet it was out of doors, except for now and again a dull
thud, as if the wind had hurled chunks of the driven snow from the
roof-tops into the street. The pauses that ensued were like death; the
white-flock carpet on the pavement swallowed up every sound.

I wanted to go on with my work, but suddenly heard the sound of
hooves, so steel clear down in the street below, one could almost see
the sparks fly.

Impossible to open the window and look out. The frame had

clinched itself to the surrounding wall with muscles of ice, and the panes were half covered with snow. All I could see was that Charousek was standing next to Aaron Wassertrum in what looked to be a friendly manner. Evidently they must just have finished a conversation. I could see the perplexed look on both their faces as they gazed, speechless, at the carriage that was still out of my range of sight.

It darted through my mind that it must be Angelina's husband! It could not possibly be she! It would have been stark madness for her to have been seen driving past my lodgings, here in the Hahnpassgasse, in open light of day! But what should I find to say if it were he indeed, and I should have to encounter him face to face?

Lie, of course. Lie like hell.

I reconstructed the case in my mind. It must surely be her husband! He had received an anonymous letter from someone—Wassertrum, of course—that she had been wont to come to this place as a rendezvous, and she had had to invent an excuse—most likely that she had ordered some stone or other from me. There! A frantic knock at my door, and—Angelina stood before me!

She was incapable of uttering one word. There was no need to. Her face was enough. Evidently the game was up.

And yet I was unwilling to accept any such idea. I simply would not and could not believe that the feeling I was going to be of use to her had been without foundation.

I led her towards my arm-chair. I stroked her hair without a word; and, like an exhausted child, she hid her face upon my breast.

We could hear the crackling of the log in the stove; we could see the red gleam of it reflected on the tiles, flaming and fading . . . flaming and fading . . . flaming and fading.

"*Where is the heart of stone, blood-red.*"

I could not get the burden of it out of my ears. . . . With a start I pulled myself together. Where am I? How long has she been sitting here in my room?

I started questioning her—gently, cautiously, very, very gingerly, that she should not wake, and I probe the smarting wounds too painfully.

Bit by bit I got at what I wanted to know, and pieced it together like a mosaic.

"Your husband knows?"

"No. Not yet. He is away."

So it must be a question of Dr. Savioli's life. Charousek had guessed right. It was to save Savioli's life, not her own, that she had come here. I realised she had ceased to think of hiding anything now.

Wassertrum had been going again to Dr. Savioli—had forced his way to his sick-bed by means of violence and threats.

What then? What next? What exactly had he wanted with him?

Wanted? What he wanted—and already she had all but guessed it to the point of certainty—what he wanted was to do her lover some vital injury.

She knew by now the reason of Wassertrum's crazy, uncontrolled hatred: "Dr. Savioli had once caused the death of his son, the ophthalmologist Wassory."

Like a flash of lightning a thought came into my mind. What if I were to rush out, then and there, to the old pawnbroker and tell him everything: how Charousek had really dealt the blow from behind, and not Savioli, who was nothing but his instrument? "Treachery, treachery!" my soul shouted at me. "Would you give over to the revenge of a scoundrel like that, poor consumptive Charousek, who wanted to help you, and her too?" I was torn by the struggle into bleeding halves. Then a detached and ice-cold voice called out to me: "Fool! The solution lies at your very hand! You've only got to pick up the file there on that table, run downstairs with it, and stick it through the old swine's throat, till one end comes out at the back of his neck!"

My cry of thankfulness went up to God.

I probed still further.

What of Dr. Savioli?

There seemed little doubt but that he would take his own life if she did not save him. The nurses in attendance never left him alone for a moment, and kept him constantly under the influence of morphia, but he might surely suddenly wake up any moment—perhaps it was happening even now—and—and—ah—she must go—she mustn't stay here a moment longer. She would write to her husband . . . confess everything to him . . . even if he took her child from her. Savioli would be saved, for then Wassertrum would be deprived of the only weapon he possessed to threaten her with.

She wanted to make a clean breast of the secret before he could give it away.

"You needn't do that, Angelina," I cried, thinking of the file; and my voice almost choked in my throat in my joy at the power that dwelt within me.

Angelina wanted now to go, but I held her fast.

"One thing more. Think carefully. Is your husband bound to believe Wassertrum without further proof?"

"But Wassertrum has proofs. He's evidently got my letters, and probably a picture of me, too . . . everything that was contained in the writing-desk in the studio."

Letters? Pictures? Writing-desk? I lost all sense now of what I was doing. I clasped Angelina to my breast and kissed her. On the mouth . . . on the brow . . . on the eyes. . . .

Her fair hair lay like a golden veil before my face.

Then I held both her little hands in mine, and, in as few words as possible, told how that devil Wassertrum had been circumvented by a poor Bohemian student, who had himself taken possession of the letters; how they had been handed over to me, and were safely in my keeping.

She fell upon my neck, laughing and weeping in one breath. She kissed me. She ran to the door . . . then turned back and kissed me again.

Then she vanished.

I stood there transfixed, feeling still the breath of her mouth upon my face.

I could hear the carriage wheels rolling over the paved street, and the lively clatter of the horses' hooves. A moment later and all was quiet. Peaceful as the grave.

So, too, was my heart.

Suddenly there was a knock on my door, and Charousek was in the room.

"Excuse me, Master Pernath. I've been knocking some time, but you didn't seem to hear."

I nodded dumbly.

"I hope you've not been thinking I've made it up with Wassertrum, just because I've been talking to him?" I could see from the sarcastic smile of him he was only indulging in a grim jest. "I'll have you know this is my lucky day! The *canaille* down below there is inclined to take me to his heart. Strange thing, the call of the blood?" He spoke softly, almost as though to himself.

I had no notion what he could mean, and thought I must have mistaken what he said. I was still acutely excited.

"He actually wanted to present me with a coat," Charousek went on. "I refused the offer, of course, with due thanks. My skin was quite hot enough as it was, I can tell you. After that he tried to press some money upon me."

"And you took it?" it was on the tip of my tongue to call out, but I stopped myself in time.

Two red spots flared out in the student's cheeks. "Of course I took it!"

"T—t—took it?" I stammered.

"I'd never have believed life had such a sensation to offer." He stopped a moment, and made a grimace. "It gives us, does it not, my brethren, a blissful feeling of uplift, when wondrous Mother Nature's divining hand is found to rule supreme, in accordance with the laws of an all-seeing Providence?"

He droned his words forth like a parson, fumbling the while, with the money in his pocket.

"How can I regard it otherwise than as a sacred duty to devote the filthy lucre bestowed upon me by so gentle a hand to the furtherance of the most noble of all ends?"

Was he drunk? Or mad?

Suddenly he altered his tone.

"When you think of Wassertrum himself paying those doctor's bills, it's remarkably like one of the Devil's own peculiar little jests, don't you think?"

I began now to have a faint suspicion of the meaning behind Charousek's remarks, and the sight of his fevered eyes frightened me more than a little.

"However, we won't worry about that now, Master Pernath. Let's attend first to 'current affairs.' First of all—that lady! '*She*,' of course? What on earth made her drive down here publicly like that?"

I explained what had happened.

"Wassertrum certainly doesn't possess any proofs," he broke in, exultant. "If he had, he wouldn't have been searching through that studio once again this morning. I'm surprised you didn't hear him. He was there—for a full hour."

I expressed my astonishment that he should know all this so precisely.

"May I?" By way of explanation, he took a cigarette from the table, lit it, and proceeded:

"Have you ever noticed, as soon as you open your door, how the draught coming up the stairs blows your cigarette smoke in the direction of the window? That is probably the only natural law known to old Wassertrum, and, with that fact in mind, he had built in the wall of the studio overlooking the street—the house belongs to him, as you know—a little concealed aperture, open to the air—a kind of ventilator—covered over with a strip of red cloth. When anyone entered that room, or left it—that is to say, whenever the door was opened, letting in the draught—Wassertrum could see it from below by the fluttering of that bit of red cloth. If it comes to that," went on Charousek drily, "I can observe it myself from the cellar in which a God who catereth for the sparrow has seen fit to lodge me. It's a comic little patent to have been invented by the aged patriarch, but its existence has been known to me for some time now."

"You're a good hater, Charousek, that I must say," I couldn't help saying. "From the way you shadow his every footstep, I gather your hatred of the old scoundrel is of pretty long standing?"

"Hatred?" Charousek gave a twisted smile. "*Hatred?* That's not the word for it. The word has yet to be invented that would serve to express my feelings against him. It's not him I hate. It's his blood. Can you understand that? I can scent in a minute—like a wild beast of the woods—if a single drop of that blood runs in a man's veins, and"—he clenched his teeth—"that happens here in the Ghetto once too often." Words failed him, so worked up had he got. He hurried to the window and stared out. I could hear his efforts to stifle his cough. For a while we were both silent.

"Hallo! What's that?" suddenly he cried, and signed to me to come. "Quick! Quick!! Have you got an opera glass?"

We peered cautiously from behind the curtains.

Jaromir, the deaf-mute, stood before the entrance of Wassertrum's shop, offering to its proprietor, so far as we could surmise from a language of signs, some small shining object that he held concealed in his hand, trying to sell it. Wassertrum pounced on it like a vulture, and retired with it to his little dirty sanctum. Next moment he was back, his face livid. He flung himself on Jaromir, and a sharp struggle ensued. Suddenly Wassertrum let go, and seemed to stand there considering, gnawing furiously at his hare-lip. Then he cast an ingratiating glance up in our direction, and, taking Jaromir by the arm, he drew him into his shop.

We waited for what seemed quite a quarter of an hour; they didn't seem able to conclude their bargain.

At last the deaf-mute emerged with smiling countenance, and went his way.

"What d'you make of it?" I asked. "It doesn't seem to amount to much. The poor devil was probably only pawning something he'd stolen."

The student made no answer, but sat down at the table without a word. But it was obvious that he, too, regarded the matter lightly, for he began, after a pause, to go on with his conversation just where he had left off:

"As I was saying, what I hate past all bearing is the blood of him. Stop me, please, Master Pernath, if I become violent. I want to keep cool. I don't want to squander away my perfectly good emotions on

his account. I'll try and keep sober. A fellow with the feeling of shame
in him that I've got ought not to pull out the pathetic stop like a whore
or a minor poet. Since the world began, no one's ever yet 'wrung his
hands for grief,' for all the play-actors have chosen to register such a
gesture as 'effective.' "

I realised he was rambling on like this to try and collect himself. He
didn't find it too easy. Nervously he paced the room, picking up at
random various objects in his hand, then setting them down again,
distracted, in the same place. Suddenly he leapt plump into the middle
of his subject once more.

"I can recognise the damned blood of him betraying itself in every
single little movement that a man makes, unconsciously. I know kids
that look like him in the face, and are supposed to be his, but I know
very well they don't come from the same stock; you can't take me in.
For a long time I had never heard that Dr. Wassory was his son, but
I *sensed* it all right.

"Even as a youngster, when I didn't know the relationship in which
I stood to Wassertrum"—he gave me a piercing look—"I possessed
this faculty. I had never been able actually to hate those who caused
me suffering. They could kick me and beat me till there was hardly a
sound spot on my body; they could let me go hungry and thirsty till I
was half crazy and took to eating the dirt in the streets—but I could
never bring myself to hate those responsible for it. I simply *could* not.
There was no more room left in me for hatred. Can you understand
that? And yet my whole being was permeated with it.

"Wassertrum had never done anything to me of any kind. I'm
bound to admit that he had never struck me or picked on me or even
insulted me in any way when I was a kid, playing around in the
streets. I realised that, too; and yet everything within me that made
for revenge and hatred rose up against him. Against him and no one
else!

"Looking back now, it's curious to think that I never played a dirty
trick on him when I was a boy. When the other boys did it, I stood
and looked on. But for hours on end I could stand in that archway
there, or hide behind the door of his house, staring through the cracks
at him, till I literally saw *black* with hatred.

"That, I believe, is the explanation of a certain clairvoyance within
me when I come in contact with any object that has had to do with
him. I know so well each and every one of his movements; how he
wears his coat, how he picks things up, how he coughs, how he drinks;
unconsciously, almost, I seem to have learnt him off by heart like a
book all that time, till it positively ate into my system and made me

able to read his traces on every single thing. Later on it became almost a mania; I would throw things from me simply because it made me vomit to think his hand might have touched them. Some things, on the other hand, I had an affection for; I cherished them like friends who wished him no good."

Charousek paused a moment. I could see him gazing absently into space, while his fingers mechanically stroked the file on the table.

"After a pair of kindly professors had sent the hat round for me, and I had studied philosophy and medicine, and even learned to think for myself, I arrived, by degrees, at the realisation of what hate was.

"No one can hate anything as deeply as I do unless it is a part of himself.

"Later on, when I came to know everything—what my mother was and—and still must be . . . if she still lives . . . and that my own body"—he turned sharply away, so that I might not see his face— "was full of his foul blood. . . . See here, Pernath, you'd better know it; he's my father! Then, at last, I had got down to bedrock. Sometimes I think it is more than a coincidence that I am consumptive and spit blood; it's my body probably, revolting against everything that pertains to *him,* and rejecting it with loathing. Often my hate would follow me into my dreams, and try to console me with every conceivable form of torture man has been known to devise, applied to him; but I always rejected them all, as they never really came within measurable distance of assuaging the thirst within me. Sometimes, when I start to analyse myself, I am surprised at the fact there is no living creature in this world whom I can bring myself to hate, or even, for that matter, mildly to dislike, except *him* and his brood. For that very reason folk might even class me within their category of 'good men.' But, by the grace of God, it is not so. As I told you just now, there's no room for it.

"Don't run away with the idea that a melancholy fate had embittered me for good and all (I didn't learn till later what it was he had done to my mother), for I have experienced at least one day of joy such as is granted to few mortal men upon this earth. I don't know whether you know what it is ever to have suffered a really *religious* experience: I had never known it before, but that day Wassory made away with himself, and I stood down there by the shop, looking on at how *he* took the news—'indifferently' anyone might have called it who wasn't an expert on the stage of life—how he stood there so long and so quiet, that blood-red hare-lip of his only a little bit more drawn back from his teeth than usual, and his look so strange and *turned inwards on itself*—then it was I could feel the fumes of the incense

swung by the angels in Paradise. Do you know the Black Madonna in
the Tein Cathedral? Well, I went and threw myself down in front of it,
and my soul was wrapped around with all the murk of Paradise."

Seeing Charousek standing there, his great dreamy eyes full of
tears, Hillel's words came into my mind—of the mystery of that darkened path trodden by the Brothers of Death.

"The outer shell of circumstance that 'justifies' my hatred, or at
least makes it comprehensible in the eyes of paid servants of the law,
will probably not interest you particularly. Outward events, after all,
are only so many milestones, of no more value than so many empty
egg-shells. They are like the popping of champagne corks, that impress simpletons at the tables of the idle rich. Wassertrum had his way
of my mother all right—the usual devilish way, apparently, that he
and his sort are accustomed to, if not worse. After which he went one
further, and sold her—*bartered* her, I tell you—to a disorderly house;
a thing quite easy of achievement to a man in with the police. But he
didn't do it because he was tired of her . . . oh, no! I know the sweet
workings of that heart of his. He sold her the very day he made the
discovery how madly he cared for her! A fellow like that may seem to
act contrary sometimes, but he's always perfectly consistent really.
The only driving force within him is the acquisitive instinct. It creaks
out of his very bones directly anyone opens the door of his junkshop
and buys something from his stock, paying gold: the obsession to hold
on. The idea of possession eats into his very soul, and, if he were
capable of forming any ideal whatsoever, it would all be summed up
in sheer *possession* as an abstract concept.

"Bit by bit the thing took hold of him, till it assumed immense
proportions and became a veritable mountain of anxiety, lest he
should fail to possess his own self; lest he should be forced to love
someone—to admit the presence within himself of someone alien,
who would secretly fetter his will, or what he chose to consider his
will. That was the beginning of it. What followed was automatic. Just
as the pike has no choice but to swallow the bait when a glittering
object swims past it at the psychological moment. Selling my mother
was really a natural consequence, so far as Wassertrum was concerned. It gratified those two qualities slumbering within his soul—
avarice and a desire for self-torture.

"You must forgive me, Master Pernath"—Charousek's voice now
sounded so harsh and self-controlled that I positively shrank from
it—"you must forgive me if I seem to be talking somewhat like a
book, but once you're at the university, and find yourself surrounded

by a wilderness of printed matter of all sorts, one is apt to fall into their foolish jargon."

Out of politeness to him, I summoned up a smile. I knew quite well he was struggling with a desire to cry.

"Somehow or other," I pondered, "I must find some way to alleviate this fellow's plight, at least as far as lies in my power." Without his seeing, I took the hundred gulden note I still had in the house out of the drawer in the commode, and slipped it into my pocket.

"A little later on, Herr Charousek," I said, trying to steer the conversation into channels more propitious, "when you have been able to settle into better surroundings, and go into practice as a doctor on your own account, you'll be more at peace within yourself. How soon will you be qualified?"

"Quite soon now. I owe that to my patrons. There's nothing in it, of course, for my days are numbered."

I was about to make some conventional statement about his being too prone to look on the black side of things, but he laughingly prevented me:

"Better so . . . better so. There would be no satisfaction in aping these medical clowns by becoming a well-poisoner with a diploma, and ending up with an honorary title. Besides," he continued, with that bitter tone still in his voice, "I'm afraid I should be precluded, for the future, from giving the Ghetto the benefit of my miracle-mongering." He picked his hat up. "But I won't disturb you any longer. Unless there was anything else you wanted to discuss with me concerning the Savioli affair? I don't think there's anything. Let me know, though, directly anything fresh happens. The best thing would be for you to hang a mirror in your window as a sign that you want me to call on you. Don't, under any circumstances, come to my cellar. I'm curious to know what *he* will do once he's seen the lady's been to you. Tell him quite simply she brought a bit of jewellery for you to repair, and, if he gets importunate, just act strange."

There seemed to be no suitable opportunity to press that bank-note upon Charousek. So I took my wax model down from its board, saying to him: "Come, and I'll go a little way downstairs with you. Hillel's expecting me." It was a lie, of course.

He stammered at that. "Is he a friend of yours?"

"I know him slightly. Do you? Or do you, perhaps"—in spite of myself, I smiled—"mistrust him too?"

"God forbid!"

"Why do you say that so earnestly?"

Charousek shivered as he stood thinking. Then he replied: "I scarcely know. It must be something unconscious. But every time I meet him I feel I want to step down from the pavement and bend the knee to him as if he were a priest carrying the Host. There's a man, Master Pernath, the exact opposite, if you like, from that fellow Wassertrum! For one thing, it's rumoured amongst the Christians in the quarter, who are usually wrongly informed on every point, that he's a miser, and a secret millionaire into the bargain. As a matter of fact, he's as poor as a church mouse."

I broke in, horrified. "Poor?"

"Oh, yes. Poorer than me, if possible. It's my opinion he's acquainted with the word 'take' only from books. When he comes out of the Jewish Council House on the first of every month, all the beggars come swarming round him, knowing he'll press into the hand of the first comer his entire miserable salary, and a couple of days later go starving, he and his daughter together. If the old legend from the Talmud's true, and, of the whole twelve Jewish tribes, ten of them are cursed and two holy, then he personifies the two holy ones rolled into one, and Wassertrum all the remaining ten. Have you ever noticed how Wassertrum goes all colours of the rainbow when Hillel goes past him? Interesting fact, that. Blood like theirs could never mix in this world; all children born of it would be born dead, provided that the mothers hadn't died of horror first. Hillel's the only man makes Wassertrum feel not quite sure of himself. He avoids him like the plague. Probably because Hillel represents for him the incomprehensible, the something he'll never understand. Probably sniffs the Kabbalist in him too, I shouldn't wonder."

By now we were going downstairs.

"Do you believe," I asked him, "that there really are such things as Kabbalists in these days? Or that there's anything in the Kabbala?" I waited in some suspense for his answer. But he did not seem to have heard. I repeated the question.

He hastily turned aside, pointing to the door of the house we were just passing, all botched up with the lids of old packing-cases.

"There you've got a new lot of lodgers, a Jew family poor as poor as can be; the old half crazy musician Nephtali Schaffraneck, with daughter, son-in-law, and grandchildren. When it's dark, and he's left alone with the little girls, a madness comes over him. He strings them together by the thumbs, so that they shan't run away from him, forces them into an old poultry-cage, and gives them 'singing-lessons,' as he calls it, so that they'll be able, later on, to earn their own living—that is to say, he teaches them the craziest songs ever invented, German texts, snatches that he's picked up somewhere or other and retained in the dim twilight of his soul—and thinks are Prussian battle-hymns, or something of the kind."

And, true enough, some strange sort of melody was wafted forth into the passage. To the accompaniment of an excruciating fiddle-bow, playing over and over again the refrain of some vulgar street-song, two childish voices could be heard singing:

> "Frau Pick,
> Frau Hock,
> Frau Kle-pe-tarsch,
> Stand in rows together,
> Gossiping and gossiping."

Tragedy and comedy here were so inextricably interwoven that for the life of me I could not help bursting out laughing.

"The son-in-law, while the wife sells pickle juice in the egg market to the schoolchildren at so much a glass, spends his days running round the offices," Charousek continued grimly, "begging for old postage stamps. He gets them all together and sorts them, and those that by chance have only been stamped on one side he puts in a heap and cuts them through. Then he sticks together all these unstamped halves and sells them as new. At first business boomed, and often he'd make nearly as much as a gulden a day, but he got cut out finally by the industrial magnates of Prague, who've taken to doing it themselves. That's taken the wind out of his sails."

"If you had more money than you knew what to do with, Charousek," I asked him quickly, "would you give to those in need?" We were now in front of Hillel's door, and I knocked.

He looked at me in surprise. "Do you suppose I'd be such a hog as not to?"

Miriam's step now drew near, and I waited till she had her hand on the latch, then quickly pressed the banknote into his pocket. "No, no, Herr Charousek, I didn't really mean my question seriously, but you must please think me equally a hog if I neglect to do it."

Before he could say a word, I had shaken him by the hand and pulled the door to behind me. While Miriam was greeting me, I was listening to hear what he would do. He stood there a moment, then sighed softly, and went slowly, tentatively down the stairs, as if he had to support himself by holding onto the banisters.

It was the first time I had visited Hillel in his room.

It was bare as a prison. The floor painfully clean, and strewn with sand. No furniture in it save a table and two chairs, together with a chest of drawers.

Miriam sat opposite to me in the window, and I worked away at my wax model.

"Must one always have the model in front of one in order to get a good likeness?" She asked the question shyly, and only, I thought, to break the silence. We avoided each other's gaze. In her confusion and embarrassment over the miserable apartment she scarcely knew where to look, and my cheeks were burning hot with reproach for not having troubled before to find out how she and her father lived.

All the same, I must say something!

"No so much in order to get the likeness as to be able to check whether one's inner vision has been correct," I replied, painfully aware of the falsity of the remark.

For years now I had been led by the nose by the foolish dictum of the painters that a man must devote himself to the direct study of Nature; the inner vision had only come to me since that night I spent with Hillel, when he had shown me how true sight only comes with closed eyelids and vanishes again directly they open to the light of day—that mysterious gift of vision which so many think to possess, and which is given to only one among millions. How could I have suggested the possibility that the true line of spiritual vision could be corrected by the coarse means of physical appearance?

Miriam, too, seemed to be thinking along my lines, to judge from the astonished look in her eyes.

"Do not take what I have said literally," I apologised.

She watched me closely while I worked the model into deeper relief. "It must be terribly difficult to cut all that exactly on to the stone?"

"That part of the work is only mechanical. More or less."

A pause.

"May I see it when it's finished?" she asked.

"The stone is destined for you, Miriam."

"Oh, no—no—you mustn't." I could see the nervous trembling of her hands.

"Won't you even accept a tiny thing like that from me?" I asked her. "I would like . . . I most certainly should . . . do so much more."

She quickly looked away. What stupid thing had I said? Evidently I'd wounded her to the quick. It had sounded as if I'd made a point of referring to her poverty!

Could I retrieve my own gaucheness? Or should I only make matters worse? I plunged wildly:

"Listen to me, Miriam. . . . Do please listen. . . . I owe your father such a tremendous debt. . . . You've no idea how much."

She looked at me irresolutely, obviously not understanding.

"You mean, because he did what he could for you, that time you fainted? That was only to be expected!"

I felt she didn't know the real link which bound me to her father. I must feel my way carefully, so as not to give away anything he chose to keep from her.

"What I really meant was something far deeper than that. I mean the spiritual influence that can radiate forth from one human being to another. Do you know what I mean by that, Miriam? It's possible to help people in their souls, not only in their bodies, you know."

"And he——?"

"Yes. That's what your father did to me." I took her hand in mine. "Can't you see how I long to be the cause of some little pleasure, however small, if not to him, then at least to someone so near to him as you are? Isn't there any desire of yours I might be the means of fulfilling?"

She shook her head. "You don't, surely, think I'm unhappy here?"

"Of course not. But perhaps there are certain worries I could help to relieve you of? You are really bound—please do hear me out—really and truly bound to let me be the sharer of them. Why do you both live here, in this dark, depressing street, when you don't have to? You're so young still, Miriam, and——"

She smilingly interrupted. "You live here yourself, Herr Pernath! What makes you stay here, if it comes to that?" I hesitated. Yes, that was quite true. Why, exactly, did I live here? I couldn't explain, even to myself. What held me to this house? Absently I kept on repeating the words to myself. I could find no explanation, and for the time being entirely forgot where I was. Suddenly I felt myself caught up and carried far, far away—into a garden! I could smell the scent of the lilac blossom . . . a view of the town lay below me. . . .

"Have I touched an old wound? Have I given you pain?" Miriam's voice came to me faintly, as from a great distance. She was stooping over me, anxiously looking into my face. I must have been sitting still in my chair like that for a long time, she seemed so concerned.

I sat there for a while, irresolute, then suddenly the old inhibition was broken down, and I was pouring out my whole heart to Miriam, as though to an old and trusted friend, whom I had known all my life and who shared all my secrets.

I told her how I had learned, through some idle chatter of Zwakh's, how I had once been mad, and lost in the process all memory of my past; how, quite recently, images had begun to come into my mind more and more frequently that must have had their roots in those olden days, and how I trembled to think of the moment that might reveal everything to me, and leave me nothing but a wreck.

But my adventure in the subterranean passages, and everything that bore upon my relations with her father, I kept from her. She had crept quite close to me, and listened to my every word with a breathless sympathy that did me more good than I could say.

At last I had found a human soul in whom I could confide when the burden of my spiritual loneliness became too hard to bear. Of course, there was Hillel himself—but his presence seemed to me somehow so infinitely remote, like a being from another world, who came and disappeared, like a beam of light, whom I could reach out for, but never grasp.

I told her that too, and she understood me. She herself regarded him like that, for all he was her father.

There was a bond between them of infinite love, and yet, she confided to me, "I feel as though there were a wall of glass dividing us, which I can never break through. It has always been so, ever since I can remember. When, in my childish dreams, I used to see him standing at the head of my bed, he was always clad in the robes of the High Priest; on his breast would be fastened the golden table of the Law of Moses, with the twelve jewels therein, and a halo of blue, shimmering light would play around his temples. I think his love is of the kind that reaches forth beyond the grave, and too great for us to comprehend. So my mother always used to say, when we talked secretly together about him." Suddenly she shuddered, and trembled in every limb. I wanted to jump up, but she prevented me. "Don't be disturbed. It is nothing. Only a memory. When my mother died—no one but myself knows how much he loved her, and I was only a child at the time—I thought the pain of it would kill me, and I ran to him, and buried my face in his coat, and wanted to cry out, but could not, as everything in me seemed to be choked up; and—and—it makes me shudder even now, to think of it—he looked at me, smiling, kissed me on the forehead, and passed his hand over my eyes. From that day to this all the pain caused by the loss of my mother vanished. The day she was buried I could not shed one tear; the sun seemed to me as the shining hand of God Himself, outstretched in the heavens, and I wondered why the people wept. My father walked close to me behind the coffin, and each time I looked up he smiled at me softly, and I could see the scandalised look on the faces of all those who saw it."

"And are you happy, Miriam—really happy? Isn't there something a little terrifying for you in the thought of having for a father a being that has grown beyond the rest of humanity?"

She shook her head, and spoke happily:

"It is like living in a blessed state of sleep. When you asked me just now, Herr Pernath, whether I had not troubles, and why we lived where we do, it was all I could do not to laugh. Is Nature so beautiful as all that? I know, of course, how the trees are green and the skies are blue, but I have only to shut my eyes to see it all before me, a thousand times more beautiful. Do you suppose I must actually stand in a meadow, in order to see it? As for a little worry and—and—privation . . . all that will be made up for by waiting and hope."

"Waiting?" I asked, astonished.

"Waiting for a miracle. Don't you know what it is to do that? Don't you? Poor man, I pity you! There are so few who seem to know. Don't you see, that is the reason I so seldom go out, or mix with people. I did once have a pair of girl friends—Jewesses, of course—but we always seemed talking together at cross-purposes. They didn't understand me, nor I them. When I talked to them of miracles, they thought at first I was joking. When they learnt that I was serious and did not mean by miracle what bespectacled German professors do, the natural laws by which grass grows, but the contrary, they would have liked to consider me mad. But against that was the fact that I am fairly skilled in logic, have learned Hebrew and Aramaic, can read the *Targum* and the *Midrash,* and other things of that sort. Finally, they decided to call me 'highly strung.'

"When I tried to explain to them that what I considered most significant and most essential in the Bible and other sacred writings was just this element of miracle, and only miracle, and not the mere ethics and morals which were nothing but the hidden path by means of which miracles are attained, they could only answer me with platitudes, for they were shy of admitting that the only part of the religious writings that they believed in were just those which could have been found in any municipal book of law. The very word 'miracle' made them feel uncomfortable. It felt, so they said, as though the ground had been cut away from beneath their feet.

"As though there could be a more blessed state than that!

" 'The world only exists for us to be thought out of existence by us,' I once heard my father say. 'Then, and only then, does Life begin.' I don't quite know what he means by Life exactly, but I do sometimes feel as though one day I shall suffer a great awakening. Though I can't tell exactly how it will be. But I am positive there will be miracles.

" 'Have you ever experienced any, that you wait for them so patiently?' my two friends would often ask me, and when I said 'no,' they would look suddenly happy and triumphant. Can you understand the workings of hearts like that, Herr Pernath? At any rate, I will not hide the fact from you that I *have* known miracles—only quite tiny ones, ever so tiny"—Miriam's eyes shone—"but miracles none the less."

I could hear how tears of joy almost prevented her from speaking.

"I wonder if you can understand me," she went on very softly, "really and truly we have often lived by means of miracles! Sometimes, when there has been no bread in the house, no food of any kind, then have I felt within myself—now—*now* it will happen! And I have sat here and waited and waited, till I could hardly hear the heart beat in my body. And then—then—just when the spirit moved me, I would run hither and thither through the streets, very quickly, so as to be back by the time my father came. And—and every time I found money! Sometimes more, sometimes less, but always enough with which to satisfy our immediate needs. Often a gulden would be lying in the middle of the street and I could see it shining, and the people treading on it, but never noticing it. Sometimes I would feel so confident that I would begin by not going out at all, but would look all over the floor in the kitchen to see if either some money or some bread had not dropped down from heaven."

An idea shot through my brain, and for the very pleasure of it I could not refrain from smiling.

She noticed it.

"Don't laugh, Herr Pernath," she implored. "Believe me, I do know that these miracles exist, and that one day they——"

"I'm not laughing, Miriam," I assured her. "How could you think such a thing? I'm only too glad that you're not like all the rest, who seek the old time-worn explanations for everything that happens upon earth, and then if it doesn't end by squaring with their formula—as, thank God, it frequently doesn't—promptly have a grievance, accordingly."

She reached me out her hand.

"And you won't ever say again, will you, Herr Pernath, that you want to help us? Especially now you know that, if you did, you would probably be depriving me of the experience of a miracle?"

I promised her. But with a certain reservation in my mind.

The door opened, and Hillel came in. Miriam embraced him, and he greeted me, friendly and cordial, yet perhaps not quite so intimately as I had hoped. I also thought he seemed a little weary. Or did I only imagine it? Perhaps it was only the evening light, with which the room was now filled.

"You have come here, I feel sure, to ask my advice," he began, so soon as Miriam had left us alone. "In the matter of the strange lady, is it not?"

Surprised, I tried to break in, but he prevented me.

"I know it from the student Charousek. I met him just now in the street, and he seemed strangely altered, I thought. He told me everything, in the fulness of his heart. Even that you had given him some money." He looked at me piercingly, and emphasised his every word in the most curious fashion, that I was completely at a loss to understand.

"No doubt heaven has seen fit to rain down upon earth another drop or two of good fortune. In which case, doubtless there is no harm done. But"—he paused to think a while—"very often these things do more harm than good. It's not so easy as you think, my dear friend, to help people. If it were, the salvation of the world would be a comparatively simple proposition. Don't you think so?"

"But don't you, too, help the poor, Hillel?" I asked him. "Sometimes everything you have?"

Smiling, he shook his head. "From the look of it, you have grown into a Talmudist overnight, judging by the way you answer one question with another! That means we're in for a fierce argument."

He paused, as though for me to reply, but again I failed to understand why it was he waited.

"To get back to our subject," he continued in a changed tone, "I do not think that your protégée—I refer to the lady—is in any imminent danger. Let things take their course. There is a proverb, 'Prevention is better than cure,' but I think it is often better still to wait and see what happens. Perhaps the opportunity will arise of a meeting between myself and Aaron Wassertrum, but it will have to come from him. The initiative must come from him. Whether to me or to you makes no difference—and then I shall talk with him. It will then be up to him whether he will follow my advice or not. I wash my hands in innocence."

I tried anxiously to read his face. I had never heard him speak so coldly, almost threateningly. Behind those dark and deep-set eyes an abyss lay hidden. . . .

"Like a glass partition between himself and me" . . . Miriam's words came into my mind.

I could only press him by the hand, without a word—and go.

He accompanied me to the door, and as I went upstairs and once again turned round, I could see that he was looking after me with a friendly gaze, for all the world like someone who would like to say something, but could not.

FEAR

I had intended fetching my cloak and hat and going for my evening meal to the Alte Ungelt, where every evening Zwakh, Vrieslander, and Prokop sat together through the watches of the night, relating one another more and more impossible stories; but scarcely had I reached my room when all desire to do so left me as if strange hands had stripped away a piece of clothing from me.

The air seemed filled with a marked degree of tension, for which I could in no way account, but which was perfectly palpable, and, in the course of a few seconds, had so got the better of me that for very nervousness I knew not what was best to do—whether to light the lamp, to shut the door behind me, to sit down, or continue walking about.

Had someone crept in during my absence, and hidden himself? Was it an involuntary fear of something I was going to see took my breath away? Was Wassertrum here, by any chance?

I groped behind the curtains, opened the doors of my cupboard, looked inside the bedroom—nobody!

Even the iron box stood untouched where I had left it. Would it not perhaps be better to give way to my sudden impulse, and burn all the letters, for safety's sake?

Already I was fumbling for the key in my waistcoat pocket. Must I do it now, this instant? Couldn't it wait till to-morrow?

Best light the lamp first!

I couldn't find the matches.

Was the door locked? I went back a couple of steps. Then stood there, waiting.

Why did I feel this terror, all of a sudden?

I wanted to reproach myself for being a coward. But my thoughts were checked at birth.

I was suddenly seized with the craziest possible impulse; to get up on the table quick as could be, seize a chair and, raising it on high, crash it on to the skull of . . . whoever or whatever it was crawling on the floor of the room—if it drew near me.

"But there's no one here," I said, out loud to myself. "Do you make a habit of panicking like this?"

It was no use. The air I breathed had now become rarefied and penetrating as the ether.

If only I could have seen something! Could I but catch one glimpse of the most horrifying sight the mind of man could conceive—then, in a trice, would my fear be dispelled!

It didn't come.

With my eyes I tried to pierce each several corner.

Nothing.

Nothing at all around me but familiar objects . . . drawers . . . the table . . . the lamp . . . my picture . . . the clock . . . old, inanimate, faithful friends. Beneath my gaze I hoped they might change their aspect, and I should find the cause of my baseless terror had been nothing but an optical delusion.

Neither did that happen. Stubbornly did they retain their accustomed shapes. There they stood in the half-light, stock still, even as I did. "They are beneath the same spell," I thought to myself: "why are they, too, afraid to make the slightest movement?"

Why wasn't the clock ticking?

All sound seemed swallowed up in this universal dumb watching.

I shook the table, and was quite surprised I could hear the noise it made.

If only the wind would start blowing round the house! There was no sign even of that. If only the firewood in the grate would crackle! But the fire was out.

And still that perpetual noiseless waiting . . . without a pause . . . without a gap . . . like the trickle of water!

I began to think I should never get over this appalling state of nerve tension. The room seemed full of unseen eyes, and waving, purposeless hands that I was unable to grasp.

This, I realised, was the very essence of terror—that ghastly, paralysing fear of nothing at all, of something devoid of form, that yet eats into the very boundaries of one's thought.

Stiffening my every sinew, I stood there, waiting. I waited quite a quarter of an hour. Perhaps IT could be deceived. I might be able to get behind it and surprise it. In a series of random leaps I encompassed the room. Nothing! That self-same devastating Nothingness that did not exist, yet filled my room with a horrible sort of life. Suppose I were to turn and flee? What was there to prevent me?

It would go too, outside with me. I knew that, somehow, for certain. Also that it would be no use my striking a light—for all which I searched for the matches, and at length found them. But the wick wouldn't burn, and refused to develop into anything but the dullest of dull glimmers—a yellow, dirty-looking, flickering tongue, like tarnished tin. Darkness was better than that.

I put the light out, and flung myself, prostrate, on my bed. I counted my heart beats . . . one . . . two . . . three . . . four . . . up to a thousand. And then all over again. It seemed to go on for hours, days, weeks, till my lips were dry, and my hair rose up on end. The same suspense. Not the least little particle of relief.

I began saying over casual words, just as they came to my tongue . . . "prince" . . . "tree" . . . "child" . . . "book" . . . and to repeat them, torturedly, till they suddenly were transformed into meaningless, terrifying noises of barbarous ancestry, confronting me, stark naked, while perforce I must strain my every nerve to force them back to their original significance. "PRINCE" . . . "BOOK" . . .

Had I gone mad? Or was I dead? I groped . . . and groped. Now I must get up, I thought. And then sit down! I sat in my arm-chair. If only I could die, here and now! If only this chill, fearsome *watching* sensation could be got rid of! "I won't! *I won't!*" I shrieked aloud. "CAN'T YOU HEAR ME?"

All my remaining strength left me then, and I collapsed. The fact that I still lived was beyond my power to grasp. I simply sat there, dully staring straight in front of me, incapable of thought or action.

"Why does he keep offering me the seeds?"

A thought flowed suddenly into my conscious mind. Then ebbed again. Ebbed and flowed: ebbed and flowed.

By degrees it was borne in upon me that a curious apparition stood before me, and had probably so stood since I had sat there. It was reaching out its hand towards me. A grey, broad-shouldered figure, the height of an average thick-set man, leaning on a knotted, spiral walking-stick of white wood. In place of a head I could only distinguish a nebulous globe of pale mist. From it stole a slightly nauseating odour of sandalwood and wet slate. A feeling of utter helplessness now deprived me almost of all consciousness. All that I had suffered in this endless period of utter nerve-rack had materialised here before me into this horrifying abortion. My instinct of self-preservation told me I should go mad from fear or horror, once I saw the phantom's face—and yet it drew me like a magnet, forcing me to gaze upon that pale sphere of mist, and find therein eyes, a nose, and a mouth.

Try as I would, there it stood, unchanged and motionless before me. All sorts of heads did I succeed in placing upon that ghostly torso—yet each time I was aware they were but the product of my own imagination. Added to which, they vanished, all of them, almost directly I had conceived them.

The one that remained longest was the head of an Egyptian ibis. The being's outline seemed to contract and expand at regular intervals, as though it were taking long breaths. This was the only visible movement that could be discerned in it. In place of feet, it stood on knobs of bone, from which the grey, anæmic flesh was drawn back in puffy rolls.

Without one sound, without moving, it held out its hand to me. It was full of little seeds, red, spotted with black, about the size of a bean.

What had that got to do with me?

In a dull, obtuse sort of a way, I now felt the weight of some colossal responsibility—some decision to be made, which far surpassed all earthly concerns, were I to blunder at this crucial moment.

I dimly apprehended how, in the world of events, two scales were laden now with the fate of a world—one of which, according to the infinitesimal quantity of my throwing, would sink down!

That, it dawned upon me, was the secret of that impalpable awfulness, lapping me around. "Don't move one finger," my reason had cried out to me, "even should Death deny you his presence, and his all-merciful release."

But then you would have made a choice. You would have rejected the seeds. There would be no turning back.

I looked round appealingly for some sign that would afford me the faintest light on what I ought to do.

Nothing. No inward inspiration in myself. Not the faintest spark of an impulse. Everything dead and dried up.

I realised—too well—how the fate of myriads of men and women lay, light as a feather, in the hand of this most terrifying and pregnant moment.

It must be well on into the night by now, for I could no longer see the walls round my room. Heavy steps were to be heard in the studio next door. I could hear chests being moved and cast upon the floor, and thought I recognised Wassertrum's voice, shrieking out curses in his familiar, raucous bass. I stopped listening. It seemed of no more import to me than the rustling of a mouse. I shut my eyes.

Slowly, human faces passed before me in endless procession. Dead masks all, with eyes fast closed; my own flesh and blood . . . my own ancestors! And, however much the type changed, it was always the same formation of skull that rose forth from its grave; heads with smooth hair parted down the middle, heads with curly hair cut short, heads with long perukes and flowing ringlets . . . century after century lined up before me, till the features, bit by bit, became more and more familiar, culminating at long last in one hideous countenance— the face of the Golem, and none other! With that my chain of forebears broke off short.

The darkness now within my room had resolved itself into infinite empty space, in the centre of which I sat in my arm-chair, the grey shadow, with its outstretched arm, still standing before me.

When I opened my eyes once more, strange forms had ranged themselves around me in semicircular formation; those on one hand clad in robes of shimmering violet, those on the other in a kind of reddish black. Creatures of an alien race, with long, attenuated forms, and faces concealed behind luminous cloths.

The very beating of my heart now told me the decisive hour had arrived. My fingers twitched towards the seeds—and a visible shudder passed through the ranks of the red-black contingent.

Should I once again refuse them? The blue-mauve semicircle was now seen to quiver. I looked fixedly at the headless man. There he stood, in the same spot, motionless as ever.

Even his breathing had ceased.

Still at my wits' end to know what to do, I raised my arm—then smote the phantom's outstretched hand, so that the seeds rolled upon the floor!

For a moment, as if I had received an electric shock, I lost consciousness, and I seemed to be falling into infinite depths—and then I was standing firmly on my feet again.

The grey presence had vanished now. So had the red-black semicircle. The bluish forms, on the other hand, had made a ring around me. On the breast of each one of them were golden hieroglyphs, and each held high betwixt its finger and thumb—dumbly, almost as though an oath were being taken—one of the red seeds that I had smitten from the hand of the headless ghost.

Outside I could hear the thunder muttering, and great hailstones beat against the window.

A winter storm full of sound and fury now hurtled on its way throughout the town. Through its howling could be heard, at rhythmic intervals, sounds as of cannon-shot in the direction of the river. The ice was breaking on the Moldau. The room was filled with the luminous glare of incessant flashes of lightning. All of a sudden I felt so weak my knees trembled, and I had perforce to sit down.

"Fear not," said a voice quite clearly in my ear. "Fear not. It is the Lelschimurim . . . the Night of Protection."

Gradually the storm died down, and the deafening noise resolved itself into the monotonous drubbing of the hailstones upon the roof.

The lassitude that now filled my limbs dulled all my senses, and as though half in a dream only did I register what went on around me.

Someone within the circle uttered the words:

"He whom you seek is not here."

The rest answered in a language I could not understand. The first speaker then spoke a sentence in which was the name: "ENOCH," but the rest of it I could not catch. The wind was too full of the groaning of the bursting ice-blocks.

Then one member of the circle came forward, stepping directly in front of me, pointed to the hieroglyphs on its breast—the same as all the rest bore—and asked me if I could read it.

And as, scarce able to speak for weariness, I shook my head, the figure stretched towards me the palms of its hands, so that the characters appeared upon my breast in letters of flaming gold, in Latin script: CHABRAT ZEREH AUR BOCHER. Gradually the characters changed into a script I could not read.

I fell into a deep, dreamless sleep, such as I had not enjoyed since the night that Hillel had released my tongue-tied soul.

URGE

The last few days had flown past me with wings. Scarcely had I seemed to have time to take my meals.

From morning to evening I sat at my table, filled with an irresistible urge towards active occupation.

I was through with the cutting of my stone, and Miriam had been as pleased with it as a child.

The letter "I," too, in the book *Ibbur* had been repaired.

Peacefully I lay back in my chair, and reviewed all the trivial happenings of the day just past.

The old woman who looked after me had told me when she came in the morning how last night's storm had broken down the old stone bridge. That was strange! Broken it down . . . probably at the identical moment that I had smitten. . . . No . . . no . . . I refused utterly to think of that! I had firmly resolved all those events should be buried deep within me till they woke up of their own accord. I was not going deliberately to interfere with them.

It only seemed the other day I was crossing that bridge, and taking stock of its stone statues—and now there it lay in ruins, the old bridge that had stood the wear and tear of so many centuries.

I could find it in my heart to feel quite sentimental when I thought that never again should I set foot upon it. Howsoever it was restored, it would never be the same old mysterious bridge of stone.

I thought of it persistently as I sat at work, and gradually a complete scene rose up in my mind, gently and inevitably, as though I had never really forgotten it; myself as a small boy, and later as a growing youth, gazing up at the carving of St. Luitgard, and all the holy men who now lay plumb beneath the raging waters. There welled up in my consciousness, too, all the little tiny nothings that in my childhood had been part of me, as well as my father, and my mother, and my numerous school-mates. The one thing I could not remember was the house I lived in.

I knew, however, that one of these days when I least expected it, it would stand revealed to me, and I rejoiced greatly in the thought.

It was so inexpressibly comforting, that feeling of everything gradually developing within me, bit by bit.

Yesterday, when I had taken the book *Ibbur* out of its iron box, it had in no way looked so inordinately strange—only an old parchment volume, adorned with precious illuminated lettering. That was all.

I could not understand now the feeling of the supernatural it had once impressed me with.

It was written all in Hebrew, and for that reason quite incomprehensible to me.

When, I wondered, would the stranger call for it again?

The joy of living, that unconsciously had crept back into my soul whilst I was at work, woke vitally within me now, and beat back the army of night thoughts that had bid fair to overwhelm me.

With a sudden impulse, I took up the picture of Angelina—I had cut off the inscription underneath—and kissed it.

Foolish and childish I knew it to be—but why not, for once in a way, at least *dream* of happiness . . . hold fast the glittering bubble of the present, rejoicing till it burst?

Was it beyond all laws of Chance that those seeds of longing sown within my heart should ever flower? Were they to be frustrate, ever and for ever? Was it so utterly unthinkable I should ever rise to fame? Become equal to her in rank, even if not in family? As far as that went, I was as good as Dr. Savioli, surely? That relief I had just carved of Miriam . . . if I were to achieve many such—even the greatest artists of all time had done nothing better; at least I was convinced of that!

Supposing . . . supposing Angelina's husband were to die suddenly?

I went hot and cold all over. One only happening, and my most audacious thought might clothe itself in actuality! Fortune, dangling above me like a ripened plum, might fall at any moment, plop into my lap!

Had not things happened to me already—and that not a few—stranger, by far, than this? Things the existence of which my fellow-creatures dreamed not at all?

Was it any wonder that within the space of a few weeks creative powers had been awakened within me that raised my work on to a completely different level—far, far higher than the average ruck?

Surely . . . surely . . . I stood on the threshold of a new existence? Had I no right to happiness?

Must mysticism be synonymous with the suppression of all desire? I stifled within me the voice that answered "yes"; only a moment . . . let me but for one instant minute enjoy the sweetness of a dream!

I lay in a brown study, with eyes wide open. The precious stones upon my table waxed and waned in size, till I was in the midst of waterfalls of every hue! Great trees formed of opals stood in groups, clustered together, streaming forth to the skies all colours of the rainbow, the radiant blue thereof iridescent as the wing of some great tropic butterfly, shimmering its way over unseen meadows, full of summer's very essence. And I, being afire with thirst, cooled my limbs in the ice-cool spray of the streams, as they rushed their way over rocky beds, like gleaming mother of pearl!

Sultry winds blew from the south, laden with the scent of blossom, intoxicating me with the fragrance of jasmine, hyacinths, narcissi, and sweet syringa. It was too much! Too much! Deliberately, I wiped my vision out. But oh . . . how thirsty I still was!

The torments of Paradise!

I flung open the window, and cooled my forehead in the spring wind.

Spring was coming. The air was full of the smell of it.

Miriam!

I couldn't keep Miriam from my thoughts. I kept on seeing her excited face telling me, with one hand against the wall for her support, how once more she had experienced a miracle—a real, unmistakable miracle! She had found a gold piece in the loaf of bread that the baker had placed through the little grille window in the kitchen that overlooked the passage-way.

I seized my purse. It was not surely too late, before the day was over, to conjure another ducat or so in the same direction!

She had been to see me every day—"to keep me company," so she said, but had scarce uttered a word all the time, so full had she been of her "miracle." The experience had stirred her to the depths of her soul, and as I recalled the way her face had blanched—just with the bare recollection, as she told it—to the very lips, almost I reeled at the thought I might have been the perpetrator of a deed whose consequences would reach out heaven knew where!

And when in this connection I called to memory those last dark words of Hillel's, my blood ran cold.

My purity of motive was no excuse, so far as I was concerned. The end did not justify the means. I saw that.

And what if, when all was said and done, my motive was only pure as a whited sepulchre? What if some insidious lie lay concealed within it? The desire—maybe unconscious—to play a benefactor's role?

I began woefully to mistrust my own self.

It was clear to me now, my judgment of Miriam had been far too superficial.

As Hillel's daughter, she would naturally be quite different from other girls.

How could I have had the audacity to probe, in my clumsy wise, the inmost depths of a personality probably infinitely superior to my own!

The very cast of her countenance, a hundred times better suited to the sixth Egyptian dynasty—and too spiritual by half even for that!—than to this workaday world, ought to have warned me where I stood.

Once I had read somewhere: "Only a fool despises appearances." How true that was! How devastatingly true!

Miriam and I were the best of friends. Should I own up to her that I myself, day after day, had been putting that ducat in the loaf of bread?

The shock of it would be too sudden. She wouldn't be able to stand it, surely? I dare not do that. But in future I would be more circumspect.

Could I, bit by bit, tone the miracle down? Instead of placing the coin in the loaf, put it on the front doorsteps, where she would find it when she opened the door—and so on and so forth? I should, I felt sure, be able to hit upon a variety of ways, each one more likely than the last, that gradually would efface the miraculous element altogether, and place the happening on an everyday plane.

Yes! Surely that was the right course to adopt!

Or should I cut the Gordian knot asunder? Should I take her father into my confidence, and ask his advice? I reddened at the very thought of it. Time enough for that, when all other means had failed.

I must get to work now, and lose no more time! I was seized with a sudden inspiration! What if I could persuade Miriam into doing something unusual, something that would take her out of her ordinary surroundings, even if only for a couple of hours?

I would order a carriage and take her for a drive! After all, who knew us, if we avoided the Jewish quarter?

Perhaps it would amuse her to go and look at the broken-down bridge?

Or perhaps old Zwakh, or one of her former girl friends, would accompany her, if the thought of me as her escort seemed too outrageous in her eyes!

I was most firmly determined not to take "no" for an answer!

On the threshold I collided with a human form! Wassertrum!

He must have been peering through the keyhole, for he was still stooping when I ran into him!

"Were you looking for me?" I asked curtly.

He stammered forth a few apologetic phrases in his unconscionable jargon, then said that he was.

I asked him to come in and sit down. But he preferred to stand by the table, convulsively grasping the brim of his hat. That implacable hatred he cherished against me was apparent in his face, and his every movement, despite his efforts to conceal it.

I had never seen the man quite so close before. It was not the revolting ugliness of him that inspired such loathing (rather, that aroused my compassion, making me think of a creature whom Nature herself has repudiated at birth, bruising, in her horror and disgust, its poor distorted face)—it was something else—something intangible, that emanated from him, and was the cause of it.

The "blood," as Charousek had so pithily phrased it.

Involuntarily I wiped the hand I had held out to him on his entrance.

Though I made it as unobtrusive as possible, he must have noticed, for all of a sudden he had to control himself to the utmost to suppress his hatred of me flaming forth in all his features.

"You've got a fine place," he began, in heavy dialect, seeing I had not the good grace to begin the conversation. But in spite of the nature of his remark he shut both his eyes—in order, probably, not to meet my gaze. Or did he fancy it lent a more prepossessing expression to his face?

It was obviously a struggle for him to speak standard German.

I felt myself in no way bound to reply, and waited for his next.

In his embarrassment, he picked up the file that—God knows why—had lain on the table ever since Charousek's visit. Next moment he had put it down as though bitten by a snake! I was all amazement, inwardly, at his refinement—however unconscious—of perspicacity.

"Of course . . . of course. You've got to keep it looking good. It's business," he mumbled. "Since you get the carriage trade." He evidently wanted to open his eyes at that point, to observe what impression his words had made, but decided the moment was premature, and quickly shut them again.

I resolved I would corner him. "You mean that lady who came here the other day? If so, say so!"

He hesitated a moment, then seized me firmly by the wrist, and tugged me over to the window.

The curious and unexpected manner of it reminded me of the way in which, some days ago, he had dragged poor deaf and dumb Jaromir into his den. With his claw-like fingers he held up something to me which gleamed:

"What do you think, Herr Pernath . . . can you do something with this?"

It was a gold hunter watch, with the cover of it so bent it almost looked as though someone had done it on purpose.

I picked up a magnifying-glass. The hinges were half twisted off, and within the lid . . . wasn't there something engraved there? It was almost illegible, having been partially erased with a number of newly made scratches. Slowly I deciphered what I could of it.

K–RL ZOTT—MANN.

Zottmann? *Zottmann*? Where had I heard that name before? Zottmann? I couldn't for the life of me remember. Zottmann?

Wassertrum all but snatched the glass out of my hand.

"There's nothing wrong with the works. I've looked at it myself. It's the case that's wrecked."

"It only needs a tap or two . . . at most a small rivet. Any competent working jeweller could see to that, Herr Wassertrum."

"Ah . . . but I want a good job made of it! What they call artistic— see?" He interrupted me hastily, almost anxiously.

"Very well, if it's so important to you."

"Important!" His voice cracked in his eagerness. "But I want to sport it myself. I want to show it and say: See . . . that's Herr von Pernath's work."

The fellow's laboured flattery nearly made me sick. He literally spat it into my face.

"If you'll come back again in an hour, it'll be quite ready for you."

Wassertrum fairly tied himself into knots. "No . . . no . . . no . . .

don't put yourself out . . . I wouldn't for the world——Say three days . . . say four days. . . .Next week is time enough. I'd never forgive myself if I thought I caused you any trouble, Herr Pernath."

What on earth made him get into such a state about it? I stepped into the adjoining room, to lock the watch in the iron box. On the top of it lay Angelina's photograph. Quickly I slammed the lid to, in case Wassertrum should have been looking in after me.

When he came back, he appeared to me to have changed colour. I looked at him closely, but dismissed my suspicion almost immediately. He *couldn't* have seen!

"Very well, then, next week," I said to him, meaning he could go.

But he seemed all of a sudden resolved to take his time, taking a chair and sitting down!

He changed his tactics now, keeping his goggle eyes wide open, and fixing them immovably on the top button of my waistcoat.

Pause.

"That bitch told you you didn't know anything about it if it came out, didn't she!" Spluttering, he suddenly delivered himself of this outburst, without the slightest preamble, as he banged the table with his fist.

There was something positively horrifying in the abrupt transition he seemed able to make between one mode of speech and another; those flattering tones converted in a trice to those of a brute. I could quite understand, now, how so many people, especially women, must find themselves beneath his thumb before they knew where they were—once he possessed the smallest weapon he could use against them.

My first impulse was to fall upon him, seize him by the scruff of his neck, and shoot him through my door; next I bethought me how far more sensible it would be to sit still and listen.

"I haven't the least idea what you mean, Herr Wassertrum," I said, looking about as obtuse a fool as I knew how, "really I haven't. As for that extremely unpleasant word—what, precisely, do you mean by it?"

"Mean by it? Mean by it? Am I supposed to teach you German?" he snarled at me. "You'll be raising your right hand in court when the cat's out of the bag. Do you understand me? I'm telling you!" He began to scream. "Can you look me in the eye and deny that she came from over there," he pointed with his thumb toward the studio, "with a cloth wrapped around her arse and nothing more, not a damned thing more!"

I began to see red. I seized hold of the swine and began to shake him.

"If you say another word of that sort, I'll break every bone in your body! Do you hear me?"

He went grey as he sank back in his chair, and stuttered:

"What now? What's the matter? I didn't mean anything."

For a moment or so I walked the room to calm myself. Of his voluble excuses I heard not a word. Then I took a chair opposite him, with the firm resolve once for all to have it out with him, at any rate so far as Angelina was concerned. If it *must* come to a passage of arms, then would I force him to commence hostilities, and shoot a few premature bolts.

Without taking the slightest notice of his repeated interruptions, I told him, with no uncertain voice, how *blackmail of any kind*—and I emphasised the word—was foredoomed to failure, as he had not a dog's chance of proving any single point, and I, on my side, could produce witnesses (if it should conceivably come to such a point) who would support me and refute him. (The welfare of Angelina was far too dear to me for me to boggle at the thought of perjury, if necessary!)

Every muscle in his face twitched, his hare-lip pushed its way up almost to his nose, he ground his teeth, and gobbled like a turkey-cock in his efforts to interrupt me:

"Listen to me . . . listen, I tell you . . . Do I want something from that bitch? I'll tell you . . ." He was half frantic with me because I had not let myself be sidetracked. "It's Savioli I want . . . Savioli . . . the God damn' filthy cur!" he suddenly burst out in his frenzy.

He gasped for air, and I held my peace. This was the point I had wanted to bring him to. But already he'd got himself under control again, and sat fixing my waistcoat button once more.

"Listen to me, Pernath." He forced himself to adopt the cold, calculating tones of a man of business. "We were speaking just now of the bitch—of the lady, were we not? Very well. She's married. Very well. And she's been carrying on with a young cocksman. What do I care? I know that." He waved his hands before my face, to and fro, finger and thumb pressed together, as though they contained a sample of salt. "I know . . . I know . . . the bitch can do as she likes. I'm a man of the world, and you're a man of the world, eh, Pernath? We both of us know what's what. But what I want is my money! Understand that, Pernath?"

I listened, astonished.

"What money? Is Dr. Savioli in your debt, then?"

Wassertrum evaded the point.

"I've had dealings with him. It will come out right."

"You mean you're going to kill him!" I cried.

He sprang up at that, in a panic, then gobbled again.

"Yes! Kill him! How much longer do we have to keep up this comedy?" I pointed to the door. "Get out!" I said.

Slowly he felt for his hat, put it on his head, and turned to go. Then, for a moment, paused, and, with a coolness for which I wouldn't have given him credit, replied:

"That's right. I wanted to leave you out of it. Good! If I don't, all right. The barbers that worry make the most cuts. I've got enough. If you had any sense—Savioli is in your way! But—now—I'm going—to make—all three of you——" —he made a gesture of strangling someone—"neckties!"

His face looked altogether so satanic, and he seemed so appallingly sure of himself, my blood ran cold to see him. Obviously he must have some weapon in his possession that I knew not of. Neither did Charousek. I felt the ground tottering beneath my feet.

"The file! The file!" Something was whispering in the back of my brain. Instantaneously I measured the distance with my eyes: one step to the table . . . two to Wassertrum. . . .I was poised for a spring when—there at the door stood Hillel, as though he had risen out of the floor!

The room swam before my eyes.

As through a mist I saw how Hillel stood there, motionless, and Wassertrum, step by step, retreated towards the wall. Then I heard Hillel speaking:

"You know the old proverb, Aaron, doubtless, how all Jews will go bail one for another? Don't make it too difficult." He added a couple of Hebrew words that I did not understand.

"What do you mean, listening at doors?" Aaron snarled at him, his lips trembling with rage.

"Whether I was listening or not is my own affair," Hillel told him. And again added a sentence in Hebrew which this time sounded like a threat. I expected an open row now, but Wassertrum stood there never saying a word. Then, after pondering a moment, he went out.

Apprehensively I looked towards Hillel. But he signed to me to be silent. Obviously he was waiting for something, for he strained his ears in the direction of the passage, I wanted to go and shut the door, but he restrained me with an impatient gesture.

After at least a minute, the junkdealer's shuffling tread was heard coming up the stairs again. Without speaking one word, Hillel went out and made way for him.

Wassertrum waited till he was out of hearing, then snarled at me, "Give me back my watch!"

WOMAN

What on earth had become of Charousek?

Twenty-four hours had passed since I put my mirror in the window, and still not a sign of him. Had he forgotten the signal we had agreed upon together? Or had he just not seen it?

I went to the window and adjusted the piece of glass so that the sun's rays on it were reflected directly towards the little barred peep-hole of his basement lodging.

Hillel's intervention yesterday had reassured me somewhat. He would surely have warned me had any danger been impending. Added to which, Wassertrum couldn't have done anything of moment since; the instant he had left me he had gone back to his shop; I glanced down towards it to make certain, and there he was, sure enough, leaning motionless behind his counter, just as I had seen him early in the morning.

This incessant waiting was getting more than my nerves could bear! The mild spring breeze that blew in from the window of the adjoining room made me quite sick with longing.

The snow was melting from the roofs! And how the little beads of water shimmered in the rays of the sun! More and more did it all seem to draw me out of doors by invisible threads. Full of restlessness, I walked up and down the room. Threw myself into a chair. Got up again.

This sickly germ of uncertain love was like a cancer eating away my breast. The whole night long it had tormented me. One time it had been Angelina nestling into my arms; then, apparently, I was talking to Miriam, quite quiet and calm, when again Angelina came and kissed me. I could smell the perfume of her hair, and the soft sable fur of her coat tickled my neck. Suddenly it began to peel off her naked shoulders, and Rosina was in her place—Rosina, dancing, half drunk, with half-closed eyes, clad in a swallow-tail coat—naked. All this in a semi-dream that was almost equivalent to being awake. A terrible kind of awakeness, sweet, evanescent, agonising. . . .

When morning broke, my doppelgänger was standing at my bed-side, the ghostly Habal Garmin, referred to by Hillel as "breath of bones." I looked him in the eyes. He was in my power, and must now reply to any question I chose to put to him to do with this or any other world. He was only waiting for me to begin. But my craving after the mysterious must perforce give way to the heat of my blood; it was no more than a weak, thin trickle, leaking through to the barren ground of my reasoning powers. I dismissed the phantom, which promptly resolved itself into the image of Angelina and finally dwindled into the letter "Aleph," only to wax once more and stand before me as the colossal female stark naked, that once I had seen emerge from the book *Ibbur*, with the pulse like an earthquake. The creature stooped towards me, and I breathed the intoxicating perfume of her hot flesh.

Was Charousek never coming? The bells were beginning to ring in the steeples. One more quarter of an hour would I wait—and then go out! I would saunter through bustling streets, full of folk dressed in their best, in the rich quarter of the town, where would be seen beautiful women with tiny hands and feet and the faces of coquettes!

Perhaps I should by chance meet Charousek there! At least, that was the excuse I muttered to myself.

I fetched down my old pack of tarot cards from the bookcase meanwhile, to while away the time.

Maybe I should get an idea from one of them for a design for a new cameo? I hunted through them for the *Pagad*. But it didn't seem to be there. Where could it have got to?

As I sat shuffling through the cards, my thoughts dwelt upon their mystic import. Especially that of the Hanged Man. What could that mean?

A man, strung on a cord betwixt heaven and earth, head down, arms bound behind him, right thigh crossed over his left leg, looking almost in the form of a cross, over an inverted triangle.

Some symbol pregnant with meaning that I could not fathom.

Ah! At last there was Charousek!

Or was it not?

Better still—Miriam!

"Do you know, Miriam, that I was just on the point of going down to you and suggesting you went for a drive with me?" The words were not, literally speaking, perfectly true, but I couldn't think of that just now. "You will, won't you? You couldn't be so cruel as to refuse? I feel in such extraordinarily good spirits to-day, and only wanted you to crown my happiness!"

"A *drive*?" She was so utterly dumbfounded that I simply had to burst out laughing.

"Is it quite such an astounding proposition?"

"No . . . no . . . But"—she was actually at a loss for words—
"remarkable . . . unusual! A drive!"

"Not in the least unusual, in the light of the fact that hundreds and
thousands of folk do it every day of their lives! And that that, most
frequently, is about all that they *do* do!"

"Ah! Other people," she admitted. But the thought of it still quite
took her breath away.

I took her by both hands.

"I want all those pleasures that come the way of other people, Miriam, to be enjoyed by you a thousandfold!"

Suddenly she went deathly white, and I could see from the glazed
look in her eyes what she was thinking of.

I felt a stab at my heart.

"Don't let it obsess you, Miriam," I pleaded. "I mean—the miraculous. Will you promise me to try not to—out of friendship to me?"

Hearing the anxious tone in my voice, she looked at me in amazement.

"If it didn't take you like this, I could rejoice in it, too, with you
. . . but . . . as it is . . . Do you know I'm very concerned about you,
Miriam? About—how shall I say it?—your spiritual health? Try and
not take me too literally, but—but I could wish there were no such
things as miracles."

I waited, expecting her to protest, but she only nodded as she stood
there, sunk in thought.

"It is devouring you, Miriam."

She answered hastily, "Sometimes I almost wish there were none."

For me her words contained at least a ray of hope. "Were I to
think," she went on, softly and dreamily, "the time would come when
I would have to live without such miracles as——"

"You might all of a sudden become rich, and not need any more."
The words rushed thoughtlessly to my tongue, but I stopped on seeing
her look of consternation. "I—I mean . . . one day you might, in the
ordinary course of things, be freed from all your worries, and the
miracles you would then experience would be of a different sort. They
would be, so to say, inner experiences."

She shook her head, and said resolutely, "Things of that kind are
not miracles. The amazing thing is that such a lot of people seem to
exist without ever having them. Ever since my childhood, day after
day, night after night, I have lived through——" She suddenly broke
off short, and I surmised she referred to something deep within her of
which I had not been told—possibly the same kind of concatenation

of strange happenings as I myself had suffered. "Never mind about that. . . . Only if someone were to stand up here and now, curing the sick by laying on of hands, that I could call no miracle. Not till the soulless earth becomes informed with spirit, and the laws of Nature set at naught, will that happen for which I have yearned since my birth. Once my father said to me: 'There are two aspects of the Kabbala, one magical, one abstract, which do not coincide.' The magical can encompass the abstract or theoretical, but the reverse can never be. The magic side is a gift, while the other may be acquired, though only with the help of a guide. And what I long and long for is this same strange gift: things that can be acquired I set no store by, and find as worthless as dust. And if I were to think"—the convulsive twisting of her hands, and the pain and grief in her voice, went to my very heart—"if once I were to believe that miracles would pass out of my life, then I think the mere possibility of such a thing would kill me, here and now."

"Is that the reason why you said just now you almost wished no miracles had happened?" I asked.

"Only partly. There's something else as well. I—I——" She stopped a moment to think. "I was not sufficiently developed to experience a miracle like that. How can I best explain to you? Let us suppose—just suppose, of course—that for a period of years I had the same dream every night, which went on and on, and in which someone—let us say a visitor from another world—instructed me, and showed me, not only my own self as in a mirror, but how far removed I was from the maturity necessary to experience a miracle; guiding me at the same time into the paths of reason, thereby giving me the key to so much that was wont to puzzle me during the day, and enabling me to put my problems to the test. . . . You, surely, will understand how great a thing that must be to come into one's life—what a difference it makes, and how far it can surpass all the joys life has to offer? For me it meant the bridge that united me to the unseen, the Jacob's ladder by means of which I could climb up out of the darkness of everyday existence. He was my friend and my guide and my sole assurance that the obscure ways my soul seemed bound to tread would not end in darkness and insanity. He was my every hope, and he had never lied to me. Then, all of a sudden, and in direct contradiction to everything he had ever told me, a miracle crossed my path! Whom now should I believe? All these years that had gone before, and meant so much to me, were they nothing but a snare and a delusion? Once my faith in them were to go, I fell into a bottomless abyss! And yet—the miracle *had* happened! I would sing for joy, if only——"

"If only?" I interrupted, breathless. Maybe she herself now would utter the one redeeming word whereby I could tell her everything!

"If only I could learn I was mistaken! That it was no miracle! But, if it were so, I know as surely as I stand here"—my heart stood still—"it would be my undoing! To fall from highest heaven to deepest earth—do you think mortal man could be called on to endure it?"

"Ask your father to help you," was all the advice that, in my distress, I could offer.

"Ask father?" She looked at me uncomprehendingly. "But when for me it is only one of two ways, how could he find a third? Do you know the one thing that could save me now? It would be for that to happen which has happened to you! If I could forget, once and for all, everything that lies behind me! Strange, is it not, that what makes you so unhappy would be for me my greatest good?"

For a long time we both were silent. Then all at once she seized my hand and laughed.

"But I don't want you, please, to distress yourself too much about it!" (That she should be comforting me . . . she, me!) "Here were you just now, so merry and bright over the coming of spring, and now I have plunged you into the depths of depression! I shouldn't have said anything about it to you. Try and pretend I have not! Dismiss it from your mind, and be cheerful once more! Like—like I am."

"You, Miriam?" My voice was bitter as I interrupted her. "You cheerful?"

She smiled resolutely at me. "Ever so cheerful! When I came up to see you I was most dreadfully cast down—I can't say why. Somehow I couldn't get it out of my head that you were in great peril of some sort"—I listened attentively—"but, instead of rejoicing, as I should have done, to find you safe and sound, here have I been depressing you with——"

I now forced myself to be merry. "You can atone for that now," I told her, "if only you'll go out with me." (I deliberately made my voice sound as cheerful as possible.) "Once in a way, Miriam, I should ever so much like to see whether I couldn't succeed in driving away those morbid thoughts of yours! Say what you like, you know, you're no Egyptian magician! You're just a young girl, and, as such, subject to the caprices of the winds of spring!"

She, too, became gay all of a sudden.

"Why, Herr Pernath, I've never seen you like this before! As for the winds of spring—our parents control them for us Jewish girls, and we must obey. It comes naturally to us. I suppose it's in our blood. Though perhaps not so much in our family," she added thoughtfully, "since my mother refused flatly to marry Aaron Wassertrum."

"*What*? Your mother? The junkdealer down below?"

Miriam nodded. "It never happened, though, thank God. Though it was a dreadful blow to the poor man."

"Poor man, you call him?" I burst forth. "The fellow's an utter rogue!"

Very seriously she nodded her head. "Of course he's a rogue. But anyone stuck in his skin would have to be a prophet if he weren't a scoundrel."

Full of curiosity, I edged nearer to her. "Do you know anything particular about him? I'm interested. Particularly so."

"Once you had seen the inside of his shop, Herr Pernath, you'd know exactly the sort of things went on in his mind. I can tell you that, for as a child I used very often to be in there. Why do you look at me so astonished? Is it so surprising? He's always been kind and friendly towards me. Once, I remember, long ago, he gave me a big stone that glittered, and which I had taken a fancy to among his things. But my mother told me it was a diamond, and I must take it back at once.

"For a long time he wouldn't take it back again, then suddenly he tore it out of my hand and threw it angrily away. But I could see the tears in his eyes as he did so, and I knew enough Hebrew to understand what he was muttering to himself: '*Everything I put my hand to is accursed.*' It was the last time I ever went to see him. He never asked me in again. I knew quite well why it was. If I hadn't tried to comfort him, it would have been all right, but just because I felt so sorry for him, and said so, he didn't want to see me any more. Can you understand that, Herr Pernath? It's ever so simple, really. He is a man obsessed; the kind of man who becomes suspicious to the point of madness directly anyone touches his heart. He thinks of himself as being far more detestable than he really is—if such a thing is possible—and that is the mainspring of all his thoughts and acts. They say his wife was very fond of him. It may have been more pity than love, but, all the same, I have heard it from a lot of people. He was the only person who thought otherwise. He goes about scenting treachery and hatred everywhere.

"The only exception he made was in favour of his son. Whether it was because he had watched him grow up and studied his every quality from childhood onwards, and could therefore find no single point in which to sow the seeds of his mistrust, or whether it was his Jewish blood concentrating all its powers for loving on its own offspring, in obedience to the old Jewish instinct lest the race die out ere the mission be achieved that slumbers still, forgotten, in the darkness of their hearts, who can tell?

"He superintended this boy's education with a judgment little short of marvellous in a man so unlettered as he. An expert psychologist could hardly have improved on it. To begin with, he sheltered him throughout his boyhood from whatever experience might develop any such thing as an active conscience, thereby safeguarding his future from the pains of remorse. As his tutor he engaged an eminent man of science with decided views as to the animal world not being liable to pain. His entire upbringing was based on the principle of squeezing the last drop of enjoyment possible from every created thing, and then casting away the shell thereof as of no further practical use. And, of course, money was represented as the be-all and end-all of existence, and the key to every kind of power. He actually hit upon a method, too, whereby his son might mystify the world, as he had done, with regard to his own wealth, without the disadvantage of the poverty-stricken appearance he himself had seen fit to adopt. He thought this would increase the sphere of his influence, and to that end he made him an æsthete, imbuing him with the insidious and pernicious 'cult of the beautiful.' I should hardly think this could have been his own unaided inspiration—more likely he was acting on the advice of some really cultured person—but the result was that the boy grew into the kind of man who deliberately affects the worship of the lilies of the field, while the true soul of him is that of a ravening vulture.

"He cherished no grievance against this son for disavowing him wherever and whenever possible. On the contrary, he preached it as a duty. For his love was devoid of self, and, as I once heard my father say, 'of the kind that reaches out beyond the grave.' "

Miriam was silent for a moment, though I could gather the trend her thoughts had taken from the changed tone of voice in which she next said:

"Strange fruits, at times, grow from the tree of Judaism."

"Tell me, Miriam," I asked her, "have you ever heard that Wassertrum keeps a wax figure somewhere in his shop? I don't know who told me—it may have been only a dream——"

"No, Herr Pernath, it was not. It is quite true. A wax figure, large as life, stands in the corner where he sleeps, on a sack of straw heaped round with every possible kind of rubbish. He took it once, so they say, from a waxworks show, on account of its likeness to some girl—a Christian—who must, I suppose, have one day been a sweetheart of his."

"Charousek's mother!" the thought flashed into my mind.

"You don't know her name, Miriam?"

She shook her head. "If you really want to know—shall I find out for you?"

"No, no, Miriam, don't bother. It really doesn't matter." I saw from the light in her eyes how worked up she had been getting, and was resolved to calm her down. "Tell me more about what you were saying just now. It interests me. I mean about the soft winds of spring. Your father surely won't tell you whom to marry?"

She laughed merrily. "Father? What are you thinking about?"

"Ah! All the better for me!"

"How so?" she asked guilelessly.

"Doesn't it increase my chances?"

It was but a joke, and she only took it as such, but she went none the less quickly to the window, so that I should not see the deep flush on her cheeks. I rambled on, to help her out of her embarrassment.

"As an old friend you must let me, of course, be present at the ceremony. Or do you think of for ever remaining unmarried?"

"No. Oh, no." She disclaimed the idea so earnestly that I smiled, in spite of myself. "One day, most certainly, I must marry."

"Of course. Naturally you must!"

She was as nervous as a flapper.

"Herr Pernath, can't you be serious for one single moment?" In obedience to her wish, I adopted the mask of a wise philosopher, and sat down close to her.

"You see, when I tell you like that I must one day marry, it is just that I have not so far worried myself a great deal about things of that sort. But it is not that I do not realise that I should miss the full meaning of life if I thought I had come into the world to remain for ever childless."

For the first time since I had known her, I saw the look of the true woman come into her eyes.

"One of my dreams," she continued softly, "is to prefigure to myself as an ultimate ideal the complete fusion of two human beings into what—have you never heard of the old Egyptian cult of Osiris?—into what the hermaphrodite stands for in the language of symbolism."

I listened now with the utmost attention. "The hermaphrodite."

"I mean by that, the magical union into one single entity of a man and a woman. Not, as I said, really as the *ultimate* goal, but as the beginning of a new way that is eternal—a way without an end."

"And is it your hope," I questioned her, "one day to find what you are looking for? May it not be that he lives in some far-off land

. . . perhaps not even upon this our planet?"

"I know nothing about that," she replied simply. "I can but wait. If we are really separated from one another both by space and time—and I can hardly believe it, for, if so, why should I be so firmly planted here in the Ghetto?—or through a mutual ignorance of one another's existence, so that I am never to find him, then is my entire life nothing but some mocking devil's dream. But please—please," she implored me, "let us speak no more of it. Once one begins to clothe one's thoughts in words, their brightness becomes obscured at once by this horrible tinge of earthliness, and I don't want——"

She broke off short.

"What don't you want, Miriam?"

She lifted up her hand, then rose quickly, saying:

"Visitors for you, Herr Pernath!"

The swish of silken skirts was now heard in the passage.

An impetuous knock. Then:

Angelina!

Miriam wanted to go, but I prevented her.

"Let me introduce . . . the daughter of an old friend . . . the Countess . . ."

"Why, it's almost impossible to make one's way along all this broken plaster in the passage. My dear Master Pernath, why ever don't you live in a place fit for human habitation? There's the snow melting away out of doors, and the heavens rejoicing thereat, and here you sit glooming away like an old frog in a mildewy cave! Only yesterday I was at my jeweller's, and he told me you were the finest artist and cutter of precious stones that exists at the present day—if not one of the greatest ever known!" Angelina sparkled on like a waterfall, and I was enchanted without more ado. Once again to behold those eyes of shining blue, those little feet in the diminutive patent leather shoes, the whimsical face peeping forth from its wilderness of fur, and the tips of her little rosy ears!

She hardly took a breath, but continued.

"My carriage is waiting round the corner. I was so afraid I shouldn't find you at home. You haven't had your lunch yet, I hope? We'll drive out to . . . well, where *shall* we drive? . . . Wait a moment! I know! We'll go into the park, or at least somewhere in the fresh air where we can sniff the rising of the sap and the bursting of the buds! Come along now . . . come along . . . get your hat! You'll lunch with me, and we'll sit and talk till evening! Get your hat, quick! What is it you're waiting for? There's a lovely thick rug in the carriage, and we'll wrap ourselves in it up to the ears, and sit close, one against another, till we're as snug as snug can be."

What was there left for me to say? "I was just talking of going for a drive with my neighbour's daughter." But Miriam had hastily withdrawn, before I could get the words out of my mouth.

I accompanied her to the door, though she tried good humouredly to prevent me.

"Listen to me, Miriam. I cannot tell you here on the stairs how much I depend on you. I would a thousand times rather go with you . . ."

"You mustn't keep the lady waiting, Herr Pernath," she insisted. "Good-bye, and—have a nice time!"

Her tone was cordial and quite sincere, but I could see the light had gone out of her eyes.

She hurried down the stairs, and for very grief I could say not a word. I felt as if I knew what it was to lose a world.

As in an intoxicating dream, I sat at Angelina's side. At a brisk pace we were driving through the overcrowded streets. It was like being plunged into the hub of the universe, a sparkling swirl of life, amid which here and there only could I distinguish bright, isolated, gleaming points: flashing jewels in ear-rings and muff-chains; stark, shiny opera-hats; white feminine gloves; a poodle dog with a scarlet collar round its neck, barking, and trying idiotically to bite our carriage wheels as they turned; immaculate steeds, foaming at the lips, snorting at us in their silver-plated harness; a shop-window filled with cases full of lustrous pearls and twinkling ornaments; costly silks that gleamed round women's hips.

And the spell of Angelina's warm body, all the more potent in its workings for the bitter wind that cut into our faces.

The police controlling the traffic stepped respectfully aside as we drove past. We turned in the direction of the bridge, past the mass of stone ruins surrounded by a crowd of gaping sightseers. I scarcely looked at it; the slightest word from the mouth of Angelina, the lashes of her eyes, the quick play of her lips, all—all—was far more momentous to me than seeing how the blocks of fallen stone checked the surging cakes of ice upon their course.

Then came the park. And with it the good earth, hard trodden. The rustle of leaves beneath the horses' hooves; the wet air; the stark branches of the trees filled with crows' nests; dead winter green of grass lawns, flecked here and there with islets of white snow—all—all of it flashed past me like a dream.

Quite suddenly, almost indifferently, Angelina had touched on the subject of Dr. Savioli with a couple of abrupt words.

"Now that the danger is past," she told me, with enchanting and child-like lack of embarrassment, "and I know he's going on so much better, everything I did then, at that time, seems to me so dreadfully boring! All I want to do now is to feel happy again, and close my eyes, and bathe in the sunshine and joy of life. I believe all women are like that although they won't admit it. Or are they so stupid they don't even know it themselves? What do you think?" But she obviously didn't listen to a word of what I said. "We women, you know, are so uninteresting, as a rule, to one another. You needn't take it to yourself for flattery, but it's absolutely true that the mere presence of a sympathetic male is worth more to my little finger than the most exciting conversation with the cleverest woman that ever was! Talks between women are always so stupid! What is there for them to talk *about*? Just . . . clothes and such . . . and the fashions don't change as often as all that, after all! I'm dreadfully frivolous, am I not?" she asked, suddenly starting to play the coquette, with the result that it was all I could do not to take her head between both my hands and kiss the nape of her neck. "Tell me that I'm frivolous!"

She nestled still closer to me, and snuggled up against me. We were out of the main drive now, and rolling along little pathways with small shrubs on either hand, swathed in straw till they looked like the rumps of strange, fantastic monsters deprived of limbs and heads.

People sat on seats in the sun, looking after us, then putting their heads together and whispering.

For a while we both took refuge in our thoughts. How different Angelina seemed now from the figure who had occupied so large a space in the world of my imagination! Was it really the same woman I had comforted that day in the Cathedral?

I simply couldn't turn my eyes away from those half-parted lips. But still she said not a word. She seemed to be forming some picture in her mind's eye.

The carriage was rolling now over a waste of moist grass. It smelt of earth awakening.

"Do you know, madame——"

"Please call me Angelina," she broke in softly.

"Do you know, then, Angelina, that I spent all last night dreaming of you?"

She made a quick little gesture, as though to withdraw her arm from mine, and looked at me with astonished eyes. "But so did I of you!" she cried. "And I was just this moment thinking of it!"

The conversation ended with a jerk, for we both realised we had been subject to the same dream.

I could feel it in the pulsing of her blood. Her arm quivered slightly on my breast. She was looking away from me, with an agonised expression on her face.

Slowly, slowly, I drew her hand towards my lips, stripping from it the white, fragrant glove, hearing as I did so the catching of her breath. Then, half crazed with love, I pressed my teeth into the ball of her little thumb.

Hours later I was making my way like a drunken man towards the town, through the evening mist. Aimlessly I went up first one street, then another, making a circle as complete as it was unconscious.

I was standing now by an iron railing close to the river, staring down at the raging waters.

I still felt Angelina's arm around my neck; I could still see the stone basin of the fountain, full of sodden elm-leaves, before which, so many, many years ago, we had parted one from another; she was wandering still with me, as she had done only a few hours ago, her head leaning on my shoulder, speechless, through the frosty twilight of her own garden.

I sit down upon a bench, pulling my hat far down over my eyes, that I may continue dreaming.

Down below the embankment, the water blustered on its way, and in the sound of its swirling was drowned the last dying murmur of a town on the verge of its nocturnal rest. When, from time to time, I drew my cloak closer around me and looked up, the river was plunged in ever deeper shadow, till at last, capitulating to the blackness of the night, it flowed on its darkened course with a track of white foam, where it fell into the lock, cutting a diagonal streak of dazzling white from shore to shore.

I shuddered at the bare thought of having to return once more to my desolate lodging.

The magic of one brief afternoon had made me for ever and ever a stranger in my own dwelling-place.

A brief span of a few fleeting weeks—days, maybe—and my bliss would be as a tale that is told, and nothing left to remind me thereof but a sweet, sad memory.

And then? Ah, then . . . I was homeless for ever and a day, this side of the river or the other.

I stood up. Just one more look would I take through the park gates at the great house where she dwelt, behind one of whose windows she was sleeping, even now. One more look, before I returned to the Ghetto. I took my bearings with regard to the direction I had come, groping my way through the thickening mist along the rows of houses, across slumbering squares, past shadowy monuments rising threateningly on their pedestals, past lonely sentry-boxes, and flourishing façades of baroque buildings. The dull glimmer of a street lamp developed into gigantic concentric rays of an attenuated rainbow hue, only to dwindle once more into dull yellow pin-pricks of light before vanishing into the mist behind me.

From the feel of it, my feet were treading broad stone steps now, strewn with gravel. Where was I? In a tunnel, with a steep slope?

To the right and left of me seemed to be smooth garden walls, over which hung the bare boughs of trees. They had the look of springing straight from the atmosphere; their trunks were blotted out by fog.

A couple of rotten, slender twigs cracked off as my hat touched them, glancing off my cloak into the grey, misty abyss in which my feet were hidden.

Suddenly a gleaming point of light; a lonely, far-off spark it seemed, poised, mysterious fashion, somewhere in infinity 'twixt heaven and earth.

I must have gone astray; that could only be from the old Castle steps on the slopes of the Fürstenberg Gardens.

Then came a long stretch of muddy ground. Then a paved path.

A massive shadow suddenly reared itself in front of me, like a head in a black, high, peaky hat. It was the Daliborka, the Hunger Tower, in which human creatures of olden time suffered a slow death, while their monarchs far beneath them hunted wild game in the park. A little twisty, twirly alley, broken here and there by arbitrary loopholes—it might almost be called a spiral passage, scarce broad enough to admit the width of a man—and I stood before a row of diminutive houses, not one of which exceeded my own height. I had only to stretch up my arm to touch their roofs.

It was the Street of the Alchemists, where the so-called "wise men" of the past had evolved their formulas for the philosopher's stone, brewing their concoctions in the watches of the night, poisoning with their noxious fumes the sweet rays of the moon.

No road led out of it but the way I had just trod. Oddly enough, I couldn't find the passage-way again through which I had emerged; I came up instead against a lattice gate. There was no help for it, I told myself; I must awaken someone and ask the way. I thought it curious that a house should be blocking up the way—a house, moreover, larger than the others, and, from the look of it, inhabited. I couldn't remember ever having seen it before.

It must surely be whitewashed all over, to stand out so clearly in this mist?

I went through the lattice gate and up the little garden path, and pressed my face against the window-panes. Everything was dark. I knocked on the window. A veritable old Methuselah of a man came then through the door, with an aged, wambling gait, till he reached the middle of the room, when he stood still, slowly turning his head towards the phials and retorts that stood on shelves around the walls, smothered in dust; next he looked musingly at the spinning-wheel in the corner, and finally his gaze fell in my direction. The shadow cast by his protuberant cheek-bones upon the sockets of his eyes was so deep it made them look as empty as the eye-holes of a mummy.

Obviously he didn't see me. I knocked again on the glass. He didn't hear. Without a sound, like a man walking in his sleep, he went out of the room again.

I waited in vain. At length I knocked on the front door. But nobody opened.

There was nothing for it now but to go on looking till I had found the entrance to the street again.

Would it not be better, I wondered, to go down below again and mix with my fellow-creatures—sit with Zwakh, Prokop, and Vrieslander at the Alte Ungelt and try and drink away, at least for a couple of hours, this gnawing desire for Angelina? Resolutely, and very quickly, I set my face in that direction.

There the three old cronies sat, their heads together over the worm-eaten table, white, slender-stemmed clay pipes between their teeth, and the whole room full of smoke.

Almost it was impossible to make out their faces, so little of the sparse light from the old-fashioned hanging lamp was reflected from the dark brown walls.

In the corner sat, as usual, the elderly waitress, flat-chested, thin as a rake, terse of speech, yellow-billed as a duck, knitting . . . knitting . . . knitting . . .with that eternally vacant look upon her face.

Thick pads were fastened on the closed doors, so that the voices of the customers in the neighbouring room filtered through only like a swarm of hiving bees.

Vrieslander, wearing on his head his conical hat with the stiff brim, looked, what with his beard and moustaches, the blue-grey tint of his skin, and the scar beneath his eye, for all the world like a drunken Dutchman of a bygone century.

Joshua Prokop had stuck a fork right into the midst of his

musician's locks, and was drumming incessantly on the table with his long, wraith-like fingers, while he looked on admiringly at Zwakh's laborious efforts to clothe a paunchy bottle of wine in the purple cloak belonging to one of his marionettes.

"That is Babinski, that is," declared Vrieslander, with the utmost gravity. "Mean to say you don't know who Babinski was? Zwakh, tell Pernath this instant who Babinski was!"

"Babinski was," Zwakh began immediately, without so much even as looking up from his work, "Babinski was one of Prague's celebrated robbers and murderers. For many a year he carried on the bloody business without anyone being aware of it. But, bit by bit, it dawned upon some of the better families of the neighbourhood as more than a little strange that, one by one, various relatives became conspicuous by their absence when it came to sitting down to table. And, though some of them argued the cloud had its silver lining in that it tended to reduce housekeeping expenses, it could not be denied that people would most probably begin to talk, and their prestige would suffer in consequence.

"The most remarkable part of these disappearances was the number of marriageable daughters involved.

"Apart from everything else, it became awkward, for, after all, every self-respecting family has a certain reputation to keep up for harmony in the home circle. The insertions in the agony column of the daily press—'*Come back: all is forgiven*'—grew more and more frequent, and were the cause of universal comment. But Babinski, thoughtless like most professional killers, had never taken this into account—and it finally attracted general attention.

"Meanwhile, he had taken the utmost pains to build himself the cosiest little country house out at Krtsch, that charming little village close to Prague. He had always been at heart an apostle of the simple life, and that little house of his was clean and bright as a new pin, and had a little garden in front of it full of scarlet geraniums.

"But as he couldn't afford to buy more land in which to conceal the dead bodies of his victims, he had, to his infinite regret, to convert this flower-bed into a grass plot, smooth and trim, that bit by bit developed into the shape of a suspicious-looking mound, increasing gradually in bulk according to how business was, or the season of the year.

"Here it was that Babinski used to sit, after the burden and heat of the day, playing all kinds of melancholy tunes on his flute, in the light of the setting sun."

"Stop a bit," Prokop broke in, and, quickly pulling his latch-key out of his pocket, held it to his mouth like a clarionet, singing: "*Zimzerlim zambusla—deh.*"

"Were you ever there, then, that you know the tune so well?" asked Vrieslander, astonished.

Prokop threw him a withering look. "I was not. Babinski was born a little too soon to have had the pleasure of my acquaintance. But, as a composer, I can be allowed to know the tunes he played, I suppose? You have nothing to say about it. You're not musical. *Zimzerlim— zambusla—busla—deh.*"

Zwakh listened attentively till Prokop had put his key back again into his pocket, and then continued:

"But the waxing of that grass mound at length aroused suspicion on the part of the powers that be, and to a certain policeman from the suburb of Zizkov, who had witnessed from afar the spectacle of Babinski throttling the life out of an ancient dame of good family, belongs the honour of having finally ascertained the nature of that worthy's extremely anti-social profession, and putting an end to it accordingly.

"Babinski was duly arrested at the privacy of his own fireside. The court brought in a verdict of guilty, and, by virtue of the prisoner's otherwise exemplary reputation, condemned him to death by hanging. The firm of Leipen Bros., wholesale and retail rope merchants, was contracted with for the provision of all the necessary outfit for the execution, so far as their particular side of it was concerned.

"But it so happened that the rope gave way at the crucial moment, and Babinski's sentence was commuted to penal servitude for life. For a period of twenty years did the murderer atone for his misdeeds behind the prison walls of St. Pancras. Not once was a single reproach heard upon his lips: indeed, such was his behaviour he is quoted as a model to this day amongst the prison officials: he was even allowed, so they say, to play his flute on the birthdays of the lords of the land."

Whereupon Prokop immediately began to search for his latch-key again, but Zwakh prevented him.

"As the result of a general amnesty, the remainder of Babinski's sentence was annulled, and he got a job as porter in the Convent of the Compassionate Heart. The work involved a certain amount of light gardening, and such was his proficiency with the spade, owing to his previous experience in another walk of life, he soon used to find himself through with it, and free for the rest of the day to devote himself to his reading, which was chosen with the greatest care, for the betterment of his soul.

"The result was most delightful. Though the Mother Superior was quite willing to allow him every Saturday evening off, to go down to the local tavern and cheer his spirits up, he always used to return punctually before nightfall, alleging that the universal degeneration of

public morals was more than he could bear to witness, and that the
sort of rabble a man met these days on the high roads was such as to
make it positively unsafe to venture out of doors at all after dark.

"It was just about then that certain wax modellers bethought themselves of making little wax effigies of Babinski, and of being sufficiently tactless as to display them in their windows, dressed, each of
them, in little red cloaks. Such an object was soon to be found in the
house of each one of the afflicted families.

"But in still greater profusion were they to be seen in the shop
windows, beneath glass cases, and nothing put Babinski into such a
fine state of frenzy as to behold one of them.

"It was, so he used to declare, an utterly unwarranted and repre-
hensible piece of impertinence that nothing could justify thus to per-
petuate a man's youthful peccadilloes before his very eyes, and he
would declare himself astounded that prompt action in high quarters
was not taken to put an end to such a disgraceful practice.

"Even on his death-bed did he deliver himself of such and similar
sentiments.

"Neither was it to no purpose, for not long afterwards the authorities actually did step in and forbid the traffic in those little Babinski
statuettes that had been the cause of such heart-burnings."

Zwakh now took a mighty pull out of his tankard of grog, while all
three of them grinned like the devil. After which, he turned his head
towards the anæmic-looking waitress, and I, for one, was witness of
the tear she was wiping from her eye.

"Well, Master Pernath, honoured friend and esteemed cutter of
stones," Vrieslander asked me, after a considerable pause, "do you
feel inclined to cap our colleague's yarn with a better of your own?
Unless, of course, you like to foot our little bill as an alternative."

I began to tell them of my wanderings through the fog. When I
came to the part where I had discovered the white house, they all
three of them, for very suspense, removed their pipes from their
mouths, and, when I ceased, Prokop smote the table with his fist, as he
cried:

"Can you beat it? Isn't that just the sort of thing that happens to
our friend Pernath here, and nobody else! And oh—by the way—that
Golem mystery—you remember that time?—has been cleared up all
right. Did you know?"

"How, cleared up?" I asked, dumbfounded.

"You know Haschile, the mad Jewish beggar? No? Well, at any
rate, Haschile was the Golem all right."

"A beggar, the Golem?"

"Yes. Haschile. Yesterday afternoon the so-called ghost was seen blissfully wandering through the streets, clothed in those disgusting old rags from the seventeenth century, if you please! He walked right through the Salnitergasse bold as brass, and the butcher's boy caught him and led him off to the station on a dog leash!"

"What on earth are you talking about? I can't make head or tail of it!" I broke in.

"I'm telling you! It was Haschile! It seems he found the old clothes some time ago, before the door of some house. But, to get back to what you were telling us about that little white house—it's extraordinarily interesting. You may not know it, but there's an old legend about a house in that very Street of the Alchemists that's only visible when there's a fog, and only then to those folk born of a Sunday! It goes by the name of 'Last Lamp House.' Whoever goes up the street by day sees only a huge grey stone, and behind it there's a sheer drop right down into the Hirschgraben. You can thank your lucky stars, Pernath, you didn't take one step more. If you had, you would have fallen into the Hirschgraben and broken every bone in your body. Beneath that stone, according to the legend, is hidden a mighty treasure. It is the foundation-stone, so they say, laid by the Order of the Asiatic Brothers, who are said to have founded the city of Prague, for a house that should one day be inhabited by a man—or, to use a better expression, a hermaphrodite; for it is to be a creature formed from both man and woman. It will carry a hare as its coat-of-arms. For the hare was apparently the symbol of Osiris, and that is the origin of our custom of the 'Easter Hare.'

"Ever since it was put there, so men tell, old Methuselah actually watches over it in person, to see that Satan doesn't come and seduce the stone and beget on it a son, the so-called Armilos. Have you never heard tell of Armilos? They even know what he would look like—that is to say, the old rabbis do—when he comes down to earth; he would have hair of gold, bound straight back from his brow; two peaks on his head; eyes in the form of sickles; and arms that reached down to his feet."

"A beauty like that should be drawn," growled Vrieslander, and fumbled for his pencil.

"So don't forget, Pernath," Prokop concluded, "if you *should* ever have the luck to be transformed into a hermaphrodite, and find the hidden treasure in passing, don't at least forget I've always been a good friend to you!"

But I was not in the mood for joking, feeling rather a prey to a faint feeling of dismay.

Zwakh must have noticed it, for all he knew not the reason, for he quickly came to my rescue:

"At any rate, it's most strange, not to say uncanny, that Pernath should have had such a vision in the very spot so closely associated with the old legend. There are hidden linkages, from whose bond certain men apparently cannot free themselves, if their souls have the faculty of seeing forms which are denied to the external senses.

"I cannot help it. The supernatural is the most fascinating subject in the world. Do you agree?"

Vrieslander and Prokop had suddenly become grave, and none of us seemed to think an answer necessary.

"What do you think, Eulalia!" said Zwakh, turning to the old waitress.

She scratched her head with her knitting needle, and snorted, with heightened colour.

"Oh, go on. You always give me a hard time."

"At any rate," Vrieslander went on, as soon as we had stopped laughing, "it's been confoundedly close to-day. So much so, I haven't been able to paint a stroke. Somehow or other I've kept on seeing Rosina, dancing in that coat."

"Has she turned up again?" I asked.

" 'Turned up' is good! The police have her on a long-term contract. Perhaps the commissioner took a fancy to her at Loisitschek's. In any case she's running wild, and contributing quite a bit to the taxation of the 'foreign trade' in the Ghetto. She's really a damned goodlooking girl!"

"It's astounding what sort of a fool a woman can make of a man once he allows himself to get fond of her," Zwakh interpolated. "That poor fellow, now—Jaromir, the deaf-mute—to get money to go to her, has become an artist overnight. He goes into the cafés and taverns all over town and cuts silhouettes of the customers."

Prokop, who had not been listening to Zwakh, now smacked his lips. "Indeed? Is she that goodlooking? Ever been favoured with one of her kisses, Vrieslander?"

In a frenzy of indignation, the waitress jumped up and flounced out of the room.

"Old hen!" growled Prokop after her. "She really needs it—offended virtue!"

"Take it easy, take it easy," Zwakh adjured him. "She didn't mean to be personal . . . and, besides, she'd just finished that stocking."

The landlord brought a fresh supply of grog, and the conversation took a turn that was *piquant*, to say the least of it. A little too much so for the abnormally fevered state of my own blood. I fought against it, but, the more I strove to detach myself from them and sit there thinking about Angelina, the hotter and more excited their talk seemed to make me. In the end, I left them somewhat abruptly.

The fog was slightly more transparent now as it sprinkled me with its fine needles of ice, but it was still too thick for me to read the names of the streets distinctly, so that I got a little out of my reckonings on my homeward way.

I had just got into the wrong street, and was about to turn back again, when I heard my name called:

"Herr Pernath! Herr Pernath!"

I looked round, and I looked up, but nobody could I see.

Above the open door of a house a little red lamp showed its unobtrusive light, and within its rays stood what seemed—to me, at any rate—a form of beauty.

Once again: "Herr Pernath! Herr Pernath!" This time, in a whisper.

I stepped, amazed, into the passage-way. In a trice, two soft female arms had wound themselves around my neck, and, by the shaft of light that flowed forth from an open doorway, I saw that it was Rosina, clinging to my body with all the warmth of hers.

TRICKERY

A raw, grey day.

I had slept on late into the morning, dreamless and impercipient as the dead.

My old charwoman had either forgotten to lay the fire or else had not come at all.

The grate was strewn with cold ashes.

Dust lay on all the furniture.

The floor was unswept.

Shivering, I walked up and down.

A nauseating smell of stale gin permeated the whole room. My cloak and all my clothes reeked of old tobacco-smoke.

I pushed the window open, but closed it again immediately. The cold, dirty breath of the street was more than I could bear.

On the lead guttering sparrows were huddling, motionless, with soaked feathers.

The whole world seemed nothing but dust and ashes; and I had a soul to suit.

Nothing looked right. How shabby and shiny that cushion seemed in the arm-chair—and all the horse-hair stuffing trickling out of it! Really, it must be sent to the upholsterers . . . ah! . . . what was the good of it all? After all, only one other fatuous existence going to pot!

Those rubbishy thread bobbles on the window . . . how vulgar and purposeless . . . how utterly tasteless the whole thing was! Why didn't I twist the whole lot of them into one single cord, and hang myself by it?

Then, at least, the damned things needn't offend my eyes any more, and the whole grey, dismal pother of life would be over, once and for all!

Yes! That was the brightest idea I'd had yet. Make an end of everything!

I'd do it to-day.

I'd do it this morning. Before I'd had my meal, even. Think of committing suicide on a full stomach! Think of lying in the wet earth, full of rotting, undigested food!

If only the sun would show its impudent face, and once again shine into my soul its damned infernal lie of *joie de vivre*!

Not much! I wasn't going any longer to be made the dupe of a clumsy-footed, purposeless God of Fate who didn't even know his own rotten job . . . who lifted me up to the heights, only to push me down into the filthy, stinking puddle of despond, and pipe the while its silly tune to me that I'd known all along . . . that every child knew . . . every dog in the street, for that matter . . . how nothing lasts on earth . . . everything passes . . . everything. . . .

Miriam! Poor, poor Miriam! If only it lay in my power to help her!

What I had to do was to make a resolve and stick to it; turn it into grim, concrete fact, before the confounded Life Force once again started dangling its pinchbeck images before my very nose!

What had it all been for—all these communications from the eternal, incorruptible world.

For nothing, by the look of it. Precisely nothing at all.

Or only, perhaps, to send me twirling and twirling round in a circle, and leave me now, earth-bound, in a veritable torment.

There was only one way out.

I reckoned up in my mind how much money I had at the bank.

That was it. That little sum, paltry though it was, probably represented the net result of any value to which all my strivings here below had attained!

I should tie up in a little parcel all the valuables that I possessed—

including that couple of precious stones in the drawer—and send it to Miriam. That ought to rid her of the worry of material cares for at least the space of two years. And I should also write a note to Hillel, confessing the whole truth to him about the "miracle."

Only he could help her.

I felt certain he would know how to advise her, somehow.

I found the stones, wrapped them up, and looked at the clock. If I were to go to the bank now, I could be through with everything in an hour's time.

And then I would buy one more bunch of red roses for Angelina! My whole being cried out with pain and wild longing. I would like to live one more day . . . just one single day more!

And then have to contend all over again with this throttling agony of despair? No! A thousand times, no! Not one single minute more would I wait! The conquering of that one moment's weakness almost left a feeling of peace within me.

I looked around. Was there anything else I ought to see to? Ah . . . that file, on the table! I put it in my pocket, meaning at last to carry out my intention of throwing it away somewhere outside in the street.

I hated the sight of it. Had it not come within an ace of making me a murderer?

Who was that, coming up to disturb me?

It was the junkdealer.

"Only a moment, Herr von Pernath," he panted out breathlessly, as I signed to him I had no time to spare. "Only just a couple of words."

The sweat was trickling off his forehead, and he was trembling all over with excitement.

"Can we talk together here, without being disturbed, Herr von Pernath? I don't want . . . I don't want that Hillel to come up again! If you'd just turn the key in the door . . . or . . . better still . . . just come into the next room . . ." In his usual grabbing fashion he started pushing me into the room with him. Then he looked cautiously round him, and whispered in his hoarse voice:

"I've been thinking things over . . . It's better that way. Nothing'll come of it. Good. What's past is past!"

I tried hard to read his eyes. But he avoided my gaze, twisting his hand on the arm of the chair, such an effort did it cost him to control himself.

"I'm glad to hear it, Herr Wassertrum," I said, in as friendly a tone as I could command. "Life is sufficiently sad, is it not, without the added bitterness of mutual hate?"

"Ah . . . He talks as nice as a book," he grunted, obviously in some relief, while he fumbled in his trousers pocket, and finally pulled out the golden watch with the bent cover to it. "And so you'll see that I mean it honestly, I want you to take this, as a present."

"Oh, but really, really!" I expostulated. "You surely don't suppose——" Then suddenly I remembered what Miriam had told me about him, and I stretched out my hand, so as not to wound him.

But he didn't see it, and quite suddenly had gone as white as the wall. Listening, he rasped:

"There . . . there! I knew he would! There's Hillel again! He's knocking!"

I listened too, and then went back into the other room, partly closing the bedroom door behind me. But it was not Hillel. Charousek entered, laying his finger on his lips as a sign that he knew who was with me. Next moment, without giving me time even to greet him, he had overwhelmed me with a torrent of verbiage:

"Ah, my esteemed and honoured friend, dear Master Pernath, how can I find words sufficient to express my delight in finding you at home, alone?" He spoke like a play actor, and his bombastic and unnatural delivery formed such a startling contrast to the distorted look upon his face that I postively recoiled in horror.

"My dear master, never would I have presumed to come and call on you here, in your own house, in the down-at-heel condition in which you have met me so often in the street—nay, rather let me say, in which you have so often done me the honour to shake me by the hand!

"And whom do you suppose I have to thank for the fact that I am able to present myself to you as I am to-day, regardless, in spotless linen and clean overcoat? Why, one of the noblest and—I regret to have to say—most misunderstood individuals in all our town! The mere thought of him moves me almost to tears! Despite the fact that his own circumstances are but humble, he has ever a helping hand to hold out to the poor and needy. For many a day now the yearning has been strong within me, when I've seen him standing mournfully before his own shop door, to go up and press him by the hand without a word.

"And then, only a few days ago, if he didn't actually call me up to him and insist on giving me money, wherewith I might purchase an overcoat on the instalment system!

"I wonder, Master Pernath, if you could ever guess the name of this, my benefactor? I'm more than proud to be able to tell you, being, as I am, the only one ever to guess what a heart of gold was beating in that bosom. It was Herr Aaron Wassertrum!"

I knew, of course, that all this play-acting on the part of Charousek was directed towards the junkdealer who was listening next door, though as yet I could not imagine what he meant by it. The flattery seemed to me so much too thickly laid on to take in a man as suspicious as Wassertrum. Charousek evidently read the dubious look in my face, for he grinned as he shook his head, and his next words were evidently intended to show me that he knew his man to a "T" and just how near he could sail to the wind.

"It's as true, believe me, as I stand here! Herr—Aaron—Wassertrum! It almost breaks my heart not to be able to tell him myself how infinitely grateful I feel towards him. But you must promise me, master, none the less, never to reveal to him the fact that I've been here and told you all about it. I know how the greed of mankind in general has embittered the poor man's soul, and planted the seeds therein of deep and ineradicable distrust—tragic, of course, but how terribly easy to understand!

"As you know, I am a professional psychologist, and I feel most strongly it's best that Herr Wassertrum should never hear—not even from my own mouth—what I really think of him. It would only sow further seeds of suspicion; at least, never let it be said that I did *that*! Better, even, he should think me ungrateful!

"Let me tell you this, Master Pernath—that from my childhood upwards I've known what it is to be lonely and deserted in this world. I don't know the name of my own father, and never even saw my dear mother face to face! She must have died very early"—a curious, forceful, and utterly mysterious note had now crept into Charousek's voice—"and was, I feel sure of it, one of those reserved, deeply sensitive natures, who can never tell another human creature the extent of their love. Aaron Wassertrum is just such another.

"I have in my possession a torn-off leaf from my mother's diary—as a matter of fact, I perpetually wear it next my heart—and on it is written how she loves my father, for all he was so repulsive, more than any mortal woman ever loved a man on earth. But she never appears to have acquainted him with the fact. Most probably for the very same reason that prevents me from speaking to Aaron Wassertrum, and makes me conceal the gratitude with which my heart is bursting.

"But there's something else, too, to be found in that torn-out page, though I can only dimly surmise the meaning of it, the writing all being smudged with tears. Whoever my father may have been—and may his memory perish from off the earth—there's no doubt he behaved like an utter swine to my mother!"

Quite suddenly Charousek crashed on to his knees, screaming out in such hair-raising tones that for the life of me I did not know whether he was really going mad or merely playing a part:

"ALMIGHTY GOD, WHOSE NAME MAY NOT BE SPOKEN BY MORTAL MEN, HERE ON MY KNEES DO I ENTREAT AND SUPPLICATE: CURSÈD, CURSÈD, CURSÈD BE MY FATHER, TO ALL ETERNITY."

He literally bit the last word in two, and for the space of a second knelt there, listening, with eyes wide open.

Then he grinned a devilish grin. From the next room, I fancied I could hear a faint groan from Wassertrum.

"Forgive me, master," Charousek went on presently, with a well-simulated choke in his voice. "Forgive me for what must seem making an exhibition of myself, but what you have just heard is the daily prayer I send up to God, early and late, that He may hold in reserve for the author of my being, whosoever he may be, the most fearful end that ever man has yet devised."

In spite of myself I tried to answer him, but he interrupted quickly:

"And now, Master Pernath, I come to the request I am going to make you. Herr Wassertrum had a certain protégé, whom he used to regard as the apple of his eye. Most probably it was a nephew of his. Some people even say it was his son, but I can scarcely believe that, for in that case he would surely have borne the same name, whereas this man was called Wassory . . . Dr. Theodore Wassory.

"It brings the tears to my eyes only to think of him. For some reason or other, he had a curious attraction for me, as though betwixt us there was some close bond of love and kinship."

At this point Charousek sobbed, as if his emotion were getting the better of him.

"Ah . . . the pity of it . . . 'that such a noble mind was here o'er-thrown!' Ah . . . ah!

"For some reason best known to himself—for I have never been able to discover it—he committed suicide. And I was one of those called to his aid . . . alas! . . . too late . . . too late! And as I stood there, by his deathbed, covering his cold, limp hand with kisses—I'm not ashamed to confess it to you, Master Pernath, for, after all, 'twas no theft—I took a rose from those that lay on his dead bosom, and pocketed the little bottle, with the contents of which the unfortunate man had cut short his most promising career."

Charousek now took a small medicine bottle from his pocket, and continued in trembling tones:

"And now . . . I am going to put both of them here . . . on your table . . . the withered rose and the little bottle. They were the only souvenirs I possessed of my dear dead friend.

"How many a time and oft, in hours of deepest depression, when I have sat wishing for death, in the loneliness of my heart, and longing for my dead mother, have I toyed with this little bottle. For it gave me a strange sense of consolation only to know *I had but to pour its contents on to a piece of cloth, and breathe its fumes,* and at once I should 'cease upon the midnight with no pain,' wafted maybe to those Elysian fields where my dearest Theodore rests from the trials and tribulations of this world!

"And that, my dear and honoured Master Pernath, brings me at long last to my point. Will you take both these things and deliver them for me to Herr Wassertrum?

"I want you to tell him, if you will be so good, that they come from somebody closely connected with Dr. Wassory, whose name you are in honour bound not to mention: maybe a lady! He will believe you, and it will be a precious souvenir for him, even as it was for me.

"That will be my secret expression of the gratitude I feel towards him. I am a poor man, and it is all that I have; none the less, it rejoices my heart to think that both these precious objects will now belong to him, and that he will never know I was the donor. I cannot tell you how incomparably sweet that thought will be to my mind.

"And now, farewell, Herr Pernath, and a thousand thanks in advance."

He grasped me by the hand, winked, and, as though even yet I might not have understood, whispered something to me that was scarcely audible.

"Stop a moment, Herr Charousek—I'll see you a little way down the stairs," I said, mechanically reading the words that were on his lips, and went outside with him.

We stood together on the dark first-floor landing, and here I wanted to part from Charousek.

"I know the meaning of all this circus, perfectly," I said, straight to his face. "You want Aaron Wassertrum to poison himself out of that bottle!"

"Of course," he assented cheerfully.

"And you actually think I am going to be a party to it?"

"That won't be necessary in the slightest degree."

"But you said just now you wanted me to give the bottle to Wassertrum!"

Charousek shook his head.

"When you go back, you'll soon see you've been forestalled."

"How on earth could you conceive such an idea?" I asked him in astonishment. "A man like Wassertrum will never kill himself in this world. He's far too cowardly, and not the sort to act on impulse."

"I see you don't know," Charousek interrupted me gravely, "the insidious power of suggestion. If I'd spoken in the language of every day, may be you'd have proved right, but the slightest tone of my every word had been carefully prepared and reckoned upon. On such a dog only pathos works, pathos of the most revolting order, laid on with a trowel! Take my word for it! I knew what I was about. I'd figured out to myself beforehand the play of his every feature. With a certain sort of mind, you simply can't overdo it, strange as it may seem. Do you suppose, if it weren't for that, the theatre wouldn't have been razed to the ground, lock, stock, and barrel, long ago? These second-rate *canaille* are known by their sentimentalities. Thousands of poor devils can die in the streets of starvation, and they won't shed a tear on their behalf, but once let a made-up ass on the stage, in the role of a stupid peasant, roll his goggle eyes at them out of his grease-painted face, and they'll howl like a dog baying the moon! Even if dear father Wassertrum forgets to-morrow the way I made his heart go pitter-pat to-day, the time will come, when the hour is ripe, in which every single word I've uttered will come alive in his soul, and make a little hell of it. At a time like that, it'll only need the least little encouragement—and I'll be responsible for that—and even his cow-ardly paws will go groping after that deadly phial. The one essential thing is for it to be at hand. Little Theodore too, maybe, wouldn't have gone so successfully the same way, if I hadn't made it easy for him, first!"

"Charousek," I cried out, horrified, "you're a devil! Haven't you any——"

Quickly he put his hand over my mouth, and forced me back into a recess in the wall. "Ssh! Here he comes!"

With tottering steps, supporting himself by the wall, Wassertrum came down the stairs, and staggered past us.

Charousek, shaking me quickly by the hand, fled after him.

Returning to my room, I saw that the flower and the bottle had gone, and in their place was laid the battered gold watch.

They told me at the bank I must wait an entire week before I could draw my money. The "customary notice must expire," so I was offi-cially informed. Whereupon I told them to send for the manager, for I was in the most God-almighty hurry, being on the point of departing for a journey. But the manager, it seemed, was engaged, and, in any case, the established practice of the bank could not be trifled with.

The fellow with the glass eye, who had come in with me through the door, seemed mightily amused.

Eight whole grey days of awfulness, waiting for death!

Surely Eternity itself could last no longer?

So utterly cast down was I, I had no idea how long I had been walking up and down in front of a café. Finally, I entered, if only to be rid of the fellow with the glass eye, who had followed me on from the bank, and was hovering around me where I stood, looking on the ground, when he saw me looking at him, as though he had lost something.

He had on a light striped suit, the coat of which was far too tight for him, and the trousers grease spotted and hanging round his legs like sacks. On the foot of his left boot was a raised egg-shaped ring of leather, almost as if he had adorned his big toe with a seal ring.

Scarcely had I taken my seat than he came in and sat down at a place near me.

At first I thought he was going to beg from me, and searched for my note-case, but then I caught sight of a large diamond gleaming on one of his fat, butcher's fingers.

For hours and hours I seemed to sit there in that café, till I thought I should go out of my senses through sheer nervousness: but where should I go? Home? Or simply amble about? Difficult to say which of these alternatives was worse.

The stale-breathed air, the incessant clatter of the billiard balls, the perpetual dry cough of a half-blind journalist sitting opposite me, together with a stork-legged infantry officer who alternatively picked his nose and combed his peaky beard with cigarette-stained fingers in front of a little pocket mirror; a sticky little clot of perspiring, chattering, expostulating Italians round the card-table in the corner, eagerly rapping their trump cards with their knuckles, as they shrilled forth exclamations, or else spat in all directions of the compass. To behold all this was bad enough, but to see it doubled and trebled in the mirrors on the walls . . . it literally caused what little life was in me to ebb away like the sap of a withered tree!

Bit by bit it began to grow dark, and a flat-footed, knock-kneed waiter poked up at the glass lustres with a long pole. But for the most part they refused to burn, and he gave it up as a bad job. Look which way I would, the lynx gaze of that squinting, glass-eyed man was for ever riveted upon me, for all he strove to hide it, ducking behind his newspaper, or dipping his grubby moustaches in his long since empty coffee-cup.

He had cocked his hat on his head in such a way that his ears stood out almost horizontally. Apparently he had settled there for the rest of his natural existence.

Not for one instant longer could this be endured.

I paid my bill, and went.

As I was about to shut the glass door behind me, someone removed the latch from my hand. I turned round. THERE HE WAS AGAIN! Blast him!

In a frenzy of annoyance, I made as though to turn to the left, in the direction of the Jewish quarter. He stepped to my side and prevented me.

"Will you stop that!" I screamed to him at the top of my voice.

His speech was sharp and curt. "Turn to the right!"

"What's that?"

He looked at me insolently. "You're Pernath!"

"I'll trouble you to say Herr Pernath!"

He laughed at that, spitefully. "I don't want any lip from you! You're coming along with me!"

"Are you off your head? And who are you, anyway?" I burst out at him.

The only reply he made was to unbutton his coat, and point circumspectly to a dilapidated metal eagle, pinned inside, on to the lining.

I understood perfectly. The wretch was a detective in plain clothes, and he now was arresting me.

"At least tell me, for pity's sake, what it's all about?"

"You come along with me, and you'll learn that quick enough," he assured me surlily. "Quick march now—to the station, and no more palaver!"

I told him I would prefer to get into a fiacre.

"Not a chance!" said he.

We went on our way to the police station.

There, a *gendarme* led me up to a door.

ALOIS OTSCHIN
Superintendent

I read, on an enamelled sign.

"Go in there," said the *gendarme*.

A couple of grubby writing-tables with high desks above them stood opposite to one another. Between them a pair of rickety chairs.

On the wall a portrait of the Emperor.

A bowl of goldfish on the counter.

Otherwise the room was quite bare.

Behind the writing-desk on the left could be discerned a club-foot, in conjunction with a thick felt shoe, from beneath a pair of grey frayed trousers.

There was a sound of rustling. Somebody murmured a word or two in Czech, and immediately the figure of the Superintendent emerged from the writing-desk on the right and confronted me.

He was a little man, with grey pointed beard, and a curious habit of clenching his teeth and grimacing before speaking, like a man looking up into the sun. Then he squinted behind his spectacles, all of which gave him an expression of contemptuous hostility.

"Your name is Athanasius Pernath . . . by profession . . . cutter of precious stones," he informed me.

Immediately the club-foot beneath the other writing-table showed signs of animation, rubbing itself against the leg of a chair, while I heard the sound of a quill pen.

"Precisely," I corroborated. "Pernath. Cutter of precious stones."

"Very good, then we agree, Herr . . . Pernath, of course . . . Herr Pernath. *Very* good . . . oh, very good indeed." . . . All of a sudden he had adopted the tone of the utmost possible friendliness, as though he had just been imparted the most joyful news in all the world. With both hands stretched out towards me, he was making the most ridiculous efforts to look benevolent.

"Tell me now, Herr Pernath; generally speaking, what do you do all day?"

"I should hardly have thought that concerned you," I answered coldly.

Whereupon he blinked his eyes and waited a moment, before he flashed forth at me, like lightning:

"Since when has this affair been going on between the Countess and Savioli?"

I had been prepared for something of the kind, and never moved an eyelash.

With all the technique of the expert, he now sought through questioning and cross-questioning to involve me in self-contradictions; but though, in my dismay, my heart had almost sunk into my boots, I managed not to give myself away, while I perpetually reiterated I had never heard the name of Savioli, that Angelina had been an old family friend of my father's, and had often been in the habit of commissioning cameos from me.

None the less, I felt convinced the whole time that the Superintendent realised the falsity of my statements, and was inwardly boiling with rage at not being able to extract from me what he wanted.

He paused a while to consider, then drew me towards him by the lapel of my coat, gesticulating with a warning thumb towards the left-hand writing-desk, and whispering in my ear:

"Come now, Athanasius! Your late father was one of my dearest friends . . . I want to save you, Athanasius . . . but you've got to tell me, first, everything that concerns the Countess! Do you hear? Everything!"

I hadn't an idea what the fellow was up to. "What do you mean . . . you want to save me?" I asked him, out loud.

The club-foot then stamped ominously on the ground. The Superintendent's face went ashen grey with rage and hatred. He bit his lips. I waited. I knew quite well he was going to spring on me again (his system of sudden attack reminded me strangely of Wassertrum), and I waited quietly, while a goat-faced man—obviously the owner of the club-foot—peered over the top of his writing-desk at me. Suddenly the Superintendent yelled at the top of his voice:

"Murderer!"

I was speechless with sheer surprise.

The goat-faced man withdrew again, gloomily, behind his desk.

The Superintendent seemed slightly put out at the calmness of my demeanour, but concealed the fact skilfully, as he drew up a chair and requested me to sit down.

"Then you flatly refuse, Herr Pernath, to give me the required information concerning the Countess?"

"It is not in my power to give it to you—or, at any rate, not in the sense you mean. In the first place, I don't know anyone of the name Savioli, and, moreover, I am completely convinced that it's sheer calumny even to hint that the Countess has been deceiving her husband."

"Are you prepared to state that upon oath?"

I suppressed a choking feeling in my throat. "Of course. Any time."

"Good. Hmm."

There ensued a long pause, during which the Superintendent seemed to be labouring to deliver himself of an idea.

When next he looked at me, comedian wise his ugly face had assumed an expression of compassion. Involuntarily I found myself thinking of Charousek, play-acting, as I heard the tearful voice addressing me:

"You can confide in me, surely, Athanasius—in me, your old family friend . . . the friend of your father . . . haven't I carried you pig-a-back." (Really, I could hardly choke down my laughter: the fellow was only ten years older than I was, at most.) "Come, come,

Athanasius . . . it was in self-defense, was it not?"

The goat-faced man now hove into sight again.

"What was self-defense?" I asked, now thoroughly nonplussed.

"Why, of course . . . *Zottmann!*" Quite suddenly the Superintendent bellowed the name into my ear.

It struck me like the blade of a dagger! ZOTTMANN! The watch! The name Zottmann was engraved inside the case! My heart sank. That scoundrel Wassertrum had given me the watch in order to fix suspicion of murder on me!

At this point the Superintendent discarded his mask, and, grinding his teeth and squinting his eyes, demanded:

"So you own up to the murder, then, Pernath?"

"It's all a mistake . . . a horrible misunderstanding! Listen to me, for God's sake! I can explain the whole thing to you, indeed I can!" I cried.

But in a trice he had interrupted me. "*Now* will you tell me everything you know relating to the Countess? Take it from me, it will improve your case!"

"I've nothing to say. I've said everything I can. I tell you, the Countess is innocent."

He ground his teeth, and turned to the goat-faced man:

"Take down: Pernath has confessed to the murder of Karl Zottmann, of the Life Assurance Co. . . ."

Quite suddenly I saw red.

"You dirty dog of a policeman!" I found myself yelling at him. "*How dare you?*"

I looked round for some heavy object to hurl at him.

Next moment two policemen seized me, and I was handcuffed.

The Superintendent blew himself out like a cock on a dungheap.

"And this watch?" All at once he was holding the identical watch in his hand. "Was the unfortunate Zottmann dead when you robbed him of this, or not?"

I was quite quiet again now, and made my statement in a clear voice.

"I received that watch from the junkdealer, Aaron Wassertrum, this morning. He gave it to me."

There was a roar of derisive laughter, and beneath the left-hand writing-table I could see the club-foot and the felt slipper dancing a joyful dance together.

TORMENT

With fettered hands, and a *gendarme* with fixed bayonet in my rear, I had now to walk through the open streets. It was evening, and the lamps were lit.

Right and left, gutter urchins ran whooping, women pushed open their windows and jeered at me with scolding tongues, waving their cooking-spoons at me. In the distance I could already see the massive stone prison by the law-courts, with the inscription overhead: "LAW CHASTISES THE GUILTY AND PROTECTS THE INNOCENT." A gigantic door then opened and swallowed me up. I passed into a passage that smelt of cooking.

A man with a long beard, and official sword, coat, and cap, but with bare feet and trousers tied together at the ankles, stood up, put down the coffee-mill that he was holding between his knees, and ordered me to remove my clothes. He then examined my pockets, took everything out that he found therein, and asked me if I harboured bugs.

After I had told him no, he took the rings from my fingers. That done, he told me I could dress again.

They took me up and up, many stories, and through diverse passages with windows, in the recesses of which stood great grey chests, with lock and key.

All along the walls were iron doors with bolts, and little barred squares, a gas flame burning over each. An enormous, military-looking guard—the first face approaching decency I had seen for some hours—unlocked one of the doors, pushed me into a dark, cupboard-like, foully smelling aperture, and locked the door behind me.

There I stood in the utter darkness, and groped my way to the right. My knee knocked up against a tin bucket. At last I discovered—the place was so narrow I could scarcely turn round in it—a latch, and finally found myself—in a cell.

Planks were fastened to the walls in twos, with straw sacks upon them. The distance between them was only a step or so. High up in the wall a barred, rectangular window allowed the dull light of the night sky to filter through.

Unbearable heat and a stink of old rotten clothing filled the room.

Once my eyes had got used to the darkness, I saw that on three of the planks—the fourth was empty—men in grey prison suits were sitting, their elbows on their knees, their faces buried in their hands.

Not one of them spoke a single word.

I sat myself on the empty bed, and waited. Waited. Waited.

An hour passed. Two hours. Three hours.

Directly I heard a step outside I sat up.

"They'll be coming now," I thought, to fetch me before the Examining Magistrate.

But each time this happened I was doomed to be disappointed. Always the steps disappeared up the passage.

I tore my collar open, feeling as though I were going to choke.

One after another I could hear the prisoners stretching themselves, and groaning.

"Can't that window be opened, up above?" I addressed the darkness despairingly, and shrank in terror at the sound of my own voice.

"Not allowed," growled a voice from one of the straw sacks.

Nevertheless, I started groping with my hand along the wall. I could feel a board fastened to it at the height of a man's breast, and on it a couple of pitchers and a few crusts of bread. Laboriously I clambered on to it, holding on to the bars of the window and pressing my face against it, to breathe in some fresh air, however little.

I stood like that till my knees began to tremble. In front of me floated the unfathomable darkness of the night. The cold iron bars seemed to sweat. It must surely be past midnight.

Behind me I heard snoring. Only one prisoner appeared not to be able to sleep; he tossed about on his straw, faintly groaning from time to time.

Would the morning never come? Ah! there was a clock striking!

I counted the hours feverishly. One . . . two . . . three! Thank heaven, only a few more hours, and then the dawn *must* come! It went on striking. Four . . . five. . . . The perspiration ran down my brow. Six . . . seven. . . . It was eleven o'clock!

Only one hour had passed since I heard it strike the last time!

Bit by bit I was able to piece my thoughts together.

Wassertrum had palmed off on me that watch of the missing Zottmann in order to get me suspected. He himself, presumably, must have been the murderer. How else could he have got possession of the watch? If he had come across the corpse somewhere or other and then robbed it, he would surely subsequently have applied for the thousand gulden reward that had been publicly offered for the dead man's discovery! But that, obviously, could not have been. The bill was still pasted on to public buildings, as I had myself seen on my way to the prison.

That the junkdealer had informed against me was perfectly clear.

Equally clear did it seem that he was in league somehow with the police. Why, otherwise, those investigations concerning Dr. Savioli?

On the other hand, it seemed pretty plain that Wassertrum was not yet in possession of Angelina's letters. I probed, and probed—and quite suddenly the whole situation was revealed to me with a hideous clarity, as though I myself had been spectator thereof.

There could be no other possible explanation. Wassertrum, when searching my room in conjunction with the police, had secretly managed to get hold of my little iron box, in which he suspected incriminating documents. Not being able to open it on the spot—as I always carried the key on my person—he had carried it back to his den, and was most probably on the point of breaking it open even as I sat here!

With the frenzy of a madman I tugged at the bars of the window, through which I could mentally see Wassertrum rummaging about among Angelina's letters.

If only I could somehow inform Charousek, so that at least he could go and put Dr. Savioli wise in time!

For a moment I seized upon the hope that the news of my arrest must spread through the Ghetto like wildfire, and I trusted in Charousek as in a kind of rescuing angel! The junkdealer hadn't a dog's chance, surely, when it came to the student's infernal cunning. . . . "I'll have him by the throat that same day he thinks to have Savioli on toast" . . . hadn't he said that to me, or something very like it? But the very next moment I had thrown all my hopes to the winds, and was a prey to the uttermost despair. What if Charousek came too late?

Angelina would be ruined then, entirely.

I bit my lips till the blood came, and tore at my breast for having been such a fool as not to burn those letters when I said I would. I swore a deadly oath that Wassertrum's last hour should come the moment I was set at liberty.

What on earth did it matter to me, if I died on the gallows or by my own hand?

I never doubted for an instant that the Examining Magistrate would believe every word I said when I told him my plausible story of the watch, and of Wassertrum's threats against me.

I must surely be free by the morning, and at least the law could do no less than arrest Wassertrum on suspicion of murder.

I counted the hours, and prayed that they might go faster, as I stared out into the murk of the night.

After what seemed an unconscionable time, the dawn began to break, and a gigantic copper face emerged from the dark, first like a black speck, then growing lighter and lighter. It was the clock-dial on an old watch-tower. *But the hands were missing!* Fresh tortures! It struck five at last.

I could now hear the prisoners waking, one by one, and talking together in muttered Czech. A familiar voice suddenly sounded in my ears. I turned round, got down from my shelf, and became aware, opposite to me, of the pock-marked countenance of Loisa, as he lay upon his plank staring at me in amazement. The other two were fellows with brazen faces, staring contemptuously at me. One of them dug the other in the ribs, and said, "Embezzler," looking at me. His comrade took no notice, except for a kind of snarl, as, rummaging about in his sack of straw, he fetched out a piece of black paper and laid it on the floor. Then he shook on to it a few drops of water out of the pitcher and kneeled down, using it as a mirror in which to comb his hair with his fingers, over his brow. After which he dried the paper again with the utmost care, and stuck it once more under his plank.

"Pan Pernath . . . Pan Pernath," Loisa was murmuring over and over again, with wide-open eyes staring straight in front of him, like someone who had seen a ghost.

"Gentlemen know one another, I see," said the first prisoner, speaking in the most ungodly Czech patois, as he made a half-bow in our direction. "Allow me to introduce. Vóssatka's my name. Black Vóssatka." And added, an octave or so lower, as if for some reason or other proud of the fact: "*Arson.*"

The amateur barber spat between his teeth, looked at me a while disgustedly, then patted himself on the chest, with the laconic remark: "Burglary."

I said nothing.

"Well, my lord Duke, and what have you been and gone and got yourself run in for?" asked the first prisoner again, after a pause. He was a Viennese, which accounted for his abominable Czech.

I considered a moment, then replied placidly: "Robbery with murder."

Whereupon they both looked up astonished; the mocking look vanished from their features, giving way to an expression of the utmost respect, as, for all the world like Tweedledum and Tweedledee, they exclaimed together:

"Pleased to meet you. Pleased to meet you."

But, seeing that no notice was being taken of them, they withdrew into their corner, and sat there, talking to each other in whispers.

Once only did the amateur barber come up to me, feeling the muscles of my forearm critically, twixt finger and thumb—then returned to his comrade again, dubiously shaking his head.

"Are you too in here under suspicion of having killed Zottmann?"
I asked Loisa, as unobtrusively as I could.

He nodded. "Long time ago."

Some moments passed in silence. I shut my eyes and pretended to
be sleeping.

"Herr Pernath! Herr Pernath!" Suddenly I heard Loisa address me,
very softly.

"Yes?" I pretended to wake up.

"Herr Pernath . . . 'scuse me . . . Herr Pernath . . . but . . . but
. . . if you could tell me where Rosina is now? Is she back home?" he
stammered. It was piteous to see him standing there, with his eyes on
fire and his fingers twisting in suspense, as he virtually hung on to my
lips.

"She is quite all right. She is . . . she's got a job . . . as waitress at
the Alte Ungelt." I lied shamelessly.

I could see him draw a deep breath of relief.

A couple of prisoners had now brought in a tray full of tin bowls
filled with some kind of sausage mess. Three of these they left in our
cell. Soon afterwards the bolt of the door was drawn back again, and
the guard conducted me before the Examining Magistrate.

My knees were positively shaking with apprehension, as we went up
and down those flights of cold stone stairs.

"D'you think it's likely I shall be set free before the day is over?" I
asked the guard awkwardly.

I could see him suppressing a smile, out of pity. "To-day, eh? Ah,
well . . . you never know."

I felt as cold as death.

And now I was reading an inscription on another door, and the
name:

KARL FREIHERR VON LEISETRETER
Examining Magistrate.

The same sort of God-forsaken room, with the same two writing-
tables with high desks.

A large, elderly man, with white beard carefully parted, black frock
coat, red puffy lips, and boots that creaked.

"Are you Herr Pernath?"

"I am."

"Cutter of precious stones?"

"Yes."

"Cell No. 70?"

"Yes."

"Suspected of the murder of Zottmann?"

"Believe me, sir, I——"

"Are you suspected of the murder of Zottmann?"

"I suppose so. So they say, at any rate . . . but——"

"Do you admit it?"

"Admit what? I am innocent."

"Do you admit it?"

"No."

"Then I remand you in custody. Guard, remove the prisoner."

"But, sir . . . sir . . . please listen to me! I have positively *got* to go back home to-day. I have most important things to arrange——"

Somebody exploded behind the second writing-desk.

Even the Magistrate sniggered. "Take the prisoner out, guard."

Day followed day, week followed week—and still I sat on and on in that cell.

At mid-day every day we had perforce to go down into the prison yard and parade round in a circle for the space of forty minutes on the wet earth, with other prisoners.

It was strictly forbidden to talk to one another.

In the middle of the yard stood a stark, moribund tree, on to the bark of which had somehow or other got itself fastened a little oval glass picture of the Virgin Mary.

Bushes of privet were planted around the walls, the leaves of which were all but black from falling soot.

All round were the barred windows of the cells, through which, sometimes, a glimpse might be caught of a putty-grey face, with bloodless lips.

Then, up we used to go again to our daily meal of bread and water and sausage soup, with an addition of decayed lentils, if it happened to be Sunday.

At length I was taken down to be examined again.

Could I produce witnesses to testify to the fact that "Herr" Wassertrum had given me the watch, as alleged?

"Yes. Herr Schemajah Hillel. That is to say . . . no . . . " (I remembered now, he had not been present at the time.) "But Herr Charousek . . . no . . . he wasn't there, either!"

"In short, nobody was there?"

"No. sir. No one was actually present."

Again that giggle from behind the writing-desk, and again:

"Guard, remove the prisoner!"

My agony over Angelina had given way now to a dull resignation.

The time was past for agonising about her. Either Wassertrum's plan had by now succeeded or else Charousek had frustrated it, I told myself.

But I worried distractedly over Miriam.

I kept on picturing her, hour by hour waiting for the "miracle" to renew itself; running, first thing every morning when the baker came, with outstretched hands to look for what should be revealed. Also I would visualise her half dead with apprehension on my account.

The thought of it at night would hound me out of my sleep, and I would clamber on to the board above, and stare dumbly at the clock's copper face, poignantly concentrating in my desire to transfer, somehow, my thoughts to Hillel—that they might shriek their commands in his ear to go straight to Miriam, and release her from this torment of waiting for a miracle that did not happen.

Then would I cast myself down on the straw again, and hold my breath till my heart nearly burst in my body—trying to force my doppelgänger to appear before me, that I might be able to send him to her for her comfort.

Once he actually appeared, and stood by my side, with the old inscription on his breast, CHABRAT ZEREH AUR BOCHER, written looking-glass wise, and for very joy I wanted to shout aloud that everything now would be all right. But before I could instruct him to go to Miriam he had vanished and sunk into the ground once more.

Why didn't I receive any news of my friends?

Was it forbidden to send letters? I asked my cell-mates.

They none of them knew. They had certainly never got any. There was nobody to write to them, they said.

The guard promised me he would enquire, if he got the opportunity.

My nails were becoming lacerated with continual gnawing; my hair was a tangled mass, for neither comb, brush, nor scissors came our way. Nor did we have water to wash with.

My skin had become a torment to me on account of scurvy—the sausage soup being flavoured with soda, instead of salt, a prophylactic, apparently, according to prison regulations, against "man's carnal desires."

Bit by bit time dragged on its way, in ghastly, drab monotony. It was like a slow wheel of torture.

At certain intervals one or the other of us would be seized by a brain-storm. It would happen suddenly, inevitably, and regularly, and the victim would rage round the cell for hours on end, like a caged beast, only to cast himself down again on the plank bed, and lie there inertly waiting . . . waiting . . . waiting . . .

As evening drew on, the bugs could be seen, creeping over the walls in streaks, like ants, and I would wonder in mild astonishment why that trousered man with the sword had troubled to put such highly personal questions to me the night of my arrival.

Perhaps the Immigration Authorities were afraid lest a foreign race of insects should be introduced and create a hybrid form?.

As a rule, every Wednesday morning a fool of a medical officer— Dr. Rosenblatt—would come in, in his slouched hat, in order to convince himself that we were all in the very flower of health. And if any of us made any complaints, he would perfunctorily write out a prescription—zinc ointment, to be rubbed on the chest.

Once we were actually visited by the judge himself—a tall, highly scented, scoundrelly-looking individual, with vice written on every particle of his countenance. He had come, so he said, to see whether "everything was in order." "To see if anyone has hung hisself," our amateur barber expressed it.

I had been about to go up to him, to make an enquiry, but he leapt behind the guard and instantly whipped out a revolver, which he held towards me. "What do *you* want?" he barked out at me. I asked him, as courteously as I could, if there were any letters for me. But all the answer I got was a push in my middle from Dr. Rosenblatt, who promptly took refuge the other side of the door. Upon which His Honour also withdrew, and jeered at me from the passage. I'd better, so he said, turn my attention to confessing that murder. I'd get no more letters in this world, else.

I had got quite used, now, to the vitiated air and the stuffiness, and was perpetually in a state of shivering, even when the sun shone.

Two of the inmates of our cell had been changed about now, more than once, but I scarcely noticed it. One week we would have a pickpocket and a highway robber, another a coiner of false money, or a receiver of stolen goods. And so it went.

I would forget to-day what I had suffered yesterday. Every other feeling was swamped by that one gnawing anxiety on Miriam's behalf. One thing only was there made a keener impression still upon my mind. Once, when I was standing on the shelf, trying to gaze up into the sky, I felt something sharp sticking into my side, and, looking closer, found it was the file that had bored its way through the lining of my pocket. It must have been hidden in the lining a long time, otherwise that man would have found it, when he examined my things on arrival.

I pulled it out, and flung it down on to my sack of straw without another thought. When I got down again it had disappeared, and I never for one instant doubted but that Loisa had taken possession of it. Some days later they came to fetch him to another cell, on a story below. It was not considered desirable, so the guard informed us, that two prisoners like we were, suspected of one and the same crime, should be sharing the same cell.

I wished with all my heart the poor fellow might succeed in making his escape with the help of that file.

MAY

To my enquiry what date it was—the sun seemed as hot as in midsummer, and even the tree in the prison yard had burst a couple of buds—the guard had whispered, after a few moments' silence, that it was the 15th May. He had, as a matter of fact, no business to say it, for it was forbidden to talk to the prisoners. Especially those who had not yet confessed to their crimes were supposed to be kept in ignorance as to the passage of time.

So I had been kept now for three whole months in prison, with no news whatsoever from the outside world!

When night fell the soft strains of a piano would often be wafted through the barred window, which on warm days was kept open. It was the daughter, so one of my cell-mates told me, of one of the prison officials.

Day and night would I lie and dream of Miriam.

What was happening to her?

Sometimes I had a strange feeling of consolation, as if my thoughts, as I slept, had made their way to her bedside, and laid their hands, soothingly, upon her brow.

Sometimes, when despair had got me by the throat, as one by one my fellow-prisoners were fetched for their trial, and only I seemed to be ignored, I would be half stifled by a dull dread lest she should be no longer living.

Then would I question the Fates: was she living, was she dead . . . was she sick or was she well . . . and read the answer in the handful of straw blades I would pull forth from my sleeping-sack. The answer, nearly every time, was in the negative, and the whole soul of me raged impotently for a glimpse into the future. I would resort to trickery to try and obtain the required answer. Would the day come, I would demand fiercely, when I should ever be happy again, and able to laugh? To this the oracle, more often than not, would answer "yes." And then, for an hour on end, I would be joyful and content.

Like the secret growth and sprouting of a plant, a great love for Miriam had wakened gradually within my soul, and I failed to comprehend now how I could so often have sat by her side, talking to her, and known it not.

The tremendous desire that she too might be thinking of me in just such a way would grow, in moments like these, to a premonition of certitude, and then, hearing steps in the corridor, outside, almost I would feel afraid lest they were coming to release me, and my dream, in contact with the rough actualities of an outer world, would evaporate into nothingness.

My sense of hearing had grown so sharp, during this long period of confinement, that the slightest noise would not escape me. In the watches of the night I would hear the dim rumbling of a carriage in the distance, and cudgel my brains as to who might be sitting inside it.

To me there was something so strange in the thought that there were human beings out there who could do or not do exactly what they wanted—who were free to go hither and thither at will, and yet not feel intoxicated with the joy of it.

As for ever again being myself one of those happy creatures, at liberty to wander through the streets in the sunshine—my mind seemed no longer capable of grasping any such idea.

That day I had held Angelina in my arms seemed now to belong to some previous existence, long, long extinct. I looked back upon it with that kind of gentle melancholy with which one opens a book and finds therein a withered flower or two once worn by the beloved of one's youth.

Was old Zwakh still to be seen every evening at the Alte Ungelt, together with Vrieslander and Prokop, bewildering poor Eulalia's soul?

Ah, no . . . this was the merry month of May—the time of year when he was wont to trudge through all the villages of the neighbourhood, with his pack of marionettes, presenting the tragic history of Bluebeard and his Eight Wives to country yokels, in a meadow setting all emerald with the spring.

I was sitting alone in my cell. Vóssatka, the incendiary, who for a week now had been my sole companion, had been fetched a couple of hours ago before the Examining Magistrate.

They seemed to have been questioning him for an unconscionably long time.

There! The bolt shot back all of a sudden, and with radiant face Vóssatka burst into the room, and, throwing a bundle of clothes down on his plank, began with lightning speed to dress himself. One by one he flung his prison garments on to the floor, with a curse at each of them.

"They didn't have a speck of proof against me, damn them," he said. "Their damned arson! It was the wind, I told them. Let them pick up the winds and charge them." He put his fingers derisively to his nose. "They've got to get up earlier than that to get Black Vóssatka. No pokey for Vóssatka tonight. I'm sprung. There's going to be a hot time at Loisitschek's." He spread out his arms and started a stamping peasant dance, bawling out in his awful patois something about gathering roses while ye may; then stopped suddenly, and clapped on to his head a stiff-peaked hat with a little blue jay's feather stuck into the crown. "Tell you what'll interest you, Duke—d'you know the latest? That Loisa pal of yours has vamoozed! I heard 'em talking about it down below. He took off last month and that's the last they've seen of him."

"Aha!" I thought to myself. "The file!" And I smiled. "And I hope, my lord Duke, as you'll be the next," the incendiarist assured me, as he held out a friendly hand. "And if it's short of cash you find yourself, just roll up to Loisitschek's and ask for Black Vóssatka. The girls all know me there. So! It was a pleasure to know you, Duke."

But even as he stood there in the doorway, the guard had thrust him on one side to introduce a new prisoner.

At first glance I recognised the fresh arrival as the man in the military cap who had once stood next me in the rain under that archway in the Hahnpassgasse. Here was a welcome surprise! Perhaps by chance he might be able to tell me something about Hillel, and Zwakh, and all the rest!

I wanted to ask him without further loss of time, but, to my infinite astonishment, he laid his finger mysteriously on his lips, and signed to me to keep silence. Nor did he start to show signs of life till the door was bolted again and the steps of the guard had died away in the corridor.

My heart nearly stopped beating with excitement.

What did he mean by it?

Did he know me? And what could he want?

The first thing the fellow did was to sit down and pull off his left boot. Then, with his teeth, he pulled a peg out of the heel and extracted from the hole thereof a little piece of bent steel, with which he dexterously ripped off the sole that was but lightly attached. He then handed them both to me, with an expression of much pride. All this in less time than it takes to tell, and without taking the slightest notice of the excited questions I addressed to him.

"With Herr Charousek's compliments."

So dumbfounded was I, not one word could I utter.

"All you need to do's to take a piece of metal and slit the soles along with it, come night-time," declared the cool card, "or any other time no one's looking. It's hollow, and you'll find a letter inside from Herr Charousek."

In my transport of delight I fairly fell on the fellow's neck, and was unable to refrain from tears.

He expostulated mildly, and even adopted a slight tone of reproach:

"Come now, Herr von Pernath, a little more self-control! We haven't a moment to lose. It might come out any moment as how I've got into the wrong cell. That fellow Franzl and I went and exchanged our numbers."

I must have looked particularly stupid, for he went on again:

"Never you mind, if you don't understand. I'm here, and 'nuff said."

"But tell me," I broke in, "tell me, Herr—Herr——"

"I'm Wenzel," he helped me out. "Handsome Wenzel, for short."

"Tell me, Handsome Wenzel, then, how is Schemajah Hillel the registrar, and his daughter?"

But he broke in impatiently. "No time for that. I'll be hauled out of here any moment now. I'm only here now 'cos I confessed to an extra robbery."

I looked at him, aghast. "You mean to say you've really been and committed a theft on my account, in order to be able to come here to me?"

He shook his head with a contemptuous grin. "If I'd really been and gone and done it, d'you suppose I'd be confessing to it? What do you take me for?"

By degrees I understood. The plucky chap had worked a trick by means of which he could smuggle in Charousek's letter to me.

"Now listen to me." He assumed an expression of supreme importance. "What I've got to do's to teach you how to throw a fit."

"Throw a——?"

He nodded. "You've hit it! Epilepsy! Pay attention now, and mark how it's done. Easy. First you get your spittle up"—here he set about making the most hideous contortions with his cheeks—"then get your lips all slobbery"—this he proceeded to do, with the most revolting realism—"stuff your thumb into your fist, bulge your eyes out"—horrifyingly he goggled at me—"and then—it isn't quite so easy—you start yauping. Mind now: Boo! Boo! Boo! And next"—he cast himself full length upon the floor with a resounding smack, saying, as he got up again: "That's epilepsy! Dr. Hulbert—may the Lord rest his soul—learned that to his Brigade all right."

"It's certainly uncommonly like," I agreed with him. "But what on earth's the point of all this?"

"Why," said Wenzel blandly. "So you can get out of your cell. Rosenblatt, the doctor, is a stupid fool. The guts could be rotting inside you and he'd pass you. Only one thing puts the fear of the Lord into *him*, and that's an epileptic fit. Once you can put *that* across him, you're for the infirmary. As for getting out of *there*—it's a shame to take the money!" He became most mysterious. "You feel the window-bars, and you'll soon see! *They're sawn through the middle.* Cracks plastered nicely round with mud. Another of the Brigade's little dodges. All you've got to do's to keep a sharp look-out nights, till one fine evening, you'll catch sight of a rope let down from the roof with a noose at the end. Then you outs the bar, as quiet as a cat, slips your shoulders into the noose, and waits for me to draw you up and let you down into the street again, on the other side."

"But," I objected timidly, "what's the point of my trying to escape out of prison when I'm innocent?"

"But that's no reason for not beating it when you could!" protested Handsome Wenzel, and his eyes, as they looked at me, seemed round as saucers with surprise.

I had to summon all my powers of eloquence in order to talk him out of this crazy plan, which he said had been mooted at the instigation of the Brigade.

It seemed to him beyond belief that I should look a gift horse like that in the mouth, and prefer to wait until I was officially released.

"None the less," I told him, "I thank you and your brave comrades from the bottom of my heart." I shook him warmly by the hand. "When my luck turns once more, I shall hope to be able to prove my gratitude to you."

"None of that," he protested cordially. "A couple of glasses of Pilsener beer and we wouldn't say no, but let it go at that. Pan Charousek, who's our Brigade treasurer, he's told us about you. Any news for him if I get out in a couple of days or so?"

"Please," I urged him hastily, "tell him to go to Schemajah Hillel and say to him how concerned I've been as to the health of his daughter Miriam, and that I hope he won't let her out of his sight! You'll be sure and not forget the name, won't you—*Hillel?*

"Hirral?"

"No. Hillel"

"Hillar?"

"No. *Hillel.*"

Wenzel nearly tied his tongue into knots to try and get the better of such an utterly un-Czech-sounding name, but at length mastered it by means of devious fantastic grimaces.

"And one other thing. If Herr Charousek would have the kindness—and tell him I'd appreciate it enormously, if he did—to make enquiries in connection with a—a certain lady. . . . He'll know what I mean."

"You mean the aristocrat who was playing around with that Niemetz, Dr. Sapolio? Well, she got a divorce and she and her kid took off with him."

"Do you know that for certain?"

I could feel the quiver in my voice. However glad I felt for Angelina's sake, the thought of it gave me a pang in my heart, none the less. To have suffered all that . . . and now . . . forgotten, just the same.

"Maybe," I thought, "she thinks I really am a robber and a murderer." The taste of life was bitter on the tongue.

With that curious sixth sense that even the veriest ragamuffins seem to possess where affairs of the heart are concerned, the fellow appeared to realise something of what I was enduring, for he looked away shyly, and made no attempt to answer.

"Can you tell me at all," I asked constrainedly, "how Herr Hillel's daughter, Fräulein Miriam, is? Do you know her?"

"Miriam? Miriam?" Wenzel wrinkled up his face in contemplation. "Miriam? Does she go around Loisitschek's nights?"

I had to smile, in spite of myself. "Oh, no. Certainly not."

"Then I don't know her," he replied laconically.

For a few moments we were both silent. I was hoping that perhaps something would be in the letter about her.

"But the Devil's fetched away old Wassertrum all right," Wenzel burst forth again, quite suddenly. "Maybe you've heard already?"

I started in horror.

"No?" Wenzel drew his finger across his throat. "He's finished, and it was a messy job. They broke open his shop after no one had seen him for a couple of days, and I was one of the first ones in. I wished I wasn't. Wassertrum was sitting there, all covered with blood, and his eyes staring. Look, I'm pretty tough, but it turned my stomach. After a while, I said to myself, 'Wenzel, don't get excited. It's only a dead man.'

"Someone stuck a file into his throat, and the shop was turned upside down. Breaking and entering, and murder."

"The file! The file!!" I could feel my breath go cold with horror. "*The file!*" So it had found its way there after all!

"I know who it was too," Wenzel continued in a hoarse whisper, after a pause. "It was that pock-faced Loisa. I found his jack-knife on the shop floor, and stuffed it into my pocket, so that the police wouldn't get wise to it. He came in through an underground passage . . . " Suddenly he broke off short, listening with every nerve in his body, then flung himself full length on to the plank bed, and began snoring for all he was worth.

Almost immediately afterwards the bolt was drawn back in the door, and the guard came in. He stood and regarded me suspiciously. But I had a face like a mask, and Wenzel was almost beyond man's power to awaken. Only after repeated thumps did he sit up, yawning, and staggered, half drunk with sleep, out of the cell, the guard behind him.

In feverish expectation I now tore open Charousek's letter, and read:

12th May.

My Very Poor Friend and Beloved Benefactor,

Week by week have I been waiting for you to be released, but always in vain. I have done all that was humanly possible to try and collect evidence for your acquittal, but without success.

I have also implored the Examining Magistrate to push on with your case, but each time he informed me what I asked was impossible, as it was now the exclusive concern of the solicitor for the prosecution. The blithering red-tape fool!

Only an hour ago, however, I came across something that I hope will be of the utmost possible use. I have ascertained that Jaromir sold to Wassertrum a gold watch that he found in his brother's bed after the latter's arrest.

At Loisitschek's, where, as you know, the detectives have a stake-out, the rumour went round that this watch—belonging to the ostensibly murdered Zottmann, whose body has never yet been discovered—was found at your place, and taken as evidence of your guilt in the matter. I then began to put two and two together . . . Wassertrum, and so on and so forth!

I have given Jaromir 1,000 florins . . .

For a moment I laid down the letter, and my eyes filled with tears of joy. None but Angelina could have given Charousek a sum like that. Neither Zwakh, nor Prokop, nor Vrieslander possessed anything like that amount. So she had not forgotten me, after all! I read on:

> . . . and will give him another 2,000 when he goes to the police and confesses that he found the watch in his brother's effects and sold it.
>
> There will not be time, however, for this to have happened before Wenzel is on his way with this letter to you. Rest assured, however, it *will* happen. And to-day. I pledge my word on that.
>
> I have not the slightest doubt that Loisa is the murderer, and the watch belongs to Zottmann.
>
> If all goes well, Jaromir knows what to do. In any case, he will identify the watch as the one found in your room.
>
> So keep patient, and do not give way to despair. The day of your release is rapidly approaching.
>
> Whether you and I will ever see one another again, that I cannot say. I am inclined to think it unlikely, for things are hastening on apace with me, and I must be on my guard lest my last hour overtake me unawares.
>
> Be it as it may, of one thing I am convinced. *We shall meet again.* Even though it be not in *this* life, nor as the dead may meet in *that* life, we shall meet when that day breaks, when the Lord, as the Bible has it, will spew out of His mouth all those that are neither hot nor cold.
>
> Do not be astonished at my writing thus. I have never talked with you about these things, and on one occasion, when you started mentioning the Kabbala, I evaded the subject, but . . . I know what I know.
>
> Perchance you may understand what I have in mind. If not, then please wash everything I have said out of your memory. Once—but I was delirious at the time—I thought I saw a certain sign upon your breast. But maybe I was half in a dream, and imagined it.
>
> Whether you understand me or no, you must know that ever since my childhood I have been possessed of a certain inner knowledge which has led me into strange paths—knowledge which coincides not at all with what the doctors of medicine teach—knowledge that is, at present, by the grace of God, a closed book to them. I hope it always will be.
>
> I have not, nevertheless, allowed my brain to stagnate as the consequence of a knowledge the highest aim of which is setting up a practice and a waiting room full of wealthy clients.
>
> But enough of this. Let me rather confine myself to telling you the succession of recent events.
>
> By the end of April things had got to such a pitch that my suggestions were working admirably upon Wassertrum. With my own eyes I saw him standing on the streets gesticulating and talking to himself aloud. And that in itself is a sure sign that a man's thoughts are in a state of fermentation, and will one day break forth and master him.
>
> Next he bought himself a note-book, and began to make notes therein. He was writing. Actually writing! Don't make me laugh!

Then he went to a lawyer. I stood below in the street, but I knew what he was doing up there. He was making his will.

What I did not know was that he was making me his sole heir! If I had, I should verily have fallen a victim to St. Vitus's dance through the sheer joy of it.

He left me all he possessed, as being the only person on earth, so he thought, whom he could really benefit. He wanted to help someone. His conscience was beginning to work.

It may have been in the hope that I should bestow my blessing upon him, once I found myself a millionaire by virtue of his generosity, and thereby revoke the curse he had heard spoken by my own mouth that day in your room.

My suggestion had evidently been working in the most potent manner possible. Strangely enough, in his innermost inner he did believe in a certain final reckoning in the world to come, and even though he had always scoffed at it. All these super-subtle, clever people are like this in reality. You can see it by the rage they get into whenever you have it out with them face to face. Always they feel themselves being found out.

From the moment Wassertrum left his solicitor I never let him out of my sight. At night I would stand listening outside the shutters of his shop, for I knew that the thing I was waiting for might happen any moment.

I believe I should have heard through the very walls that sweet, longed-for sound of gentle dropping, following on the cork being drawn out of that bottle. Maybe only one little hour now stood between me and the fulfilment of my whole life's work.

Then if some fool meddler didn't get in and murder him! With a file!

Wenzel will tell you all the details. It would be too bitter for me to set them down on paper.

Call it superstition if you will, but when I saw the blood of him, dripping all around—most of the things in the shop had got smeared with it—it seemed to me as though his soul had escaped me after all!

Something within me—some instinct that cannot lie—tells me it is not the same thing if a man die by the hand of a stranger, or by one of his own kin. My mission could only have been fulfilled if Wassertrum had taken his own blood down into the grave with him. And, now that it has happened otherwise, I feel myself in the nature of an outcast, a mere tool considered as unworthy by the Angel of Death.

But I will not spend myself in useless resistance. *My hate is of the kind that reaches out beyond the grave,* and I still have my own blood within me that I can shed as I will, that it can go, together with his, step by step, into the Kingdom of Shadow.

Ever since the day they pitched him into his grave I sit down there in the cemetery, close to him, pondering in my own soul what I had best do. I think I know it already, but I will wait first till that inward word within me makes itself clear. We humans are an impure race, and often require much watching and fasting ere we can hear the whispers of our souls.

Last week I had official notice from the courts that Wassertrum had made me his sole heir. I need not, of course, tell you that I shall use not a single stiver of it for my own personal ends. I'm never going to give him a handle against me in the next world.

The house property he left me will be sold by auction; the actual objects that he himself touched will all of them be burned. The money realised will be left, after my death, to the extent of one-third to you, personally. I see you, in the spirit, jumping up to expostulate, but, believe me, you have no cause. You are acquiring nothing that is not yours by actual right, restored to you once more, plus compound interest. I have known for some time now that Wassertrum fleeced your father and his family of everything they possessed, though I have only recently been in a position to prove it by actual documents.

Another third is to be divided between those twelve members of the Brigade who were known to Dr. Hulbert personally. I want each one of them to be well off, and in a position to enter what is known as the "good society" of Prague.

And the last third is to be divided in equal parts between the next seven robber-murderers to be arrested in this country, who, for lack of sufficient evidence against them, have to be released.

Why, after all, should I not have my little joke?

And that, I think, is all.

And now, my dear, dear friend, farewell, and think of me sometimes.

Your sincere and always grateful
Innocence Charousek.

I laid the letter down, deeply moved.

I could no longer rejoice even over the news of my probable early release.

Charousek! Poor, poor fellow! He had been troubling himself about my future as if I were his own brother. And all because I had once given him one hundred florins! If only once more I could shake him by the hand!

But I felt he was perfectly right. That day would never come. His image rose up before me: the strange flicker in his eyes, the tubercular shoulders, the high, noble forehead.

And perhaps everything might have been different in that frustrated life if only one helping hand had been held out to him soon enough.

Once again I read his letter through. What a vast lot of method lay in Charousek's madness! After all, was he mad? I felt ashamed, now, even to have entertained such a thought for an instant.

Didn't the very trend of this man's character speak for itself? He was a man, obviously, of the same kidney as Schemajah Hillel; like Miriam; like me, too, if it came to that; a man whom his own soul had mastered; by whose intrinsic force he had been raised far, far above the slough of this our life, up, up beyond the snow-capped peaks of a land untrodden yet by mortal man.

He who all his life had brooded upon murder, stood out, surely, as a figure of purity, crystal-clear, against the drab background of those whose lives were circumscribed by sterile rule-of-thumb submission to some unknown mythical prophet about whose laws they "made much argument," and evermore "came out by that same door wherein they went."

He had acted at the dictates of a command delivered by some power beyond and above him, without one lingering thought of a reward, this side the grave or beyond it.

After all, what was the thing he had done but the uttermost fulfilment of a pious duty, in the most hidden sense of the word?

Treacherous . . . cowardly . . . vicious . . . abnormal . . . pathological . . . criminally insane—I could literally hear all the muttered comments of public opinion, the mumblings of the masses, groping in the innermost recesses of his soul with the dim horn lanterns of their unilluminated minds—the mob, "clapping their chopped hands" and "throwing up their sweaty night-caps," and "uttering a deal of stinking breath" to pass judgment on the patrician—those proletariat minds for ever and for ever unable to comprehend the beauty of the deadly nightshade, growing wild in the hedgerow, a thousandfold more beautiful and nobler than the harmless, necessary chive of the herb garden.

Once more the bolt was drawn back in the door, and I could hear a man being pushed over the threshold. But, for the moment, I did not turn round, so deeply was I thinking of the contents of the letter.

There was no word at all in it of Angelina, nothing whatsoever of Hillel. Obviously Charousek must have written it in the utmost hurry. His very writing betrayed that fact.

Would by any chance another letter be brought in to me in secret fashion from the outer world? To-morrow; perhaps, during general exercise in the prison yard? That would afford the easiest opportunity by far for a member of the Brigade to communicate with me.

A very soft voice aroused me from my broodings:

"Sir, might I take the liberty of introducing myself to you? My name is Laponder. Amadeus Laponder."

I turned round.

A little, slender, still youngish man, carefully clad, though without his hat, like all newly introduced prisoners, stood bowing politely before me.

He was clean shaven, like an actor, and his large, almond-shaped eyes, with a bright green gleam in them had the strange peculiarity of not seeming to see me, for all they gazed at me so directly. Almost as though his spirit were absent from the body.

I murmured my own name as I bowed in my turn, wanting to turn away again, and yet being unable to remove my eyes from this curious being, so strange was the effect he wrought on me with his *Pagad*-like smile, derived from the upturned curve at one corner of the finely formed lips.

Almost he looked like a Chinese statue hewn out of rose quartz, with the nearly transparent skin devoid of wrinkles, the small girlish nose, and the sensitive nostrils. "Amadeus Laponder . . . Amadeus Laponder . . . " I kept on repeating to myself.

What on earth might he have done?

MOONLIGHT

"Have you been examined yet?" I asked him, after a pause.

"Just this moment. I hope I shall not be a nuisance to you here for too long," Herr Laponder replied, in the most friendly manner possible.

"Poor devil," thought I. "He doesn't know yet what he's up against."

I thought it best slowly to prepare him.

"You get used, you know, to sitting still and waiting, after the first few hard days have passed."

He gave me the look of a man much obliged.

Another pause.

"Did your examination last long, Herr Laponder?"

He smiled a little vaguely.

"Oh, no. They only asked me whether I was guilty, and made me sign the statement I had made."

"But did you sign yourself as guilty?" I couldn't help asking him.

"Of course I did."

He said it as though there could be no other possible alternative.

It couldn't be anything so very awful, I thought to myself, or he surely wouldn't be so placid about it. Perhaps he'd called somebody out in a duel, or something of the kind.

I sighed involuntarily.

"Personally, I have been here such a long while now, it seems like a whole lifetime." He made a gesture of the utmost sympathy. "I sincerely hope, Herr Laponder, the same thing will not happen to you. From the look of it, I should think you would quite soon be released."

"That's as may be." He answered quite quietly, but with a faint trace of a double meaning in his words.

"You don't think?" I asked, with a smile. He shook his head.

"What am I to make of that, I wonder? What can you have done so very dreadful? Believe me, Herr Laponder, it's out of sheer sympathy I ask—not curiosity, in the least. You must forgive my impertinence."

He hesitated a moment, then, without one quiver of the eyelid, said: "Rape—and murder."

It was just as though he had hit me with a club over the head! For very horror and revulsion I was unable to utter one sound.

He seemed to be aware of this, and looked tactfully away from me, but not the least play of feature on that automatically smiling face of his betrayed that he was in the slightest degree upset at this sudden change on my part.

Our conversation had now ended with a jerk, and we silently avoided each the other's glance.

When night came on, and I began to undress, he at once followed my example, carefully hanging his clothes on to the nail on the wall, stretching himself out full length on his plank, and apparently, from the regular, peaceful breathing of him, falling into a deep sleep almost instantaneously.

But I tossed and turned the whole night long.

The horror of having such a creature as that at close quarters, and having to breathe the same infected air, was so perturbing, and altogether so hideous, that it completely drove out of my head the rest of the day's impressions—even the thought of Charousek's letter.

I lay down in such a way that I could keep the figure of the murderer in full view, for the thought of his presence behind me would have been more than I could bear.

The cell was fitfully lit by the glimmer of the moonlight, and I could see the strange, still way Laponder was lying there, almost like a corpse. His features, too, had something of the dead about them, and his half-open mouth only enhanced the impression.

For hours on end he lay there prostrate, without making the slightest movement. Not till towards midnight, when an attenuated moonbeam cast its light upon his face, did he move his lips, without a sound, like someone talking in his sleep. Over and over again did he seem to repeat the same phrase of two syllables, perhaps, "Leave me . . . leave me . . . leave me."

The next few days passed away without my taking any further notice of him, and he, on his part, made no attempt to break the silence.

His attitude towards me was consistently amiable. When the mood took me to pace up and down, he would at once realise it, and punctiliously draw his feet back out of the way when I passed his plank bed, on which he would be sitting. I almost began to reproach myself for my boorish behaviour, and yet, with the best will in the world, I could not get the better of that feeling of repulsion. However hard I tried to get used to the feeling of his proximity, it simply was no use.

At night-time, even, it would keep me awake. Hardly a quarter of an hour's consecutive sleep could I get.

Evening after evening, the same ritual would be repeated, with the utmost precision. He would wait respectfully till I had laid myself down, then remove his clothes, folding them meticulously as he did so, hanging them up on their nail, and so on and so forth.

One night—it must have been about two o'clock—I was standing positively worn out with sleeplessness, gazing up, from that shelf on the wall, at the full moon, whose beams fell like luminous oil across the copper face of the old tower clock, and thinking, in most melancholy wise, of Miriam.

Suddenly, behind me, I heard her voice, softly talking!

In an instant I was awake—more than awake—and listened, turning round.

A moment passed.

Already I was beginning to think it a delusion of mine when it happened again. I couldn't exactly make out the words, but it sounded something like:

"Ask me. Ask me."

Not a doubt of it—it was Miriam's voice!

Shaking with terror, I got down on to the floor, and, as softly as I could, crept up to Laponder's bed.

The moon's rays fell full upon his face, and revealed the fact that his eyelids were wide open, though only the whites of his eyes were visible.

It was easy to see from the rigidity of his cheek muscles that he was sound asleep. The lips, however, were beginning to move once more, and by degrees I made out the words they were uttering:

"Ask me. Ask me."

It was Miriam's voice to the very life!

"Miriam! Miriam!" I shouted, on the impulse of the moment. But next moment I had dropped my voice, so as not to wake the sleeper.

I waited until his face assumed the rigidity of sleep, and repeated, in a low voice, "Miriam, Miriam!"

Scarcely audible, yet entirely unmistakable, came the sound from his lips in response:

"Yes?"

I laid my ear close to his mouth.

After a little while I could hear Miriam's voice whispering—so terribly her voice, and no other, I shuddered from head to foot.

So greedily did I drink in the words that it was only the bare gist of them I seemed to take in. She spoke to me of love, and of the unspeakable happiness we had at last found, she and I, that could part us nevermore, and she spoke rapidly, without a pause, like someone who fears to be interrupted, and is anxious to make use of every moment.

Soon it came at rarer intervals; then, bit by bit, ceased altogether.

"Miriam," I asked, trembling all over with fear, as I caught my breath at the very thought, "Miriam, are you dead?"

For a long time there was no answer.

Then, almost inaudible:

"No. I am alive. I am asleep."

That was all.

I listened . . . and listened . . .

But all in vain. Nothing more happened.

In my fear and emotion I must needs clutch on to the edge of the plank bed, so as not to fall down, across Laponder.

So complete had the hallucination been, I had every moment expected to see Miriam lying before me in the flesh, and had perforce to use all my self-control not to press a kiss upon the murderer's lips.

"Enoch! Enoch!" I suddenly heard him begin to murmur confusedly, and then, clearer and more distinct: "Enoch! Enoch!!"

Hillel's voice! I recognised it at once!

"Is that you, Hillel?"

No answer.

I remembered now to have read how, when a man is talking in his sleep, questions should be addressed to him, not by means of his ear, but to the solar plexus.

This I accordingly did.

"Hillel?"

"Yes? I hear you!"

"Is Miriam all right? And do you know—all there is to know?" I asked him quickly.

"Yes, I know everything. Fear not, Enoch, and do not worry."

"Can you forgive me, Hillel?"

"I told you not to worry."

"Shall we see one another soon?" I was terribly afraid I was no longer going to understand the answers, for the last sentence had been scarcely more than breathed.

"I hope so. I will wait . . . for you . . . if I can . . . then I must . . . to the land. . . . "

"Where? What land?" I just missed, now, falling on to Laponder. "What land? *What land?*"

"Land . . . Gad . . . South . . . Palestine . . . "

The voice faded away.

My brain was positively seething with questions. Why did he call me Enoch? Zwakh . . . Jaromir . . . the watch . . . Vrieslander . . . Angelina . . . Charousek . . .

"Farewell, and think of me sometimes." The sentence came from the murderer's lips quite suddenly and clear. Moreover, it was in the tone of Charousek's voice, though somehow I myself seemed to have uttered the words.

I remembered now. They were the last words of Charousek's letter.

Laponder's face was already in darkness again. The moonbeam had crept to the head of his straw sack. One more quarter of an hour and it would have disappeared from the cell altogether.

I put question upon question, but got no more answers.

The murderer lay there motionless as a corpse, and the lids of both his eyes were shut.

I now tortured myself with reproaches for not having been able to discover the real man in Laponder behind the criminal.

Obviously, after what I had just seen, he was an acute case of somnambulism—the kind of person highly susceptible to the influence of the full moon.

Perhaps he had committed his crime in one of these queer states of mental transition. Yes. I felt quite sure he had.

By the time the day dawned, all his features had relaxed, and he had regained his usual expression of peaceful contentment.

A man couldn't sleep like that, thought I to myself, with a murder of that kind on his conscience.

I could hardly wait for the moment of his awakening.

Would he, or would he not, know what had happened?

At last he opened his eyes, met my gaze, and looked away.

But at once I went up to him, and shook him by the hand.

"Herr Laponder, I must ask you to forgive me for not having behaved particularly well to you. It—it was only that I was somewhat taken aback——"

"Oh, my dear sir, please, please—I understand perfectly," he interrupted me at once. "I realise only too well how revolting it must be to you to be shut up with a murderer and rapist."

"Please don't talk of it," I begged him. "I turned the whole matter over in my mind last night, and couldn't help coming to the conclusion that perhaps——"

"You think I am ill." He helped me out.

"Yes," I affirmed. "Through symptoms that came to my notice I—I——May I ask you a personal question, Herr Laponder?"

"Please do."

"It may strike you as a little strange, but—would you tell me what you dreamed of last night?"

He smiled as he shook his head. "I never dream."

"But you were talking in your sleep."

He looked up, astonished, then thought a moment, and said very decidedly:

"That could only have happened if you asked me a question." I admitted the truth of that. "You see . . . as I said . . . I never actually dream. I . . . I wander sometimes." He said this after a little pause, softly, as though to himself.

"You wander? What am I to understand by that?"

But he didn't seem to want to talk further, and that being the case, I felt the only thing to do was to tell him my reasons for wishing to know. As briefly as I could, I related to him what had passed the previous night.

"There is one thing you can rely on," he said to me earnestly, when I had finished, "and that is that everything I said to you in my sleep rests on a foundation of truth. When I said to you just now I never dreamed, but only *wandered,* it was my way of trying to explain that my actual dream existence is different from that of normal men—for lack of a better expression. If you like, we will call it an 'absence of the spirit.' Last night, for instance, I found myself in the most curious room possible, to which the only entrance was a trap-door up through the floor."

"What did it look like?" I interpolated quickly. "Was it uninhabited? Quite empty?"

"No. There was furniture in it, but not much. And a bed, in which a young girl lay sleeping, so soundly she almost looked to be dead. A

man was sitting next her, with his hand laid upon her forehead."
Laponder then described both their faces. Not a doubt of it, it was
Hillel and Miriam.

I scarce dared to breathe for suspense.

"Please go on telling me. Was there no one else in the room?"

"Anyone else? Wait a moment. . . . No . . . there was no one else
in the room. There was a seven-branched candlestick burning on the
table. I went down through a winding stairway."

"All broken and shattered, was it not?" I asked him.

"Oh, no . . . it was in quite good repair. There was a little room
leading off it, and inside it sat a man with silver buckles on his
shoes—a queer specimen, such as I don't remember having seen before. He had a strange yellowish face, with eyes that slanted, and he
was bending over something in a kind of expectant attitude. As
though waiting to be told something."

"And wasn't there a book—didn't you see an old book somewhere
lying about, very old and large?" I pressed him.

Whereupon he rubbed his forehead. "Ah, you're right there! There
was a book lying on the floor. It was made all of parchment, and open
at a page that began with the letter 'A.' "

"You mean the letter 'I,' do you not?"

"No. It was 'A.' "

"Are you quite sure of that? Sure it wasn't an 'I'?"

"I am quite sure it was an 'A.' "

I shook my head, and now began to doubt. Obviously, somehow or
other Laponder had managed during his sleep to penetrate my subconscious self, and was now reproducing the result at random—Hillel,
Miriam, the Golem, the book *Ibbur,* and the subterranean passage.

"Have you possessed this faculty of 'wandering,' as you call it, for
long?" I asked.

"Since my twenty-first year." He stopped short, and seemed unwilling to speak of it. Then, all of a sudden, an expression of the utmost
amazement came into his face, and he stared hard at my breast, as
though he saw something there.

Without so much as noticing my astonishment, he seized me impul-
sively by the hand, and demanded almost imploringly:

"For the love of heaven, tell me *everything!* This is the very last day
I shall ever spend with you. At any moment now I may be taken away
to hear my sentence of death pronounced."

I broke in, appalled:

"But you must call upon me to witness in your behalf! I shall testify
to the fact that you are sick! The moon influences you! They simply

can't condemn you without having investigated the state of your mind! Please, please be reasonable."

But he deprecated the whole affair with the utmost indifference. "It is all so trivial. Now, please tell me."

"What is it you want me to tell you? Let us talk, rather, of you and——"

"Listen. You must—I realise now—have experienced certain strange things which concern me nearly—far more nearly than you know. I implore you to tell me!" he begged.

I could hardly tolerate the fact that my life should mean more to him at the moment than his own imperative affairs; but in order to calm him down, I told him of all the inexplicable occurrences of which, up to now, I had been a part.

At each strange fact I retailed he nodded, well pleased, like someone who at long last has succeeded in piercing to the heart of some dark mystery.

When I came to the part where the headless apparition had stood by my side, holding out to me the black-red seeds, he could hardly wait to hear me out till the end.

"So you struck them out of his hand?" he murmured thoughtfully to himself. "Never would I have believed that a third way could have been found."

"It can scarcely be called a third way," I protested; "it was the same thing, surely, as if I had refused to take the seeds?"

He smiled.

"Don't you think so, Herr Laponder?"

"If you had refused them, then would you most certainly have chosen the path of life, but the seeds, that signify the powers of magic, would not in that case have remained behind. You tell me they rolled on the ground. That is to say, they stayed behind here, and will be in the custody of your forefathers until the time of their ripening. Then will the faculties still latent within you spring into being."

I could not understand. "My forefathers . . . you say, those seeds will be in their custody?"

"All those things you have experienced," explained Laponder, "you must partly interpret in the way of symbol. That circle of blue luminous entities that closed you around was the chain of the diverse inherited personalities each mother's son is born into the world with. The soul is not 'one and indivisible'; it will ultimately become so, and thereby attain what is called immortality; your soul consists of infinite component parts—egos innumerable, like an ant-heap is composed of multitudinous ants. You bear within yourself the *spiritual vestiges* of thousands of your forebears, the original progenitors of the race from which you sprang. It is the same with all creation. How otherwise could a chicken hatched from an incubator instantly seek forth its own peculiar nourishment, did it not contain, innate within itself, the accumulated experience of hundreds of centuries? The presence of 'instinct' reveals in both one's body and one's soul the undeniable fact of our own ancestors. But forgive me. I did not mean to interrupt you."

I told him all the rest I had to tell. Also what Miriam had said concerning the hermaphrodite.

As I stopped and looked up at him, I noticed his face had gone white as the lime-wash of the wall behind him, and tears were pouring down his cheeks.

I rose quickly, pretending not to notice, and walked up and down the cell, waiting till he had controlled himself.

After which, I sat down opposite to him, and used all the eloquence at my command to convince him how essential it was to prove the abnormal condition of his mind to the jury that tried him.

"If only you hadn't confessed to the murder," I ended up.

"Oh, but I had to. They put me on my oath," he replied naïvely.

"Do you consider it worse, then, to perpetrate a falsehood than . . . your kind of murder?" I asked in perplexity.

"Generally speaking, maybe not, but in my case, certainly. You see, when the Examining Magistrate put the question to me, the strength was given me to tell the truth. It was, so to say, within my choice to lie or not to lie. When I committed my crime—and, please, I will ask you to spare me the relation of the details—it was so hideous, I think the mere remembrance of it would kill me to live through again. But I had no choice in the matter. I *had* to commit it, though I was fully conscious at the time of what I did. Something inside me, of which I had had no previous knowledge, came to life, and was stronger than I was. Do you suppose I'd have committed a murder like that, if it had been left to me to choose? I, who had never taken life—not even that of the smallest insect . . . and wouldn't be able to . . . even now. . . .

"Just try and imagine to yourself, for a moment, murder as the law of the land, and *not* to murder as capital offence—as it is in wartime. I should have been guilty, and condemned instantly, for the simple reason that I should have had no choice. When I committed my crime, it happened to be the other way round."

"All the more," I urged him, "now that you feel yourself in very truth another human being, ought this to be included in your evidence."

He made a deprecatory gesture. "That's where you're wrong. From their point of view, my judges are perfectly right. How can they let a man such as I am loose on the streets? So that to-morrow, or the next day, the same thing might happen all over again?"

"No, but you ought to be confined in a mental home for special cases of this kind. That's all I mean!"

"If I were insane, then you'd be right," Laponder replied indifferently. "But I'm not. What I am is something quite different from madness, though, on the face of it, it bears the same aspect. Listen to me . . . you'll understand in a moment. You were talking just now of a phantom without a head: that, of course, is purely symbolical, and, if you think hard enough, you'll soon be able to find the key to it. But I, too, have experienced precisely the same vision! *Only, I took the seeds!* So I, by the same token, must tread the path of death. All that is most sacred in my soul must respond to that ideal—that all my actions be dictated by this holy of holies within me, blindly, and full of trust, wheresoever the way may lead, to the gallows or to the throne, to poverty or riches. Never once have I hesitated yet, when the choice lay in my hand. That is why I did not lie when I had the choice of doing so.

"Do you know the words of the Prophet Micah—'He hath showed thee, O man, what is good; and what doth the Lord require of thee'? I should have lied then, had I done so, as a responsible agent. I was no such thing when I committed the murder; that was but the working out of some dormant principle, long hidden within my being, over which I possessed no power.

"Therefore are my hands pure. Now that the holy of holies within me has turned me into a murderer, now that it has led to my execution, now that it has driven me to the gallows, that moment sees the final rupture of the bond betwixt us. Henceforth I am free!"

"The man is a saint," I thought to myself, and I could feel the spleen within me rise at the realisation of my own nauseating pettiness.

"You were telling me," he went on, "how some physician, through hypnotism, has robbed you of the memory of your early youth. But that is the sign—the holy stigmata—of all those bitten by the Snake of the Kingdom of the Spirit. It almost looks as if two lives must be found together in us, like the mistletoe and the oak, before the miracle of awakening can take place. What is usually accomplished by death, the separation of the two selves, has resulted here from extinction of the memory—or sometimes by a sudden internal reversal and upheaval.

"With me, it certainly seemed to happen that way. When I was twenty-one, I apparently woke up, one morning, completely and absolutely changed. Everything I had cared for up to then seemed all of a sudden to have no value for me. Life appeared to me as colourless as a tale that is told, and to have lost all touch with actuality. Dreams were transformed into certainty—a powerful, demonstrable reality—and my everyday life of hitherto was relegated to the status of a dream.

"Every man on earth could do the same did he but possess the key. And the key consists in simply and solely this: that a man, during sleep, shall become conscious of his ego-form, his *skin,* so to say, and aware of that infinitesimal rift through which his conscious self presses in that transition state which lies betwixt waking and deep sleep.

"And that is why I say 'I wander' instead of 'I dream.'

"Our struggle to attain immortality is our struggle to gain ascendancy over those unruly ghosts and warring elements innate within our being. We await the crowning of the true I, which is the same as the Messiah.

"The ghostly Habal Garmin, whom you have beheld, the 'Breath of Bones' of the Kabbala—that was the King. So soon as he is crowned will the bonds be rent in two that shackled you to the world by means of your bodily senses and your reason.

"You want, I know, to ask me how it is that I, despite the detachment I have achieved from the web of life, could be transformed in a night into the most vicious kind of murderer? I will tell you. Human beings are like tubes made of glass, through which many coloured balls may roll. Most men are restricted to one colour only. Should the ball be red, the man is branded as 'bad'; if yellow, then is he 'good.' Should two balls pursue their passage through the same tube, one yellow and one red, then that man has 'an unstable character.' But we who have been bitten by the Serpent compress within ourselves the experience of a whole race within an age. Coloured balls rush wildly on their way through the glass tube, and when it ends, then are we 'prophets,' and the mirror of very God himself."

Laponder was now silent. As for me, I could not say one word. His talk had well-nigh stupefied me.

"But why," I at last began again, "did you question me just now so feverishly about my own experiences, when you yourself are so far, far above me?"

"That is where you are wrong," answered Laponder. "I am infinitely below you. I questioned you because I felt you possessed the key I lacked."

"I? A key? O God!"

"Yes. You. And, what's more, you have given it to me. I think there is no happier man on earth to-day than I am."

There was a noise of feet outside. The bolt was drawn back. Laponder scarcely noticed.

"What you told me about the hermaphrodite, *that was the key!* Therefore do I rejoice that even now they come to fetch me, for yet a little while, and I shall have attained my goal."

I could not see Laponder's face any more for my own tears, but I could hear the smile in his voice.

"Good-bye, now, Herr Pernath. Please think tomorrow, or whenever it may be, that the gallows will know nothing but my outer garments. Through you has been revealed to me the ultimate and most beautiful of all. This is my bridal day." He rose, and followed the guard out of the cell. "And with it my crime is closely knit," were the last words I heard him utter, and could but darkly comprehend.

Every night, now that the full moon shone in the heavens, I thought to see once again Laponder's sleeping face lying there on the grey bedding.

In the course of the next few days after his removal from my cell I would often hear the sound of hammering from the execution yard near by, and frequently it would last until the break of day.

I surmised the cause of it, and would stand there despairingly, with my fingers thrust into my ears.

Month followed month. I could register the fleeting footsteps of summer on the sickly foliage in the prison yard. Each time I passed the withered tree, with the glass picture of the saint so curiously incorporated in its trunk, I could not refrain from making a comparison with the face of Laponder, so deeply graven on my mind. Never did I seem able to dismiss the memory of that smooth-skinned Buddha countenance, with the strange, fixed smile.

Once only—during September—had the Examining Magistrate sent for me, and asked me suspiciously how I could account for having said, when I went to my bank, that I was most urgently compelled to make a journey, and why had I been in such a disturbed frame of mind before my arrest, and why had I done up all my precious stones and concealed them on my person?

When I replied I had done all this with the intention of taking my own life, the usual derisive snigger from behind the writing-desk had not been lacking.

Up to now I had had my cell to myself, and could let my thoughts

roam at will—of Laponder, of my grief concerning Charousek, who I
felt must long since be dead, and of my longing for Miriam.

Then fresh prisoners were thrust upon me; little thieving clerks with
dissipated faces; pot-bellied bank cashiers; 'strays' of all sorts, as
Black Vóssatka would have termed them, infecting both the atmosphere and my own mood.

One of them, one day, chose to work himself up into a state about
a certain murder of a particularly bestial kind, committed in the town
some little while ago. By the grace of God, he said, they had got on
the scoundrel's tracks almost at once, and made short work of *him!*

"His name was Laponder, the dirty bastard," shrilled forth a fellow
with a visage like a beast of prey's, who was doing fourteen days for
mistreating a child. "The lamp got knocked over, and the house was
burnt out. The girl's body was so charred that they still don't know
who it was. Laponder wouldn't talk. All they could tell was that
she had black hair and a small face. If I got a chance at him, do you
know what I would do? I'd skin him alive and rub salt on him. That's
what they're like, the fine lords. Murderers, every one of them. As if
there ain't enough other ways if you want a woman——" he added
with a cynical smirk.

My blood boiled within me, and for two pins I'd have stretched the
fellow on the ground.

Night after night he would lie snoring in Laponder's bed. The room
felt more than a little cleaner when he'd been disposed of.

None the less, I couldn't free myself from him. His words still stuck
in my gullet like a sharp-baited fish-hook.

Almost incessantly, and most of all in the darkness of the night, I
was consumed inwardly by a gnawing fear lest Laponder's victim
should have been Miriam!

And the more I strove against it, the deeper the notion gripped me,
till it became almost an obsession in my mind.

Sometimes—and especially when the moon shone brightly through
the window-bars—the pain would lessen; I could live over then, in the
spirit, those hours I had passed with Laponder, and the thought of
them soothed me accordingly, but in due course the horrifying image
would rise up in front of my eyes of Miriam a charred and bleeding
corpse, till for sheer agony I thought I would go mad.

The very slenderness of the only proofs I could produce to substan-
tiate my theory seemed, if anything, to accentuate the whole process
in my mind. Day by day the picture became more and more detailed,
and more and more ghastly.

One evening towards ten o'clock, at the beginning of November, when it was already pitch dark, and despair had reached to such a point in my heart that I was forced to bite my straw sack like a demented animal, the guard suddenly opened the door of my cell and ordered me out, to appear before the Examining Magistrate. So weak did I feel that I staggered, rather than walked, before him.

The hope of ever again leaving this terrible place had died in me long ago.

All I was prepared for at this moment was the usual formal question, followed, in the approved manner, by the stereotyped giggle from behind the desk, and a final relegation to outer darkness once again.

My friend Baron Leisetreter being snug within the bosom of his family at this time of night, the only occupant of the room was an elderly, round-shouldered little clerk with spider-like fingers.

I waited in silence for anything that might befall me.

I was dimly aware of the fact that the guard had come into the room with me, and was twinkling at me in a benevolent sort of way, but I was far too crushed to interpret the true significance of any of these facts.

"CASE CARL ZOTTMANN. The summary proceedings go to show," began the clerk, sniggered, clambered on to a chair, and started fidgeting about with a sheaf of papers, before continuing: "the summary proceedings go to show that the aforesaid Carl Zottmann, prior to his decease, as the result of a clandestine relationship with one Rosina Metzeles, a registered prostitute, known to the police as 'Redheaded Rosina,' subsequently associated with a certain deaf-mute of the name of Jaromir Kwasznitschka, silhouette-artist, now under police supervision, and at this present date living in open shame as concubine to Prince Ferri Athenstädt, was conveyed surreptitiously, and with fraudulent intent, to an underground cellar in house No. 7 of the Hahnpassgasse, there concealed under lock and key, and presumably left to die a lingering death of hunger and cold. The proceedings further go to show," the clerk droned on, looked up for a moment over the top of his glasses, and started fumbling again with the papers

. . . .

"The proceedings further go to show that, presumably subsequent to his decease, the aforesaid Carl Zottmann was robbed of his gold hunter watch"—here he held up the watch from the table by its chain—"slightly damaged about the cover, with lettering inside partially obliterated, together with the rest of his portable property. The declaration made on oath by the aforesaid Jaromir Kwasznitschka, orphan son of the seventeen years deceased baker of consecrated wafers of the same name, that he found the watch in the bed of his brother Loisa, who has since absconded, and that he took it to the shop of one Aaron Wassertrum, householder, subsequently deceased, and handed over the aforesaid watch in return for an agreed sum of money, has been dismissed, owing to the improbable nature of the story.

"The proceedings further go to show that the corpse of the aforesaid Carl Zottmann had on it, at the time of its discovery, in the left-hand trouser pocket, a notebook in which he had, presumably several days prior to his decease, made certain entries tending to throw light upon the crime, and render possible the apprehension of the criminal.

"Loisa Kwasznitschka, at the time a fugitive from justice, having, in consequence of the entries by the aforesaid Carl Zottmann, incurred grave suspicion, has engaged the attention of the police authorities.

"It is therefore directed that the detention pending trial of Athanasius Pernath, cutter of precious stones, shall come to an end, and that the proceedings against him be abandoned.

"PRAGUE,

"*July,*

"*Signed*: DR. FREIHERR VON LEISETRETER."

The ground swam beneath me, and for the space of a moment I lost consciousness. . . .

When I came to, I found myself sitting on a chair, with the guard clapping me solicitously on the back.

The clerk was sitting unperturbed, taking snuff and sneezing, and finally informing me:

"The reading of the statement had to be postponed till to-day in consequence of your name beginning with a 'P.' Naturally the cases have to be dealt with in alphabetical rotation." After which he continued reading:

"We, moreover, beg to inform the aforesaid Athanasius Pernath, cutter of precious stones, that he has been made heir to a third part of the estate of the late Innocence Charousek, medical student, now defunct, in consequence of a will drawn up in his favour by the aforesaid, and he is hereby requested to set his hand by way of signature to this present statement."

Wherewith the clerk dipped his pen into the inkpot, and started making blots on the paper.

I sat there, waiting for the accustomed snigger to follow. But it never came.

"Innocence Charousek," I repeated after him, a little vacantly.

The guard stooped, and whispered in my ear:

"Shortly before his death, Dr. Charousek called here to enquire for you. He asked me to be sure and convey his warmest greetings to you. But of course I could not at the time do anything of the kind. It is strictly against all rules. The poor Doctor came to a terrible end. He took his own life. They found him dead, lying flat on his face in the cemetery, over the grave of Aaron Wassertrum. He dug two deep holes in the ground, cut his wrists and put his arms in the holes and bled to death. He must have been crazy, that Dr. Char——"

The clerk had now pushed his chair back noisily, and was handing me the pen for me to sign with.

After which he drew himself up, and, with all the dignity of an underling, dressed in a little brief authority:

"Guard, take the man away."

Again—as once before, eons ago—the man with the sword and baggy trousers in the hall had taken the coffee-mill off his lap. But this time, instead of searching me, he had given me back my packet of precious stones, and my note-case with the ten gulden in it, together with my cloak, and all my other belongings.

After which, I was in the street again!

Miriam! Miriam! At last I would see her! It was all I could do to suppress a wild shout of joy.

It must surely be midnight. The moon was shining dully in the clouds, like a great plate of pale brass, behind a veil of mist.

The pavement was covered with a coating of sticky mud.

I signed to a *drosky*, that loomed out of the night air like some dilapidated prehistoric monster. My legs, it seemed to me, didn't know their job any more. I had forgotten how to walk, and could only stumble, walking on numbed soles, like a man sick of the palsy.

Hahnpassgasse, coachman, as quick as you can—No. 7. Do you hear? No. 7!"

FREE

After a few yards, the man pulled up.

"Was it Hahnpassgasse, sir, you said?"

"Yes . . . yes . . . quickly!"

We went on a little way. Then stopped again.

"For God's sake! What's the matter?"

"It was Hahnpassgasse, sir, wasn't it?"

"Yes, you fool. Go on!"

"Can't drive down Hahnpassgasse, sir."

"Why not?"

"It's ripped up, sir. The Jewish quarter is being rebuilt."

"Take me as far as you can, then. But, for heaven's sake, get along!"

The *drosky* leapt forward with a bound, then almost immediately subsided into a jog-trot.

I let down the rackety window, and greedily filled my lungs with the night air.

Everything seemed to have become so strange to me, so curiously new—the houses, and the streets, and the shops with closed shutters.

A miserable white dog was trotting along the pavement. I gazed after it. How odd! A dog! I had forgotten there were such things! I found myself calling out after it, like a happy child; "Hey, hey! Don't be such a sourpuss!"

What on earth would Hillel say when he saw me? And Miriam! Only a few moments more, and I should be with them! Not for one minute would I stop knocking at their door till I had waked them both up!

Everything was going to be all right now . . . all the trials and tribulations of this past year over at last!

It would be like Christmas night! But this time I wouldn't sleep through it.

Just for a fleeting instant I was paralysed with the old horror. The words of the prisoner with the bestial face sounded in my ears. The charred face . . . that hideous murder. But, no . . . a thousand times, no! I shook it off with all the strength that was in me. It simply *could* not be! Miriam was alive! I had heard her very voice, from the mouth of Laponder.

One little minute more . . . half a minute . . . and then!

The *drosky* pulled up before a heap of ruins. Barricades of paving blocks all round, everywhere, with little red lanterns alight.

In the glare of torchlight a gang of workmen were busily employed. They were digging and shovelling.

The way was blocked by heaps of rubbish and bricks. I began to climb over them, and sank up to my knees.

Could this really and truly be the Hahnpassgasse?

Wearily I tried to take my bearings. But I was surrounded with nothing but ruins.

Could my old house have been pulled down?

The front of it certainly had been.

I clambered on to a mound of earth. In place of what had once been the street, a black-walled passage lay beneath me. I looked up. Rooms yawned above me in all their nakedness, like so many gigantic cells in a hive, lit, half by the moon, half by the flickering light of the torches.

That room over there must have been mine. I recognised it by the colour of the walls.

But only the tiniest portion of it still remained.

Next to it was Savioli's studio! A strange feeling of emptiness came into my heart. How curious it seemed! Angelina! So far removed, so infinitely remote, did it all appear to me now.

I turned round. Not one stone remained of the house where Wassertrum had lived. It had literally been razed to the ground . . . the junkshop . . . Charousek's cellar . . . lodging . . . everything . . . every single thing . . .

"Man perisheth as a vain shadow," a phrase I had read somewhere, suddenly came into my mind.

I asked one of the workmen whether he knew where the people who used to live here had gone; whether he knew Hillel the Registrar.

"No speak German," was the answer. I gave him a gulden and his knowledge immediately improved. But he could give me no information. The same was true of the other workmen.

I asked them did they think I might learn anything down at Loisitschek's?

Loisitschek's, they told me, was shut. Closed for remodeling.

But surely there was somebody in the neighbourhood I could wake up and ask?

"Not even a cat lives around here," one of the men volunteered. "It's forbidden. Typhus."

"The Alte Ungelt? Is it open?"

"Closed."

"Sure?"

"Dead sure!"

I mentioned a couple of other people, tobacconists, residents in the neighbourhood: then Zwakh, Vrieslander, Prokop.

But each time he shook his head.

"Do you, by any chance, know Jaromir Kwasznitschka?"

At that he pricked up his ears.

"Jaromir? Deaf mute?"

Thank God! At last someone I knew!

"Yes. Deaf and dumb. Where does he live?"

"Does he cut pictures out? Of black paper?"

"Yes! That's the fellow. Where can I find him?"

As best he could the man described to me a certain night café in the heart of the town, and started to go on with his shovelling again.

For the space of an hour I stumbled over fields of rubble, crossed sagging planks, and crawled through piles of timber that blocked the streets. The whole Jewish quarter was one waste of earth and rubbish, just as though an earthquake had passed over it.

At last—breathless, bedraggled, and torn—I had found my way out of the labyrinth.

The dirty little public-house in question was a couple of rows of houses away. Over the doorway was written "Café Chaos."

The saloon bar was practically empty. It was also very small, with scarcely enough room for a couple of tables fastened to the walls.

A waiter was snoring on top of the three-legged billiard table that stood in the middle of the room.

A market woman, with her vegetable basket in front of her, sat in the corner nodding over a glass of beer.

At last it dawned upon the waiter to get up and ask what I wanted. Only from the insolent look with which he scanned me from top to toe did it dawn on me how disreputable must my appearance be.

Horrified, I looked at myself in the glass. Out of it stared at me an entirely unfamiliar face—wrinkled, pasty, grey as putty, with scrubby beard, and long, tangled hair.

I ordered some black coffee, and asked if Jaromir had been there that evening.

"Not turned up yet," yawned the waiter, and laid himself down on the billiard table once more, to sleep.

I took the "*Prager Tagblatt*" from the wall and . . . waited.

The letterpress ran about all over the page, like ants, and I understood not one word of what I read.

The hours passed and that curious dark-blue light was beginning to steal through the window-panes that in a gas-lit café is the equivalent of daybreak.

Now and again a couple of helmets with shimmering cock's feathers would be poked round the door, but the policemen that owned them would soon make the best of their way outside again, with slow, heavy tread.

Three weary-looking soldiers trailed into the room.

A crossing-street-sweeper came in for a brandy.

And at long last—Jaromir.

He had changed so much, I scarcely knew him at first. His eyes were glazed, he had lost his front teeth, his hair was all tousled, and there were deep hollows behind his ears.

So delighted was I to see a familiar face once more, after so long a time, that I sprang up and seized him by the hand.

But he seemed extraordinarily timid, and kept looking towards the door. Through every possible means in my power I tried to convince him how glad I was to have come across him. For a long time he seemed unable to take it in.

As for the questions I put to him—every single one of these received the same helpless gesture of incomprehension.

How, oh, how, could I make myself intelligible?

Ah! An idea!

I asked for a pencil, and drew, one by one, the faces of Zwakh, Vrieslander, and Prokop.

"What? None of them in Prague any longer?"

He brandished his arms about in the air violently, made a gesture as of counting out money, then set his fingers walking across the surface of the table, and slapped the back of his hand. I understood. They had probably all three of them come into some money from Charousek, and were touring with their Marionette Company, on an increased scale, as a going concern.

"And Hillel? Where does he live, now?" I drew his face, then a house close to it, then a large note of interrogation.

The question mark meant nothing to him. He couldn't read. But he understood what I wanted, for he picked up a match, threw it deliberately up into the air, and then caught it, juggler-fashion, so that it disappeared.

What could that mean? Had Hillel gone away, too?

I now drew the Jewish Council House.

"Hillel isn't there any more?"

"No." (Shake of the head.)

"Where is he, then?"

Business again with match.

"He mean's the gentleman's gone away, and he doesn't know where," the crossing-street-sweeper joined in informatively. He had been looking on at the whole proceeding with the utmost interest.

My heart leapt into my mouth! Hillel gone! I was all alone in the world, then!

All the things in the room began to dance before my eyes.

"And Miriam?"

My hand trembled so that for a long time I couldn't draw any face that was like her.

"Has Miriam gone too?"

"Yes. Gone. Quite gone."

I groaned aloud, and paced back and forth around the room. The three soldiers looked at each other enquiringly.

Jaromir now tried to calm me, and made painful efforts to communicate something else he seemed to know. He laid his head down on his arm, like somebody sleeping.

Whereat I held on to the table. "Christ! Is Miriam dead?"

He shook his head, and again repeated the gesture of sleep.

Had she been ill? I drew a medicine bottle.

Another headshake. And again he laid his head down on his arm.

Bit by bit it grew lighter, and the gas-jets began to be turned out. But still I could not make out what that gesture was intended to convey.

I gave it up, and sat thinking.

The only thing that remained to me was to go to the Jewish Council House, and there make enquiries where Hillel might have gone to, with Miriam.

Wherever it was, I must go after him.

Without one word, I sat there, close to Jaromir. As deaf and as dumb as he was.

Looking up, after a long interval, I saw him cutting a silhouette out of a piece of paper.

I recognised the profile as Rosina's. He passed it over the table to me, then laid his hand before his eyes, and began to cry silently.

Suddenly he leapt to his feet, and staggered out of the room precipitately.

Schemajah Hillel, the Registrar, had apparently left the neighbourhood one day and never returned: his daughter he had presumably taken with him, for nobody had since caught a glimpse of her. That was what they told me at the Jewish Council House. And that was all they could tell me.

There seemed to be not one trace of where they might have gone.

As for my money, it still lay at the bank, hedged in by legal restrictions, but every day now they were expecting to be in a position to pay it over to me.

I must also comply with the necessary legal formalities with regard to Charousek's legacy, and the whole soul of me was now filled with burning impatience to get through with it, realise everything I had got, and start off on my search for Hillel and Miriam.

I sold my precious stones, that I still had in my pocket, and with the proceeds hired a couple of tiny furnished attic rooms in the Altschulgasse—the one remaining street in the Ghetto that did not seem to have been condemned.

By some curious law of coincidence it turned out to be precisely the same house as that in which the Golem was said to have taken refuge, according to the old legend. I made enquiries among my neighbours—for the most part small shopkeepers and artisans—as to the truth of the yarn concerning the "room with no entrance," and all of them laughed at me. Fancy believing a thing like *that*! was the general attitude.

My own experiences in that connection had long faded, during imprisonment, to the pale hues of a vanished dream. I now wiped them completely from the tablets of my mind, as mere empty symbols void of all manner of life.

Laponder's words, which I would frequently hear as clearly as though he sat opposite talking to me, only strengthened my feeling that maybe I had but seen, with the inward eye of vision, something that at the time had seemed tangible reality.

Wasn't everything gone and vanished now that once I had possessed?

The book *Ibbur*, the ghostly game of tarot, Angelina, and even my old friends Zwakh, Vrieslander, and Prokop!

It was Christmas Eve, and I was taking back to my rooms a little tree with red candles. For once I longed to be a boy again, with the glitter of lights around me, and the fragrance of pine-needles and burning wax.

Before the year was over I should most likely have started on my pilgrimage, and be scouring the towns and villages, or wherever the spirit moved me to go, in my quest for Hillel and Miriam.

By degrees all impatience had departed from my soul, and I feared no more lest Miriam should be murdered. For I knew in my heart that I should find both her and her father.

I was fulfilled now with a feeling of happy contentment—the sweet peace of a man who, after many wanderings, returns to his home, and sees from afar the spires of his native town. Strange.

I had turned in at the little café house to try and collect Jaromir to spend Christmas evening with me. But they told me he never went there any more now. I was going somewhat sadly away again when an old itinerant pedlar came in, hawking his trumpery little wares.

I rummaged about among all the odds and ends in his pack, turning over crucifixes, hair-combs, rubbishy brooches—and suddenly found myself picking up a heart-shaped stone, strung on a piece of silk. In amazement I recognised it as the identical red heart that Angelina once, when she was a little girl, had given me as a parting present, down by the fountain in the old garden at her castle.

In a flash my youth stood revealed to me—in miniature, as though I gazed at it through a peep-show on a small scale.

For a long, long time I stood there, gazing and gazing at the little red heart in my hand.

I was sitting in my little attic room now, listening to the faint crackle of the pine-needles, when here and there a little twig would be set alight by one of the candles.

Most probably old Zwakh at this very moment, somewhere or other, was producing his Christmas Eve play, in terms of marionettes. I pictured the scene to myself, declaiming in hushed tones the verses of his favourite poet, Oskar Wiener:

> Where is the heart of stone, blood-red,
> That hung upon a silken thread?
> Give, oh give it not away,
> For I did love him, and I served
> Seven years to win this heart, nor ever swerved
> From faithful service, night and day.

Why did I feel so awe-struck all of a sudden?

The candles had all burned down by now. Only one was still flickering. Small rings of smoke hovered in the air.

Suddenly, as though a hand had clutched me, I turned, and:

MY OTHER SELF STOOD ON THE THRESHOLD. MY DOPPELGÄNGER. IN A WHITE CLOAK. A CROWN UPON ITS HEAD.

For one fleeting moment.

Then, through the wooden door flames burst, and the room was filled with a hot smother.

Fire had broken out in the house! Fire! FIRE!

I tear open the window. I climb out on to the roof.

The sharp clatter of the fire brigade can already be heard in the distance.

Gleaming helmets and short, sharp words of command.

Then the ghostly, rhythmical squelch of the pumps, as though the Demon of Water were making ready to spring on its arch-enemy—Fire!

Next, the smashing of glass, and red tongues of flame shooting forth from all the windows.

Mattresses are flung on to the ground below, till the whole street seems full of them, and of human creatures jumping down on them, and being carried away, injured.

As for me, I am filled with a wild kind of jubilant ecstasy. Why, I do not know. My hair positively stands on end.

I rush to the chimney, to escape from the flames that are pursuing me.

A chimney-sweep's rope is fastened round it.

I coil it up, twist it round ankle and leg as we had been taught to do at "gym" in school, and let myself quietly down the side of the house.

I am passing by a window. I am peering in.

It is all brightly lit up inside.

And there I see . . . THERE I SEE . . .

My whole person is transformed into one great cry of joy:

HILLEL! MIRIAM! HILLEL!

I try to clutch hold of the bars . . .

But in my clutching I leave hold of the rope . . .

For a moment I hang there, head twisted back, and with legs crossed, betwixt heaven and earth . . .

The rope twangs under the strain. I hear the strands stretching and groaning.

I fall.

I lose consciousness.

I try to grasp the window-sill in my falling, but my hand slithers off. Nothing to hold . . .

The stone is smooth . . .

SMOOTH LIKE A LUMP OF FAT!

END

" . . . like a lump of fat!"

That is the stone, that looks like a lump of fat!

The words are shrilling in my ears still. Then I sit up, and force myself to realise where I am.

I am in bed. I am staying in a hotel.

My name is not Pernath, at all.

Has it all been just a dream?

No. Dreams are not like that.

I look at the clock. I have scarcely been asleep half an hour. It is half-past two.

And there hangs the hat which is not mine, which I took by mistake in the Cathedral to-day, when I attended High Mass.

Was there a name inside?

I pick it up, and read, in golden letters on the white silk lining, the name which is not my name, and yet so oddly familiar by now:

ATHANASIUS PERNATH

There is no question of rest for me any more now. I dress rapidly, and run downstairs.

"Porter! Unlock the door! I'm going out for an hour!"

"*Out,* sir?"

"Yes. Into the Jewish quarter. Hahnpassgasse. There's a street of that name, isn't there?"

"There *is* a street." The porter smiles, disagreeably. "But it's not the Jewish quarter any more now, sir, in a manner of speaking. It's all been rebuilt long ago."

"It doesn't matter. Where is the Hahnpassgasse?"

"Here, sir." The fat thumb of the porter points it out to me on the map.

"And the café—"Loisitschek's?"

"Just here, sir."

"Give me a large sheet of brown paper, will you?"

"Very good, sir."

In it I wrap up Pernath's hat. Strange; it is almost new, spotlessly clean, and yet as fragile-looking as if it were extremely old.

I ponder, and ponder, as I go on my way.

Obviously I had experienced, within my dream, everything that Athanasius Pernath had lived through. Everything have I witnessed, heard, and felt, within the space of one night, as though I had been he. But then why, in that one brief moment, when the cord broke, and he had called out "Hillel! Hillel!"—why did I not know now what it was he had seen behind that barred window?

I realise that must have been the moment in which he and I were separated.

Come what come may, I must find this Athanasius Pernath, if I have to search for three days and three nights on end without stopping.

So *that's* the Hahnpassgasse?

Never for one instant had I seen it like that in my dreams!

Just a lot of new-built houses.

A moment later, and I am seated in the Café Loisitschek. A quiet, fairly clean little place it seems to be.

There is, as a matter of fact, a kind of estrade up at the back, with a wooden railing in front, and a certain resemblance to the old Loisitschek's of my dreams is not to be denied.

"What can I get you, sir?" a buxom waitress comes and asks me. She seems literally bursting out of her hot red velvet frock.

"One cognac, please . . . thanks. Please . . . Fräulein?"

"Sir?"

"Whom does this café belong to?"

"To Herr Kommerzialrat Loisitschek, of course. The whole house belongs to him. He's a very well-to-do gentleman."

Ah! I remember. The individual with the boar's teeth upon his watch-chain. I remember, perfectly.

I have a brain-wave. Surely, I shall get on to it now.

"Fräulein!"

"Sir?"

"When was it the stone bridge broke down?"

"Thirty-three years ago." *

"Oh! Thirty-three years ago!" I ruminate. In that case, my friend Pernath must be getting on for ninety now.

"Fräulein!"

"Sir?"

"Isn't there anybody here amongst your regular customers who can remember how it was the old Jewish quarter used to look? I am an author, and interested in things of that sort."

She thinks a moment. "Any of our customers . . . n-no. . . . At least . . . there's that old billiard marker playing billiards over there with the young student . . . the old fellow with the hooky nose . . . see him? He's always lived here, and would be able to tell you all about it. Shall I fetch him when he's done?"

I follow the girl's glance.

Over there by the mirror a thin white-haired old man is chalking the end of his cue. An emaciated face, but somehow very appealing. What is it he reminds me of?

"What's the marker's name, Fräulein?"

The waitress is now leaning both her elbows on the table, and, licking the end of her pencil, rapidly writes her name over and over again on the marble top, rubbing it out each time, as quickly, with her finger. The gesture is accompanied by a series of glances in my direc-

---

* The chronology is awry. The bridge was damaged in 1890, at which time Pernath was said to have been in his forties and Athenstädt a young man. [E.F.B.]

tion, of varying degrees of suggestiveness, according to the reception they meet with. And of course she does not omit to arch her eyebrows the while, or do anything else to accentuate the magic of her appeal.

"What is the marker's name, Fräulein?" I ask again. I know quite well, as I look at her how much she would prefer another question: "Fräulein, why haven't you on nothing but a swallow-tail coat?" . . . or words to that effect. But I don't put it. I am far too taken up with my dream.

"Called?" she pouts. "Oh . . . *called!* . . . why, he's Ferri—Ferri Athenstädt."

"Indeed? Ferri Athenstädt? Ah! Then he's an old acquaintance.

"Go on, my dear," I wheedle her—for all I have to fortify myself first with another cognac. "It's good to hear the sound of that pretty little voice of yours." . . . Lord, how I do detest myself at this moment!

She stoops down, unnecessarily close to me, so that her hair tickles my face, as she whispers:

"Ferri, he was a real big wheel in his day. Some say he came from the old nobility—but I'll bet that's just a story, because he doesn't have a beard—and he was rolling in money. A red-headed Jewess—real hot stuff——" she wrote her name a couple of times more—"stripped him bare. I mean money. And when he was broke, she up and married a fine gentleman. He was"—and she whispered some name in my ear, but I didn't catch it. "The gentleman had to give up his rank and you couldn't call him Ritter any more. That's all right. But he still couldn't wash away that she used to be on the streets. Do you know what I think?"

"Fritzi! Check, please!" someone called down from the estrade.

Left alone, my gaze roams all round the café, when suddenly I hear behind me a tiny metallic sound, like the chirping of a grasshopper.

I turn round enquiringly. It is all I can do to believe my eyes.

There is old Schaffranek sitting in the corner, actually old blind, hoary-headed Nephtali Schaffranek, aged as Methusaleh, sitting, shrunk into himself, face to the wall. His trembling, skeletal hands fingered a small music box. As he turned the handle, twanging noises emerged.

I go up to him.

Immediately he begins singing to himself, confusedly,

> "Frau Pick,
> Frau Hock,
> Und rote blaue Stern
> die schmusen allerhand.
> Von Messinung, an Raucherl und Rohn."

"Waiter, can you tell me the name of this old man?" I ask a waiter who is scurrying by.

"No, sir. Nobody here knows his name any more. He's forgotten it himself. He's all alone in the world. He's one hundred and ten years old. He comes in every evening, and we give him a cup of coffee."

I bend down over the old creature, and call a word into his ear: "Schaffranek!"

It goes through him like a stroke of lightning. He murmurs something, and rubs his hand over his forehead, as if trying to think.

"Do you understand me, Herr Schaffranek?"

He nods.

"Try hard and listen. I want to ask you something about old days. If you can tell me what I want to know, I shall give you that gulden on the table, there."

"Gulden!" The old man repeats, parrot-wise, and begins to turn the handle of his hurdygurdy madly.

I take his hand, and hold it fast. "Try and think a moment! Did you ever hear, three and thirty years ago, of a gemcutter called *Pernath?*"

"Hadrbolletz! Breeches-maker!" he wheezes asthmatically, and then laughs all over his face, under the impression I've told him something extraordinarily funny.

"No . . . no . . . not Hadrbolletz! *Pernath!*"

"Pereles?" He literally shouts with glee.

"No. *Not* Pereles! PERNATH!"

"Pascheles?" He crows with delight.

In bitter disappointment, I give it up.

"You want to speak to me, sir?" Ferri Athenstädt, the billiard marker, is confronting me with a distant bow.

"Yes. That's right. I thought we might have a game, perhaps?"

"Hundred up? Give you ninety handicap, if it's agreeable. . . . For money, sir?"

"Done! For a gulden. You begin, if you like, marker."

His Highness takes the cue, aims, muffs it, and pulls a face. I know perfectly well what he is doing. Letting me get up to ninety-nine, then running out in one break.

But more and more is my curiosity at boiling-point. I go straight to the point now.

"Tell me, marker . . . do you happen to remember, a long time ago . . . somewhere about the time the old stone bridge collapsed, probably . . . a certain Athanasius Pernath who lived in the Jewish quarter, as it stood then?"

A man in a red and white striped linen jacket, with squinting eyes and small golden ear-rings, sitting on a chair against the wall and reading a newspaper, stares at me and crosses himself.

"Pernath? *Pernath?*" the marker repeats, and racks his brains to try and think. "Pernath? Medium height, slender, wasn't he? Brown hair . . . pepper and salt beard . . . cut pointed?"

"Yes. That's right."

"About forty years old, at that time? Looked like——" Suddenly His Highness stops, and gazes at me in amazement:

"Are you related to him, may I ask, sir?"

The man with a squint crosses himself again.

"I? A relative? No! Only I happened to be interested in him. Is there anything else you know?" I ask nonchalantly, for my heart feels like a lump of ice.

Ferri Athenstädt once more puts on his thinking-cap.

"If I'm not mistaken, they used to say that he was mad. Pernath once said, yes I believe he once said his name was—let me think—Laponder—and at other times he'd give himself out for a certain . . . Charousek!"

"It's all a pack of lies!" breaks in the man with a squint.   "Charousek was a real man all right. My father came into a couple of thousand florins through him."

"Who is this man?" I ask the marker softly.

"He's a boatman, and his name's Tschamrda. All I seem to remember about Pernath is that later on in life he married a very beautiful Jewess—at least, I *think* he did."

"Miriam!" I tell myself, and am so overcome with emotion that my hands are trembling and I can play no longer.

Once again the squint-eyed man crosses himself.

"What's the matter with you, Herr Tschamrda?" asks the marker in astonishment.

"Pernath never did live!" shouts the squint-eyed, in a frenzy, at us. "I don't believe it!"

I at once make the man take a cognac with me, to get him talking.

"Some people say," declared the boatman, "that Pernath is still alive . . . that he cuts combs . . . and lives up at the Hradschin!"

"Where, on the Hradschin?"

Once more the boatman crosses himself.

"That's where you're asking! He lives where no living man *could* live! At '*Last Lamp House*'!"

"Do you know the house, then, Herr . . . Herr . . . Herr Tschamrda?"

"I wouldn't go up there for all the money on God's earth!" protests he. "What do you take me for? Jesus, Mary and Joseph!"

"But you could show me the way to it, I suppose, Herr Tschamrda?"

" 'Spose I could," growls the boatman. "If you wait till six in the morning, when I go down to the Moldau. But I warn you! You'll have no luck! Likely as not, you'll fall over into the Hirschgraben and break your neck! Holy Mother of God!"

We walk together through the early morning air. A fresh wind is blowing up from the river. So full of expectation am I, I can hardly feel the ground beneath my feet.

Suddenly I am confronted by the house in the Altschulgasse.

I recognise the window at once: the bent guttering . . . the iron bars . . . the stone sill . . . slippery . . . like a lump of fat. . . .

"When was this house on fire?" I ask the squint-eyed. There is a dull buzzing in my ears, as I wait for the reply.

"On fire? Never!"

"But it was burned. I know it was!"

"It never was."

"But it *was*! Will you bet me?"

"How much?"

"A gulden."

"Done." And Tschamrda proceeds to fetch the concierge. "Has this house ever been on fire?"

"Oh, come on!" The man laughs.

Can I believe it? Yes, and no.

"I've lived in this house come seventy years," the man informs us. "I should know, shouldn't I?"

Strange . . . strange . . . strange!

With grotesque, jerky movements the boatman rows me over the Moldau in his little boat, consisting of eight rough, unplaned boards. The yellow water foams up against its timber sides. The roofs of the Hradschin gleam red in the morning sun. My soul seems possessed with a strange feeling of solemnity. A faint, indefinable feeling rises up within me as of something proceeding from another life than this— some previous enchanted existence: the whole world, in fact, seems enchanted, seen through a haze of dreamy recognition, as though I had lived already at many times, and in many places, simultaneously.

I get out of the boat.

"How much, Herr Tschamrda?"

"One kreuzer. If you'd wanted to help with the rowing—it would have been two!"

Once again I tread the same road I had trodden in my last night's dream—and climb the same lonely steps, that lead towards the Castle. My heart beats rapidly: I know beforehand I shall see the leafless trees whose boughs reach over the wall.

But no. It is strewn with white blossom.

The air is full of the sweet scent of lilac.

Beneath me is spread the town, in the early morning light, like a vision of the Promised Land.

No sound. Nothing but scent and gleam.

With my eyes shut I could have found my way through the quaint old Street of the Alchemists, so familiar has every inch of it suddenly become to me.

But instead of the little wooden lattice gate that had formerly led up to the glimmering white house, another one now stands—a magnificent affair, all in lines of curving gold, shutting off the entrance to the street.

Two sombre yew-trees rise up from a shrubbery, and stand as sentinels on either hand of the entrance door to the garden wall, directly behind the lattice gate.

I stand on tiptoe, trying to see over the bushes, and am immediately dazzled by fresh splendour.

The garden wall is all covered with decoration in mosaic, of a beautiful Turkish blue background, set with gold, highly stylised frescoes depicting the Egyptian cult of the god Osiris.

The swinging door is the God himself: a hermaphrodite in two halves, the right female, the left male. The figure is seated on a flat, radiant throne of mother of pearl, in semi-relief, and its golden head is in the form of a hare. The ears of it stand up high and close together, giving the semblance of two pages of an open book.

The atmosphere is filled with the freshness of dew, and the fragrance of hyacinths is wafted over the wall.

I stand there petrified, for a long time, staring. It is like the entrance to an unknown world. An old gardener, or servant of some sort, with a ruffle round his neck, silver buckles on his shoes, and a coat of most curious cut, now appears from the left hand side behind the golden gate, and asks me through the bars what it is I want.

Without a word, I hold out to him the hat of Athanasius Pernath.

He takes it, and goes through the swinging doors.

As they open, I catch a glimpse behind of a marble house, with all the aspect of a temple, on the steps of which is standing:

ATHANASIUS PERNATH

and leaning up against him:

MIRIAM!

They are both gazing down at the town below them. Just for an instant Miriam turns in my direction, sees me, smiles, and whispers something to Athanasius Pernath.

Her beauty holds me spellbound.

She is so young—just as I had seen her in my dream of yesternight.

Athanasius Pernath turns slowly towards me, and my heart stops beating:

So like is he to myself, it is as though beholding my own face and figure in the glass!

Then the swinging doors are closed once more, and all I can see is the gleaming hermaphrodite.

The old servant hands me my hat, saying—and his voice sounds to me as though proceeding from the bowels of the earth:

"HERR ATHANASIUS PERNATH'S COMPLIMENTS AND THANKS, AND HE HOPES YOU WILL NOT THINK HIM INHOSPITABLE NOT TO INVITE YOU INTO THE GARDEN, BUT FOR MANY A DAY IT HAS BEEN AGAINST THE RULES OF THE HOUSE.

"HE ALSO WISHES ME TO SAY HE HAS NOT WORN YOUR HAT, HAVING IMMEDIATELY DISCOVERED A MISTAKE HAD BEEN MADE.

"HE ONLY HOPES HIS HAT MAY NOT HAVE GIVEN YOU A HEADACHE."

A CATALOG OF SELECTED
DOVER BOOKS
IN ALL FIELDS OF INTEREST

A CATALOG OF SELECTED DOVER
BOOKS IN ALL FIELDS OF INTEREST

CONCERNING THE SPIRITUAL IN ART, Wassily Kandinsky. Pioneering work by father of abstract art. Thoughts on color theory, nature of art. Analysis of earlier masters. 12 illustrations. 80pp. of text. 5⅜ x 8½.   23411-8 Pa. $4.95

ANIMALS: 1,419 Copyright-Free Illustrations of Mammals, Birds, Fish, Insects, etc., Jim Harter (ed.). Clear wood engravings present, in extremely lifelike poses, over 1,000 species of animals. One of the most extensive pictorial sourcebooks of its kind. Captions. Index. 284pp. 9 x 12.   23766-4 Pa. $14.95

CELTIC ART: The Methods of Construction, George Bain. Simple geometric techniques for making Celtic interlacements, spirals, Kells-type initials, animals, humans, etc. Over 500 illustrations. 160pp. 9 x 12. (USO)   22923-8 Pa. $9.95

AN ATLAS OF ANATOMY FOR ARTISTS, Fritz Schider. Most thorough reference work on art anatomy in the world. Hundreds of illustrations, including selections from works by Vesalius, Leonardo, Goya, Ingres, Michelangelo, others. 593 illustrations. 192pp. 7⅛ x 10¼.   20241-0 Pa. $9.95

CELTIC HAND STROKE-BY-STROKE (Irish Half-Uncial from "The Book of Kells"): An Arthur Baker Calligraphy Manual, Arthur Baker. Complete guide to creating each letter of the alphabet in distinctive Celtic manner. Covers hand position, strokes, pens, inks, paper, more. Illustrated. 48pp. 8¼ x 11.   24336-2 Pa. $3.95

EASY ORIGAMI, John Montroll. Charming collection of 32 projects (hat, cup, pelican, piano, swan, many more) specially designed for the novice origami hobbyist. Clearly illustrated easy-to-follow instructions insure that even beginning papercrafters will achieve successful results. 48pp. 8¼ x 11.   27298-2 Pa. $3.50

THE COMPLETE BOOK OF BIRDHOUSE CONSTRUCTION FOR WOOD-WORKERS, Scott D. Campbell. Detailed instructions, illustrations, tables. Also data on bird habitat and instinct patterns. Bibliography. 3 tables. 63 illustrations in 15 figures. 48pp. 5¼ x 8½.   24407-5 Pa. $2.50

BLOOMINGDALE'S ILLUSTRATED 1886 CATALOG: Fashions, Dry Goods and Housewares, Bloomingdale Brothers. Famed merchants' extremely rare catalog depicting about 1,700 products: clothing, housewares, firearms, dry goods, jewelry, more. Invaluable for dating, identifying vintage items. Also, copyright-free graphics for artists, designers. Co-published with Henry Ford Museum & Greenfield Village. 160pp. 8¼ x 11.   25780-0 Pa. $10.95

HISTORIC COSTUME IN PICTURES, Braun & Schneider. Over 1,450 costumed figures in clearly detailed engravings–from dawn of civilization to end of 19th century. Captions. Many folk costumes. 256pp. 8⅜ x 11¾.   23150-X Pa. $12.95

STICKLEY CRAFTSMAN FURNITURE CATALOGS, Gustav Stickley and L. & J. G. Stickley. Beautiful, functional furniture in two authentic catalogs from 1910. 594 illustrations, including 277 photos, show settles, rockers, armchairs, reclining chairs, bookcases, desks, tables. 183pp. 6½ x 9¼. 23838-5 Pa. $11.95

AMERICAN LOCOMOTIVES IN HISTORIC PHOTOGRAPHS: 1858 to 1949, Ron Ziel (ed.). A rare collection of 126 meticulously detailed official photographs, called "builder portraits," of American locomotives that majestically chronicle the rise of steam locomotive power in America. Introduction. Detailed captions. xi + 129pp. 9 x 12. 27393-8 Pa. $13.95

AMERICA'S LIGHTHOUSES: An Illustrated History, Francis Ross Holland, Jr. Delightfully written, profusely illustrated fact-filled survey of over 200 American lighthouses since 1716. History, anecdotes, technological advances, more. 240pp. 8 x 10¾. 25576-X Pa. $12.95

TOWARDS A NEW ARCHITECTURE, Le Corbusier. Pioneering manifesto by founder of "International School." Technical and aesthetic theories, views of industry, economics, relation of form to function, "mass-production split" and much more. Profusely illustrated. 320pp. 6⅛ x 9¼. (USO) 25023-7 Pa. $9.95

HOW THE OTHER HALF LIVES, Jacob Riis. Famous journalistic record, exposing poverty and degradation of New York slums around 1900, by major social reformer. 100 striking and influential photographs. 233pp. 10 x 7⅞. 22012-5 Pa. $11.95

FRUIT KEY AND TWIG KEY TO TREES AND SHRUBS, William M. Harlow. One of the handiest and most widely used identification aids. Fruit key covers 120 deciduous and evergreen species; twig key 160 deciduous species. Easily used. Over 300 photographs. 126pp. 5⅜ x 8½. 20511-8 Pa. $3.95

COMMON BIRD SONGS, Dr. Donald J. Borror. Songs of 60 most common U.S. birds: robins, sparrows, cardinals, bluejays, finches, more–arranged in order of increasing complexity. Up to 9 variations of songs of each species. Cassette and manual 99911-4 $8.95

ORCHIDS AS HOUSE PLANTS, Rebecca Tyson Northen. Grow cattleyas and many other kinds of orchids–in a window, in a case, or under artificial light. 63 illustrations. 148pp. 5⅜ x 8½. 23261-1 Pa. $5.95

MONSTER MAZES, Dave Phillips. Masterful mazes at four levels of difficulty. Avoid deadly perils and evil creatures to find magical treasures. Solutions for all 32 exciting illustrated puzzles. 48pp. 8¼ x 11. 26005-4 Pa. $2.95

MOZART'S DON GIOVANNI (DOVER OPERA LIBRETTO SERIES), Wolfgang Amadeus Mozart. Introduced and translated by Ellen H. Bleiler. Standard Italian libretto, with complete English translation. Convenient and thoroughly portable–an ideal companion for reading along with a recording or the performance itself. Introduction. List of characters. Plot summary. 121pp. 5¼ x 8½. 24944-1 Pa. $3.95

TECHNICAL MANUAL AND DICTIONARY OF CLASSICAL BALLET, Gail Grant. Defines, explains, comments on steps, movements, poses and concepts. 15-page pictorial section. Basic book for student, viewer. 127pp. 5⅜ x 8½. 21843-0 Pa. $4.95

BRASS INSTRUMENTS: Their History and Development, Anthony Baines. Authoritative, updated survey of the evolution of trumpets, trombones, bugles, cornets, French horns, tubas and other brass wind instruments. Over 140 illustrations and 48 music examples. Corrected and updated by author. New preface. Bibliography. 320pp. 5⅜ x 8½. 27574-4 Pa. $9.95

HOLLYWOOD GLAMOR PORTRAITS, John Kobal (ed.). 145 photos from 1926-49. Harlow, Gable, Bogart, Bacall; 94 stars in all. Full background on photographers, technical aspects. 160pp. 8⅜ x 11¼. 23352-9 Pa. $12.95

MAX AND MORITZ, Wilhelm Busch. Great humor classic in both German and English. Also 10 other works: "Cat and Mouse," "Plisch and Plumm," etc. 216pp. 5⅜ x 8½. 20181-3 Pa. $6.95

THE RAVEN AND OTHER FAVORITE POEMS, Edgar Allan Poe. Over 40 of the author's most memorable poems: "The Bells," "Ulalume," "Israfel," "To Helen," "The Conqueror Worm," "Eldorado," "Annabel Lee," many more. Alphabetic lists of titles and first lines. 64pp. 5$\frac{3}{16}$ x 8¼. 26685-0 Pa. $1.00

PERSONAL MEMOIRS OF U. S. GRANT, Ulysses Simpson Grant. Intelligent, deeply moving firsthand account of Civil War campaigns, considered by many the finest military memoirs ever written. Includes letters, historic photographs, maps and more. 528pp. 6⅛ x 9¼. 28587-1 Pa. $12.95

AMULETS AND SUPERSTITIONS, E. A. Wallis Budge. Comprehensive discourse on origin, powers of amulets in many ancient cultures: Arab, Persian Babylonian, Assyrian, Egyptian, Gnostic, Hebrew, Phoenician, Syriac, etc. Covers cross, swastika, crucifix, seals, rings, stones, etc. 584pp. 5⅜ x 8½. 23573-4 Pa. $12.95

RUSSIAN STORIES/PYCCKNE PACCKA3bl: A Dual-Language Book, edited by Gleb Struve. Twelve tales by such masters as Chekhov, Tolstoy, Dostoevsky, Pushkin, others. Excellent word-for-word English translations on facing pages, plus teaching and study aids, Russian/English vocabulary, biographical/critical introductions, more. 416pp. 5⅜ x 8½. 26244-8 Pa. $9.95

PHILADELPHIA THEN AND NOW: 60 Sites Photographed in the Past and Present, Kenneth Finkel and Susan Oyama. Rare photographs of City Hall, Logan Square, Independence Hall, Betsy Ross House, other landmarks juxtaposed with contemporary views. Captures changing face of historic city. Introduction. Captions. 128pp. 8¼ x 11. 25790-8 Pa. $9.95

AIA ARCHITECTURAL GUIDE TO NASSAU AND SUFFOLK COUNTIES, LONG ISLAND, The American Institute of Architects, Long Island Chapter, and the Society for the Preservation of Long Island Antiquities. Comprehensive, well-researched and generously illustrated volume brings to life over three centuries of Long Island's great architectural heritage. More than 240 photographs with authoritative, extensively detailed captions. 176pp. 8¼ x 11. 26946-9 Pa. $14.95

NORTH AMERICAN INDIAN LIFE: Customs and Traditions of 23 Tribes, Elsie Clews Parsons (ed.). 27 fictionalized essays by noted anthropologists examine religion, customs, government, additional facets of life among the Winnebago, Crow, Zuni, Eskimo, other tribes. 480pp. 6⅛ x 9¼. 27377-6 Pa. $10.95

FRANK LLOYD WRIGHT'S HOLLYHOCK HOUSE, Donald Hoffmann. Lavishly illustrated, carefully documented study of one of Wright's most controversial residential designs. Over 120 photographs, floor plans, elevations, etc. Detailed perceptive text by noted Wright scholar. Index. 128pp. 9¼ x 10¾. 27133-1 Pa. $11.95

THE MALE AND FEMALE FIGURE IN MOTION: 60 Classic Photographic Sequences, Eadweard Muybridge. 60 true-action photographs of men and women walking, running, climbing, bending, turning, etc., reproduced from rare 19th-century masterpiece. vi + 121pp. 9 x 12. 24745-7 Pa. $10.95

1001 QUESTIONS ANSWERED ABOUT THE SEASHORE, N. J. Berrill and Jacquelyn Berrill. Queries answered about dolphins, sea snails, sponges, starfish, fishes, shore birds, many others. Covers appearance, breeding, growth, feeding, much more. 305pp. 5¼ x 8¼. 23366-9 Pa. $8.95

GUIDE TO OWL WATCHING IN NORTH AMERICA, Donald S. Heintzelman. Superb guide offers complete data and descriptions of 19 species: barn owl, screech owl, snowy owl, many more. Expert coverage of owl-watching equipment, conservation, migrations and invasions, etc. Guide to observing sites. 84 illustrations. xiii + 193pp. 5⅜ x 8½. 27344-X Pa. $8.95

MEDICINAL AND OTHER USES OF NORTH AMERICAN PLANTS: A Historical Survey with Special Reference to the Eastern Indian Tribes, Charlotte Erichsen-Brown. Chronological historical citations document 500 years of usage of plants, trees, shrubs native to eastern Canada, northeastern U.S. Also complete identifying information. 343 illustrations. 544pp. 6½ x 9¼. 25951-X Pa. $12.95

STORYBOOK MAZES, Dave Phillips. 23 stories and mazes on two-page spreads: Wizard of Oz, Treasure Island, Robin Hood, etc. Solutions. 64pp. 8¼ x 11. 23628-5 Pa. $2.95

NEGRO FOLK MUSIC, U.S.A., Harold Courlander. Noted folklorist's scholarly yet readable analysis of rich and varied musical tradition. Includes authentic versions of over 40 folk songs. Valuable bibliography and discography. xi + 324pp. 5⅜ x 8½. 27350-4 Pa. $9.95

MOVIE-STAR PORTRAITS OF THE FORTIES, John Kobal (ed.). 163 glamor, studio photos of 106 stars of the 1940s: Rita Hayworth, Ava Gardner, Marlon Brando, Clark Gable, many more. 176pp. 8⅜ x 11¼. 23546-7 Pa. $12.95

BENCHLEY LOST AND FOUND, Robert Benchley. Finest humor from early 30s, about pet peeves, child psychologists, post office and others. Mostly unavailable elsewhere. 73 illustrations by Peter Arno and others. 183pp. 5⅜ x 8½. 22410-4 Pa. $6.95

YEKL and THE IMPORTED BRIDEGROOM AND OTHER STORIES OF YIDDISH NEW YORK, Abraham Cahan. Film Hester Street based on Yekl (1896). Novel, other stories among first about Jewish immigrants on N.Y.'s East Side. 240pp. 5⅜ x 8½. 22427-9 Pa. $6.95

SELECTED POEMS, Walt Whitman. Generous sampling from *Leaves of Grass*. Twenty-four poems include "I Hear America Singing," "Song of the Open Road," "I Sing the Body Electric," "When Lilacs Last in the Dooryard Bloom'd," "O Captain! My Captain!"—all reprinted from an authoritative edition. Lists of titles and first lines. 128pp. 5³⁄₁₆ x 8¼. 26878-0 Pa. $1.00

THE BEST TALES OF HOFFMANN, E. T. A. Hoffmann. 10 of Hoffmann's most important stories: "Nutcracker and the King of Mice," "The Golden Flowerpot," etc. 458pp. 5⅜ x 8½. 21793-0 Pa. $9.95

FROM FETISH TO GOD IN ANCIENT EGYPT, E. A. Wallis Budge. Rich detailed survey of Egyptian conception of "God" and gods, magic, cult of animals, Osiris, more. Also, superb English translations of hymns and legends. 240 illustrations. 545pp. 5⅜ x 8½. 25803-3 Pa. $13.95

FRENCH STORIES/CONTES FRANÇAIS: A Dual-Language Book, Wallace Fowlie. Ten stories by French masters, Voltaire to Camus: "Micromegas" by Voltaire; "The Atheist's Mass" by Balzac; "Minuet" by de Maupassant; "The Guest" by Camus, six more. Excellent English translations on facing pages. Also French-English vocabulary list, exercises, more. 352pp. 5⅜ x 8½. 26443-2 Pa. $9.95

CHICAGO AT THE TURN OF THE CENTURY IN PHOTOGRAPHS: 122 Historic Views from the Collections of the Chicago Historical Society, Larry A. Viskochil. Rare large-format prints offer detailed views of City Hall, State Street, the Loop, Hull House, Union Station, many other landmarks, circa 1904-1913. Introduction. Captions. Maps. 144pp. 9⅜ x 12¼. 24656-6 Pa. $12.95

OLD BROOKLYN IN EARLY PHOTOGRAPHS, 1865-1929, William Lee Younger. Luna Park, Gravesend race track, construction of Grand Army Plaza, moving of Hotel Brighton, etc. 157 previously unpublished photographs. 165pp. 8⅞ x 11¾. 23587-4 Pa. $13.95

THE MYTHS OF THE NORTH AMERICAN INDIANS, Lewis Spence. Rich anthology of the myths and legends of the Algonquins, Iroquois, Pawnees and Sioux, prefaced by an extensive historical and ethnological commentary. 36 illustrations. 480pp. 5⅜ x 8½. 25967-6 Pa. $10.95

AN ENCYCLOPEDIA OF BATTLES: Accounts of Over 1,560 Battles from 1479 B.C. to the Present, David Eggenberger. Essential details of every major battle in recorded history from the first battle of Megiddo in 1479 B.C. to Grenada in 1984. List of Battle Maps. New Appendix covering the years 1967-1984. Index. 99 illustrations. 544pp. 6½ x 9¼. 24913-1 Pa. $16.95

SAILING ALONE AROUND THE WORLD, Captain Joshua Slocum. First man to sail around the world, alone, in small boat. One of great feats of seamanship told in delightful manner. 67 illustrations. 294pp. 5⅜ x 8½. 20326-3 Pa. $6.95

ANARCHISM AND OTHER ESSAYS, Emma Goldman. Powerful, penetrating, prophetic essays on direct action, role of minorities, prison reform, puritan hypocrisy, violence, etc. 271pp. 5⅜ x 8½. 22484-8 Pa. $7.95

MYTHS OF THE HINDUS AND BUDDHISTS, Ananda K. Coomaraswamy and Sister Nivedita. Great stories of the epics; deeds of Krishna, Shiva, taken from puranas, Vedas, folk tales; etc. 32 illustrations. 400pp. 5⅜ x 8½. 21759-0 Pa. $12.95

BEYOND PSYCHOLOGY, Otto Rank. Fear of death, desire of immortality, nature of sexuality, social organization, creativity, according to Rankian system. 291pp. 5⅜ x 8½. 20485-5 Pa. $8.95

A THEOLOGICO-POLITICAL TREATISE, Benedict Spinoza. Also contains unfinished Political Treatise. Great classic on religious liberty, theory of government on common consent. R. Elwes translation. Total of 421pp. 5⅜ x 8½. 20249-6 Pa. $9.95

MY BONDAGE AND MY FREEDOM, Frederick Douglass. Born a slave, Douglass became outspoken force in antislavery movement. The best of Douglass' autobiographies. Graphic description of slave life. 464pp. 5⅜ x 8½. 22457-0 Pa. $8.95

FOLLOWING THE EQUATOR: A Journey Around the World, Mark Twain. Fascinating humorous account of 1897 voyage to Hawaii, Australia, India, New Zealand, etc. Ironic, bemused reports on peoples, customs, climate, flora and fauna, politics, much more. 197 illustrations. 720pp. 5⅜ x 8½. 26113-1 Pa. $15.95

THE PEOPLE CALLED SHAKERS, Edward D. Andrews. Definitive study of Shakers: origins, beliefs, practices, dances, social organization, furniture and crafts, etc. 33 illustrations. 351pp. 5⅜ x 8½. 21081-2 Pa. $8.95

THE MYTHS OF GREECE AND ROME, H. A. Guerber. A classic of mythology, generously illustrated, long prized for its simple, graphic, accurate retelling of the principal myths of Greece and Rome, and for its commentary on their origins and significance. With 64 illustrations by Michelangelo, Raphael, Titian, Rubens, Canova, Bernini and others. 480pp. 5⅜ x 8½. 27584-1 Pa. $9.95

PSYCHOLOGY OF MUSIC, Carl E. Seashore. Classic work discusses music as a medium from psychological viewpoint. Clear treatment of physical acoustics, auditory apparatus, sound perception, development of musical skills, nature of musical feeling, host of other topics. 88 figures. 408pp. 5⅜ x 8½. 21851-1 Pa. $11.95

THE PHILOSOPHY OF HISTORY, Georg W. Hegel. Great classic of Western thought develops concept that history is not chance but rational process, the evolution of freedom. 457pp. 5⅜ x 8½. 20112-0 Pa. $9.95

THE BOOK OF TEA, Kakuzo Okakura. Minor classic of the Orient: entertaining, charming explanation, interpretation of traditional Japanese culture in terms of tea ceremony. 94pp. 5⅜ x 8½. 20070-1 Pa. $3.95

LIFE IN ANCIENT EGYPT, Adolf Erman. Fullest, most thorough, detailed older account with much not in more recent books, domestic life, religion, magic, medicine, commerce, much more. Many illustrations reproduce tomb paintings, carvings, hieroglyphs, etc. 597pp. 5⅜ x 8½. 22632-8 Pa. $12.95

SUNDIALS, Their Theory and Construction, Albert Waugh. Far and away the best, most thorough coverage of ideas, mathematics concerned, types, construction, adjusting anywhere. Simple, nontechnical treatment allows even children to build several of these dials. Over 100 illustrations. 230pp. 5⅜ x 8½. 22947-5 Pa. $8.95

DYNAMICS OF FLUIDS IN POROUS MEDIA, Jacob Bear. For advanced students of ground water hydrology, soil mechanics and physics, drainage and irrigation engineering, and more. 335 illustrations. Exercises, with answers. 784pp. 6⅛ x 9¼.
65675-6 Pa. $19.95

SONGS OF EXPERIENCE: Facsimile Reproduction with 26 Plates in Full Color, William Blake. 26 full-color plates from a rare 1826 edition. Includes "The Tyger," "London," "Holy Thursday," and other poems. Printed text of poems. 48pp. 5¼ x 7.
24636-1 Pa. $4.95

OLD-TIME VIGNETTES IN FULL COLOR, Carol Belanger Grafton (ed.). Over 390 charming, often sentimental illustrations, selected from archives of Victorian graphics—pretty women posing, children playing, food, flowers, kittens and puppies, smiling cherubs, birds and butterflies, much more. All copyright-free. 48pp. 9¼ x 12¼.
27269-9 Pa. $7.95

PERSPECTIVE FOR ARTISTS, Rex Vicat Cole. Depth, perspective of sky and sea, shadows, much more, not usually covered. 391 diagrams, 81 reproductions of drawings and paintings. 279pp. 5⅜ x 8½. 22487-2 Pa. $7.95

DRAWING THE LIVING FIGURE, Joseph Sheppard. Innovative approach to artistic anatomy focuses on specifics of surface anatomy, rather than muscles and bones. Over 170 drawings of live models in front, back and side views, and in widely varying poses. Accompanying diagrams. 177 illustrations. Introduction. Index. 144pp. 8⅜ x11¼. 26723-7 Pa. $8.95

GOTHIC AND OLD ENGLISH ALPHABETS: 100 Complete Fonts, Dan X. Solo. Add power, elegance to posters, signs, other graphics with 100 stunning copyright-free alphabets: Blackstone, Dolbey, Germania, 97 more–including many lower-case, numerals, punctuation marks. 104pp. 8⅛ x 11. 24695-7 Pa. $8.95

HOW TO DO BEADWORK, Mary White. Fundamental book on craft from simple projects to five-bead chains and woven works. 106 illustrations. 142pp. 5⅜ x 8. 20697-1 Pa. $4.95

THE BOOK OF WOOD CARVING, Charles Marshall Sayers. Finest book for beginners discusses fundamentals and offers 34 designs. "Absolutely first rate . . . well thought out and well executed."–E. J. Tangerman. 118pp. 7¾ x 10⅝. 23654-4 Pa. $6.95

ILLUSTRATED CATALOG OF CIVIL WAR MILITARY GOODS: Union Army Weapons, Insignia, Uniform Accessories, and Other Equipment, Schuyler, Hartley, and Graham. Rare, profusely illustrated 1846 catalog includes Union Army uniform and dress regulations, arms and ammunition, coats, insignia, flags, swords, rifles, etc. 226 illustrations. 160pp. 9 x 12. 24939-5 Pa. $10.95

WOMEN'S FASHIONS OF THE EARLY 1900s: An Unabridged Republication of "New York Fashions, 1909," National Cloak & Suit Co. Rare catalog of mail-order fashions documents women's and children's clothing styles shortly after the turn of the century. Captions offer full descriptions, prices. Invaluable resource for fashion, costume historians. Approximately 725 illustrations. 128pp. 8⅜ x 11¼. 27276-1 Pa. $11.95

THE 1912 AND 1915 GUSTAV STICKLEY FURNITURE CATALOGS, Gustav Stickley. With over 200 detailed illustrations and descriptions, these two catalogs are essential reading and reference materials and identification guides for Stickley furniture. Captions cite materials, dimensions and prices. 112pp. 6½ x 9¼. 26676-1 Pa. $9.95

EARLY AMERICAN LOCOMOTIVES, John H. White, Jr. Finest locomotive engravings from early 19th century: historical (1804–74), main-line (after 1870), special, foreign, etc. 147 plates. 142pp. 11⅜ x 8¼. 22772-3 Pa. $10.95

THE TALL SHIPS OF TODAY IN PHOTOGRAPHS, Frank O. Braynard. Lavishly illustrated tribute to nearly 100 majestic contemporary sailing vessels: Amerigo Vespucci, Clearwater, Constitution, Eagle, Mayflower, Sea Cloud, Victory, many more. Authoritative captions provide statistics, background on each ship. 190 black-and-white photographs and illustrations. Introduction. 128pp. 8⅞ x 11¾. 27163-3 Pa. $14.95

EARLY NINETEENTH-CENTURY CRAFTS AND TRADES, Peter Stockham (ed.). Extremely rare 1807 volume describes to youngsters the crafts and trades of the day: brickmaker, weaver, dressmaker, bookbinder, ropemaker, saddler, many more. Quaint prose, charming illustrations for each craft. 20 black-and-white line illustrations. 192pp. 4⅝ x 6. 27293-1 Pa. $4.95

VICTORIAN FASHIONS AND COSTUMES FROM HARPER'S BAZAR, 1867–1898, Stella Blum (ed.). Day costumes, evening wear, sports clothes, shoes, hats, other accessories in over 1,000 detailed engravings. 320pp. 9⅜ x 12¼. 22990-4 Pa. $15.95

GUSTAV STICKLEY, THE CRAFTSMAN, Mary Ann Smith. Superb study surveys broad scope of Stickley's achievement, especially in architecture. Design philosophy, rise and fall of the Craftsman empire, descriptions and floor plans for many Craftsman houses, more. 86 black-and-white halftones. 31 line illustrations. Introduction 208pp. 6½ x 9¼. 27210-9 Pa. $9.95

THE LONG ISLAND RAIL ROAD IN EARLY PHOTOGRAPHS, Ron Ziel. Over 220 rare photos, informative text document origin (1844) and development of rail service on Long Island. Vintage views of early trains, locomotives, stations, passengers, crews, much more. Captions. 8⅞ x 11¾. 26301-0 Pa. $13.95

THE BOOK OF OLD SHIPS: From Egyptian Galleys to Clipper Ships, Henry B. Culver. Superb, authoritative history of sailing vessels, with 80 magnificent line illustrations. Galley, bark, caravel, longship, whaler, many more. Detailed, informative text on each vessel by noted naval historian. Introduction. 256pp. 5⅜ x 8½. 27332-6 Pa. $7.95

TEN BOOKS ON ARCHITECTURE, Vitruvius. The most important book ever written on architecture. Early Roman aesthetics, technology, classical orders, site selection, all other aspects. Morgan translation. 331pp. 5⅜ x 8½. 20645-9 Pa. $8.95

THE HUMAN FIGURE IN MOTION, Eadweard Muybridge. More than 4,500 stopped-action photos, in action series, showing undraped men, women, children jumping, lying down, throwing, sitting, wrestling, carrying, etc. 390pp. 7⅞ x 10⅝. 20204-6 Clothbd. $27.95

TREES OF THE EASTERN AND CENTRAL UNITED STATES AND CANADA, William M. Harlow. Best one-volume guide to 140 trees. Full descriptions, woodlore, range, etc. Over 600 illustrations. Handy size. 288pp. 4½ x 6⅜. 20395-6 Pa. $6.95

SONGS OF WESTERN BIRDS, Dr. Donald J. Borror. Complete song and call repertoire of 60 western species, including flycatchers, juncoes, cactus wrens, many more—includes fully illustrated booklet. Cassette and manual 99913-0 $8.95

GROWING AND USING HERBS AND SPICES, Milo Miloradovich. Versatile handbook provides all the information needed for cultivation and use of all the herbs and spices available in North America. 4 illustrations. Index. Glossary. 236pp. 5⅜ x 8½. 25058-X Pa. $7.95

BIG BOOK OF MAZES AND LABYRINTHS, Walter Shepherd. 50 mazes and labyrinths in all—classical, solid, ripple, and more—in one great volume. Perfect inexpensive puzzler for clever youngsters. Full solutions. 112pp. 8⅛ x 11. 22951-3 Pa. $4.95

PIANO TUNING, J. Cree Fischer. Clearest, best book for beginner, amateur. Simple repairs, raising dropped notes, tuning by easy method of flattened fifths. No previous skills needed. 4 illustrations. 201pp. 5⅜ x 8½. 23267-0 Pa. $6.95

A SOURCE BOOK IN THEATRICAL HISTORY, A. M. Nagler. Contemporary observers on acting, directing, make-up, costuming, stage props, machinery, scene design, from Ancient Greece to Chekhov. 611pp. 5⅜ x 8½. 20515-0 Pa. $12.95

THE COMPLETE NONSENSE OF EDWARD LEAR, Edward Lear. All nonsense limericks, zany alphabets, Owl and Pussycat, songs, nonsense botany, etc., illustrated by Lear. Total of 320pp. 5⅜ x 8½. (USO) 20167-8 Pa. $7.95

VICTORIAN PARLOUR POETRY: An Annotated Anthology, Michael R. Turner. 117 gems by Longfellow, Tennyson, Browning, many lesser-known poets. "The Village Blacksmith," "Curfew Must Not Ring Tonight," "Only a Baby Small," dozens more, often difficult to find elsewhere. Index of poets, titles, first lines. xxiii + 325pp. 5⅜ x 8¼. 27044-0 Pa. $8.95

DUBLINERS, James Joyce. Fifteen stories offer vivid, tightly focused observations of the lives of Dublin's poorer classes. At least one, "The Dead," is considered a masterpiece. Reprinted complete and unabridged from standard edition. 160pp. 5³⁄₁₆ x 8¼. 26870-5 Pa. $1.00

THE HAUNTED MONASTERY and THE CHINESE MAZE MURDERS, Robert van Gulik. Two full novels by van Gulik, set in 7th-century China, continue adventures of Judge Dee and his companions. An evil Taoist monastery, seemingly supernatural events; overgrown topiary maze hides strange crimes. 27 illustrations. 328pp. 5⅜ x 8½. 23502-5 Pa. $8.95

THE BOOK OF THE SACRED MAGIC OF ABRAMELIN THE MAGE, translated by S. MacGregor Mathers. Medieval manuscript of ceremonial magic. Basic document in Aleister Crowley, Golden Dawn groups. 268pp. 5⅜ x 8½. 23211-5 Pa. $9.95

NEW RUSSIAN-ENGLISH AND ENGLISH-RUSSIAN DICTIONARY, M. A. O'Brien. This is a remarkably handy Russian dictionary, containing a surprising amount of information, including over 70,000 entries. 366pp. 4½ x 6⅛. 20208-9 Pa. $9.95

HISTORIC HOMES OF THE AMERICAN PRESIDENTS, Second, Revised Edition, Irvin Haas. A traveler's guide to American Presidential homes, most open to the public, depicting and describing homes occupied by every American President from George Washington to George Bush. With visiting hours, admission charges, travel routes. 175 photographs. Index. 160pp. 8¼ x 11. 26751-2 Pa. $11.95

NEW YORK IN THE FORTIES, Andreas Feininger. 162 brilliant photographs by the well-known photographer, formerly with *Life* magazine. Commuters, shoppers, Times Square at night, much else from city at its peak. Captions by John von Hartz. 181pp. 9¼ x 10¾. 23585-8 Pa. $12.95

INDIAN SIGN LANGUAGE, William Tomkins. Over 525 signs developed by Sioux and other tribes. Written instructions and diagrams. Also 290 pictographs. 111pp. 6⅛ x 9¼. 22029-X Pa. $3.95

ANATOMY: A Complete Guide for Artists, Joseph Sheppard. A master of figure drawing shows artists how to render human anatomy convincingly. Over 460 illustrations. 224pp. 8⅜ x 11¼. 27279-6 Pa. $11.95

MEDIEVAL CALLIGRAPHY: Its History and Technique, Marc Drogin. Spirited history, comprehensive instruction manual covers 13 styles (ca. 4th century thru 15th). Excellent photographs; directions for duplicating medieval techniques with modern tools. 224pp. 8⅜ x 11¼. 26142-5 Pa. $12.95

DRIED FLOWERS: How to Prepare Them, Sarah Whitlock and Martha Rankin. Complete instructions on how to use silica gel, meal and borax, perlite aggregate, sand and borax, glycerine and water to create attractive permanent flower arrangements. 12 illustrations. 32pp. 5⅜ x 8½. 21802-3 Pa. $1.00

EASY-TO-MAKE BIRD FEEDERS FOR WOODWORKERS, Scott D. Campbell. Detailed, simple-to-use guide for designing, constructing, caring for and using feeders. Text, illustrations for 12 classic and contemporary designs. 96pp. 5⅜ x 8½. 25847-5 Pa. $3.95

SCOTTISH WONDER TALES FROM MYTH AND LEGEND, Donald A. Mackenzie. 16 lively tales tell of giants rumbling down mountainsides, of a magic wand that turns stone pillars into warriors, of gods and goddesses, evil hags, powerful forces and more. 240pp. 5⅜ x 8½. 29677-6 Pa. $6.95

THE HISTORY OF UNDERCLOTHES, C. Willett Cunnington and Phyllis Cunnington. Fascinating, well-documented survey covering six centuries of English undergarments, enhanced with over 100 illustrations: 12th-century laced-up bodice, footed long drawers (1795), 19th-century bustles, l9th-century corsets for men, Victorian "bust improvers," much more. 272pp. 5⅜ x 8¼. 27124-2 Pa. $9.95

ARTS AND CRAFTS FURNITURE: The Complete Brooks Catalog of 1912, Brooks Manufacturing Co. Photos and detailed descriptions of more than 150 now very collectible furniture designs from the Arts and Crafts movement depict davenports, settees, buffets, desks, tables, chairs, bedsteads, dressers and more, all built of solid, quarter-sawed oak. Invaluable for students and enthusiasts of antiques, Americana and the decorative arts. 80pp. 6½ x 9¼. 27471-3 Pa. $8.95

HOW WE INVENTED THE AIRPLANE: An Illustrated History, Orville Wright. Fascinating firsthand account covers early experiments, construction of planes and motors, first flights, much more. Introduction and commentary by Fred C. Kelly. 76 photographs. 96pp. 8¼ x 11. 25662-6 Pa. $8.95

THE ARTS OF THE SAILOR: Knotting, Splicing and Ropework, Hervey Garrett Smith. Indispensable shipboard reference covers tools, basic knots and useful hitches; handsewing and canvas work, more. Over 100 illustrations. Delightful reading for sea lovers. 256pp. 5⅜ x 8½. 26440-8 Pa. $7.95

FRANK LLOYD WRIGHT'S FALLINGWATER: The House and Its History, Second, Revised Edition, Donald Hoffmann. A total revision–both in text and illustrations–of the standard document on Fallingwater, the boldest, most personal architectural statement of Wright's mature years, updated with valuable new material from the recently opened Frank Lloyd Wright Archives. "Fascinating"–*The New York Times*. 116 illustrations. 128pp. 9¼ x 10¾. 27430-6 Pa. $12.95

PHOTOGRAPHIC SKETCHBOOK OF THE CIVIL WAR, Alexander Gardner. 100 photos taken on field during the Civil War. Famous shots of Manassas Harper's Ferry, Lincoln, Richmond, slave pens, etc. 244pp. 10⅝ x 8¼. 22731-6 Pa. $9.95

FIVE ACRES AND INDEPENDENCE, Maurice G. Kains. Great back-to-the-land classic explains basics of self-sufficient farming. The one book to get. 95 illustrations. 397pp. 5⅜ x 8½. 20974-1 Pa. $7.95

SONGS OF EASTERN BIRDS, Dr. Donald J. Borror. Songs and calls of 60 species most common to eastern U.S.: warblers, woodpeckers, flycatchers, thrushes, larks, many more in high-quality recording. Cassette and manual 99912-2 $9.95

A MODERN HERBAL, Margaret Grieve. Much the fullest, most exact, most useful compilation of herbal material. Gigantic alphabetical encyclopedia, from aconite to zedoary, gives botanical information, medical properties, folklore, economic uses, much else. Indispensable to serious reader. 161 illustrations. 888pp. 6½ x 9¼. 2-vol. set. (USO) Vol. I: 22798-7 Pa. $9.95
Vol. II: 22799-5 Pa. $9.95

HIDDEN TREASURE MAZE BOOK, Dave Phillips. Solve 34 challenging mazes accompanied by heroic tales of adventure. Evil dragons, people-eating plants, blood-thirsty giants, many more dangerous adversaries lurk at every twist and turn. 34 mazes, stories, solutions. 48pp. 8¼ x 11. 24566-7 Pa. $2.95

LETTERS OF W. A. MOZART, Wolfgang A. Mozart. Remarkable letters show bawdy wit, humor, imagination, musical insights, contemporary musical world; includes some letters from Leopold Mozart. 276pp. 5⅜ x 8½. 22859-2 Pa. $7.95

BASIC PRINCIPLES OF CLASSICAL BALLET, Agrippina Vaganova. Great Russian theoretician, teacher explains methods for teaching classical ballet. 118 illus-trations. 175pp. 5⅜ x 8½. 22036-2 Pa. $5.95

THE JUMPING FROG, Mark Twain. Revenge edition. The original story of The Celebrated Jumping Frog of Calaveras County, a hapless French translation, and Twain's hilarious "retranslation" from the French. 12 illustrations. 66pp. 5⅜ x 8½. 22686-7 Pa. $3.95

BEST REMEMBERED POEMS, Martin Gardner (ed.). The 126 poems in this superb collection of 19th- and 20th-century British and American verse range from Shelley's "To a Skylark" to the impassioned "Renascence" of Edna St. Vincent Millay and to Edward Lear's whimsical "The Owl and the Pussycat." 224pp. 5⅜ x 8½. 27165-X Pa. $5.95

COMPLETE SONNETS, William Shakespeare. Over 150 exquisite poems deal with love, friendship, the tyranny of time, beauty's evanescence, death and other themes in language of remarkable power, precision and beauty. Glossary of archaic terms. 80pp. 5³⁄₁₆ x 8¼. 26686-9 Pa. $1.00

BODIES IN A BOOKSHOP, R. T. Campbell. Challenging mystery of blackmail and murder with ingenious plot and superbly drawn characters. In the best tradition of British suspense fiction. 192pp. 5⅜ x 8½. 24720-1 Pa. $6.95

THE WIT AND HUMOR OF OSCAR WILDE, Alvin Redman (ed.). More than 1,000 ripostes, paradoxes, wisecracks: Work is the curse of the drinking classes; I can resist everything except temptation; etc. 258pp. 5⅜ x 8½. 20602-5 Pa. $5.95

SHAKESPEARE LEXICON AND QUOTATION DICTIONARY, Alexander Schmidt. Full definitions, locations, shades of meaning in every word in plays and poems. More than 50,000 exact quotations. 1,485pp. 6½ x 9¼. 2-vol. set.
Vol. 1: 22726-X Pa. $17.95
Vol. 2: 22727-8 Pa. $17.95

SELECTED POEMS, Emily Dickinson. Over 100 best-known, best-loved poems by one of America's foremost poets, reprinted from authoritative early editions. No comparable edition at this price. Index of first lines. 64pp. 5 5/16 x 8¼.
26466-1 Pa. $1.00

CELEBRATED CASES OF JUDGE DEE (DEE GOONG AN), translated by Robert van Gulik. Authentic 18th-century Chinese detective novel; Dee and associates solve three interlocked cases. Led to van Gulik's own stories with same characters. Extensive introduction. 9 illustrations. 237pp. 5⅜ x 8½. 23337-5 Pa. $7.95

THE MALLEUS MALEFICARUM OF KRAMER AND SPRENGER, translated by Montague Summers. Full text of most important witchhunter's "bible," used by both Catholics and Protestants. 278pp. 6⅝ x 10. 22802-9 Pa. $12.95

SPANISH STORIES/CUENTOS ESPAÑOLES: A Dual-Language Book, Angel Flores (ed.). Unique format offers 13 great stories in Spanish by Cervantes, Borges, others. Faithful English translations on facing pages. 352pp. 5⅜ x 8½.
25399-6 Pa. $8.95

THE CHICAGO WORLD'S FAIR OF 1893: A Photographic Record, Stanley Appelbaum (ed.). 128 rare photos show 200 buildings, Beaux-Arts architecture, Midway, original Ferris Wheel, Edison's kinetoscope, more. Architectural emphasis; full text. 116pp. 8¼ x 11. 23990-X Pa. $9.95

OLD QUEENS, N.Y., IN EARLY PHOTOGRAPHS, Vincent F. Seyfried and William Asadorian. Over 160 rare photographs of Maspeth, Jamaica, Jackson Heights, and other areas. Vintage views of DeWitt Clinton mansion, 1939 World's Fair and more. Captions. 192pp. 8⅞ x 11. 26358-4 Pa. $12.95

CAPTURED BY THE INDIANS: 15 Firsthand Accounts, 1750-1870, Frederick Drimmer. Astounding true historical accounts of grisly torture, bloody conflicts, relentless pursuits, miraculous escapes and more, by people who lived to tell the tale. 384pp. 5⅜ x 8½. 24901-8 Pa. $8.95

THE WORLD'S GREAT SPEECHES, Lewis Copeland and Lawrence W. Lamm (eds.). Vast collection of 278 speeches of Greeks to 1970. Powerful and effective models; unique look at history. 842pp. 5⅜ x 8½. 20468-5 Pa. $14.95

THE BOOK OF THE SWORD, Sir Richard F. Burton. Great Victorian scholar/adventurer's eloquent, erudite history of the "queen of weapons"–from prehistory to early Roman Empire. Evolution and development of early swords, variations (sabre, broadsword, cutlass, scimitar, etc.), much more. 336pp. 6⅛ x 9¼.
25434-8 Pa. $9.95

AUTOBIOGRAPHY: The Story of My Experiments with Truth, Mohandas K. Gandhi. Boyhood, legal studies, purification, the growth of the Satyagraha (nonviolent protest) movement. Critical, inspiring work of the man responsible for the freedom of India. 480pp. 5⅜ x 8½. (USO)　　　　24593-4 Pa. $8.95

CELTIC MYTHS AND LEGENDS, T. W. Rolleston. Masterful retelling of Irish and Welsh stories and tales. Cuchulain, King Arthur, Deirdre, the Grail, many more. First paperback edition. 58 full-page illustrations. 512pp. 5⅜ x 8½.　　26507-2 Pa. $9.95

THE PRINCIPLES OF PSYCHOLOGY, William James. Famous long course complete, unabridged. Stream of thought, time perception, memory, experimental methods; great work decades ahead of its time. 94 figures. 1,391pp. 5⅜ x 8½. 2-vol. set.
Vol. I: 20381-6 Pa. $13.95
Vol. II: 20382-4 Pa. $14.95

THE WORLD AS WILL AND REPRESENTATION, Arthur Schopenhauer. Definitive English translation of Schopenhauer's life work, correcting more than 1,000 errors, omissions in earlier translations. Translated by E. F. J. Payne. Total of 1,269pp. 5⅜ x 8½. 2-vol. set.
Vol. 1: 21761-2 Pa. $12.95
Vol. 2: 21762-0 Pa. $12.95

MAGIC AND MYSTERY IN TIBET, Madame Alexandra David-Neel. Experiences among lamas, magicians, sages, sorcerers, Bonpa wizards. A true psychic discovery. 32 illustrations. 321pp. 5⅜ x 8½. (USO)　　22682-4 Pa. $9.95

THE EGYPTIAN BOOK OF THE DEAD, E. A. Wallis Budge. Complete reproduction of Ani's papyrus, finest ever found. Full hieroglyphic text, interlinear transliteration, word-for-word translation, smooth translation. 533pp. 6½ x 9¼.
21866-X Pa. $11.95

MATHEMATICS FOR THE NONMATHEMATICIAN, Morris Kline. Detailed, college-level treatment of mathematics in cultural and historical context, with numerous exercises. Recommended Reading Lists. Tables. Numerous figures. 641pp. 5⅜ x 8½.
24823-2 Pa. $11.95

THEORY OF WING SECTIONS: Including a Summary of Airfoil Data, Ira H. Abbott and A. E. von Doenhoff. Concise compilation of subsonic aerodynamic characteristics of NACA wing sections, plus description of theory. 350pp. of tables. 693pp. 5⅜ x 8½.　　　　　　　　　　　　　　60586-8 Pa. $14.95

THE RIME OF THE ANCIENT MARINER, Gustave Doré, S. T. Coleridge. Doré's finest work; 34 plates capture moods, subtleties of poem. Flawless full-size reproductions printed on facing pages with authoritative text of poem. "Beautiful. Simply beautiful."–*Publisher's Weekly.* 77pp. 9¼ x 12.　　22305-1 Pa. $7.95

NORTH AMERICAN INDIAN DESIGNS FOR ARTISTS AND CRAFTSPEO-PLE, Eva Wilson. Over 360 authentic copyright-free designs adapted from Navajo blankets, Hopi pottery, Sioux buffalo hides, more. Geometrics, symbolic figures, plant and animal motifs, etc. 128pp. 8⅜ x 11. (EUK)　　　25341-4 Pa. $8.95

SCULPTURE: Principles and Practice, Louis Slobodkin. Step-by-step approach to clay, plaster, metals, stone; classical and modern. 253 drawings, photos. 255pp. 8⅛ x 11.
22960-2 Pa. $11.95

THE INFLUENCE OF SEA POWER UPON HISTORY, 1660–1783, A. T. Mahan. Influential classic of naval history and tactics still used as text in war colleges. First paperback edition. 4 maps. 24 battle plans. 640pp. 5⅜ x 8½. 25509-3 Pa. $14.95

THE STORY OF THE TITANIC AS TOLD BY ITS SURVIVORS, Jack Winocour (ed.). What it was really like. Panic, despair, shocking inefficiency, and a little heroism. More thrilling than any fictional account. 26 illustrations. 320pp. 5⅜ x 8½. 20610-6 Pa. $8.95

FAIRY AND FOLK TALES OF THE IRISH PEASANTRY, William Butler Yeats (ed.). Treasury of 64 tales from the twilight world of Celtic myth and legend: "The Soul Cages," "The Kildare Pooka," "King O'Toole and his Goose," many more. Introduction and Notes by W. B. Yeats. 352pp. 5⅜ x 8½. 26941-8 Pa. $8.95

BUDDHIST MAHAYANA TEXTS, E. B. Cowell and Others (eds.). Superb, accurate translations of basic documents in Mahayana Buddhism, highly important in history of religions. The Buddha-karita of Asvaghosha, Larger Sukhavativyuha, more. 448pp. 5⅜ x 8½. 25552-2 Pa. $12.95

ONE TWO THREE . . . INFINITY: Facts and Speculations of Science, George Gamow. Great physicist's fascinating, readable overview of contemporary science: number theory, relativity, fourth dimension, entropy, genes, atomic structure, much more. 128 illustrations. Index. 352pp. 5⅜ x 8½. 25664-2 Pa. $8.95

ENGINEERING IN HISTORY, Richard Shelton Kirby, et al. Broad, nontechnical survey of history's major technological advances: birth of Greek science, industrial revolution, electricity and applied science, 20th-century automation, much more. 181 illustrations. ". . . excellent . . ."–*Isis*. Bibliography. vii + 530pp. 5⅜ x 8¼. 26412-2 Pa. $14.95

DALÍ ON MODERN ART: The Cuckolds of Antiquated Modern Art, Salvador Dalí. Influential painter skewers modern art and its practitioners. Outrageous evaluations of Picasso, Cézanne, Turner, more. 15 renderings of paintings discussed. 44 calligraphic decorations by Dalí. 96pp. 5⅜ x 8½. (USO) 29220-7 Pa. $4.95

ANTIQUE PLAYING CARDS: A Pictorial History, Henry René D'Allemagne. Over 900 elaborate, decorative images from rare playing cards (14th–20th centuries): Bacchus, death, dancing dogs, hunting scenes, royal coats of arms, players cheating, much more. 96pp. 9¼ x 12¼. 29265-7 Pa. $12.95

MAKING FURNITURE MASTERPIECES: 30 Projects with Measured Drawings, Franklin H. Gottshall. Step-by-step instructions, illustrations for constructing handsome, useful pieces, among them a Sheraton desk, Chippendale chair, Spanish desk, Queen Anne table and a William and Mary dressing mirror. 224pp. 8⅛ x 11¼. 29338-6 Pa. $13.95

THE FOSSIL BOOK: A Record of Prehistoric Life, Patricia V. Rich et al. Profusely illustrated definitive guide covers everything from single-celled organisms and dinosaurs to birds and mammals and the interplay between climate and man. Over 1,500 illustrations. 760pp. 7½ x 10⅛. 29371-8 Pa. $29.95

Prices subject to change without notice.

Available at your book dealer or write for free catalog to Dept. GI, Dover Publications, Inc., 31 East 2nd St., Mineola, N.Y. 11501. Dover publishes more than 500 books each year on science, elementary and advanced mathematics, biology, music, art, literary history, social sciences and other areas.